THIEVES' WORLD™

is a unique experience: an outlaw world of the imagination, where mayhem and skulduggery rule and magic is still potent; brought to life by today's top fantasy writers, who are free to use one another's characters (but not to kill them off . . . or at least not too freely!).

The idea for Thieves' World and the colorful city called Sanctuary™ came to Robert Lynn Asprin in 1978. After many twists and turns (documented in the volumes), the idea took off—and took on its own reality, as the best fantasy worlds have a way of doing. The result is one of F&SF's most unique success stories: a bestseller from the beginning, a series that is a challenge to writers, a delight to readers, and a favorite of fans.

Don't miss these other exciting tales of Sanctuary: the meanest, seediest, most dangerous town in all the worlds of fantasy....

THIEVES' WORLD
(Stories by Asprin, Abbey, Anderson, Bradley, Brunner, DeWees, Haldeman, and Offutt)

TALES FROM THE VULGAR UNICORN
(Stories by Asprin, Abbey, Drake, Farmer, Morris, Offutt, and van Vogt)

SHADOWS OF SANCTUARY
(Stories by Asprin, Abbey, Cherryh, McIntyre, Morris, Offutt and Paxson)

STORM SEASON
(Stories by Asprin, Abbey, Cherryh, Morris, Offutt and Paxson)

THE FACE OF CHAOS
(Stories by Asprin, Abbey, Cherryh, Drake, Morris and Paxson)

WINGS OF OMEN
(Stories by Asprin, Abbey, Bailey, Cherryh, Duane, Chris and Janet Morris, Offutt and Paxson)

THE DEAD OF WINTER
(Stories by Asprin, Abbey, Bailey, Cherryh, Duane, Morris, Offutt and Paxson)

SOUL OF THE CITY

LYNN ABBEY, C. J. CHERRYH,
AND JANET MORRIS

ACE FANTASY BOOKS
NEW YORK

SOUL OF THE CITY

An Ace Fantasy Book/published by arrangement with
the authors

PRINTING HISTORY
Ace Fantasy edition/January 1986

ISBN: 0-441-77581-0

Ace Fantasy Books are published by The Berkley Publishing Group,
200 Madison Avenue, New York, New York 10016.
PRINTED IN THE UNITED STATES OF AMERICA

CONTENTS

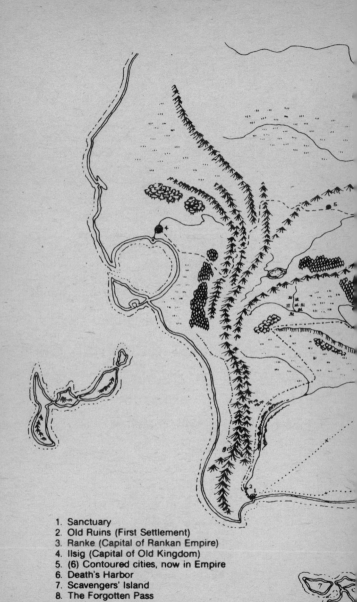

1. Sanctuary
2. Old Ruins (First Settlement)
3. Ranke (Capital of Rankan Empire)
4. Ilsig (Capital of Old Kingdom)
5. (6) Contoured cities, now in Empire
6. Death's Harbor
7. Scavengers' Island
8. The Forgotten Pass

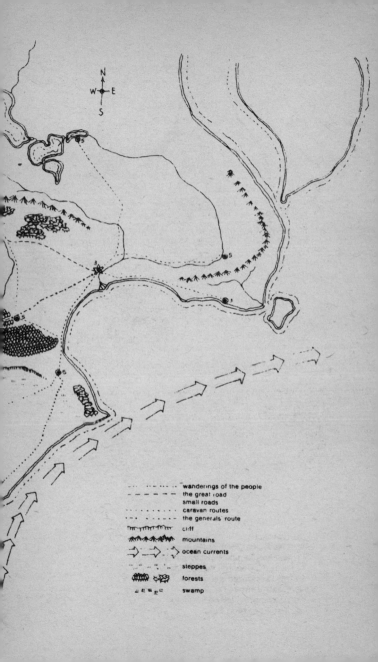

wanderings of the people
the great road
small roads
caravan routes
the generals' route
cliff
mountains
ocean currents
steppes
forests
swamp

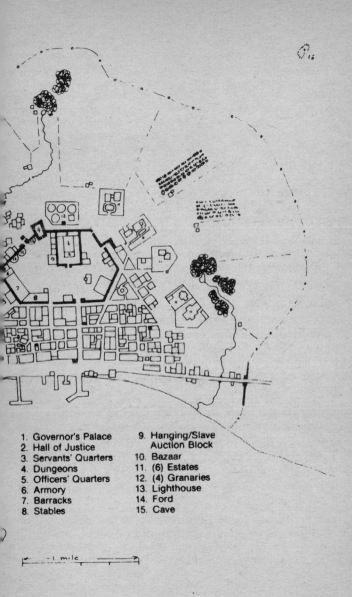

1. Governor's Palace
2. Hall of Justice
3. Servants' Quarters
4. Dungeons
5. Officers' Quarters
6. Armory
7. Barracks
8. Stables
9. Hanging/Slave Auction Block
10. Bazaar
11. (6) Estates
12. (4) Granaries
13. Lighthouse
14. Ford
15. Cave

├─── 1 mile ───┤

SOUL OF THE CITY

Dramatis Personae

The Townspeople

DUBRO, *Bazaar blacksmith and husband to Illyra.*
ILLYRA, *half-blood S'danzo seeress with True Sight.*
ARTON, *their son, marked by the gods and magic as part of an emerging divinity known as the Stormchildren.*
LILLIS, *Arton's twin sister.*

JUBAL, *prematurely aged former gladiator. Once he openly ran Sanctuary's most visible criminal organization, the hawkmasks; now he works behind the scenes.*

MORUTH, *king of the Downwind beggars.*

ZIP, *bitter young terrorist and Sanctuary native. Lover of Kama and leader of the Popular Front for the Liberation of Sanctuary (PFLS), an anarchist group supported by Roxane's Death Squads and funded by Nisibis money.*

The Magicians

AŠKELON, *The Entelechy of Dreams, a magician so powerful that the gods have set him apart from men to rule in Meridian, the source of dreams. Once betrothed to Jihan; now married to Tempus's sister, Cime.*

DATAN, *Supreme of the Nisibisi wizards; slain by the Stepson and Randal. His globe of power, which now belongs to Randal, was the foremost of such artifacts manufactured along Wizardwall.*

ISCHADE, *necromancer and thief. Her curse is passed to her lovers who die from it.*
HAUGHT, *her apprentice. A Nisibisi dancer and freed slave.*
KOTILIS, *partner of Shiey and actual cook at the Peres house.*

MOR-AM, *Ischade's servant. A Hawkmask she saved from certain death, whose pain and torment she holds at bay in exchange for other services.*

MORIA, *Mor-am's sister, also once a Hawkmask but now chatelaine of Ischade's uptown establishment, the Peres house. Haught, stealing Ischade's magic, has transformed her from an Ilsigi street-wench into an aristocratic, Rankan beauty.*

SHIEY, *one-handed cook and thief sent by Moruth to supervise the servants at the Peres house.*

STILCHO, *one of the Sanctuary natives chosen to replace the Stepsons when they followed Tempus to Wizardwall. He was tortured and killed by Moruth, then reanimated by Ischade, whom he has served as ambassador to Hell.*

ROXANE; DEATH'S QUEEN, *Nisibisi witch. Heiress to all Nisi power and enemies. Her nearly fatal weakness was her love for the Stepson, Nikodemos.*

SNAPPER JO, *a fiend summoned and controlled by Roxane. Employed by the Vulgar Unicorn as a bouncer.*

Others

BRACHIS, *Supreme Archpriest of Vashanka, companion of Theron.*

MRADHON VIS, *Nisibisi mercenary, adventurer, and occasional spy.*

THERON, *new military Rankan Emperor. A usurper placed on the throne with the aid of Tempus and his allies.*

The nobility of Sanctuary

GYSKOURAS, *one of the Stormchildren, conceived during an ill-fated Ritual of the Ten Slaying, a commemoration of Vashanka's vengeance on his brothers.*

SEYLALHA, *his mother, a temple dancer chosen to be Azyuna in the Ten Slaying Rite.*

PRINCE KADAKITHIS, *charismatic but somewhat naive half-brother of the recently assassinated Emperor, Abakithis.*

MOLIN TORCHOLDER; TORCH, *Archpriest and architect of Vashanka; Guardian of the Stormchildren.*

HOXA, *his secretary. An Ilsigi merchant's son, born and raised in Sanctuary.*

ISAMBARD, *a young Rankan priest loyal to Molin.*

SHUPANSEA; SHU-SEA, *head of the Beysib exiles in Sanctuary; mortal avatar of the Beysib mother goddess.*

TASFALEN LANCOTHIS, *Rankan noble of jaded and sophisticated pleasures.*

The Military within Sanctuary

RANKAN 3RD COMMANDO, *mercenary company founded by Tempus Thales and noted for its brutal efficiency.*

KAMA; JES, *Tempus's barely acknowledged daughter. Tactical liaison between the 3rd and both the PFLS and the Stepsons.*

STEPSONS; SACRED BANDERS, *members of a mercenary unit dedicated to Vashanka and under the command of Tempus Thales.*

ABARSIS; THE SLAUGHTER PRIEST, *founder of the Stepsons; castrated and enslaved by Rankan conquerors, he was rescued by Tempus and formed the Stepsons as a token of personal, rather than imperial, loyalty. He sacrificed his life so that Tempus might have vengeance on Jubal and was seen to ascend into heaven by those Stepsons who attended his funerary games.*

CRITIAS; CRIT, *left-side leader paired with Straton. Estranged from Straton because of Straton's love-alliance with Ischade. Second in command after Tempus.*

JANNI, *Nikodemos's right-side partner; tortured and killed by Roxane. Raised to heaven by Abarsis and restored to a semblance of life by Ischade.*

JIHAN, *daughter of the primal god, Stormbringer. Created from an ocean storm as a mate for Aškelon, she has since fallen in love with Tempus and has accepted the inconvenience of reality in order to be with him and the other Stepsons.*

NIKODEMOS; NIKO; STEALTH, *Bandaran Adept skilled in mental and martial disciplines. Once a captive of Roxane and Datan.*

RANDAL; WITCHY-EARS, *the only mage ever trusted by Tempus or admitted into the Sacred Band.*

STRATON; STRAT; ACE, *right-side partner of Critias. Enamored of Ischade and, so far, immune to her curse.*

TEMPUS THALES; THE RIDDLER, *nearly immortal mercenary, a partner of Vashanka before that god's exile; commander of the Stepsons; cursed with insomnia and a fatal inability to give or receive love.*

WALEGRIN, *Rankan army officer assigned to the Sanctuary garrison where his father had been slain by the S'danzo many years before. Half-brother of the seeress, Illyra.*

THRUSHER, *his lieutenant.*

CYTHEN, *a former Hawkmask now allied with Walegrin. The only woman living in the garrison barracks.*

ZALBAR, *captain of the Hell-Hounds which, since the arrival of the Beysib exiles, have lost most of their influence.*

The Gods

MOTHER BEY, *the many-aspected goddess of the Beysib exiles. Within the Beysib Empire she has demoted all male deities to the status of heroes within her cult.*

STORMBRINGER, *primal stormgod/wargod. The pattern for all other such gods, he is not, himself, the object of organized worship.*

VASHANKA, *stormgod/wargod of the original Rankan lands; vanquished and exiled beyond the reach of his onetime worshipers.*

POWER PLAY

Janet Morris

Tempus, a mercenary general in the service of Ranke's new emperor, was knee-deep in the bloody purges marking the first winter of Theron's accession to the Rankan throne when the sky above the walled city began to weep black tears.

By the time dawn should have broken, ashen clouds massed to the very vault of heaven so that not even the Sun God's sharpest rays could pierce the arrayed armies of the night. The city of Ranke, once the brightest jewel of the Rankan empire, shuddered in the dark, her ochre walls stained dusky from the storm's black and ugly might.

Thunder growled; winds yowled. Black hail pelted Theron's palace, shattering windows and pounding doors. On temple streets and cultured byways it bounced, sharp as diamonds and large as heads, bringing impious priests to their knees and cheap nobles to charity in slick streets covered with greasy slush freezing to ice as black, some said, as their emperor Theron's heart.

For all knew that Theron had come to power in a coup instigated by the armies—he was a creature of blood, a wild beast of the battlefield. And the proof of this was in the allies who had brought him to the Imperial palace: Nisibisi witches, demons of the black beyond, devils of horrid aspect, even the feared near-immortals of the blood cults—Aškelon, the lord of dreams, and his brother-in-law Tempus, demigod and favorite son of Vashanka, the Rankan wargod, to name but two— had lent their strength to Theron's cause.

Did not Tempus still labor at his gory task of purging the disloyal—all who had been influential in Abakithis's court? Did not women still wake to empty beds and find pouches made of human skin and filled with thirty gold soldats (the Rankan price for one human life) nailed to their boudoir doors?

Did not those few remaining adherents of Abakithis, former emperor of Ranke (now deceased, unavenged, much cursed in his uneasy grave), still scuttle even through the deadly, knife-sharp hail with bulging pockets to the mercenaries' guildhall to leave their fortunes at the desk with scrawled notes saying, "For Tempus, to distribute as he wills, from the admiring and loyal family of So-and-So," while servants spirited noble wives and children out back ways and slumyard gates in beggars' guise?

Thus it was whispered, as the storm raged unabated into its second day, that Theron and his creature Tempus were to blame for this black blizzard straight from hell.

It was whispered by a woman to Critias, Tempus's first officer and finest covert actor, who had infiltrated the noble strata of the imperial city.

And Crit, with a wry twitch of lips that drew down his patrician nose and a rake of his swordhand through dark, feathery hair, replied to the governor's wife he was bedding: "No one gives a contract for a sunrise, m'lady. No *man*, that is. Theron is no more than that. When gods throw tantrums, even Tempus listens."

Crit had fought in the Wizard Wars up north and the woman knew it. His guise was that of a disaffected officer who had renounced his commission after Abakithis's assassination at the Festival of Man and now, like so many others of the old guard, scrambled from allegiance to allegiance in search of safety.

So the governor's wife just ran a finger along his jaw and smiled commiseratingly as she said, "You men of the armies . . . all alike. I suppose you're telling me that this is good? This storm, this hail black as hell? That it's a sign we poor women cannot read?"

And (thinking of the prognosticators—bits of hair and silver and bone and luck—nestled in the pouch dangling from his belt that, with the rest of his clothes, lay in a heap at the foot of another man's bed) Crit replied in Court Rankene, "When the Storm God returns to the armies, wars can be won—not just fought interminably. Without Him, we've just been marking time. If He's angry, He'll let us know on what account. And I'd bet it won't be Theron's—or Tempus's. One's a general whom the soldiers chose exactly because the god had abandoned us during Abakithis's reign; the other is . . ."

It was not the woman's hand, reaching low, which made

him pause. She wanted Crit's protection; information was what he'd sought here in return. And gotten what he'd come for, and more from this one—all a Rankan lady had to give. So he thought—in a moment of unaccustomed tenderness for one who would likely entertain, on his account, the crowds who'd throng the execution stands when the weather broke—to explain to her about Tempus. About what and who the man Crit had sworn to serve was, and was not.

He settled for ". . . Tempus is what Father Enlil—Lord Storm to the armies—wills, and cursed more than Ranke and all her enemies put together. By gods and men, by magic and mages. If there's hell to pay because of Theron's reign, rest assured, lady, it's he who'll suffer in all our steads."

The Rankan woman, from the look on her face and the hunger on her lips, had lost interest in the subject. But Crit had not. When he left her, he marked her door with a sign for the palace police without even a second thought to the fine body behind it which would soon be lifeless.

The sky was still black as a witch's crotch and the wind was chorusing its judgment song in a many-throated voice Crit had heard occasionally on the battlefield when Tempus's non-human allies took a hand in this skirmish or that—choraling the way it used to when wizard weather blew in Sanctuary, where Crit's partner and his brothers of the Sacred Band were now, down at the empire's most foul and egregious southernmost appurtenance.

By the time Crit had retrieved his horse, his fingers were playing with the luck charms in his beltpouch. Normally, he'd have pulled them out, squatted down, shaken and thrown them in the straw for guidance.

But the storm was guidance enough; he didn't need to ask a question he wouldn't like the answer to. If his partner Strat had been on his right tonight, he'd have bet his friend any odds that, when the weather broke, Tempus would come rousting Crit without so much as an explanation and they'd be heading south to Sanctuary where the Sacred Band was quartered for the winter.

Not that he didn't want to see Strat—he did. Not that he wasn't happy that the Storm god Vashanka, God of the Armies, of Rape and Pillage, of Bloodlust and Fury and Death's Gate, was manifest—he was. What he'd told the Rankan bitch was true—you couldn't win a war without your god. But Vashanka, the Rankan Storm God, had deserted the Stepsons, Crit's unit, in their need. So the unit had taken up with another, perhaps greater, god: Father Enlil.

And the black, roiling clouds above, the voices which spoke thunder over the fighter's head, were telling a man who didn't like gods much better than magic and who was first officer to a demigod who meddled with both, that Vashanka might not be too pleased with the fickle men who once had slaughtered in His name and now did so in Another's.

Things were so damned complicated whenever Tempus was involved.

Grabbing a tuft of mane, Crit swung up on his warhorse and reined it around so hard it half-reared and then, finding itself headed toward the mercenaries' guild and its own stall, safety and comfort in the storm, fairly bolted through the treacherous, slushy streets of Ranke.

Despite the darkened ways and chancy footing, Crit let the young horse run, trusting pedestrians, should there be any, to scatter, and armed patrols to recognize him for who and what he was. The horse had a right to comfort, where it could find some. Crit couldn't think of a thing that would do the same for him, now that the gods had dropped one shoe and all he could do was wait until Tempus dropped the other.

The storm didn't exactly break, but on the fourth day it mellowed.

By then, Theron and Tempus had summoned Brachis, High Priest of the Variously Named Wargods of Imperial Ranke, and concocted a likely story for the populace.

Executions, held in abeyance for the first three days of the storm, were resumed. "More purges, obviously, Your Majesty," Brachis had suggested, unctuous to the point of insult, managing by his exaggerated servility to mean the opposite of what he said, "will appease the hungry gods."

And Theron, old and as gray as the shadows in this newly acquired but not yet conquered palace full of politicians and whores, gave Brachis a stare fully as black as the raging sky outside and said, "Right, priest. Let's have a dozen of your worst enemies bled out in Blood Square by lunch."

Tempus stayed an impulse to touch his old friend Theron's knee under the table.

But Brachis didn't rise to Theron's bait. The priest bowed

his way out in a swish of copper-beaded robes.

"God's balls, Riddler," said the aging general to the ageless one, "do *you* think we've angered the gods? More to the point, do you think we've *got* one to anger?"

Theron's jaw jutted so that the pitting of age made it look like a walnut shell, or the snout of the moth-eaten geriatric lion he so much resembled from his thinning, unkempt mane to his scarred and twisted claws. He was a big man still, his power no mere memory, but fresh and flowing in corded veins and leathery sinews—big and powerful in his aged prime, except when seen in close proximity to Tempus, the avatar of Storm Gods on earth, whose yarrow-honey hair and high brow free from lines resembled so much the votive statues of Vashanka still worshiped in the land. Tempus's eyes were long and full of guile, his form heroic, his aspect one of a man on the joyous side of forty, though he'd seen empires rise and fall and fully expected to see the end of this one—to bury Theron as he had and would so many other men, with all their might ranged round them. And Theron knew the truth of it—he'd known Tempus since both were seemingly of an age, fighting the Defender on Wizardwall's skirts when the Rankan Empire was just a babe. The two were honest with one another when it was possible; they were careful when it was not.

"Got a god to anger? We've got *something* mad enough to spit, I'll own," Tempus replied. Now, Tempus knew, was not the time to raise false hopes of Vashanka the Missing God's return in a warrior who'd willingly and knowingly come to a throne whose weight would kill him. It was the dirtiest of jobs, was kingship, and Theron had become the man to do it by default. "If it's Vashanka, then it's a matter between Him and Enlil. Theomachy tends to kill more men than gods. Don't be too anxious to get the armies' hopes up—the war with Mygdonia won't end by gods' wills, any more than it will by Nisibisi magic."

"That's what you think this infernal darkness is, then— magic? Your nemesis, perhaps . . . the Nisibisi witch?"

"Or yours, the Nisibisi warlocks. What matter, gods or magic? If I thought he had the power, I'd pick Brachis as the culprit. He'd do without both of us well enough."

"We'd do without all of his well enough. But we're stuck with one another, for the nonce. Unless, of course, you've a suggestion . . . some way to rid me, as the saying has gone from time immemorial, of all meddlesome priests?"

The two were fencing with words, neither addressing the real problem: the storm was being taken as an omen, and a bad one, on the nature of Theron's rule.

The aging general fingered a jeweled goblet whose bowl was balanced upon a winged lion and sighed deeply at almost the same time that Tempus's rattling chuckle sounded. "An omen, is it, old lion? Is that what you *really* want—an omen to make this a mandate from the gods, not a critique?"

"What *I* want?" Theron thundered in return, suddenly sweeping up the artsy, jewel-encrusted goblet of state and throwing it so hard against the farther wall that it bounced back to land among the dregs spilled from it and roll eerily, back and forth in a circle, in the middle of the floor.

Back and forth it rolled, first one way and then the other, making a sound like chariot wheels upon the stone floor, a sound which grew louder and melded with the thunder outside and the renewed clatter of hailstones which resembled horses' hooves, as if a team from heaven was thundering down the blackened sky.

And Tempus found the hair on his arms raising up and the skin under his beard crawling as the wine dregs spattered on the floor began to smoke and steam and the dented goblet to shimmer and gleam and, inside his head, a rustle—familiar and unfamiliar—began to sound as a god came to visit there.

He really hated it when gods intruded inside his skull. He managed to mutter "Crap! Get thee hence!" before he realized that it was neither the deep and primal breathing of Father Enlil—Lord Storm—nor the passionate and demanding boom of Vashanka the Pillager which he was hearing so loud that the shimmer and thunder and smoke issuing from the goblet and dregs before him were diminished to insignificance. It was neither voice from either god; it was comprised of both.

Both! This was too much. His own fury roused. He detested being invaded; he hated being an instrument, a pawn, the butler of one murder god, the batman of another.

He fought the heaviness in his limbs which demanded that he sit, still and pop-eyed, like Theron across the table from him, and meekly submit to whatever manifestation was in the process of coalescing before him. He snarled and cursed the very existence of godhead and managed to get his hands on the stout edge of the plank table.

He squeezed the wood so hard that it dented and formed round his fingers like clay, but he could not rise nor could he banish the babble of divine infringement from his head.

And before him, where a cup had rolled, wheels spun—golden-rimmed wheels of a war chariot drawn by smoke-colored Trôs horses whose shod hooves struck sparks from the stones of the palace floor. Out of a maelstrom of swirling smoke it came, and Tempus was so mesmerized by the squealing of the horses and the screech of unearthly stresses around the rent in time and space through which the chariot approached that he only barely noticed that Theron had thrown up both hands to shield his face and was cowering like an aged child at his own table.

The horses were harnessed in red leather that was shiny, as if wet. Beyond the blood-red reins were hands, and the arms attached were well-formed and strong, brown and smooth, without hair or scar above graven gauntlets. The driver's torso was covered by a cuirass of enameled metal, cast to the physique beneath it, jointed and gilded in the fashion chosen by the Sacred Band at its inception.

Tempus did not need to see the face, by then, to know that he was not being visited by a god, nor an archmage, nor even a demon, but by a creature more strange: as the chariot emerged fully from the miasma around it and the horses snorted and plunged, dancing in place, and the wheels screeched to a halt, Tempus saw a hand raise to a brow in a greeting of equals.

The greeting was for him, not for Theron, who cowered with wide eyes. The face of the man in the chariot smiled softly. The eyes resting upon Tempus so fondly were as pale and pure as cool water. And as the vision opened its mouth to speak, the god-din in Tempus's ears subsided to a rustle, then to whispers, then to contented sighs that faded entirely away when Abarsis, dead Slaughter Priest and patron shade of the Sacred Band, wrapped his blood-red reins casually around the chariot's brake and stepped down from his car, arms wide to embrace Tempus, whom Abarsis had loved better than life when the ghost had been a man.

There was nothing for it, Tempus realized, but to make the best of the situation, though seeing the materialization of a boy who had sought an honorable death in Tempus's service wrenched his heart.

The boy was now a power on his own—a power from

beyond Death's Gate, true, but a power all the same.

"Commander," said the velvet-voiced shade, "I see from your face that you still have it in your heart to love me. That's good. This was not an easy journey to arrange."

The two embraced, and Abarsis's upswept eyes and high curved cheeks, his young bull's neck and his glossy black hair, felt all too real—as substantial as the splinters that had somehow gotten under Tempus's fingernails.

And the boy was yet strong—that is, the shade was. Tempus, stepping back, started to speak but found his voice choked with melancholy. What did one say to the dead? Not "How's life?" surely. Certainly not the Sacred Band greeting. . . .

But Abarsis spoke it to Tempus, as he had said it so long ago in Sanctuary, where he'd gone to die. "Life to you, Riddler, and everlasting glory. And to your friend . . . to *our* friend . . . Theron of Ranke, salutations."

Hearing his name shook Theron from his funk. But the old fighter was nearly speechless, quaking visibly.

Seeing this, Tempus recovered himself: "You scared us half to death. Is this *your* darkness, then?" Tempus stepped back and waved a hand toward the sky beyond the corbeled ceiling overhead. "If so, we could do without it. Scares the locals. We're trying to settle in a military rule here, not start a civil war."

A shadow passed quickly over the beautiful face of the Slaughter Priest and Tempus, seeing it, wanted to ask, "Are you real? Are you reborn? Have you come to stay?"

The shade looked him hard in the eye and that glance struck his soul and shocked it. "No. None of that, Riddler. I am here to bring a message and ask a favor—for favors done and yet to be done."

"Ahem. Tempus, will you introduce me? It's my palace, after all," the emperor growled, bluffing annoyance, straining for composure, and casting covetous glances at the horses—if such they were—which stood at parade rest in their traces, ears pricked forward, just a bit of steam issuing from their nostrils. "Favors," Theron murmured, "done and yet to be done. . . ."

"Theron, Emperor of Ranke, General of the Armies and so forth, meet Abarsis, Slaughter Priest, former High Priest of Vashanka, former—"

"Former living ally," Abarsis cut in, smooth as a whetted

blade, "and ally still, Theron. We've a problem, and it lies in Sanctuary. Speaking through priests is a matter for gods; my mandate is different. Tempus, whom we both love, must listen to gods, not priests, but on this occasion, I am . . . well equipped . . ." His grin flashed as it had once in life: ". . . to interpret." Then he shifted and his gaze caught Tempus's and held: "The message is: the globes of Nisibisi power must be destroyed; all the gods will rejoice when it is done. Destroyed in Sanctuary, where there are tortured souls of yours and mine to be released. The favor is: grant Niko's wish in a matter of children . . . yours and Ours."

Ours? There was no mistaking the upper-case tone Abarsis had used—a tone reserved for deific matters and one word spoken by the dead High Priest of Vashanka who had come so far to utter it. Liking the smell of things less and less, Tempus took a step backward and sat upon the table's edge, thinking, *For this, he comes to me. Wonderful. Now what?*

For Tempus, who could refuse a god and obstruct an archmage, knew, looking at Abarsis, that he could refuse this one nothing. It was an old debt, a mutual responsibility stretching far beyond such trifles as life and death. It was a matter of souls, and Tempus's soul was very old. So old that, seeing Abarsis yet young, yet beautiful in his spirit and his honor in a way Tempus no longer could be, the man called the Riddler felt suddenly very tired.

And Tempus, who never slept—who had not slept since he had been cursed by an archmage and taken solace in the protection of a god three centuries past—began to feel drowsy. His eyelids grew heavy and Abarsis's words grew loud, echoing unintelligibly so that it seemed as if Theron and Abarsis spoke together in some room far away.

Just before he collapsed on the table, snoring deeply in a sleep that would last until the weather broke the following day, Tempus heard Abarsis say clearly, "And for you, Tempus, whom I love above all men, I have this special gift . . . not much, just a token: on this one evening, my lord, I have haggled from the gods for you a good night's rest. So now, sleep and dream of me."

And thus Tempus slept, and when he woke, Abarsis was long gone and preparations for Theron, Tempus, and a hand-picked contingent to depart for Sanctuary were well under way.

Trouble was coming to Sanctuary; Roxane could feel it in her bones. The premonition cut like a knife to the very quick of the Nisibisi witch, once called Death's Queen, who now huddled in her shrouded hovel on Sanctuary's White Foal River, beset from within and without.

Once she had been nearly all powerful; once she had been a perpetrator, not a victim; once she had decreed Suffering and marshalled Woe upon human cattle from Sanctuary's sorry spit to Wizardwall's wildest peaks.

But that was before she'd fallen in love with a mortal and paid the ancient price. Perhaps if that mortal had not been Stealth, called Nikodemos, Sacred Bander and member in good standing of Tempus's blood-drenched cadre of Stepsons, it would not seem so foolish now to have traded in immortality for the ability to shed a woman's tears and feel a woman's fleeting joy.

But Niko had betrayed her. She should have known; if she'd been a human woman she would have—no man, and most especially no thrice-paired fighter who'd taken the Sacred Band oath, would feel loyalty or honor toward a woman when it conflicted with his bond with men.

She should have known, but she hadn't even guessed. For Niko was the tenderest of souls where women were concerned; he loved them as a class, as he loved fine horses and young children—not lasciviously, but honestly and freely. Now that she understood, it was an insult: She was no waif, no fuddle-headed twat, no inconsequential piece of fluff. And there was injury to add to insult's sting: Roxane had given up immortality to love a mortal who wasn't capable of appreciating such a gift.

She had been betrayed by her "beloved" over a matter that should have been towering only in its insignificance: the "life" of a petty mageling, a would-be wizard called Randal, a flop-eared, freckled fool who fooled now with forces beyond his ability to control.

Yes, Niko had dared to trick Roxane, to distract her with his charms while this posturing prestidigitator, whom she'd thought to have for dinner, got away.

And now Niko lurked in priestholes, palaces, and princely bedrooms, protected by Randal (who had a Globe of Power similar to Roxane's own, and more powerful) and the counter-magical armor given Niko by the entelechy of dreams. Not once did sweet Stealth venture riverward, though his de facto commander, Straton of the Stepsons, rode this way on evenings to visit another witch.

This other witch, too, was an enemy of Roxane's—Ischade the necromant, whom by rights the Stepsons should have hated more than they did Roxane, vilified in their prayers as they nightly did Death's Queen.

There was some irony to that: Ischade, a tawdry soul-sucker with limited power and unlimited lust, was a friend of the Stepsons, ally of the mercenary army that was all that stood between Sanctuary and total chaos now that the town was divided into blood feuds and factions as the Rankan Empire's grasp grew weak and the Rankan prince, Kadakithis, was barricaded in his palace with some salmon-eyed Beysib slut from a fishy foreign land.

And Roxane, who'd been Death's Queen on Wizardwall and flown high, ruler of all she once surveyed, was shunned by Stepsons and even by lesser factions in the town—all but her own death squads, some truly dead and raised from crypts to do her bidding, some only a hair's-breadth away from mossy graves like One-Thumb, the Vulgar Unicorn's proprietor, a.k.a. Lastel, and Zip, guttersnipe leader of the PFLS (Popular Front for the Liberation of Sanctuary) rebels who couldn't get along without her help.

And Snapper Jo, of course, her single remaining fiend—a warty, gray-skinned, wall-eyed beast, snaggle-toothed and orange-haired, whom she'd summoned from a nearby hell to serve her—she still had Snapper, though lately he'd been taking his spy's job of day-barkeep at the Vulgar Unicorn too much to heart, thinking silly thoughts of camaraderie with humans (who'd no more accept a fiend as one of them than the Stepsons had accepted Roxane).

And she had her snakes, of course, a fresh supply, whom she could witch into human form for intervals (though Sanctuary's snakes weren't bred for masquerading and turned out small, sleepy in cold weather, and even more dull-witted than the northern kind).

Still, it was a pair of snakes—a butler-snake and a bodyguard—whom she called to build a fire in her witching room, to bring her chalcedony water bowl and place it on a column of porphyry near the hearth, to stay and watch and wait with her while she poured salt into the water and words came from her mouth to make the salt into her will and the water bowl into the open wounds in Sanctuary. Not wounds of flesh, but wounds of spirit—the arrogance of loyalty given and withheld, the gall of greed, the acne of innocence, the lacerations of love, the pustules of passion which prickled such hearts as Straton's, as Randal's, as those of the prince/governor and his flounder-faced consort, Shupansea (fool enough to keep snakes herself, thinking that Beysib snakes might be immune to Nisibisi snake magic), and even as Niko's own consuming compassion for a pair of children he wet-nursed like some useless Rankan matron.

And the water in her bowl took chop as the salt hit it, then began to cloud and then to bubble as if salt had turned to acid in hearts all around the town. The color of the water grew grayer, more opaque, and outside her skin-covered window, snow began to fall in giant flakes.

"Go, snakes," she crooned, "go meet your brothers in the palace of the prince. Meet and eat them, then defeat the peace between the Beysib and her Rankan host. And find those children, both, and bite them with the poison of your fangs, so that death beats down on midnight wings and Niko will be forced to come to me . . . to me to save them." Almost, she didn't get those last words out, because a chuckle rose to block the speech's end—especially the word "save."

For as she'd looked into the bowl she'd seen a vision, then another. First she'd seen riders, and a boat with a lion rampant on its prow: one rider was her ancient enemy, Tempus, called the Sleepless One, avatar of godly mischief; another was Jihan, a more potent enemy, Froth Daughter, princess of the endless sea, a copper-colored nymph of matchless passion, a sprite with all the strength of moon and tides between her knees; another was Critias, Strat's partner and better half, the coldest and boldest of the Stepsons, and the only man among the lot of them who didn't need more-than-mortal help to do his job. And on the boat, now seeming like a wedding gift, all wrapped in gilt and gloriously colored sails as it drew nearer, was a man she'd helped become a king, one who owed an unequivocal debt to Death's Queen—Theron, Emperor of Ranke, who was so anxious to pay Roxane's price he was trekking to the empire's anus to bow his knee.

Oh, yes, she thought then. Trouble, let it come. For Roxane, once the visions were cleared from the salted water of her bowl by an impatient, dusky hand, had an idea—a thought, an inspiration, a vengeful task to undertake fitting to all the harm past and present denizens of Sanctuary had done her: She'd seen the error of her ways, and now she'd seen a new solution. She'd given up too much for Nikodemos, who'd turned on her and spurned her. She'd trade this batch of hapless souls to get back what she'd so foolishly bargained away.

And then it was left to her only to dismiss the snakes, drink the water in the bowl, and settle down spread-legged in the middle of her summoning room floor, awaiting the Devils of Demonic Deals, the Negotiators of Necromancy, the Underworld's Underwriters, to appear, to take the bait a witch could offer and then, when sated, be tricked into giving Roxane back immortality in exchange for the deaths of a pair of children who might be gods if ever they grew up, and that of Nikodemos, who deserved no better if he'd thought to spurn the witch who loved him and survive it. Of course, she'd throw in Tempus, too, for fun. He'd make an undead of choice to send raping and pillaging up and down the streets of Sanctuary of an evening, streets so thick with hatred and slick with blood no one would even think to worry about what kind of death they got.

For Sanctuarites cared only for this life, not the next. They were ignorant of choices made beyond the grave, or given up today for trifles. They didn't know or care that an eternity of hell could be had for cheap, or that the gods offered out another way.

This was why she liked it here, did Roxane. Even once she'd sacrificed Niko and his ilk—the entire Sacred Band and unpaired Stepsons, if she got lucky—she'd stay around. Once there was no more Ischade to interfere, no silly priests like the Torchholder to try to resurrect a dead god's cult, the place would let her have her way.

And so, decided, she crooked a finger and, from nowhere visible, a sound like hellish hinges squeaking reverberated through her chamber, a non-door swung down, and a Globe of Power could be glimpsed, spinning gently on its axis of golden glyphs, its stones beginning to glow as its song of sorcery spun louder and, from hells Sanctuary wasn't used to accommodating, a demon choir began to chant.

It was the old way, the only way: evil for evil, tenfold. And she'd promised hell to pay, visited upon this town for its offenses and its slights.

There remained only to touch flesh and nail to the globe spinning larger, closer, right before her eyes.

She reached out and braced herself, for a demon lover would come with contact: One did have to pay as one went, even if one was Nisibis's finest witch.

Her nail screeched into the high peaks' clay, and a demon screeched into existence between her knees, and a hellish gale whose like was known as wizard weather up and down the land stretched from Sanctuary's southernmost tip up along the Rankan seaboard where the imperial ship was under way.

And everywhere men remarked that, even for wizard weather, the gale was fierce and loud, and full of sounds the like of a goddess being raped in some forgotten passion play.

Sanctuary promised nothing of the sort to Critias, who'd ridden downcountry at an ungodly rate with Tempus and his inhuman consort, Jihan, daughter of the primal power men called Stormbringer (when they were so unlucky as to have to call Him anything at all).

The ride—across No Man's Land, a shortcut full of shades and mirages through a desert the party shouldn't have been able to cross in twice the time—hadn't been the sort of trip Crit liked. It was too fast, too easy, too full of magic—or whatever the equivalent was when power was fielded not by a human mage, but by Jihan, daughter of Stormbringer, lord of wind and wave.

Now that they'd nearly reached the town, it was too late for Crit to ask his commander questions—whether, as rumor had it, Abarsis had really appeared to the Riddler in Theron's palace; why, even if that were true, Tempus had seen fit to split his forces: the three of them were worth more than the score of fighters accompanying Theron on his ocean voyage.

But straight answers were lacking in the Rankan Empire this season, and Tempus, with Jihan around, was more obscure than usual.

So it came to pass that Tempus said to Crit as they came down the General's Road to the ford at the White Foal River: "Make your own way henceforth, Stepson, among the pigs in their mire. Find Straton and reconvene your covert actors: I want the whereabouts of Roxane and her power globe by midnight."

"Is that *all?*" Crit asked, sarcasm finding its way into his

tone—no disrespect, but gods whispered in the Riddler's ears
and never spoke to Critias at all, so that orders like these always
seemed impossible, issuing from nowhere, though he'd hardly
ever failed to carry through a task, however vague, that the
Riddler set him.

But this time, as his sorrel stallion pawed the White Foal's
mud and lewdly eyed the blue roan Jihan rode, Crit was more
than usually defensive: Down in Sanctuary, across the Foal
somewhere, was Kama, Tempus's daughter, whom Crit had
got with child. It had been in the Wizard Wars, against the
Riddler's orders, and ill had come of it for everyone involved.
He'd not thought of her—an act of will, not fortune—until
this moment, but looking out across the Foal where the lights
of Sanctuary's whorehold, the Street of Red Lanterns, were
twinkling in the dusk, suddenly the mercenary fighter could
think of nothing else.

And Tempus, who understood too much too often, who
healed from every mortal cut he took, who buried everyone he
loved in time and enjoyed the confidence of gods and shades,
said softly in a voice like the river coursing gravel, "No, not
all. A start. Take a unit of your choosing, find Straton, use
what he has, destroy Roxane's power globe by dawn, then seek
me in the palace."

"And is *that* the whole of it, Commander?" Crit asked la-
conically, as if the task were simple, not a death sentence or
an invitation to mutiny.

Crit saw even Jihan's feral eyes go wide. The Froth Daughter, achingly attractive to a fighter with her form clothed in
scale armor shining like the dusk, looked between the two men
and whispered something to the Riddler, then looked back at
Crit.

The long-eyed Riddler did not, just stroked his gray's arched
neck. "It's enough," replied the man Crit served and often had
thought he'd die to please.

That evening, later, riding alone through the Common Gate
in search of Straton, Critias was no longer so sure that an
honorable death would be a privilege—not when it was here.

Sanctuary hadn't changed, or if it had, the change was for
the worse. There were checkpoints everywhere and Crit had
to bully his way through two of them before finding a soldier
he knew—someone who had an armband he could comman-
deer.

By then he'd skirted the palace, green-walled because some sort of fungus or moss was growing there, and entered the Bazaar where illicit drugs, girls and boys, and even lives were hawked openly in twisting streets.

His back unguarded, his sorrel spooked and dancing, he was heading for the Maze, a deeper slum than this one, against his better judgment because he didn't want to look for Strat where his erstwhile partner probably could be found—lying in with the vampire woman who held sway in Shambles Cross and used the White Foal to dispose of victims.

From between two produce stalls Critias heard a hiss and a low whistle—old northern recognition signs. Adjusting the armband (a dirty rainbow of cloth specked with long-dried blood), he looked about: to his right was a fortune-teller's tent—a S'danzo girl, Illyra, worked there. He saw her standing in the door.

They'd never met, yet she waved—a hesitant gesture, part warding sign, part blessing.

The last thing Crit wanted was his fortune told: he could feel it in his pouch, where amulets grew heavy; on his neck, where hairs stood on end; in his gut, which had frozen solid when Tempus had calmly ordered him to his death on a flimsy pretext. Crit had never thought the Riddler'd held a grudge about his daughter and her miscarried child. But there was no other reason to send Stepsons up against a witch like Roxane.

Was that, then, what Abarsis had come to say to him? That it was time a few more Sacred Banders made their way to heaven? Was Abarsis lonely for his boys? Before Tempus had led the Band, Crit had fought for the Slaughter Priest. But in those days Abarsis had been of flesh and blood, even if obsessed with tasks done for the gods.

"Psst! Crit! *Here!*"

Between the stalls, opposite the fortune-teller's tent, were too many shadows. Crit sat his horse, arm crooked over his pommel, and waited, watching where his mount's ears pricked like dowsing rods.

Out from the gloom came a hand, white and long—a woman's, despite the leather bracer.

Crit squeezed with his right knee and the sorrel ambled forward—one pace, two. Then he said, "Hello, Kama. What's that you've got there, friend or captive?"

Beside the woman half in shadow was a waif—a flat-faced boy with almond eyes and scruffy beard who wore a black rag bound across his brow.

The boy didn't matter; the woman, crossbow pointed half to port so that its flight would skewer Crit's belly if she pulled its trigger mechanism back, mattered more than Crit liked.

Tempus's daughter laughed the throaty laugh that had gotten Crit in trouble long ago. "Looking for someone?" Kama never answered stupid questions. She was as sharp as her father, in her way. But not as ethical.

"Strat," he said simply, to make things clear.

"Our 'acting' military governor, now that Kadakithis lies abed with Beysibs? The leader of the militias and their councils? The vampire's fancy man? You know the way—down on the White Foal. But do take an unfortunate or two to appease her hunger—for old time's sake, I'll warn you."

Crit didn't react to Kama's acid comments on Strat's faring—for all he knew, it might be true; and he'd never show her she could still reach him, let alone hurt him. He said, "How about this pud you've got here? Will he do?" For the signs of something intimate between the woman and the street tough were clear to see—hips brushed, though Kama held the crossbow; whispers went back and forth through motionless lips.

And the youth was armed—slingshot on one wrist, dagger at his hip. The slingshot was arrogantly aimed at Crit's eyes by the time Kama said, "Don't make the mistake of thinking you understand what you're seeing, fighter. You'll need help. If you're smart, you'll remember where and how to get it—Strat's part of Sanctuary's problem, not its solution."

Everyone found comfort where they could in wartime, and Sanctuary was war's womb, a microcosm of every horror man could foist upon his brother—worse now with factions holding checkpoints and militias ruling blocks whose inhabitants were never certain. The idea of Strat being a part of Sanctuary's problem nearly made him draw his own bow—Crit knew Kama well enough to know, if quarrels were loosed, his would find its mark first: her woman's hesitation would be her last.

And he might have, right then, no matter what her provenance, but for the pud who didn't know him and didn't like any northern rider, especially one talking to *his* girlfriend. The slingshot grew taut, the boy's eyes steady as his stance widened.

So there was that—a deadly interval of stalemate broken only when a drunk caromed off a nearby doorway and knelt down, retching in the street.

Then Crit cleared his throat and said, "If you're still a member of the Stepsons, woman, I'll want you at the White Foal bridge two hours before dawn. Spread the word among the Third Commando, too; I'll need some backup on this—*if* the Third's still led by Sync, and *if* he's not succumbed to Sanctuary's blight, I should be able to expect it."

"Old debts? Words of honor?" Kama rejoined. "Honor's cheap in thieves' world. Cheapest this season, when everyone has a power play to field."

"Will you take my message, soldier?" He gave her what she wanted—recognition, though he'd rather call her whore and take her over bended knee.

"For you, Crit? Anything." Teeth flashed, a chuckle sounded, and he heard her mutter, "Zip, relax; he's one of us," and the youth behind her grumbled a reply before he slouched against a daub-and-wattle wall. "Before the break of day—we'll be there. . . . How many would that be you'll need?"

And Crit realized he didn't know. He hadn't a plan or a glimmer. What would it take to wrest the Globe of Power from Roxane, the Nisibisi witch? "Randal'll know—if he's still our warrior mage. Don't ask questions woman—not here. You know better. And Niko, find him—"

"Seh," the young tough behind her swore. "This one's walking wounded, Kama. *Niko?* Why not ask the—"

"Zip. Hush." The woman stepped out a pace from shadows, smiling like her father—a show of teeth with no humor in it. "Critias . . . friend, you've been away too long, doing what high-born officers do in Rankan cities. If not for . . . past mistakes . . . I'd ride with you and explain. But you'll find out enough, soon enough, from your beloved partner. As for Niko, if you want him, he's in the palace these days, playing nurse-maid to kids the priesthood loves."

Before he could escalate from shock to anger, before he thought to move his horse in tight and take her by the throat and shake her for playing women's games when so much was on the line, she melted back into her shadows and there was a grating sound, followed by scrabbling, a square of light that came and went, and when his horse danced forward, both Kama and the boy called Zip were gone—if they'd ever been there.

Riding Mazeward on a horse suddenly and unreasonably skittish, he cursed himself for a fool. No proof that it *was* Kama—what he'd seen could have been some apparition, even the witch, Roxane, in disguise. He'd touched nothing; only seen something he *thought* was Kama—there were undeads in Sanctuary who resembled the forms they'd had in life, and some of those were Roxane's slaves. Though if any such had happened to Kama, he told himself, Strat would have sent word to him. At least, the Strat he *used* to know would have. Right then, Critias could count the things he knew for certain on the fingers of one hand.

But he knew he was going to the vampire woman's house to find his partner. It was just a matter of time; Kama's allegations were already eating at his soul. He had to learn the truth.

Kadakithis's palace was full of fish-eyed Beysibs: Beysib men with more jewelry on their persons than Rankan women from uptown or Ilsigi whores; Beysib women—female shock troops with bared and painted breasts and poison snakes wound about their necks or arms—who seemed never to blink and gave Tempus gooseflesh.

Kadakithis wanted to introduce Tempus and Jihan to his Beysib flounder, Shupansea; before Tempus could protest, in the prince/governor's velvet-hung chamber, that he needed no more women in his life, the Rankan prince had called the woman forth.

Jihan, beside him, took Tempus's arm and squeezed, sensing what passed on first glance between her beloved Riddler and the lady ruler of the Beysib people.

For Tempus, noises lessened, the world grew dim, and in his heart a passion rose, while in his head a voice he'd not heard clear for years urged: *Take her. For Me. Ravage the slut upon this spot!*

The woman's fish-eyes widened; a snake slithered on her arm. Her breasts were fair and gilded; they stared at him with come-hither charms and it was only Jihan who restrained him, prince or no, from doing what Vashanka wanted then and there.

What *Vashanka* wanted? Tempus, who never backed away from any fight, took three retreating steps as Jihan whispered,

"Riddler, my lord? What is it? Has she witched you? I will tear her legs off one by—"

"No, Jihan," he muttered through clenched teeth in Nisi, a tongue neither prince nor consort understood. He shook Jihan's grasp from his arm and rubbed the depressions her fingers had made: the Froth Daughter's strength nearly equaled his own. But neither of them was a match for Vashanka who, Tempus was now certain, in some way had come again. He was here— more infantile, more tempestuous than ever, but here.

And what that meant to a man who'd forsaken the Pillager and taken up with Enlil to balance a curse no longer so sure upon his head Tempus couldn't say. But there was no doubt in him that soon he'd take some woman—this one if Vashanka had His way of it—and consecrate whatever wench into the service of the god.

He just stepped forward, on his best behavior where the prince could see, one palm sweating on the hilt of the sharkskin-pommeled sword, and took her hand. "My lady, Shupansea, men call me Tempus—"

She interrupted: "The Riddler. We have heard tales of thee."

And then from behind a curtain came Isambard, acolyte and priestly apprentice to Molin Torchholder, running without regard to his priestly dignity, calling out: "Quickly! My lady! My lord! There are dead snakes in the palace! There are *more* snakes than there ought to be! And in the children's rooms, where Nikodemos is . . . he's cut one of the sacred snake's heads off!"

Isambard skidded to a stop an arm's length from Tempus's chest and lapsed into panicked silence until his master entered the chamber. Molin Torchholder, ever-mindful of his position and demeanor, did not immediately clarify his acolyte's exclamations but appraised the assembly as if they, not he, were the breathless intruders.

"Ah, Tempus. Back in town at last?" Sanctuary's hierarch inquired, his voice carefully modulated to conceal the manifold anxieties which that man's unexpected presence caused him.

"That I am." Tempus detested priests, especially this one. And so he grinned once more, thinking that Brachis, when he arrived with Theron's sailing party, would put this foul, dark-skinned priest in his proper place. "Well, Torch, your minion seemed to have a problem moments ago. Surely you've got it as well?" His sword was out by then, and Jihan's also.

Kadakithis was scratching his golden curls, his handsome but vacant face inquiring: "What's this, Molin? Dead snakes? Is your state-cult out of hand again? I told you Nikodemos was no fit guardian for those children. I—"

The Beysib monarch interjected smoothly: "Let me see these dead snakes, priest. And mind you, I'm never sure that these troubles aren't made by the Rankans who announce them."

By then Tempus and Jihan were running down the hall, toward secret passages Tempus knew like the back of his sword-hand or Jihan's female mysteries, which led to the lower chambers where, near the dungeons, Niko and the children—whom some said were more than that—were being kept.

Ischade's Foalside house was more home than haunt, less forbidding than Roxane's to the south, but hardly an inviting place to visit.

Unless, of course, one was Straton, her lover whom she'd guided to de facto power in Sanctuary's factionalized streets, or an undead such as Janni or Stilcho (both of whom had once been Stepsons), or a mageling such as Haught, who learned what he could from the witches and sought to wake the power in his Nisibisi blood.

Strat had been with Ischade hardly long enough for a candle to burn low when Haught, whom Straton hated, came gusting in the door.

The place was softly lit and full of colors; precious gems and silks and metals strewed the floor.

Straton was, by then, the finest thing she had, though—a human man, with all his prowess, not an animated corpse or witchling.

She could love him, could Ischade, with a finer passion than the rest. But she could feel in him a struggle, one that made shoulders sweat and muscles twitch. She'd known that, hold him though she would, the day must come when holding Straton would be hard.

His narrow Rankan eyes were haunted, deep-set, his jaw squared with indecision lately when he came. And now, rolling off her at the sight of Haught, a hated, half-understood rival, a symptom of all about Ischade Strat couldn't justify or wish away, he reached for a robe she'd found him, shrugged it on and, with just his swordbelt, stalked outside.

"When you're done with...it, him, whatever...I'll be seeing to my horse."

Strat still grieved for his lost bay warhorse; its death was something she could and would undo, if only she thought Straton could handle the revelation that death was no barrier to Ischade.

Oh, he'd seen Janni, seen Niko embrace an undead partner. And Strat had not reacted well.

"What is it, Haught?" she asked, impatient. She didn't like the hubris growing in this Nisi child. He was difficult, growing stronger, growing bold. And she wanted to get back to Straton, who served her ends, who worked her will and excused her wiles and helped her hold her interests in the town. Ischade's interests were important. And they were too tied up with Strat now to let Haught get in the way.

So she thought to dance around the Nisi ex-slave, freed by her but not free of her. She'd only started her mesmerizing when a sanguine hand reached out and grasped her wrist.

Impertinent. This one soon would need an object lesson. She swallowed his will with a stare and let him see he couldn't even blink without her say-so. She whispered, "Yes? Your business, please."

And Haught, so pretty, so fiery underneath his slave's face, said, "I thought you'd want a warning. His boyfriend's coming...." Haught's chin jutted Mazeward. "What use he'll be once Crit's come hence, you might not like. So if you want, I could—"

There was murder in the slavebait's eyes. Murder sure of itself and offered teasingly, a sexual ploy, a sensuous violence.

She denied it, not telling Haught that Strat was so much hers that Crit couldn't get between them...because she wasn't sure. But she was sure that Straton's leftside leader, Critias, could not be murdered by one of hers. Not ever. Not and allow Ischade to keep what she had now—subtle power over more factions than any other had, even those who dwelled in the winter palace and looked to gods to aid them.

The dusky wraith that was Ischade said a second time, "I don't *want*, Haught. I *never* want. *You* want. I *have*. And I have need of both Stepsons—of Straton and his...friend. Go back uptown, see Moria, talk to Vis; we'll have a party for returning heroes tomorrow evening—in the uptown house.

Wherever Crit is, Tempus is as well. Find the Band's best and invite them all. We'll play a different game this season; you tread carefully, do you hear?"

Haught, motionless and unblinking till she loosed him, sought the door with the slightest inclination of his head and the most refined swirl of his cloak.

Trouble, that one, by and by.

But in the meantime, if she must fight for Straton, would she? She didn't know. She had a horse to raise, now, to see for certain what would happen. Strat would have more decisions to make tonight than one.

Niko was holding one child under either arm when Tempus and Jihan came upon them in the nursery.

One babe, Arton, had thumb in mouth; the other, Gyskouras, gave a single cry on seeing the interlopers.

Then Gyskouras—god-child, Niko was certain—held out his tiny hands and Jihan, mayhem forgotten, stepped over a decapitated snake oozing ichor, her own arms outstretched and the red fires of Stormbringer's passion in her eyes.

"Give him here, Stealth," Jihan crooned, calling Niko by his war-name. "My comfort's what he seeks."

Niko's gaze flickered questioningly to Tempus, who made a sour face and shrugged, sheathing his sword and squatting down to examine the snake.

Niko gave the child up to Jihan and shifted Arton, who immediately began to wail. "Me, too! Me, too! Take Arton, or tears come! Take Arton!"

In moments, Jihan held both children, the dark-haired and the fair, and Niko was kneeling opposite Tempus, the snake between them.

"Greetings, Commander. Life to you."

"And to you, Stepson. And glory." The words were only formula tonight, an afterthought from Tempus, who had out a dagger and with it turned the snake's head toward him.

"How did you kill this thing, Stealth?" asked the Riddler.

"How? With my sword. . . ." Niko's brows knit. His canny smile came and went and his hazel eyes grew bleak as he slipped his weapon from its sheath and laid it across his knee. "With this sword, the one the dream lord gave me. You mean it's not an ordinary snake?"

"That's what I mean. Not a Beysib snake, anyway. Look

here." He turned the snake and Niko could see tiny hands and feet, as if the snake had been starting to turn into a man when Niko's stroke had killed it.

And the ichor, now, was steaming, eating like acid into the stone of the palace floor.

"Why did you kill it?" said the Riddler gently. "What made you think it would attack you? Did it threaten? Did it rear up? What?"

"Because . . ." Niko sighed and tossed back ashen hair grown long enough to flop into his eyes. He'd shaved his beard and looked too young for what he was and what he'd been through; his scars were pale and the haunted look he bore made Tempus glance away. These two were each other's misery: Niko loved the Riddler and feared the consequences; Tempus saw in the youthful fighter the curse of a man the gods desire.

"Because," Niko said again, voice low and heavy with words he didn't want to say, "Arton told me to. Arton—the dark-haired—he's the prescient one. He knows the future. He protects the god-child. I'm glad you're here, Commander. It's hard trying to—"

But Tempus got abruptly to his feet. "Don't say that. You can't know it, not for sure."

"I know it. My Bandaran . . . my *maat* knows what it sees. *Maat*—my balance, my perception—shows me too much, Commander. We have things to talk over; decisions must be made. These childlren must go to the western isles, else there'll be havoc. I don't want the blame of it. Gyskouras, he's yours . . . your son—or your god's. I prayed. . . . Did the gods inform you?"

Tempus turned away from the young fighter and the words came back over his shoulder to Niko and hit as hard as a blow from the Riddler's hand. "Abarsis. He came and told me. Now we're all down here. Why in any god's name didn't you just take them and go, if that's the answer? Theron will be here by and by." He turned on his heel and faced Nikodemos. "You're sequestered here like a babysitter while Sanctuary is torn by the wolves of civil war? Are you no longer a Sacred Bander? Do you command some regiment, a cadre of your own? Or did Strat give you leave to—"

"It was by *my* order, Sleepless One," came an unctuous voice from behind: Molin Torchholder. The priest was accompanied by Kadakithis and by the prince's side was the Beysib woman, streaming tears, holding a dead and definitely Beysib snake in her arms and weeping over it as if over a stricken child.

"*Your* order, Molin?" Tempus said and shook his head. "I own I didn't think you'd have the nerve."

"He's trying to help, Tempus," said Kadakithis, looking worried and drawn, trying to comfort the weeping Beysib monarch and keep peace as best he could. "You've been away too long to judge this at face value. Nikodemos has been of exceptional help to the State and we thank you for his loan." The prince's eyes strayed to Jihan, a child on each hip and a beatific look in her inhuman eyes. "Let's go to the great hall and talk about this over food and drink. I warrant you're all tired from your long journey. We have much to decide and little time. Did I hear that Theron is coming? Tempus," Kadakithis's princely smile was strained and worried, "I hope you've told him good things of me—I hope, in fact, that you'll remember your oath. I wouldn't want to end up like my relatives in Ranke—spitted and bled out like pigs in the town square."

If the curse—or its ghost—was still in effect, it would mean that all the Riddler loved were bound to spurn him and those who loved him doomed to perish.

It was this that bothered him as he put a hand on Kadakithis's shoulder and assured the prince that Theron would look with kindness on Kadakithis's particular problems here in Sanctuary, that "he's coming because the Slaughter Priest manifested in the Rankan palace and told a soldier to look to the souls of his soldiers. That's why we're all here, boy—and lady."

He didn't tell them not to fear. Both the prince/governor and the Bey matriarch were too familiar with statecraft to have believed him if he had.

It wasn't until after dinner that everyone realized there were too many dead Beysib snakes in the palace for Niko—or the single snake he'd killed—to be responsible. And by then, it was nearly too late.

Strat's horse was at the gate. The bay horse he'd loved so well, who'd carried him through so many campaigns. And Ischade was standing in her doorway, where night blossoms bloomed, watching with that look she had which cut through the shadows of her hood.

She'd healed the horse, obviously. She had the healing touch, when she wanted to, had Ischade. He was so glad to see the bay, who nuzzled in his pockets for a carrot or the odd sweet-meat, it took him a while to clear his throat and make sure his eyes were dry before he turned to thank her: "It's wonderful having him back. There's not another in my string to equal him—not his size, his stamina, his conformation. But why didn't you tell me? I'd not have believed he could be . . ." His words slowed. He looked harder at her. ". . . healed. That's what you did, isn't it? Spirited him away somewhere after I had to leave him for dead, and nursed him back to health?" The horse's teeth felt real enough, nipping his arm for attention. "Ischade, tell me that's what you did."

Her words were wispy as the wind. "I saved him for you, Straton. A parting gift, if this visitor of yours . . ." She pointed up the road, where a figure could be seen if one looked hard through the moonlight—a rider so far away the sounds of his horse's hooves were yet masked by the breathing of the bay. "If this visitor makes an end to what is—was—between us. It's yours to say."

With that, she turned and went into her house and the door closed, of its own accord, with an all-too-final sound.

He'd never heard it close that way before.

He examined the bay from head to tail, from poll to fetlock, waiting for whoever it was Ischade said was coming, but he couldn't find a scar. It was bothering him more and more. He'd seen Janni, once a Stepson, now a decomposing thing motivated by revenge upon its Nisibisi murderers; he'd seen Stilcho, in better shape but still not one to be mistaken for a living man. But the bay was just exactly what he'd been—all horse, all muscular quarters and deep-hearted chest. The bay couldn't be a zombie horse. At least he didn't think it could.

He was just thinking to mount up and see how it went when the approaching rider drew close enough to halloo: "Yo! Strat, is that you?"

And that voice froze Straton like a witch's curse: it was Critias. Critias, his leftside leader; Critias, to whom he'd sworn his Sacred Band oath. "Crit! Crit, why didn't you tell me you were coming?"

Crit just kept riding toward him, inexorable on a big sorrel. Crit, seeking him here. That meant that Crit had heard. That he knew, or thought he knew, the hows and whys of something Straton barely understood himself.

They'd come together to Ischade's house the first time—
met her together. Then, Crit had tried to "protect" Straton from
the necromant. Now, if damage there was, it was done.

Crit said, "Am I too late?" crooking one leg over his saddle
and fishing in his pouch for the makings of a smoke. In Ischade's garden there was always a weird light and it underlit
the line officer's face so that Strat couldn't tell what Crit was
thinking. Not that he ever could.

Something inside him tensed. He said, because there had
been no Sacred Band greeting between them, "Look, Crit. I
don't know what you've heard or what you think, but she's
not like that. . . ."

"Isn't she? Still got your soul, Ace? Or wouldn't you know?"
Crit's eyes were slitted and he fingered the crossbow hanging
from his saddle.

Strat noticed that there was an arrow nocked, and that the
bow would fire, from that position, straight into him at the
click of a safety and the touch of a trigger. He tried to shrug
away the suspicion he felt, but he couldn't. "You're here to
save me from myself? She's the only reason we've survived
here—the Band, the real Stepsons—while you and the Riddler
have been upcountry playing your palace games. I'm not asking
you where you've been. Don't ask me how I've spent my time.
Unless, that is, you're ready to be reasonable."

"I can't. I haven't time. Riddler wants us to roust Roxane,
get the Globe of Power and destroy it by sunup. Maybe your
soul-sucking friend'll have a few ideas as to how to help us,
if she likes you so well. If she does, maybe I'll let her live
until you can explain. Otherwise . . ." Crit lit the smoke he'd
rolled and the spark illumined a carefully arranged face that
Straton knew wasn't one to argue with. "Otherwise, I'm going
to burn her ass to a crisp and then do what I can to beat some
sense back into you . . . partner. Before it's too late. So, you
want to call her out? Or just come with me and we'll die like
we're supposed to, shoulder to shoulder, fighting the Nisibisi
witch."

Strat didn't have to call Ischade; she was beside him, somehow, though he hadn't heard the door open or seen light spill
out and he didn't think Crit had, either.

She was so tiny in her cowl and long black cloak. He wanted
to put an arm around her shoulder, dared not, then dared. "She's
on our side, Crit. You've got to—"

"The hell I do," Crit said, and shifted his gaze to her. "I bet I don't have to explain one whit to you, honey. I just hope you're not too hungry to wait awhile. We've got something on that's just your style."

"Critias," said Ischade with more dignity than Strat would ever have, "we should talk. No one has been hurt, no one has to be. You come—"

"—to get my partner. We can leave it at that."

"And if he is unwilling to leave?"

"Doesn't have squat to do with it. I've got responsibilities; so does he, even if he's forgotten them. I'm here to remind him. As for you, we can use you. Come help out, and I'll let you have your say—later. Right now, I've got orders. So does he." Critias gestured to Strat, who looked at Ischade and could not, in front of Critias, plead with her for patience, for help, or even for his partner's life.

But Ischade didn't strike Crit dead, or mesmerize him. She nodded primly and said, "As you wish. Straton, take the bay horse. He'll serve you well in this. I'll ride your dun. And we'll give Critias what he wants—or what he thinks he wants." She turned then to Crit.

"And you, afterwards, will give me the courtesy of a hearing."

"Lady, if any of us can hear anything after sunrise, I'll be more than willing to listen," said Crit as Ischade raised a hand and Strat's dun trotted toward her.

Roxane had been waked abruptly from exhausted sleep when Niko lopped the head from her finest minion—she would miss the bodyguard snake. And Stealth would regret what he had done.

She'd paid a heavy price this evening; her thighs ached and her buttocks smarted as she got out of her bed and felt her way through the dark.

Her Foalside home was small sometimes, large at others. Tonight, it was cavernous with all the forces she'd disturbed.

She found her witching room and and sluiced the sweat from her body as she filled her scrying bowl herself.

Then, trembling with pain and fury, she spoke the spell to open the well that held the power globe, and another to summon a fiend of hers—the slave named Snapper Jo who spied for her in the Vulgar Unicorn where he tended bar.

Before the fiend arrived, she spoke her spell of utmost power and in the bowl she saw a fate she didn't understand.

Men were there, and the cursed Beysa, and a goddess called Mother Bey locked in love or hate with Jihan's terrible father, Stormbringer. And these two deities straddled the winter palace while, inside, Niko played with children and Tempus with the fates of men.

She trembled, seeing Tempus and Niko in one place—the very place where her surviving snake (more talented than most) slithered corridors in Beysib-snake disguise, biting and killing where he could.

Good. Good, she thought, and brought back Niko's face to the surface of her bowl. But this time, the vision was not of him alone. Over one of Niko's shoulders she could see the Riddler—or the Rankan Storm God, whose aspect was the same; over the other, a woman's face and that face was comely in an awful way—her own.

The meaning of it, remaining hidden, chilled her.

She could do only so much; she had certain words to say.

She said them and the dark witching room was lit with balefire. The light touched the globe in its hidey-hole of nothingness and the globe began to spin.

If there was some bond of fate between her and egregious Tempus, the thread must be cut. Even if it were Niko's life, she must do the deed. And the baby god could not be suffered to survive. Both children's lives and souls were promised to a certain demon of her recent, intimate acquaintance.

And the cold she felt, which raised gooseflesh on sanguine Nisi skin as smooth as velvet, which drew back lips as beautiful as any that had ever spoken death for men—that cold had to do with failing and winning, with perishing and surviving.

As the door to her outer chamber shivered from something scratching on its farther side, she decided.

She let the globe spin faster, let the colors from its stones bathe her in their light.

A rushing wind filled the scrying room and in its midst was a woman's form, changing shape.

Black mist spun around the comeliest of female guises. Black wizard hair grew long and covered limbs cut clean and meant to hypnotize any man. Her fine long nose grew chitinous, then hooked; her firm flesh sprouted feathers.

And by the time Snapper Jo, still wiping his claws on his

barman's apron, thought he'd better open up the door himself, an eagle with a wingspan ten feet wide stood where Roxane was before.

And Snapper, her spy among the Sanctuary denizens, who tended bar at the Vulgar Unicorn, clacked prognathic jaws together and wrung his clawed and warty hands.

"Mistress," he gurgled in his fiendish, grating voice, "is that you?" His eyes that looked every which-way squinted at the eagle swathed in dusky light. He squatted down, gray gangly limbs akimbo in submission. "Roxane?" said the fiend again. "Call Snapper, did you? Here I be, for what? Some murder? Murder do, tonight?"

And the eagle cocked its head at him and let out a screech no fiend could misconstrue, then took wing and flapped by him, out the door, leaving him bleeding from a flesh wound made by claws much sharper than his own.

Muttering, "Damn and damn and murder damned," the fiend scuttled after her. Looking askance at her black shadow in the moonless sky, Snapper Jo chewed a long orange lock of hair in dark frustration. To be human was his wish; to be free of Roxane his hidden dream. But sometimes he thought he never would be free of her.

And the trouble was, at times like these, he didn't care. He was hungry as the night for blood; just the thought of carnage made him giddy.

So he scuttled on, following the eagle in the night, cackling wordlessly under his breath as Roxane, in eagle's guise, led him toward the winter palace, then lost him in Shambles Cross when he came across a fresh and bleeding morsel of a corpse.

Jihan was alone with the two children, her scale-armor discarded, cuddling one to either breast on Niko's bed in the nursery when the snake, man-sized but silent, slithered in.

The Froth Daughter was not human, but she was lonely. Tempus was no man for progeny—he considered nothing but himself.

Jihan had wanted children of her own and been refused by him. Now, thanks to her father, fate, and Niko, she had two fine boys to care for—one of them Tempus's own.

She would never give them up. She was ecstatic in her joy, and drowsy.

Thus she didn't see the snake until it reared, fangs wide and gaping, and struck like lightning, biting Arton on the arm.

Then, wide awake with two terrified babes to hold, one wounded and screaming, the other howling just as loudly, she cowered.

To reach her sword or freeze the snake, arching high above the bed and glaring fire-eyed down upon her, she'd have to put down one or both children.

This the frustrated mother could not do. She tried to shield Gyskouras with her body, interpose her own arm, even force it like a gag into the snake's gaping jaws.

But the snake was wise and quick and its jaws unhinged, so that it bit right through Jihan's arm and punctured the god-child's flesh and shook the Froth Daughter and the child, stapled together by its fangs.

Jihan wailed in rage and agony—a sound the like of which had not been heard in Sanctuary since Vashanka battled Storm-bringer in the sky at the Mageguild's fête.

And that brought help, though she barely knew it as her body fought the poison and her arms, about the snake's neck, grew weaker as she wrestled it. Even Tempus and Niko paused in horror at the sight of Jihan locked in bodily combat with the viper, the god-child being crushed in between.

Beside Tempus, Niko drew a breath and then reached out: "Riddler! Quickly! Take this dagger."

The dagger, like Niko's sword, was dream-forged and it felt hot in the Riddler's hand.

He raced his Stepson, on his right, to reach the snake and the two of them began to hack away.

With every stroke acid ichor spouted, so that Tempus's skin sizzled, blistered, and peeled.

There was no time to fear for Niko, beside him as if they were once more a bonded pair.

Jihan was wound in coils, protecting one child who was absolutely silent. The other, Arton, was curled up moaning, forgotten on the floor except when ichor struck him and he squealed at the pain.

The snake didn't flail or shrink from the damage Niko's sword did, though Tempus's deeper cuts could give it pause.

The Riddler realized just in time what must be wrong—just as the snake was tensing and Jihan, mouth open and eyes bulging as the breath was squeezed from her, called his name and the viper fixed Niko with a gaze that pushed Stealth backward and made him drop his sword.

For no snake, not even a Nisibisi snake, should be growing larger and bolder as it fought and bled.

Tempus looked up and around and saw the source of the snake's supernatural power: an eagle perched, bating, in the bolthole of the palace wall.

Beside him, Niko faltered, his face blistered, his ankles entangled in the ever-growing coils of the snake.

Tempus knew he risked Stealth's life as he stepped out of striking range and raised his knifehand.

His eyes met the eagle's and it called softly, a cry like a baby's, and raised its head and clacked its beak.

Then the dagger Stealth had loaned him flew through the air and struck the eagle's breast.

A screech like a witch burning at the stake resounded, so that Niko lost his footing, hands clapped to either ear, and fell among the deadly coils.

But it was a chance Tempus had had to take.

And as he strode forward, faster than anything else within that room because, at last, his wrath had brought the gods awake and power rose within him, the eagle overhead burst into flame.

The flames began around the dagger in its breast and licked hot and higher as the bird took wing.

But Tempus had no more time for watching birds or taking chances; he heard a dagger fall from the bolthole's height as he waded amid the coils—first to Stealth, who still fought gamely though ichor had burned one eye shut and his limbs were bound with writhing snake.

Pitting all his strength against the failing power of the snake— now shrinking but perhaps not fast enough—the Riddler struggled.

Vaguely he heard voices behind him as palace praetorians gathered. "Stay back!" he shouted without looking.

He was watching Jihan's eyes pop, her more-than-mortal hands clutching the noose of snake still at her throat.

The damned thing was dying and as it did it was whipping back and forth, tossing Niko like a hook on a fishing line, crushing Jihan. And somewhere, in that thrashing mess of green slime and human limbs, a child was lost.

His child, Niko had said. But that wasn't why the Riddler hacked as if splitting cordwood with Niko's dream-forged sword.

He'd never fought harder than he did then to free Stealth—if
there was kinship between him and any here, it was strongest
for his partner.

Admitting this, while all around pieces of snake flew like
steaks from the block of a master butcher and smoke rose as
ichor ate at stone, Tempus found reserves of strength in anger.

This youth, foolish Stealth, was not going to die on his
account and leave the Riddler with that weight to bear eternally.
Jihan and the god-child born of a ceremonial rape—both of
them were more than mortal. Niko was just a human fool and
human foolishness—honor, valor, sacrifice, and love—were
things Tempus could not ever claim.

He didn't notice when Beysib and human help pitched in
beside him—his god-given speed made them seem too slow
and the task too great to make them matter.

But Jihan, once he'd cut through the widest coil at her throat,
was help worth having.

And once she was free, and it was clear that she'd saved
the child from certain death, the Beysibs and the Rankan priest
and Kadakithis all crowded round the Froth Daughter and the
child.

Which suited Tempus, who finished cutting the yet-quivering
coils from the Stepson who'd fought beside him and helped
Niko to his feet.

Only when the boy, through his one good eye, put a hand
on Tempus's shoulder and said, "Life to you, Commander—
and thanks," and collapsed into Tempus's arms did Niko's left-
side leader have time for snake-bitten children or Jihan.

For he'd found out, there among the butchered chunks of
snake and royal ranks of confusion, that the bond Niko and he
once shared was stronger than it had ever been.

Jihan limped over to him, where he lay Stealth down, and
frowned at the burns on Niko's face and his acid-eaten eye.
"The placenta of a black cat, powdered at midnight, Riddler—
that will heal his eye. The rest, I can do."

The Froth Daughter's hand was gentle on Tempus's face,
turning it away from the boy. "We have children who are worse
hurt," Jihan said. "Both poisoned by the snake who bit them."
Her chest was heaving, her muscles torn; flaps of skin hung
loose from her thighs as if a man-wide rope had burned her.

But the children—Arton and Gyskouras, who might be his
or perhaps just the offspring of the god—had crowds to care

for them and all of Sanctuary's priesthood to pray for them, while Stealth had only what a Stepson could expect.

Tempus sat flat on the floor, knees crossed under him, ignoring ichor slick which smarted and caused his skin to hiss and curl. "Get me what medicine you can, Jihan. You and I must heal this one. He wouldn't want life returned by magic."

They exchanged glances—one immortal and mortally tired, one feral and full of the fire of fierce and forgotten gods.

Then Jihan nodded, rose up, and said, "Your dagger skewered the eagle-witch. I saw it. She's wounded, maybe gone for good."

But it didn't please him, not at the price Niko always seemed to pay for others' folly.

Sometime in that interval, because Niko was conscious and could hear, Tempus affirmed and renewed their pairbond so that he had a rightside partner once again. And so that Niko, should it matter, would know that he was not alone.

Down by the White Foal Bridge, the gathered Stepsons waited: Kama was there, with a dozen hand-picked fighters from Sync's 3rd Commando.

It made Crit uncomfortable to command the Riddler's daughter's unit, so he gave them the periphery, made them the watch guards, kept what distance from her he could.

Strat, on the other hand, was comfortable with everything coming out of the dark that evening—with his bay horse, with paired Stepsons riding up, holding torches, with Ischade's whispered council, with men who once were Stepsons and now were no longer men—men who stayed in shadows when Crit looked at them straight on.

Strat had "explained" about Stilcho and Janni and Ischade's talent for raising uneasy dead. Strat said it was a favor she did them, a gift to those who'd died with their honor blighted.

Crit hadn't argued—there wasn't time. Strat was addled, bewitched, and if he got through this he was going to beat some sense into the big fool as soon as possible, do something final about Ischade or make her loose her hold on Strat.

If.

Something puffed and popped and Crit's horse shivered. Looking to his right, Crit saw Randal, the Stepsons' warrior mage, decked out in Niko's armor.

"Greetings, Crit. I heard you'd like some help." The flop-eared mage looked older, more fearsome tonight in dream-forged battle gear. He caught Crit staring at his cuirass. "This?" Randal touched his chest. "It's Niko's, still. Just a loan. We . . . have an understanding, but no pairbond." The freckled face aped a smile that was wan in torchlight as his horse reared and Crit realized it wasn't quite a horse at all—it was definitely transparent, though horselike in every other respect.

"Help. Right. Well, Randal, you know the Riddler's orders, if you're here. Any advice? Or should we ride right in there, storm the place, burn it to the ground?"

At his knee came a touch as soft as a butterfly landing. "I told you, Critias, just walk right in and take it—walk in by my side, if you will. . . . She's not at home and, if my guess is right, quite indisposed."

Crit looked from Ischade to Randal for confirmation. Randal nodded. "That's my best guess as well." The mage scratched one ear. "Only, I'll go in with Ischade. Roxane's my enemy, not yours—at least not so much so. And you don't trust Ischade . . . no offense, dear lady."

"None taken. Yet," said the woman whose head reached only to Crit's knee, but who seemed taller than anyone else about.

Strat rode up, concerned, looking at Crit as if to say, 'You'd better not start trouble now, partner or not. Don't push your luck.'

"I'm going," Crit said. "I have my orders."

"Into a witch's house?" Strat shook his head. "You may be my partner, but these are my men, until we've worked things out. We needn't risk them, or you. We've got friends to deal with magic who deal with it routinely. Ischade. Randal. Please be our guests—" As he spoke, Strat bowed in his saddle and, one hand outstretched in a sweeping gesture, motioned the mage and the necromant to precede the fighters up the cart-track to Roxane's house. And as his gesturing hand neared Crit's horse, it snatched a rein, and held it.

"Strat," Crit warned. "You're pushing matters."

"Me? I thought it was you, mixing in what you don't yet understand."

"Let go of my horse."

"When you let go of your anger."

"Fine," Crit sighed, holding up empty hands and feigning a smile. "Done."

Strat stared a moment at him, then nodded and freed the horse. "Let's go, then . . . partner?"

"After you, Strat. As you say, you're in command—at least till morning."

Inside Roxane's Foalside home was a smell like burning feathers and a glow as if the whole place smouldered.

Ischade was well aware that any instant, the premises might burst into flame. She said so to Randal.

They'd never worked this close, the Tysian Hazard and the necromant.

It was an eerie feeling, especially when Randal drew his *kris*, a recurved blade, and said, "It directs fire. Don't worry, Ischade. I didn't fight the Wizard Wars for nothing," in his tenor voice.

They walked over boards that creaked as if the place had been abandoned for eternity and Ischade's neck grew cold with trespass.

Randal said, waxing more the fighter with a woman watching, more the expert First Hazard of the Mageguild with a famous witch pacing by his side, "I'll open the rent where she keeps it, get it out for you. But you'll have to destroy it. I can't."

"Can't?" she said, disbelieving.

"Shouldn't, really. You see, I've got one of my own. I wouldn't want it to think I'd turned hostile. You should understand."

She did.

It was odd to work so closely with a rival mage of rival power. She wondered if there would be a price.

And there was, of sorts, though it did not fall on them directly.

When Randal had made the requisite passes with his hands and a flap in space fell down and the globe lay revealed, Ischade's soul wrenched: she loved beauty, baubles, precious trinkets, and the power globe was all of those and more. It was the most beautiful, potent piece she'd ever seen. If not for Randal, here and witness, even despite Strat she would have claimed it for her own.

When he got it out, the floorboards creaked and the roof above began to smoke.

She could see that it singed him and that he'd expected that, now with the timbers above flaring like tarred torches.

In the ruddy light, Randal knelt down, and she did also, and he told her what words to speak.

Then he said, "Reach out and set it spinning—just a push with your palm will do."

As she touched the globe, Ischade felt a shock more intense than any she'd known for ages—this was not a matter of raising dead or ordering the lives of lesser mortals. This was a matter of power great enough to flout the gods.

And there was a bite to all Nisi magic, a corrosion different from her own. She rocked back upon her heels, nearly mesmerized herself though nothing less could have done it to her.

Randal pulled unceremoniously at her elbow. "Up, my brave lady. Up and out before the beams fall down and roast us or she . . . comes back . . . somehow."

And then Ischade realized that her sense of Roxane's presence might be more than just echoes from the globe.

Quick as smoke she got her feet under her and ran, Randal beside her, toward an open window.

Once they'd scrambled through, there was a roar as deep as any dragon's and the whole house burst apart in flames.

And in the middle of the blaze Ischade could see the globe, still spinning, spitting colored fire of its own and spouting tongues of purer fire that licked up towards the heavens.

Horses thundered, coming near.

Strat was there, lifting her up onto the bay's rump as if she were a child, and Crit did the same for Randal.

Neither asked if the task was done. All could see the globe, spinning brighter, whirling larger, consuming the lesser flame of burning wood and stone and thatch and blazing like a star.

The horses were glad to be reined back; the heat was singeing. You couldn't hear a word or even the trumpets of mounts who hated fire as they reared and walked backwards on hind legs.

For it seemed, as the house collapsed, that the sky itself caught fire. Demons of colored light slunk through that wider blaze and slipped away.

Wings of lightning beat against the firmament where a rising sun was dwarfed to dullness by their light.

And down from purple lightning and clouds that came together, combusting to form a great cat-thing with hell-red eyes who swiped at it as it came, flew an eagle.

A flaming eagle, descending from the sky, chased by a giant cat of roiling cloud so black it swallowed all the heat, as if a house cat chased a sparrow in the dwelling of the gods.

The bird plummeted, wings bent. The cat struck, sent it spinning, struck again.

A scream like heaven rending issued from one, a growl like hell's bowels settling came from the other.

And the bird tumbled, then righted, then darkened and streaked, shrinking, into the lessening flame that had been the witch's house.

Ischade saw that bird dive among the timbers where a Globe of Power was now melted, fragments of white hot clay and parboiled jewels, and take a fragment in its beak and speed away.

When she looked away, she saw that Randal, face beaded with sweat and freckles standing out black as soot, had seen it too.

The mage gave an uneasy shrug and smiled bleakly. "Let's not tell them," he whispered, leaning close. "Maybe it's not . . . her."

"Perhaps not," Ischade replied, looking up at the smouldering sky.

The morning after the sky caught fire, Tempus was sitting with Niko when Randal came to call.

"I'll see to him, Commander," said the mage, who touched his *kris,* from which healing water could be wrung.

Jihan had applied the powdered placenta of some unlucky cat, and Niko's eye was healing.

But these wounds would take a while, even with magic to help them.

And beside the stricken fighter, in the nursery, two children lay in sleep from which no one had yet managed to rouse them.

That, Tempus knew, was really what Randal must do here. But he had to say, "Stealth and I have reaffirmed our pairbond. Can you tend him in good conscience, with a minimum of magic?"

Randal himself had once been paired with Stealth, at the Riddler's order, and loved the western fighter still.

The mage looked down, then up, then squared his shoulders. "Of course. And the children, too . . . if I have their father's permission?"

"Ask the god that; he's the stud, not me," Tempus snapped and stormed out.

He had a woman to rape to placate the god within him, a necromant to thank in person, and a welcome to prepare for Theron, emperor of Ranke, when he arrived.

But Jihan found him before he could find a likely wench on the Street of Red Lanterns. Her eyes were glowing and she squeezed his arm and wanted to know, "Just what kind of houses are these?"

He had half a mind to show her, but not the time: she'd come to get him to mediate between Crit and Strat in matters of command and to ask whether they could all attend a "fête for returning heroes" being given by friends of Ischade's who lived uptown, and whether he'd noticed anything strange about Strat's bay horse.

And since he had troubles enough of his own, and Jihan was one, he agreed to come with her, gave permission for the Band and Stepsons to attend the fête, and lied about the horse, saying he hadn't noticed anything strange about it at all.

DAGGER IN THE MIND

C. J. Cherryh

"My lady—" Stilcho said, ever so quietly. The dead Stepson hesitated in the doorway of the back room of the riverhouse. Hesitated longer. Ischade sat in the chair before the fire with her hands clasped between her black-robed knees and gazed there, the fire leaping and casting light on her face, on the bright scatter of cloaks and trinkets that made the house like some garish carnival.

And Ischade, a darkness in it, fire-limned. The wind rushed in the chimney. The fire roared up with a dizzy sibilance. The candles burned brighter so that Stilcho flinched back. Flinched and flinched again in the other direction, for he encountered a body behind him and a hard hand on his shoulder.

He turned and looked by mistake straight into Haught's dark Nisi eyes. A muscle jumped in his jaw. His throat grew paralyzed. Haught's grip burned him, numbed him; and there was no sound in all the world but the roar of the fire and no sight in the world but Haught laying a cautionary finger to his lips and drawing him away, quietly.

Back and back into the tangle of silks and drapes and shadow that was that over-small room he shared with Haught.

And in this privacy Haught seized his shoulders and put his back to the wall, in the slithery touch of the silken hangings. Haught's eyes held his like a serpent's.

"Let me go," Stilcho said. The voice came through jaws that tried to freeze, that tried to turn to the cold unburied meat and bone that they were without Her influence. No pain, no agony. Just a dreadful cold as if something very solid had come between him and his life-source. "L-let me g-g-go, She s-said—" *You weren't to touch me with magic*—that was the part that stuck behind his teeth. There were just the eyes.

"Hear it?" Haught asked. "Feel it, dead man? She's worried. She's unweaving her magics. Souls are winging back to hell tonight. Do you feel yours slipping?"

"Get your ha-hands from me."

Haught's hands slid up his shoulders and held there. "She's forgotten you tonight. I haven't. I'm holding you, Stilcho. *I.* And I can peel you like an onion. Or save your wretched soul. Do you feel it now?"

"Ish—"

Haught's grip tightened, that of his hands and that on his soul. The paralysis grew, and Haught's voice sank deeper and deeper, so that it was not sound at all, only the dazzle of winter cold, was snowflakes falling on dark wind.

The Queen of Death is dethroned. Power is free tonight. Fragments of it drift on the winds, sift through the air, fall on the earth.

It slays the dead.

It casts down the powerful.

Stilcho shivered, his living eye widened and the dead one saw abysses.

He tottered on the edge, reached up hands cold as clay and held to Haught as to his last and only hope.

There is something that shines and I see it, dead man.

It beckons the powerful with an irresistible lust.

And she dares not.

The dust shines and shimmers and falls everywhere and she dares not gather that power up. She seals up the ways. She burns it with fire.

Nisi power. She loathes it and desires it.

I am Nisi, dead man. And I will have that thing. She sits blind and deaf to me—what we say she cannot know. That is my power. And it needs one thing.

Things will change, Stilcho. Consider your allegiances. Consider how you fare when she forgets you.

He had a very clear picture then what Haught wanted. He held the image of a shining globe that spun and shimmered. Lust was part of it, in the same way that light was. It was raw power. It was dangerous, dangerous as some spinning blade, as some terrible juggernaut let loose. That shining, spinning thing was a humming regularity that beat like a pulse, that held all the gates of hell and creation in harmony with itself, all beating away with the same thump-thump of a living heart, that was the tiniest imperfection in this spinning. If it were perfect there would be nothing.

The universe exists on a flaw in nothing at all.

A little wobble in the works.

He caught at his chest, feeling an unaccustomed hammering. He felt it as threatening at first, and then he realized that it was a thin, occasional beat in a perfect stillness. It was his own heart giving a little thump of life. And he felt it because for a moment it had been utterly silent.

"You know," Haught said, "you understand it now, what I want." Haught's fine hand touched his face, and a little chill numbed him. "Now forget it, dead man. Just forget it now. Until I need you. . . . I want to talk to you, Stilcho. Just a moment. Privately."

Stilcho blinked. It was the living eye he saw from now. It was his enemy Haught, a Haught looking uncommonly void of malice, a Haught holding him gently by the shoulder.

"I've wronged you," Haught said. "I know that. You have to understand, Stilcho—we were both victims. I was yours; you were their pawn. Now I have a certain power and it's you who are the slave. A sweet difference for me; and a bitter one for you. But—" The hand moved softly and warmth spread from it, like life through clay, so poignant a pain that Stilcho's vision came and went. "It need not be bitter. You so scarcely died, Stilcho. Earth never went over you; fire never touched you. Just a little slip away from the body, a little slip and she caught you in her hands before you could get much beyond the merest threshold of hell, drew you back to your body in the next breath; and this flesh of yours—this is solid, it bleeds if cut—however sluggishly; it suffers pain of flesh. And pain of pride; and pain of fear—"

"Don't—"

"And when mistress wants you, it does infallibly what a man's body ought—tell me: does it feel anything?"

Stilcho gave a wrench of his arm. It was no good. The paralysis closed about his throat and stopped the shout; Haught's eyes caught his and held and the arm fell leaden at his side.

"I have the threads that hold you to life," Haught said. "And I will tell you a secret: she has never done as much for you as should be done. She *can't,* now. But she could have. The power that could have done it is blowing on the wind tonight, is falling like dust, wasted. Do you think that she would have thought twice of you? Do you think that she would have said to her-self—Stilcho could benefit by this, Stilcho could have his life back? No. She never thought of you."

Liar, Stilcho thought, fighting the silken voice; but it was hard to doubt the hand that held the threads of his existence. *Liar*—not that he believed Ischade had ever thought of him; that he did not expect; but he doubted that there had ever been such a chance as Haught claimed.

"But there was," said Haught softly, and something fluttered and rippled through the curtains of his mind. "There was such a chance and there still is one. Tell me, Stilcho—ex-slave speaks to slave now—do you *enjoy* this condition? You'll trek to hell and back to preserve that little thread of life of yours; you'll whimper and you'll go like a beaten dog because even death won't make you safe from her, and your life won't last a moment if she forgets you the way she's forgetting those others. But what if there were another source of life? What if there were someone to hold you up if she neglected you—do you see the freedom that would give you? For the first time since you died, poor slave, you can choose from moment to moment. You can say—this moment I'm hers; or: for these few I'm his. And if anything should happen to me—that choice will be gone again. Do you understand?"

There was warmth all through him. Warmth and the natural give of his stiffened ribs—it *hurt*, like cramped muscle. His heart beat at a normal rate and the socket of his eye ached with a stab of pain that was acute and poignant and for a moment giddy with strength.

Haught caught him as it faded and the river-cold came back. Stilcho shivered, a natural shiver; and Haught's face before him was pale, beaded with sweat: "There," Haught gasped, "*there*, that's what I could do for you if I were stronger."

Stilcho only stared at him, and the living eye wept at the memory and the dead one wept blood. It was a seduction as wicked as any ever committed in Sanctuary, which was going some: and he knew himself the victim of it. Of drugs and temptations he had sampled in his life, of ghassa and krrf and whatever lotos-dreams the smoke of firoq gave, there was no sensation to equal that moment of painful warmth, and it was going away now.

He needs a focus, Stilcho thought; he had learned his gram-marie in bitter and terrible lessons and knew something of the necessities of black sorcery. *He wants a familiar. Nothing so simple as snake or rat, not even one of the birds—he wants a man, a living man. O gods, he's lying. He knows what I'm thinking. He's in my skull—*

Yes, came a soft, soft voice. *I am. And you're quite right. But you also taste what my power would be. I'm still apprentice. But to hide a thing is another of my talents. And Mistress doesn't see me. I've learned the edges of her power, I've mapped it like a geography, and I simply walk the low places, the canyons and the chasms of it. She's committed an error great mages make: she's lost her small focus. Her inner eye is set always on the horizons, and those horizons grow wider and wider, so the small, deft stroke can pass her notice; I can sit in a small place and listen to the echoes her power makes. It makes so much noise tonight it has no sense of a thing so small and soft. And I approach mastery. It lacks one thing. No, two. You are one. The thought will remain. I will seal it up now, I will seal it so you needn't fear at all; all that will remain is a knowledge that I am not your true enemy. Wake up,* "Stilcho—"

Stilcho blinked, startled for a moment as he found himself face to face with Haught. Something was very wrong, that he was this close to Haught and feeling no fear. It was a situation that produced fear of its own. But Haught let him go.

"Are you all right?" Haught asked with brotherly tenderness.

Witchery did not obliterate memory of past injury. It only made things seem, occasionally, quite mad.

And the fire still roared in the front room, where he had no wish to go.

Ischade herded another soul home. This one was a soldier, and wily and full of tricks and turns—one of Stilcho's lost company who had deserted in the streets and hid and lurked down by the shambles, where there was always blood to be had. Janni, she thought; *that* was a soul she sought. It wailed and cursed its feeble curses; *not* Janni, but a Stepson of the later breed. She overpowered it with a thrust that shriveled its resistance and the only sign of this exertion was a momentary tension of her closed eyelids and a slight lift of her head as she sat with hands clasped before the fire.

She had grown that powerful. Power hummed and buzzed deafeningly in her veins, straining her heart.

Small magics stirred about her, which she supposed was Haught at his practice again; but she paid it no heed. She might summon the Nisi slave and use him to take the backload, but that led to a different kind of desire, and that desire was already maddening.

There was Stilcho. There was that release, which was not available with Straton. But what was in her tonight even a dead man might not withstand; and she had sworn an oath to herself, if not to gods she little regarded, that she would never destroy one of her own.

She hunted souls through the streets of Sanctuary and never budged from her chair, and most of all she hunted Roxane.

She smelled blood. She smelled witchery, and the taint of demons which Roxane had dealt with. She felt the shuddering of strain at gates enough for a mortal soul, but not yet wide enough for things which had no part or law in the world to linger.

One there was which Roxane had called. It was cheated, and vengeful, and demanded the deaths of gods which a mage tried to prevent. It had intruded into the world and wanted through again.

One there was which ruled it, for which it was only viceroy, and that power tried the gates in its own might: it was more than demon, less than god; but since she had never bargained with gods or demons it had no hope with her.

Mostly she felt the slow sifting of power everywhere on the winds, profligate and dangerous.

Leave it to me, she had said to Randal, who had enough to do to cheat a demon of his prey. She felt Randal too, a little spark of fire which gave her location and a sense of Randal's improbable self, cool blue fire which lay at the heart of a dithering, foolish-looking fellow whose familiar/alterself was a black dog: friendly, flop-eared hound that he was, there was wolf in his well-shielded soul; there was the slow and loyal heart of the hound that lets children pull its ears and trample it under knees and hug it giddy: but that same hound could turn and remember it was wolf; and the eyes which were not slitted green lit with a redder fire and a human-learned cunning. Wolf was clever in a wild thing's way; dog on the hunt was another matter. *That* was Randal. She shed a little touch his way and flinched at once, hearing the thunder rumble and feeling the raw edges of nature gone unstable.

Warning, warning, warning, he sent; and she gathered it up and felt the rising of the unnatural wind.

Get the dead hence, send them home. A god lies senseless, at the edge of raving. And he is prey to demons and their minions.

She located another soul, a lost child. It was glad to go. And another, who loved a man in the Maze. She drove that one away with difficulty; it was wily as the mercenary and more desperate.

She found a minor-class fiend hiding in an alley; it tried desperately to pretend it was a man. Know you, know you, it protested, *does what you want, oh, does everything you want.* ... It wept, which was unusual for a fiend, and hid in a tumble of old boxes as if *that* could save it from the gates. *I find HER*, it snuffled.

That saved it. That *Her* was Roxane. The fiend knew instinctively what she wanted. It proposed treachery (which was its fiendish part) and hoped for mercy (which was its human vulnerability).

FIND, she told it. And the orange-haired fiend leapt up and gibbered with that hope for mercy. It went loping and shambling off shattering boxes and wine bottles and scaring hell out of a sleeping drunk behind the Unicorn.

Ischade's head tilted back; the breath whistled between her clenched teeth and the lust came on her with fever-pulse, let loose by this magical exertion. She had expended a certain kind of energy. It had gone far beyond desire, went toward *need;* and she hunted the living now, hunted with a reckless, hateful vengeance.

Nothing petty this time. No inconsequential, unwashed victim picked up in the streets, slaking need with something so distasteful to her it was self-inflicted torment.

She wanted the innocent. She wanted something clean. And restrained herself short of that. She looked only for the beautiful and the surface-clean, something that would not haunt her.

And a lord of Ranke, who got up to close the shutters against the sudden and importunate wind, inhaled the stench that swept up from riverside and suffered a physical reaction of such intensity he dreamed awake, dreamed something so intense and so very real that it mingled with the krrf-dream he had taken refuge in this storm-fraught night. It had something of terror about it. It had everything of lust. It was like the krrf, destructive and infinitely desirable in that way that knowledge of other worlds, even death, has a lust about it, and a soul trembles on the edge of some great and dangerous height, fascinated by the flight and the splintering of its own bone and the spatter of its own blood on the pavings—

Lord Tasfalen took in his breath of a sudden and focused in horror at the starlit pavings of his own courtyard, realizing how close he had come to falling. And how desirable it had been. He blamed it on the krrf and flung himself away and back to the slave who shared his bed, vowing to have a man whipped for the krrf that must have something in it beyond the ordinary. He experienced a taint of fear, stood there in his bedroom with the slave staring up at him in purest terror that the handsome lord was suffering some kind of seizure, that he had perhaps been poisoned, for which she would be blamed, and for which she would die. Her whole life passed before her in that moment, before Tasfalen sank down on the bed in a convulsion he shared with a woman a far distance from his ornate bedchamber.

That was the extent to which Ischade's power had swelled. It hunted like a beast, and left Tasfalen shaking in a lust he could not satisfy, though he tried, with the slave, who spent the hour in a terror greater than any she had yet experienced in this gilt prison, with this most jaded of Rankene nobles.

Ischade leaned back and shut her eyes, lay inert for a long time while the thunder rumbled and rattled above the house and a flop-eared, freckled mage labored to save a god and a seer. Sweat bathed her limbs, ran in trails on her body beneath the robes. She felt the last impulses of that convulsion, tasted copper on her tongue, rolled her eyes beneath slitted lids and thanked her own foresight that she had sent Straton to Crit this night.

Not yet for this fine nobleman. Sweets were for prolonging. She lay there with the fires sinking in the hearth and on the candles round the room; and in her blood. She stretched out the merest tendril of will and wrapped it about the house, ran it like lightning along the old iron fence and up to the rooftree, where a small flock of black birds took flight.

She sent it pelting gustlike down the chimney and scouring out across the floor with the roll of a bit of ember.

"Haught!"

Haught was there, quickly, catfooted and sullen-faced as

ever, standing in the doorway of the room he shared with Stilcho. Ex-slave and ex-dancer. She gazed at him through slitted eyes, simply stared, testing her resolve; and beckoned him closer. He came a foot or two. That was all. Cautious Haught. Wary Haught.

"Where's Stilcho?"

Haught nodded back toward the room. The fires were silent. Every word seemed drawn in ice, written on the still air inside and the stormwind without.

"This is not a good night, Haught. Take him and go somewhere. No. Not just somewhere." She pulled a ring from her finger. "I want you to deliver this."

"Where, Mistress?" Haught came and took it, ever so carefully, as if it were white-hot; as if he would not hold it longer than he had to. "Where take it?"

"There's a house fourth up and across the way from Moria. Deliver it there. Say that a lady sends to Lord Tasfalen. Say that this lady invites him to formal dinner, tomorrow at eight. At the uptown house. And tell Moria there'll be another place for dinner." She smiled, and Haught found sudden reason to clench his hands on the ring and back away. "You're quite right," she said, faintest whisper. *"Get out of here."*

She lay back a moment, eyes shut in her dreams (and Tasfalen's) as she heard the door open and shut. She felt the tremor in the wards which ringed the place about and sealed its gates.

Come with me, Randal had said, knowing what he faced in god-healing. *Ischade, I need you—*

And Strat: *Ischade—for the gods' sake—*

For no gods' sake. No god's.

She had fled Straton's presence as she would have fled the environs of hell . . . fled running, when she had left that place and left him and the ruin of Roxane's house, in utmost confusion and dread, her heart pounding in terror of what was loose, not in the night, but in her own inner darkness—a thing which made her shun mirrors and the sight of her eyes. So she sat before her hearth and hurled magic into the fires and into the wind and into the gates of hell until she had exhausted the power to control that power and direct it; then the fire went into her bones and inmost parts and smouldered there.

Thunder rumbled again, instability in the world, fire in the heavens.

She drew a shuddering breath, tormented the dreams of the

fairhaired Rankan and thrust herself to her feet, took up her cloak and put it on with careful self-discipline.

The door opened with a crash, fluttering the candle flames, which blazed white for a moment and subsided.

So hard it was to manage the little things. The merest shrug was lethal. The gaze of her eyes might do more than mesmerize. It might strip a soul. She flung up the hood and walked out into the wind and the night.

The door crashed shut behind her and the iron gate squealed violently as it banged open. The wind took her cloak and played games with it, with a power that might have leveled Sanctuary.

"Damn it, *no*. Let me be." And Straton left the mage-quarter room and headed down the outside stairs.

Left Crit, with argument echoing in the room and the dark.

Crit came to the door, came out onto the landing. "Strat," Crit said; and got only Strat's back. *"Strat."*

Straton stopped then and looked up at his left-side leader, at the man he owed his life to a dozen times and who owed *him*. "Why didn't you shoot? Why didn't you damn well pull the trigger when you came into the yard if you're so damn convinced? Ask *me* why things in Sanctuary have gone to hell—come in damn well late and find fault with *me* when I've kept this town alive and kept the blood from running down the damn gutters—"

Crit came down the steps and leaned on either wooden railing. "That's not what I'm talking about. It's your choice of allies. Strat, dammit, *wake up*."

"We're public. We'll talk about it later. Later isn't tonight."

Crit came a step further, checked him on the step. "Listen to me. We've got the witch-bitch *out*. The other one's got you. Command of this city, hell, you lost it, Ace, you lost it a long time ago. I don't know how the hell you're still alive but if the Riddler gets his hands on you now you're done—*dammit*, Strat, where's your sense? You know what she is, you know what she does—"

"She killed me weeks ago. I'm a walking corpse. *Sure*, Crit. I'm best at full of moon. Dammit, that woman's why we're clear of the Nisi witch, she's why you had a city left down here, and why the empire has a backside left at all. I'll tell you what it is with you, Crit; it's knowing your partner was damn well *right* and you were wrong; it's having your mind made

up before you got here and riding in there to haul me out for
a traitor—that's what you came to do, isn't it? To shoot me
down without a chance if I went for your throat? It's not catching, Crit. It's not even true. They blame her for every body
that turns up in the alleys; in the *Maze*, for the gods' sake—
as if corpses never happened before she came to town. Well,
I've been with her when those stories spread; I know damn
well where she was at night; and they *still* blame her—"

"—like they blame lambs on wolves; *sure,* Strat; but a
wolf's still a wolf. And you're damn lucky this far. I'm telling
you. The Riddler will *order* you. Stay the hell out of there."

"Stay the hell out of my business!" Strat slammed an offered
hand aside and ran the steps down to the bottom.

"Strat!"

He looked up in mid-turn. By the tone there might have
been a weapon. There was not. He hardly broke stride as he
went for the stable, flung the door open, and fumbled after the
lantern that hung there. A soft whicker sounded. Another, row-
dier, sounded off loud and two steelshod hooves hit the stall:
Crit's sorrel, ill-tempered and fighting the rein every step of
the way into the stable, bucking and banging boards and making
itself heard upstairs.

"Shut up!" It was the same as yelling at Crit. About as
useful. The hooves hit the boards again.

And Crit arrived in the stable doorway, stood there dark
against the starlight on the cobbles outside. Straton ignored
him and made another attempt at the light. It took. He adjusted
the wick and hung the lamp on its peg, and did what he knew
might be fatal. He turned his back on Crit and walked away
down the aisle.

Not a quarrel between friends. It was nothing private.
Tempus's orders were involved. *Tempus* disavowed him, disavowed everything he had done, everything he had set up,
every alliance he had made; and told him (through Crit) to
break off with his woman and own up to failure. Sent his own
leftside leader to kill him.

He gave Crit the chance. He walked the stable aisle and got
his tack off the rail, flung it up onto the rim of the bay's box
stall. He kept listening through the sorrel's ruckus, for the soft
stir of straw that would be Crit walking up behind him.

Try it. From dispirited suicide, to a gathering determination
to fight back, to the imagination that he could beat Crit, beat

him to the ground, sit on him and make him listen. *Not* kill him when he could. Then Crit would come to sanity. Then Crit would be sorry. Then Crit would go and tell Tempus it was all a mistake, and his partner had done the best that any man could do, tried his damn heart out and done what no one else had been able to do, gods, had held the Nisi witch at bay, had worked out at least a fragile truce with the key factions, had patched the whole hellhole of Sanctuary together and held onto it.

He deserved thanks, by the gods. He deserved *something* besides a partner trying to murder him.

Come on, Crit, dammit. Not a sound in the straw, not a move.

He turned around and looked. Crit was not there at all; had gone—somewhere. Upstairs again, maybe. Maybe to pass an order.

Straton turned and flung the blanket on the bay, stroked its shoulder. The horse bent its head back and delicately nipped at his sleeve, nosed his ribs. He flung his arms about its neck, which indignity the bay protested by backing and fidgeting; gave the warm neck a hug and a slap and tried to stop the stinging of his eyes and the pain in his heart by holding onto something that simply loved him.

She loved him that way. Supported him. Helped him. Never contested with him for credit for this or credit for that, handed it all into his lap with a whispered: *But I don't want that, Strat. You're the mind behind it, you tell me what you need. I do it for your sake. No other in all the world. Yours is the only judgment in the world I trust more than my own. You're the only man I've ever trusted. The only one, ever.*

She was quiet, was safety, she understood what he needed and when he needed it. She was the only woman who knew him the way Crit had known him; knew what he did, knew he was the Stepsons' interrogator, unraveled his own pretense that cruelty gave him no sexual thrill at all: took the body-knowledge which was his skill at interrogation *and* at lovemaking and bent him round again till he could see the torment he inflicted on himself, inner war against his own sensibilities. She took all these things and knit them up and let him turn gentle and sentimental with her, which was his deepest, darkest secret—it was this fragile, inner self she got to, which Crit rarely had. That he could deliver himself to her inside and out, and sleep

in her arms in a way he never slept with his lovers—not without
an eye and an ear alert, somehow—alert in the way a cynic
never sleeps, never trusts, never hopes. Ischade's embrace was
a drug, the gaze of her eyes a well in which Straton the Stepson
became Strat the man, the young man, Strat the wise and the
brave—

Strat the fool to Crit. Strat the traitor to Tempus. Strat the
butcher to everyone else he knew.

He flung the saddle up and the bay which was her gift stood
quietly while Crit's damn sorrel kicked a stall to ruin and Crit
did not come to see to the animal.

He checked the bridle and turned the bay and led it out into
the stable aisle, from there to the door.

Perhaps Crit would be waiting there, having known his
chances slipping up on him. Perhaps it would be one fast bolt
through the ribs and never a chance at all to tell Crit he was a
fool and a blackguard.

Strat leapt up to the bay's back and ducked his head, sending
the bay flying out that door with a powerful drive of its hind-
quarters. If a bolt flew past he never saw it. The bay scrabbled
for a tight turn on the dirt of the little yard and lit out down
the cobbles of the alley, never pausing until he reined it to a
walk a block away.

Where he was going he had no idea. Stay away, Ischade
had said. He had believed her then, the way he believed implicitly when she spoke in that tone to him, that it was something she understood and he did not. It was something to do
with Roxane. It was something that brought a wildness to her
eyes and meant hazard to her; but it was a witch-matter, not
his kind of dealing. Nothing he could help her with. And he
and Ischade had the kind of understanding he had once with
Crit, an understanding he had never looked to have with any
woman: an unspoken agreement of personal competencies.
Witchery was hers. The command of the city was his. And he
would not go there tonight, though that was where every bone
in him ached to go, to reassure himself that she was well, and
that it was not some misapprehension between them that had
driven her away. Things had changed. Crit being back, and
Tempus—gods knew what was in her mind.

If this visitor makes an end to what is—was—between us—
It's yours to say—

His to say. His to say, by accepting her command to stay

away tonight? or by defying it?—He suspected one and then the other with equal force; he agonized over it and called up every nuance of her voice and body and behavior over weeks and months, trying to know what she had meant, whether it was keeping that unspoken pact with her inviolate or defying it and risking (he sensed) his life to pass those wards tonight— that would cancel that doubt he had felt in her. Or confirm it.

Damn Crit. Damn Tempus's coming now, late, when he had everything virtually in hand. Damn their arrival that suddenly undermined everything he had built and poisoned the air between himself and Ischade, the only (he suddenly conceived of it as such), the only unselfish passion he had ever owned, the only peace he had ever conceived of having in the world.

The bay horse picked up its pace again, moved with astonishing quiet over the cobbles and down the long street where the scars of factional violence still lingered.

Factions and powers. He waked suddenly, as if he had been numb since Ischade flung him at Crit and Crit flung him away again. He heard Ischade's voice whispering in his brain:

The only man—the only one who understands how fragile things are—

The only one who stands a chance of holding this city—

The only one who might make something of it yet—truer than the weakling prince, truer than priests and commanders who serve other powers—

You're the only hope I have, the only hope this city has of being more than the end of empire—

You might not have their love, Strat, but you have their respect. They know you're an honest man. They know you've always fought for this town. Even Ilsigis know that. And they respect you if nothing else of Ranke—

—Ilsigis! he had laughed.

You are the city's champion. The city's savior. Believe me, Straton, there is no other man could walk the line you've walked, and no other Rankan they know fights for this town. . . . They respect you if nothing else of Ranke.

Tempus counted him a failure. Tempus arrived in the midst of Roxane's death throes and laid that chaos to his account.

Let Tempus see the truth, let Tempus see that he could pull strings in this web, let him hand peace with the factions to Tempus and let Tempus deal with gods: Tempus was not inclined to tie himself down to one town, one place; Crit loathed the place—but one of Tempus's men next in line, one of Tempus's *trusted* men—could find that answer to everything he wanted.

Ischade and Sanctuary.

There had been disturbance downstairs, a door had opened, and Moria hugged the quilts to her in her lonely bed, lay hardly daring to lift her head. The whole night was terrifying with thunders, with the fitful, fretful character of a sky which promised no rain and perhaps the renewed warfare of witches, Her with the Nisi witch. The full scope of disasters possible in *that* eluded gutter-born Moria; Moria the elegant, the beautiful, curled into a fetal ball in the soft down comforters and the satin and the lace of the mansion Ischade provided Her most pampered (and hitherto least used) servant. But the depth of Moria's imagination was better than most—who had seen the dead raised, the fires blaze about Ischade and pass harmless to her—but not to others. And she had every Ilsigi's reason for terror—a dead man had turned up one morning, outside her very door: the skies arced lightnings overhead, terrible storms haunted Sanctuary nights, and there were wails and scratchings round about the house and the shutters, thumps in the pantry and the basement which sent even the hardened staff shrieking down the halls in terror of ghosts and haunts—a murdered man had lived here; he manifested in the basement all wrapped in his shroud, to Cook's abject terror and the ruin of a whole jug of summer pickles. A ghostly child sported in the hall of nights and once Moria had wakened to the distinct and most horrible feeling that *something* had depressed a body-shaped nest on the feather-mattress beside her. (For that, she had sent a terrified message to Ischade, and the manifestations abruptly stopped.) If that were not enough, there were pitched battles in the streets downhill, fires, maimed men carried past in bloodsoaked litters—a fiend had rampaged through the house of the very Beysib lady Moria had visited on Ischade's orders, and Moria knew all too much about the Harka Bey and their dreadful snakes and their way of dealing with people who brought harm to one of their own. She feared jars, jugs, and closets of late; she feared packages and baskets brought in from market (on those days market functioned): she was sure that some viper might lurk there, some Beysib horror come to find Ischade's helpless agent in some moment that Ischade was elsewhere occupied—the Mistress would take a terrible vengeance for such an attack: Moria believed that implicitly; but it was also possible that Moria would be dead and unable to appreciate it.

And, o Shipri and Lord Shalpa, patron of a one-time thief and Hawkmask, even the dead were not safe from Ischade, who might well raise her up to let her go on like poor Stilcho, like the Stepson-slave Ischade took to her bed and performed gods-knew-what with because he was dead and could not succumb to Ischade's curse—could not die as every man died who had sex with Ischade—or Stilcho died nightly and Ischade raised him up from hell (though how her living and latest lover, the Stepson Straton, had survived beyond one night she could not guess; or did guess, in lurid imaginings of exotic practices and things that she dared not ask Haught—*does he, does Haught, with Her? Would he, could he, has he ever—?* with direst jealousy and helpless rage; for Haught was *hers*). It was all too confusing for Moria, once-thief turned lady.

And now the Emperor was dead in Ranke, the world was in upheaval, and back from the Wizard Wars the Stepsons came scouring through the streets, all grim in their armor and on their tall horses; back in Sanctuary again and determined to set things into their own concept of order.

Make the house presentable, Ischade had sent word through Haught; and told her the house had to host the chiefest of these devils, including Tempus, who was an Ilsigi's direst enemy; an Ilsigi hostess had to entertain these awful men, with what end to the business Moria could not foresee.

A door had opened downstairs. It closed again. She lay between terror and another thought—for Haught came to her now and again. Haught came wherever he liked and *sometimes* that was to her bed. It was Haught who had made her beautiful, it was Haught who cared for her and made her imprisoned life worth living.

It was Haught who had prised a knife from her fingers and prevented her from suicide a half a year ago, then kissed those fingers and made gentle love to her. It was Haught who stole a little of the Mistress's magic for her and cast a glamor on her that had never yet gone away. Perhaps the Mistress tacitly approved. But the Mistress had never laid eyes on her new self; and *that* might happen tomorrow night—

That *would* happen. Oh, if there were a way to make herself invisible she would do it. If that were Haught—it *must* be

Haught, coming up the stairs so quietly.

A shiver came over her. She remembered the *thing* which had been in bed with her. She remembered the cold in the air and the steps which used to come and go in the basement, which might pass a door in the middle of the night and come padding up the stairs—

The latch of her room gave gently. The hinge creaked softly. She lay with her back to these sounds in that paralysis that a bad dream brings, in which a thing will not be real until one looks and sees it standing by one's bed—

The step came close and lingered there. There was a water-smell, a river-smell, a beer-smell unlike Haught's perfumed, wine-favoring self. It was *wrong, wrong*—

She spun over the edge of the bed and came up with the knife she kept there on the floor, as someone dived across the bed at her. She leaped back with that knife held with no uptown delicacy: she was a knife-fighter, and she crouched in her be-ribboned lace and satin whipping the tail of her gown up and aside to clear her legs. A ragged shape hulked on its knees amid her bed, silhouette in light from the hall. It held up its hands, choked for air.

"M—mo-ri-a," it said, wept, bubbled. "Mo-ri-a—"

"O *gods!*"

She knew the voice, knew the smell of Downwind, knew the shape and the hands suddenly, and fled for the door and the lamp to borrow light in the hall, her hands atremble and the straw missing the wick a half a dozen times before she lit the lamp and brought it back again in both hands, the knife tucked beneath her arm.

Mor-am her brother huddled like a lump of brown rag amid her satin sheets. Mor-am stinking of the gutters, Mor-am twisted and scarred by fire and the beggar-king's torture, as he was when She withdrew her favor.

"M-moria—M-m-moria?"

He had never seen her like this, never seen the glamor on her. She was an uptown lady. And he—

"O gods, Mor-am."

He rubbed his eyes with a grimy fist. She found the lamp burning her hands and set it on a bureau, taking the knife from beneath her arm. "Gods, what *happened?* Where have you *been?*" But she needn't ask: there was the reek of Downwind and liquor and the bitter smell of krrf.

"I—been—lost," he said. "I w-went—H-Her business."
He waved a hand vaguely away, riverward, toward Downwind
or nowhere at all, and squinted at her. The tic that twisted his
face did so with a vengeance. "I c-c-come back. What h-ha-
hap-pened t' you, M-m-mo-ria? Y-y-you don't *look*—"

"Makeup," she said, "it's makeup, uptown ladies have
tricks—" She stood and stared in horror at the kind of dirt and
the kind of sight she had grown up with, at the way Downwind
twisted a man and bowed the shoulders and put hopelessness
in the eyes. "Lost. Where, *lost?* You could've sent word—
you could have sent something—" She watched the tic by Mor-
am's mouth grow violent: it was never that way when Ischade
prevented it. Ischade was *not* preventing it. For some reason
Ischade had stopped preventing it. "You're in trouble with Her,
aren't you?"

"I—t-tr-tried. I tried to do what she w-wanted. Then I—l-
lost the m-m-money."

"You mean you drank it! You gambled it, you spent it on
drugs, you fool! Oh, damn you, damn you!"

He cringed. Her tall, her once-handsome brother—he
cringed down and his shoulderblades were sharp against the
rags, his dirty hands were like claws clutching his knees as he
crouched rocking in the cream-and-lace of her bed. "I got to
have m-m-money, Mo-ri-a. I got to go to Her, I got to make
it g-g-good—"

"Damn, all I've got is *Her money,* you fool! You're going
to take Her money and pay Her back with it?"

"You g-g-got to, you g-g-got to, the p-pain, Moria, the
pain—"

"Stay here!"

She set the knife down and fled, a flurry of satin and ribbons
and bare feet down the polished, carpeted stairs, down into the
hall and back where even in this night Cook's minions labored
over the dinner—the infamous Shiey had acquired a partner
with a monumental girth and a real skill, who co-ruled the
kitchen: one-handed Shiey managed the beggar-servants and
Kotilis stirred and mixed and sliced with a deft fury that put
an awe into the slovens and dullards that were the rule in this
house. They thought She had witched this cook, and that the
hands that made a knife fly over a radish and carve it into a
flower could do equally well with ears and noses: that was
what *Shiey* told them. And work went on this night. Work went

on in mad terror; and if anyone thought it was strange that one more beggar went padding in the front door at night (with a key) and Little Mistress came flying downstairs in her nightgown to rummage the desk in the hall for the money not one thief in the house dared steal—

No one said a thing. Shiey only stood in the door in her floured apron, and Kotilis went on butchering his radishes, while Moria ignored them both, flying up the stairs again with the copper taste of a bitten lip and stark fear in her mouth.

She loved her brother, gods help a fool. She was bound to him in ways that she could not untangle; and she stole from Her to pay Her, which was the only thing she could do. It was damnation she courted. It was the most terrible ruin in the world.

It was for the arch-fool Mor-am, who was the only blood kin she had, and who had bled for her and she for him since they were urchins in Jubal's employ. It was not Mor-am's fault that he drank too much, that he smoked krrf when the pain and the despair got to be too much; he had hit her and she forgave him in a broken-hearted torment—all the men she loved had done as much, excepting only Haught, whose blows were never physical but more devastating. It was her lot in life. Even when Ischade clothed her in satin and Haught touched her with stolen glamor. It was her lot that a drunkard brother had to show up wanting money; and adding to the sins that she would carry into Ischade's sight tomorrow. It was men's way to be selfish fools, and women's to be faithful fools, and to love them too much and too long.

"Here," she said, when she had come panting up the stairs, when she had found Mor-am huddled still amid her bed, weeping into his thin, dirty hands. "Here—" She came and sat down and put her hand on his shoulders and gave the gold to him. He wiped his eyes and snatched it so hard it hurt her hand; and got up and shambled out again.

He would not go to Ischade. He would go to the nearest dope-den; he would give it all to some tavernkeeper who would give him krrf and whatever else the place offered to the limit of that gold; and maybe think to force food down him; then throw him out on the street when he had run through his account.

And when Ischade knew where he was—if Ischade got on

his track and remembered him among her other, higher business—

Moria sank down on her soiled bed and hugged her arms about herself, the satin not enough against the chill.

She saw the bureau surface. The ivory-and-silver knife was gone. He had stolen it.

The starlit face of Tasfalen's mansion was buff stone; was grillwork over the windows, and a huge pair of bronze doors great as those which adorned many a temple. The detail of them was obscured in the dark and the windows were shuttered and barred against the insanity of uptown.

But Haught had no trepidation. "Stay here," he told Stilcho, and Stilcho turned a worried one-eyed stare his way and wrapped his black cloak tighter about him, melting into the ornamental bushes with which (unwisely) Lord Tasfalen's gardener decorated the street side.

Haught simply walked up to the door and took the pull-ring of the bell-chain, tugged it twice and waited, arms folded, face composed in that bland grace which he practiced so carefully. A dog barked in some echoing place far inside; was hushed; there was some long delay and he rang again to confirm it for them—no, it was no drunken prankster.

And now inside there had to be a consultation with the major domo and perhaps even with the master himself, for it was not every door in Sanctuary that dared open at night.

Eventually, in due course, there came a step to the door, an unbarring of the small barred peephole in the embrace of two bronze godlets. "Who is it?"

"A messenger." Haught put on his most cultivated voice. "My mistress sends to your master with an invitation."

Silence from the other side. It was a message fraught with ambiguities that might well make a nobleman's nightwarder think twice about asking what invitation and what lady. The little door snapped shut and off went the porter to more consultation.

"What are they doing?" Stilcho asked—*not* a frequenter of uptown houses, or one who had dealt with nobility in life or death. "Haught, if they—"

"Hush," said Haught, once and sharply, because more steps were coming back.

The peephole opened again. "It's an odd hour for invitations."

"My mistress prefers it."

A pause. "Is there a token?"

"My mistress' word is her token. She asks your master to attend tomorrow night at eight, at a formal dinner in the former Peles house; dinner at sundown. Tell Lord Tasfalen that my lady will make herself known there. And he will want to see her, by a token he will know." He reached up and handed a black feather toward the entry, a flight-feather of one of Sanctuary's greater birds. "Tell him wear this. Tell him my lady will be greatly pleased with him."

"Her name?"

"She is someone he will know. I will not compromise her. But this for taking my message—" He handed up a gold coin. "You see my lady is not ungenerous."

A profound pause. "I'll tell my lord in the morning."

"Tell him then. You needn't mention the gold, of course. Good rest to you, porter."

"Good night and good sleep, young sir."

Young sir. The peephole closed and a tight small smile came to the ex-slave's face; a fox's smile. He stepped briskly off the porch with a light swirl of his russet cloak and a wink of his sword-hilt in the starlight.

"Gods," Stilcho said, "the *ring*— the *ring*, man—"

"Ah," Haught said, pressing a hand to his breast. "Damn. I *forgot* it." He looked back at the door. "I *can't* call them back—that wouldn't impress them at all."

"Dammit, what are you up to?"

Haught turned and extended a forefinger, ran it gently up the seam of Stilcho's cloak, and dragged him a safe distance from the door. "You forget yourself, dead man. Do you need a lesson here and now? Cry out and I'll teach you something you haven't felt yet."

"For the gods' sake—"

"You can be with me," Haught said, "or you can resign this business here and now. Do you want to feel it, Stilcho? Do you want to know what dying *can* be like?"

Stilcho stepped away from him, his eye-patched face a stark pale mask under black hood and black fall of hair. He shook his head. "No. I don't want to know." There was a flash of panicked white in the living eye. "I don't want to know what you're doing either."

Haught smiled, not the fox's smile now, but something darker as he closed the distance between them a second time. He caught Stilcho's cloak between thumb and forefinger. "Do me a favor. Go to Moria's place. Tell her expect one more for dinner tomorrow; and wait for me there."

"She'll kill you."

Moria was not the *She* Stilcho meant. There was terror in the single eye. Stilcho's scarred mouth trembled.

"Kill *you*," Haught said. "That's what you're afraid of. But what's one more trip down there, for you? Is hell that bad?"

"Gods, *let me alone*—"

"Maybe it is. You ought to know. *Tell* the Mistress, dead man, and you lose your chance with me." Haught inhaled, one great lungful of Sanctuary's dust-ridden air. "There's power to be had. I can *see* it, I breathe it—you like what I can do, don't deny it."

"I—"

"Or do you want to run to Her, do you really want to run to Her tonight? She told us to leave Her alone—But you've dealt with Her when the killing-mood is on Her, you know what it's like. You heard the fires tonight; have you ever heard them burn like that? She's taken Roxane, she's drunk on that power, the gates of hell reel under her—do you want *that* to take you by the hand tonight and do you want *that* to take you to Her bed and do what She's done before? You'll run to hell for refuge, man, you'll go out like a candle and you'll rot in hell—whatever there is left of you when She's done."

"No—"

"No, She wouldn't, or No, you won't go there, or Yes, you're going to do exactly what I asked you to do?"

"I'll take your message." Stilcho's voice came hoarse and whispered. And in a rush: "If you get caught it's *your* doing, I won't know anything, I'll swear I had no part in it!"

"Of course. So would I." He tugged gently at Stilcho's cloak. "I don't ask loyalty of you. I have ways to ensure it. *Think* about that, Stilcho. She's going to kill you. Again. And again. How long will your sanity take it, Stilcho? Shut your eyes. *Shut them.* And remember everything. And do it."

Stilcho made a strangled sound. Flinched from him.

Stilcho remembered. Haught took that for granted; and smiled in Stilcho's distraught face.

Before he swept the russet cloak back, set a fine hand on the elegant sword, and walked on down the street like a lord of Sanctuary.

Straton stood still and blindfolded as the door closed behind, as the little charade played itself out. He heard the tread of men on board and the scrape of a chair and smelled the remnant of dinner and onions in this small, musty room.

"Do I take this damn thing off?" he asked, after too much of this shifting about had gone on.

"He can take it off," a deep voice said. "Get him a chair."

So he knew even then that his contact had not played him false; and that it was Jubal. He reached up and pulled off the tight blindfold and ran a hand through his hair as he stood and blinked at the black man who faced him across a table and a single candle—a black man thinner and older than he ought to be, but pain aged a man. White touched the ex-slaver's temples, amid the crisp black: lines were graven deep beside the mouth, out from the flaring nostrils, deep between dark, wrinkle-set eyes. Jubal's hands rested both visible on the scarred tabletop; those of the hawknosed man in the chair beside him were not visible at all. And Mradhon Vis, who lately sported a drooping black mustache to add to his dusky sullenness, sat in the corner with one booted foot on the rung of the next chair and elbow on knee, a broad-bladed knife catching the candle-light with theatrical display.

A man shoved a chair up at Straton's back; he turned a slow glance that way, took the measure of that man the same as he had of the two more in the corner. Thieves. Brigands. Ilsigis. A Nisi renegade. Jubal from gods knew where. And himself, Rankan; the natural enemy of all of them.

"Sit down," Jubal said, a voice that made the air quiver. Straton did that, slowly, without any haste at all. Leaned back and put his hands in his belt and crossed his ankles in front of him.

"I said I had a proposal," Straton said.

"From you or from the witch? Or from your commander?"

"From me. Privately. In regard to the other two."

Jubal's square-nailed finger traced an obscure pattern on the aged wood. "Your commander and I have a certain—history."

"All the more reason to deal with me. He owes the witch. She owes me. I want this town quiet. Now. Before it loses whatever it's got. If Tempus is here he's here for reasons more than one."

"Like?"

"Like imperial reasons."

Jubal laughed. It was a snarl, a slow rumbling. He spoke something in some tongue other than Rankene. The man by him laughed the same. "The Emperor, is it? Is it treachery you propose? Treachery against your commander?"

"No. Nobody benefits that way. You make your living in this town. I have interests here. My commander has interests only in getting out of here. That's in your interest. You can go back to business. I get what I want. My commander can get out of here without getting tied down in a fight in Sanctuary streets. All that has to happen is a few weeks of quiet. Real quiet. No theft. No gangs. No evidence of sedition."

"Stepson, if your commander heard you promise that he'd have your guts out."

"Give me the quiet I need and I'll give you the quiet *you* need. You and I understand each other. You won't have a friend left in our ranks—if I fall. Do you understand me?"

"Do I understand you've got your price, Rankan?"

"Mutual advantage." Heat rose to his face. Breath came shorter. "I don't give a damn what you name it, you know where we all are: trade's slowed to a stop, shops are closed, taverns shut down—are you making money? Merchants aren't; you aren't; no one's happy. And you know and I know that if this PFLS craziness goes on we've got a town in cinders, trade gone down the coast, revolutionary fools in control *or* martial law as long as it takes, and corpses up to the eaves. You see profit in that?"

"I see profit everywhere. I *survive,* Rankan."

"You're not fool enough to go up against the empire. You make *money* on it."

Bodies stiffened all around the room. Strat folded his arms across his chest and recrossed his ankles top to bottom.

"He's right." Jubal snapped his fingers. "He said the right word. Let's see if he goes on making sense. Keep talking."

There was disturbance on the Street of Red Lanterns; but the crowd that gathered did it in the discreet way of Red Lantern crowds: peered through windows and out of doorways of brothels and taverns and just stopped in ordinary passages down the Street if they were far enough away. It was glitter and drama, was this district; and a great deal of the tawdry, and in this thunder-rattling night and the bizarre quiet in town since the fire, it was a rougher-than-usual place, the clients that showed up being the sort who were less delicate about their own safety, the sort who took care of themselves. So the whores on the Street were unsurprised at the commotion down by Phoebe's: the small office where Zalbar and the remaining Hell-Hounds served quiet duty as policemen on the Street—that office was unastonished too, and tried to ignore the matter as long as possible. Zalbar in fact was deliberately ignoring it, since rumor had spread *who* was on the Street.

He poured himself another drink, and looked up as a rider on a sorrel horse went clattering past his office as if that man had business.

Stepson. He was relieved, and took a studied sip of the drink he had poured, feeling his problem on its way to resolution without him. The disturbance was far from the house in which he had a personal interest; and that rider headed down the Street was one of Tempus's own, which interference stood a much likelier chance of curtailing the trouble down the street. So it was wise to have sat still a moment and trust the problem to go away; the screams went on, but they would stop very shortly, only one life was in the balance, and the madam of the house (if not the whore) would probably agree that this intervention was better than police.

They were nothing if not pragmatic on the Street.

"Well," said Jubal. "I *like* your attitude. I like a sensible man. Question is, is your commander going to like you tomorrow?"

"An empire runs on what works," Straton said. "Or it doesn't run. We can be very practical."

Jubal considered a moment. A grin spread on his dark, lined face, all theater. "This is my friend." He looked left and right at his lieutenants, and his voice hit registers that ran along the spine. "This is my *good* friend." Looking back at Straton. "Let's call it a deal—friend Straton."

Straton stared at him, with less of relief than of a profound sickness in his gut. But it was a victory. Of sorts. It just did

DAGGER IN THE MIND 65

not come with parades and shouting crowds. It came of common sense. "Fine," he said. "Does this include a deal about that stupid blindfold? Where's my horse?"

"At the contact point. I'm afraid it doesn't include my whereabouts, friend. But I'll send you back with a man you know, how's that? Vis."

Mradhon Vis slipped his knife into sheath and let the front legs of his chair meet the floor as he got up.

It was not the man Strat would have chosen to go with, blindfolded and helpless, down an alley. Protesting it sounded like complaint and complaint did nothing for a man's dignity in this situation that had little enough of dignity about it and precious little leeway. Straton stood up, his arms at his sides as a man behind him took the chair away. Another man put the blindfold back in front of his eyes and tied it with no less uncomfortable firmness. "Dammit, watch it," Straton muttered.

"Be careful of him," Jubal's deep voice said. But no one did anything about the blindfold.

It was less trouble finding Tempus than Crit had anticipated when he talked to Niko and knew where Tempus had gotten to. He reined in at Phoebe's Inn (so the sign said) and shoved the sorrel's reins through a ring at the building's side. There were bystanders; and part of their interest diverted to him, who added himself to the diversion—he scowled blackly and glanced around him with the quiet promise what would befall the hand that touched his horse or his gear. Then he walked on into Phoebe's front room and confronted the proprietor, a fat woman with the predictable amount of gaud and matronly decorum. "Seen my commander?" he asked directly.

She had. Chins doubled and undoubled and painted mouth formed a word.

"Where?"

She pointed. "T-two of them," she said. "F-foreign lady, sh-she—"

That took no guesswork. "Tell my commander Critias is downstairs. *Do it.*"

There was another scream from upstairs. Of a different pitch. For a whorehouse the desertion of the front room was remarkable. Not a whore of either gender came out of the alcoves. The madam ran the stairs and went careening down the upstairs hall, vanishing into the dark.

And still not a beaded curtain shadowed in the downstairs. Not a sound, except upstairs: a knock at a door, the madam's voice saying something unintelligible.

A door opened finally. A heavier tread sounded in the upstairs and Crit looked up as Tempus appeared at the head of the stairs—looked up with a stolid face and a moil of trepidation in his own gut that was only partly due to disturbing Tempus at this particularly agitated moment.

He watched Tempus come down the stairs; stood quietly with his hands in his belt and composed himself to inner quiet.

And it occurred to him, staring Tempus eye to eye, that he had been a fool and that he might have just killed the partner he was trying to save, because it was not reason he saw there.

"What?" Tempus asked with economy.

"Strat—after we cleaned up on riverside, the witch—left. Strat and I parted company. He's gone missing. He's not back at riverside."

Of a sudden it seemed like *his* problem, like something he never should have brought here. He seemed like a thoroughgoing fool. There was another tread on the stairs now, and that was Jihan coming down, trouble in duplicate. But Tempus's face got that masklike look, his long eyes gone inward and deep as he looked aside, a frown gathering and tightening about his mouth.

"How far—missing?" Tempus asked with uncomfortable accuracy and looked him straight in the eye.

"He told me to go to hell," Crit said, had not wanted to say, but Tempus did not encourage reticence with that look. "Commander, he'd listen to you. She's got him—bad. You, he'd listen to. Not me. I'm asking you."

For a long, long moment he reckoned Tempus was going to tell him go to hell too. And assign him there. But he was a shaken man, was Critias. He had seen the most practical-minded man he knew go crazy and desert him. Possession he could have coped with; he might have put an end to Strat the way he would have dispatched a comrade in the field, gut-wounded and suffering and hopeless; a man dreamed about a thing like that and never forgot it, but he did it. Not this time. Not with Strat cursing him to his face and telling him he was wrong. He was accustomed to regard Strat when he said *wrong* and *stop*, and *hold it, Crit, Crit, stop it*—. Straton the level-headed. Straton who seemed at one moment coldly rational and in the next rode off on—whatever that bay horse had become.

"Where did you leave him?"

"Mageguild post. He left me. He rode off. I—lost track of him. He wasn't at Ischade's. I thought he'd come to you. Niko said not. Niko said—find you."

Tempus exhaled a long breath, took the sword he was carrying and hung it where it belonged. Thunder rattled. The inn echoed with it as Jihan came on down the steps.

"Barracks, maybe," Jihan said.

"I don't think so," Crit said.

"Where *do* you think he's gone?" Tempus asked.

"To do something," Crit said, and out of that fund of knowledge a pairbond held: "To prove something."

Tempus took that in with a grave and quiet look. "To whom?"

"To me. To you. He's being a fool. I'm asking you—"

"You want an order from me? Or you want *me* to find him?"

Of a sudden Crit did not know what he wanted. One seemed too little; the other, fatal.

"I'll find him," Crit said. "I thought you'd better know."

"I know," Tempus said. "He's still in command of the city. Tell him he'll be at Peres on time. And he *won't* have done anything stupid; tell him that too."

A horse snorted softly, hooves shifted on cobbles; and Straton heard the sound of their steps between narrow walls, knew before the hands left his arms that they had come back to the alley and the little stable-nook where he had left the bay. He felt the grip lift, heard retreating steps as he raised his hands and pulled the blindfold off. The bay whickered softly. A trio of cloaked figures went rapidly down the alley, one more than had brought him; the third would be the man who had kept the horse safe in the interval.

He walked over and patted the bay's neck, finding his hands shaking. Not from any fear of violence. Even Vis's personal grudge did not do that to him. It was himself. It was knowing what he had done.

He took the reins and swung up to the bay's back, reined about to ride out of the alley and caught his balance as the bay rose up under him: a cloaked shadow had slipped round the corner in front of him.

"That horse isn't hard to find," Haught said as the bay walked backward and came down on four feet again, still shying.

Strat reined him out of it, and held him, hand to the sword he had never given up.

"Damn you—"

Haught held up something between two fingers. "Calm yourself. *She* sent me. With this."

Strat reined the bay quieter, still too wary to bring his horse alongside a man who might have a knife. He slid down to his own feet, keeping the reins in hand, met the ex-slave on a level and took the object Haught offered at arm's length.

A ring lay in his palm. It was Ischade's.

"She wants you—*not* at the uptown house tomorrow. Stay away. Come to the riverhouse. After midnight."

He closed his hand on the ring. A shudder ran through him with a reaction he had no wish to betray to the slave's amusement. He kept his face cold and his voice steady. "I'll be there," he said.

"I'll tell her that," Haught said with uncommon civility, and whisked himself around the corner again.

Strat slipped the ring on his littlest finger, and suffered a spasm that took his sight away. The bay horse pulled the reins from his hands and then, sheepish, stood there with the reins adangle while his master recollected his sight and got his heart settled from its pounding.

It was apology, from Ischade. It was invitation as plain as ever witch or woman sent a man. His heart pounded as he climbed up to the saddle and clenched his fist on the ring that had now the slow sweet bliss krrf never matched.

He fought his head clear, knew that what the slave asked— what *she* asked—was trouble, trouble not with Crit this time. Trouble that might take everything he had done and his life and sweep everything away, but the witch knew that, but Ischade wanted him and by this gift he knew how much she wanted him; he felt it continually and the world swam in front of his eyes.

What are you doing? he asked her in absentia. *Do you know what you're asking?*

And in the gnawing doubt that had been between them at the beginning and now again: *Does it matter to you?*

The bay moved, and the alley passed in a blur of starlit cobbles, the glare of a lantern. Things passed in and out of focus.

And in a profound effort he took the ring from off his finger and put it in his pocket where it was only mildly euphoric.

Sweat ran on his body. He mopped at his face, raked his hair back and tried to think despite the erotic mist that hazed the seeping brick, the effluvium of rubbish and the gutter. The bay's steps clopped along with a distant, dazed echo in the alley's wending transformation into a street where a dope den and a tavern maintained half-open doors and a clutch of krrf-dazed sleepers sitting in the mire outside. Music wailed; strings needed tuning. No one cared, least of all the player. The alley meandered on. The horse did, while the mist came and went.

Tempus would want him at that gathering at Peres. Tempus would want to talk to him, want sense out of him, would look at him with that piercing stare of his and spit him with it till he had spilled everything. *That* was what Ischade knew.

That was why Ischade wanted him out of there.

But then what, when he had fought with Crit and defied his commander and dealt with Jubal and through Jubal, with the gangs. There were ways and ways to die. He had invented one or two himself. Lying to Tempus offered worse. Desertion, dereliction. *Treason.*

He felt a stab of ecstasy, and one of utmost terror; and knew he ought to take that ring and fling it in the mud and go confess everything to Tempus, but that was against his very nature— he had never run for help, had never thrown himself at anyone's feet, never in his life. Fixing things took nerve. It took the raw guts to hang on to a situation long after it stopped being safe.

He was no boy, no twenty-five-year-old in shining armor, head full of glory-stories. He had worked the Stepsons' shadowy jobs for a decade. He had just never had to think that Tempus himself might be involved in a mistake. The man the gods chose—But gods had self-interest right along with the rest of creation; *gods* might trick a man—might trick an empire, play games with souls, with a man who served their cause.

Tempus could be wrong. Gods know he could be wrong. He doesn't care for this town. I do. I can give it to him. Is that treason?

An empire runs on what works, doesn't it?

I've just got to live to get it working. Prove it to Crit. Prove it to Tempus. If it takes staying out of their way till I can get this thing organized—I know holes Crit doesn't.

Damn, no. *They'll go for her.*

He gripped the ring in his pocket, suffered a twinge that

dimmed his vision and reminded him it was no small power the Stepsons might take on in Ischade. There would be fatalities. Calamity on both sides.

He made up his mind, then, what he had to do.

The sun was a glimmer of red-through-murk above Sanctuary's east when Ischade came to the simple little shop in the Bazaar; she came after a trek through Sanctuary's streets and in a sordid little room in the Maze left a dead man the world would little miss. That man left her disgusted, pricklish, *soiled;* and such was the charge of energies in the air of Sanctuary that she hardly felt that ebb of power his death made, felt not even a moment's relief from what ran along her veins and suffused her eyes and made that victim, in the last moment of his life, wish he had never existed at all.

It left not the least satisfaction; more, it left a gnawing terror that nothing would *ever* be enough, that there was no man in all the world sufficient to ease that power which threatened to break loose in the muttering storm and in her vitals. She blinded herself: she saw too much of hell and not enough of where she was going, and if a gang of Sanctuary's predatory worst had confronted her and seen her eyes this moment, at dawn's breaking, they would have stopped cold and slunk away in terror. She had become—known. Victims were harder to come by. Only fools approached her. And they were without sport and without surprise.

Tasfalen. Tasfalen. She clung to that name and that promise as to sanity itself—a prey that offered wit, and hazard, and difficulty.

Tasfalen could be savored, over days. Put off and extended for a week—

She might, she reasoned with herself, make Strat understand.

She might—yet—get through that shell of unbelief Strat made around himself, teach him the things he had to know. He was ready for that. His infatuation was sufficient. That her hunger threatened him, this, *everything*—was unbearable.

It was weakness. And she had not yet accounted for Roxane. No scouring of the town had discovered her. That the dimwitted fiend had not found her tracks, but that she had discovered nothing to indicate that Roxane had not perished—did not make her secure in her present weakness. It was exactly the moment and the mode in which the Nisi would seek her out. . . .

. . . Strike through Strat, through this stranger Tasfalen, through anything at all she least expected; most of all through a weakness. . . .

And she was blind.

Knowing that, she came here, after a fruitless murder and a night's searching all of Sanctuary for Roxane's traces. . . .

. . . To find the traces Roxane left on the future.

A light burned inside the little shop. So someone was astir this dawn. She rapped at a door she might have opened, waited like any suppliant at the fane.

Heavy steps came to it; someone opened the peephole and looked out and shut it rapidly.

She knocked a second time. And heard a higher voice than belonged with that tread, before the bar thumped back and the door opened inward.

The S'danzo Illyra stood to meet her, and that shadow to the side was Dubro, was a very distraught Dubro; and Illyra's face was tearstreaked. The S'danzo wrapped her fringed shawl about her as at some ill wind sweeping through her door.

"So the news has come here," Ischade said in a low voice; and was pricklingly conscious of Dubro to the side. She forced herself to calm, concentrating on the woman only, on a mother's aching grief. "A mage is with your son since last night, S'danzo; I would be, but my talents are—awry tonight. Perhaps later. If they need me."

"Sit down." Illyra made a feverish movement of her hands, and Dubro cleared a bench. "I was making tea. . . ." Perhaps the S'danzo conceived this as a visit of condolence, some sign of hope; she wiped at her eyes with brisk moves of a thin hand and turned to her stove, where a pot boiled. It was placatory hospitality. It was something else, perhaps.

"You see hope for your son in me?"

"I don't See Arton. I don't try." The S'danzo poured boiled tea through a strainer, one, two, three cups. Brought one to her and ignored the other two. *I don't try.* But a mother might, whose son lay sick in the palace, in company with a dying god. Priests or some messenger from Molin had been here already. *Someone* had told the S'danzo; or she had Seen it for herself, scryed it in the fracturing heavens, or tea leaves, gods knew.

And consolation might make a clearer mind in her service.

"Do you think they'll slight your son," Ischade asked, and sipped the tea, "for the other boy? Not if they value this city. I assure you. Randal's very skilled. You certainly needn't doubt which side the gods are on in your son's case. Do you?"

"I don't know . . . I *can't* see."

"Ah. My own complaint. You want to know the present. I can tell you that." She shut her eyes and indeed it was little work to do, to sense Randal at work. "I can tell you the children are asleep, that there is little pain now, that the strength of the god holds your son in life. That a—" Pain assaulted her, an acute pain behind the eyes. Mage-fire. "Randal." She opened her eyes on the small, cluttered room again, on the S'danzo's drawn face. "I may be called to help there. I don't know. I have the power. But I'm hampered in using it. I need an answer. *Where is Roxane?*"

The S'danzo shook her head desperately. Gold rings swung and clashed. "I can't See that way—it's a *present* thing; I can't—"

"Find her tracks in the future. Find mine. Find your son's if you can. That's where she'll go. A man named Niko. She'll surely try for him. Tempus. Critias. Straton. Those are her major foci."

The S'danzo went hurriedly aside, snatched at a small box on the shelf. "Dubro—please," she said when the big man moved to interfere; and he let her alone as she sank down on her knees in the middle of the floor and laid out her cards.

Nonsense, Ischade thought; but something stirred, something twitched at the nape of her neck, and she thought of the magic-fall that still swept the winds, recalling that prescience was *not* her talent, and she had not a way in the worlds and several hells to judge what the S'danzo did, how much was flummery and how much self-hypnosis and how much was a very different kind of witch.

The cards flew in strong, slim fingers, assumed patterns. Re-formed and showed their faces.

Illyra drew her hand back from the last, as if she had found the serpent on that card a living one.

"I see wounds," Illyra said. "I see love reversed. I see a witch, a power, a death, a castle; I see a staff broken; I see temptation—" Another card went down. *Orb.*

"Interpret."

"I don't know how!" Illyra's fingers hovered trembling over

the cards. "There's flux. There's change." She pointed to a robed and hooded figure. "There's your card: eight of air, Lady of Storms—hieromant."

"Hieromant! Not I!"

"I see harm to you. I see great harm. I see power reversed. The cards are terrible—Death and Change. Everywhere, death and change." The S'danzo looked up, tears flowing down her cheeks. "I see damage to you in what you attempt."

"So." Ischade drew a deep breath, teacup still in hand. *But for my question, fortune-teller: Find me Roxane!*"

"She is Death. Death in the meadow. Death on the path of waters—"

"There are no meadows in Sanctuary, woman! Concentrate!"

"In the quiet place. Death in the place of power." The S'danzo's eyes were shut. Tears leaked from beneath her lashes. "Damage and reversal. It's all I can see. Witch, don't touch my son."

Ischade set the cup aside. Rose and gathered her cloak over her shoulder as the S'danzo gazed up at her. She found nothing to say of comfort. "Randal's with them," was the best that occurred to her.

She turned and went out the door. The power was still a tide in her blood, still unabated. She inhaled it in the wind, felt it in the dust under her feet. She could have blasted the house in her frustration, raised the fire in the hearth and consumed the S'danzo and her man to ash.

It seemed poor payment for an innocent woman's cup of tea. She banked the inner fire and drank the wind into her nostrils and considered the daybreak.

"I can't, I can't, I can't!" Moria cried, and went down the hall in a cloud of skirts and satin—till Haught caught her up, and took her by the arms and made her look at him. Tears streaked Moria's makeup. A curl tumbled from her coiffure. She stared at Haught with blind, teared eyes and hiccuped.

"You'll manage. You don't have to say where I am or where I went."

"Then take him with you!" She pointed aside to the study, where a dead man sat drinking wine in front of her fire and getting progressively more inebriate. "Get him *out* of here, I can't do anything with the staff, they know what he is—for the gods' sakes get him *out!*"

"You'll manage," Haught said. He carefully put the curl where it belonged and adjusted a pin for her while she snuffled. He wiped her cheeks with his thumbs, careful of her kohl-paint, and of her rouge, and tipped up her face and kissed her gently on salty lips. "Now. There. My brave Moria. All you have to do is not mention me. Say I delivered my messages. Say Stilcho's with me and we're going to go down to a shop and see about that lock you want for your bedroom—now won't that fix it? I promise you—"

"You could witch it."

"Dear woman, I might, but you don't do a thing with an axe when a penknife will do. You don't want your maid blasted, do you? I doubt you want that. I'll find a lock *I* can't pick and see if you can. If it suits, I'll have it installed on your door within the week. I promise. Now go upstairs, fix your make-up—"

"I want you *here!* I want you to tell Her what you did to me, I want you to tell Her you made me beautiful!"

"Now, haven't we been over that? She won't care. I assure you she has quite a many things on her mind, and you are the very least, Moria. The very least. Do your job, be gracious, be everything I've helped you be, and the Mistress will be *very* happy with you. Don't ruin your makeup. Smile. Smile at everyone. Don't smile too much. These men have been a long time out of a house like this. *Don't* attract them. Behave yourself. There's a love." He kissed her on the brow and followed the sudden panicked dart of her eyes, the appearance of a shadow in the study doorway.

Stilcho leaned there reeking of wine, his thin, white face uncommonly grim with its eye-patch and comma of dark hair. "My lady," Stilcho said wryly. "Very sorry to distress you."

Moria just stared, stricken.

"Come on," Haught said, and caught Stilcho by the arm, heading him for the door.

"I can't find him," Crit said, reporting in to the palace where Tempus had appropriated an office, down the hall and up a stair from the uneasy business Crit had no wish to know about.

Tempus made a mark on a map. The place was a litter of scrolls and books and the plunder of the map room. They lay on the floor as well as the desktop and afternoon light shone wanly through the window, a murky afternoon, beclouded and rumbling with rain that never fell. He rose, walked to the window, hands locked behind him—stared out into the roiling cloud beyond the portico. Lightning flashed. Thunder followed.

"He'll show," Tempus said finally. "You've tried the witch's place again."

"Twice. I . . ." There was a moment of silence that brought Tempus around to face the man. ". . . went as far as the door," Crit said, much as if he had said *gate of hell*. Stolidly. Eyes carefully blank. Tempus frowned.

"King of Korphos," Crit said then.

"I remember." A king invited his enemies to reconcile. Archers turned up round the balcony at dinner and killed them all. Witchfire might serve. And: *Nothing new under the sun,* an inner voice said; while another voice recalled dead comrades: *tortured souls of yours and mine which must be released. . . .* At times the world went giddy, skidded between past and present. Korphos and a Sanctuary mansion. A missing Stepson, and a sorely wounded one, both prey to witches. A thing that had happened, would happen, inevitably happened? Sometimes he had run risks from mere expediency. Or perversity. He did not take his men into it to no purpose.

Crit stood there, statue-quiet. Too damn willing. A snake had gotten in among them, and Stepson hunted Stepson and stood there with that look that said Anything you order.

"I've no doubt the witch can find him," Tempus said. "If he doesn't show up. Don't worry about it." He gestured toward the door. Crit took the hint, and Tempus walked as far as the hall beside him. "Just see you're on time."

"Is Niko—"

"Better."

Maybe the tone invited nothing further. Crit went. Tempus stood there with his hands slipped into the back of his belt until Crit had dwindled into a shape of light and shadow on the white marble stairs that led to outer doors.

Niko was where Niko had no business being, that was where Niko was.

He struck his hand against his leg and headed down another stairs, past priests who plastered themselves and their armfuls of linen and simples to the narrow walls.

Through doors and doors and doors, till the thunder overhead diminished and the last door gave way to a *sanctum sanctorum* deep in the palace bowels. He stepped inside, saw the cluster around the bed, a half dozen priests, the mage, with enough incense palling the room to choke a man. A child whimpered, a thin, faint sound. And Tempus's eye picked out his partner standing in that group. "Get Niko," he said as a priest passed him, and the priest scuttled into the cloying room where he had no personal wish to go. The stuff offended his nose, gave him the closest thing to a headache he was wont to have. He stood there with the pressure throbbing in his temples which might be rage at Niko or the whole damned business of priests and mummery and a mage's ill-smelling concoctions, or just the world gone awry. He stood there while the priest snagged Niko and led him into reach, Niko walking as if he would break, one eye running and filmed with gelatinous stuff, the other patched.

"Damn," Tempus snarled at the priest, "does it need the smoke?" He took Niko by the arm and led him out into clean air, closed the door. "I'm not asking this time; get to bed."

"Can't sleep," Niko said. The ashbrown hair fell loose across his brow, trailed into Jihan's unspeakable unguents. "No use—"

"You're raving." He took Niko's arm willy-nilly, led him on.

"I saw Janni," Niko said, mumbled, in a sick man's disjointed way. "I saw him here—"

"You don't see a damn thing, you're not *going* to see a damned thing if you don't get out of that foolery and leave those brats to the priests."

"Randal—"

"—can take care of it." He reached Niko's appointed bedchamber, opened the door and led him as far as the rumpled bed. "Now stay there, or do I have to set a guard?"

"Eyes aren't that bad," Niko murmured. But he felt of the bedside and sat down like a man with too many bruises.

Tempus had none. They healed. Everything slid off him and vanished. Only Niko had the bandages, Niko had the scars, Niko was fragile as all he loved. "Stay there," he said, too sharply. "I've too much else. I don't need this."

Niko subsided quietly. Lay back with his eyes shut. It was not what he had meant to say or do. He walked over and pressed Niko's hand, walked out then.

Call off the damn dinner, he thought. What's to be gained? How did I agree to that?

It was *before* hell broke loose; it was to calm a nervous town. It was to get the measure of a witch and her intentions. And to discover the threads that Strat had run here and here and here through the town. In that regard it made more sense than not. The affair was a stone in motion, downhill, and it would say something now to the town to break off this engagement. ". . . Souls of yours and mine . . ." Straton was one of those souls at imminent risk. And if there was a thing which might pull Straton into reach it was this, his own witch-lover's arranging.

Why meet with them? Why this courting of Stepsons?

That was the insane question. He thought of Korphos again; and the arrows. And poisoned wine. And the Emperor.

He was not accustomed to direct challenge, but it was still possible.

The door stayed open to a steady stream of martial guests, arrivals afoot and ahorse out front, with the clank of swords in the foyer, the inpouring of wolfish men who towered and clattered with weapons they did *not* give up at the door. Hand after huge hand took Moria's as she stood sentry at the door of her borrowed house, a powdered, perfumed mannequin that said over and over *How kind, thank you, welcome, sir* and smiled till her teeth ached. Hands which could have crushed her fingers lifted them to lips smooth, bearded, mustached, olive-skinned and white-skinned and unmarked and scarred; and each time she recovered her hand and stared a moment too long into the eyes of this or that man she felt the blue satin dress too low and the perfume too much and her whole self estimated for value right along with the vases and the house silver. And *she* was the thief!

Man after man and not a woman in the lot until a tall woman with one long pigtail came strolling in and crushed her hand in a grasp rougher than the men's. "Kama," that one said. Her hand was callused as the men's. Her eyes were smouldering and dreadful. "Pleased," Moria breathed, "thank you. Do come in. Dining hall to your right under the stairs." She worked her fingers and thrust out her hand valiantly to the next arrivals, seeing more on the street. More and more of them. There could *not* be enough wine. A stray lock of her coiffure slipped and strayed down her neck, bouncing there. She borrowed both hands up to stab it back into place with a hairpin, realized the tall soldier in front of her was staring down her decolletage and desperately thrust out her hand. "Sir. Welcome."

"Dolon," that one said, and headed in the wake of the woman with the pigtail while others came up the steps.

O Shalpa and Shipri, where's the Mistress, what am I *doing* with these Rankans? They know I'm Ilsigi, they're laughing at me, they're all laughing. . . .

A man arrived who was not a soldier, who came with servants: she mistook him for a passerby until he abandoned the servants and came up the steps, seized her hand and kissed it with a flourish of his cap.

He looked up. His hair was fair brown, his eyes were blue; he was Rankan of the Rankans and noble and he stared into her eyes as if he had discovered some strange new ocean.

"Tasfalen Lancothis," he murmured, and never let go of her hand. *"You* are the lady—"

"Sir," she said, quite paralyzed by a nobleman who stared into her eyes in that way. And she was further baffled when he plucked a black feather from his cap and offered it to her. "How kind," she murmured, blinking at him and wondering whether she had gone totally mad or was another Rankan here to make sport of her. She put it in her decolletage, having no better place, and saw his eyes follow that move and lift to hers again with profoundest concentration. "My lady," he said, and kissed her hand a second time, which meant men standing in line behind him. Her heart raced in a sense of impending disaster, the Mistress's dire displeasure. Heat and cold chased one another from her breast to her face. "Sir—"

"Tasfalen."

"Tasfalen. Thank you. Please. Later. The others . . ."

He let go her hand. She turned desperately to the men next, passed them through with a hand to each and caught her breath as she stared at the tall pair next, the taller one with the face that she had seen only at distance, riding through the streets on a fine horse. His clothing was plain. His face was smooth and cold and he was younger than she had thought until he took her hand and she looked up into his eyes by accident.

She stood there in mortal terror, mumbled something and surrendered a limp hand to the man next—"Critias," he named himself. "Moria," she said, never taking her eyes from the man who walked through the hall, an apparition as dreadful as anything the house had yet hosted. *O gods, where is She? Is She*

*going to come at all? They'll steal the silver, they'll drink down
the wine and wreck the house and come at me next, they'll kill
me, they will, to spite Her. . . .*

Thunder rumbled above the house, the light outside was
stormlight, and never a drop of rain spotted the cobbles. She
looked outside in mortal terror, expecting more apparitions.
Wind skirled, committed indiscretion with her skirts. She held
her threatened hair and watched wide-eyed as a last man came
from around the corner where the horsemen had turned in,
where the beggar-stableboys Ischade had provided did service
with the horses, in the little stable-nook to the rear of the house.
The man wore cloak and hood. For a moment she thought it
was Stilcho and held onto her coiffure and dreaded his approach. But it was not, it was a different man, who came up
the step with a matter-of-fact tread and looked up at her with
an expression different than the rest—with an expression as if
she were a wall in his way and he had suddenly realized something was in front of him. For a moment as he threw his hood
back he looked confused, which in these grim men was different
in itself.

"I'm due here," he said.

She liked this one better. He was human. She stared at him
and blinked in the wind and got out of his way. "Down the
hall," she called after him, and seized the door, seeing no one
else on the street, and pulled it to. Caught her skirt and freed
it and got the door shut. By that time he was gone down that
hall, had found the dining hall for himself.

There was a sudden quiet when he passed that door. She
stopped in her own rush toward the hall, terrified that there
was something going on, rushed on, waving frantically at Shiey,
who appeared be-aproned and floured in the doorway. "Food?"
Shiey asked.

"Wait on the Mistress," she hissed. "When the Mistress
comes." And then she eased through that dining room door
where a great deal of quiet had fallen. The last-come stood still
in the doorway, the Commander was at the other end of the
hall, and the two were staring at each other.

"Straton," Tempus said. So she knew who it was; she felt
the cold; she heard the thunder rumbling over the roof and these
great men with their swords all a-bristle with some offense that
had to do with this man and his presence. Only Tasfalen stood
nonplussed, holding his wine glass and staring at Tempus as if

he had suddenly realized he was in very dangerous and exclusive company.

"Commander." Straton came unfixed from the doorway and walked into the room. It was all slipping out of control. Moria took a quick step forward, her throat paralyzed with fear and her wits with doubt.

"Our hostess," Tasfalen said, and swept in to seize her hand. She drew a great breath, strangled by the lacings of the gown, and the air felt thin and strained and charged, her head swirling with sleeplessness and the smell of wine she had not even drunk. She took a hesitant step with Tasfalen clasping her hand.

"Please," she said. Her voice came out a hoarse breath. "Please sit down. Shiey—" No, no, one did not shout for Cook in a formal party. She struggled to free her hand. "Please."

Tempus moved. A mountain might have moved at her wish and amazed her no less. She saw to her dizzy relief all the men moving toward their seats, all of them moving in on the double tables which did, miraculously, have room enough and to spare. . . .

Tempus took a seat. Tasfalen led her inexorably forward, past the rows of chairs, toward the head of the table. Straton— *Her* Straton—walked on the other side of the tables, got as far as Critias and Tempus, slung his cloak onto a pile of others in the corner, and quietly stood behind a chair he chose. Not looking at them. Or at her. She might have been walking the edge of a chasm.

Tasfalen delivered her to the place centermost of the head table. She shook her head furiously, desperately, with Tempus standing next to that chair, the Mistress's chair; she belonged at the door, she had forgotten to take their cloaks, they had draped them off in the corner in a pile on an unused bench or hung them over the backs of their chairs; Cook delayed with the food, she had to go back to the kitchen and get Cook into motion. . . .

Eyes shifted from her toward the door. She turned, clutching the finials of the carved chair, and saw Ischade in the doorway—an Ischade without her cloak; in a deep-necked gown of deepest blue; the sparkle of sapphire at her tawny throat, her black, straight hair in upswept elegance.

Straton left his place, walked through that vast silence and offered his hand to Ischade. Quietly she took it, and he walked her the whole long distance up the tables in mortal silence.

Moria caught a breath, having forgotten to breathe. The effort strained the limits of the corset and dizziness tightened her hands on the chair as Tasfalen's hand left her waist. Ischade had paused in her walking to offer her hand to him, leaving Straton's. The silence trembled there, and Moria desperately transferred her grip to the next chair over, displacing Tasfalen to endmost. She caught the edge of that glance: Ischade's nostrils were white about the edges and her mouth set in an anger carefully controlled.

He's Hers, Moria thought, weak-kneed. *Tasfalen's Hers—* with all that meant. With absolute terror that stole the strength from her knees and made her wish that she could bolt from the room. She felt the feather ride between her breasts with every breath. Felt—something terrible in the air. Straton stood there, motionless, his face frozen. No one had moved.

"Lord Tasfalen," Ischade said, and turning that glance smoothly to Moria and reaching out her hand. "Moria, my dear." Ischade's hand closed on hers. Drew her close, closer, so close that the musk of Ischade's perfume was in her nostrils, Ischade's hand firm on hers, Ischade's lips dry and cool on her cheek. "How splendid you look."

Moria swayed on her feet. Ischade's hand ground the bones of her hand together and sent pain through her; Ischade's eyes caught hers and for a moment gulfs opened at her feet.

Then Ischade released her hand and offered it past her toward Tempus. Moria turned her head, clutched the chair again, staring in helpless terror as she had view of Tempus's face and the terrible delicacy with which he lifted Ischade's small hand in his. Power and Power. She felt the hair rise on her nape as if the whole air were charged.

"I owe you thanks," Tempus said. "So I'm told. In the matter of Roxane."

There was the smallest delay, another prickling of storm. "Welcome to Sanctuary, Commander. How fortunate your arrival."

O my gods—

But Ischade turned then and let Tempus and then Straton draw her chair back. She sat. Everyone settled into chairs. Moria fumbled weakly at hers before realizing Tasfalen was drawing it back for her. She gathered her skirts, sat down as her knees went to water.

Tasfalen seated himself and slipped his hand to hers beneath the table and held with firm strength. Straton passed to Ischade's other side, took the chair at Tempus's left, next to Critias. By some mercy, men had started talking to each other. Then by a further one, the kitchenside door swung open and food started coming.

Tasfalen's hand rested on her thigh. She failed to care. She stared down the long tables, listened to Tempus and Ischade speaking quiet banalities about wine and food and weather—

O gods, get me out of here! Haught!

She would have hurled herself even into Stilcho's arms.

"I don't know where she is," Ischade was saying, again, in a voice not meant to carry. "I've searched. I've spent the night searching. I had hoped for better news."

"How much *do* you know?" Tempus asked.

A pause. Perhaps Ischade looked his way. Moria drank a mouthful of wine and tried not to shiver. "I know," Ischade said. And reached for Moria's hand again beneath the table.

"Who told you?"

Another profound silence. "Commander. I *am* a witch."

Thunder rolled and cracked overhead. "Damn," Tasfalen said. And reached for Moria's hand again beneath the table.

Gentle man, she thought. *Gentleman. He doesn't understand this. He doesn't understand what he's into, he's as lost as I am*—Ischade invited him, she must have. Oh, what are they talking about, priests and searching and a demon? O gods, where's Haught? It was a lie about the lock, he's not off on any errand, not now, with Her like this and the storm and the house full of Rankan soldiers—Why was Stilcho with him? What could *he* have to do with Stilcho?

She took another glass of wine. A third when that ran out. The room swam in a haze, and the voices buzzed distantly in her ears. She picked at food and picked at another course and drank another cup until she could stare about the room without more than a distant trepidation. The conversation about the hall grew more relaxed. Tasfalen whispered invitation in her ear and she only blinked and gave him a dazed look at close range, lost for a moment in blue eyes and a masculine scent unlike Haught's, whose clothes always smelled of Ischade.

Doomed, she thought, *damned. Dead. Gods save this man. Gods save me.* And she held his hand until his closed on hers with painful force.

"My lady," Tasfalen whispered once, "what's wrong? What's happening here?"

"I can't say," she whispered back; while Ischade said something else to Tempus, which made less sense than before. Of a sudden she realized they were speaking some foreign tongue.

And there was no laughter. There was sudden quiet all about the table. No word from Straton or the man next to him. Critias. The men nearest caught that contagion and it spread down the table. Wine stayed untouched.

"It's sufficient," Ischade said at last. "Your pardon." And rose.

Tempus got to his feet. Straton was next. The whole company began to rise, and Moria thrust herself from her seat, tangling her legs and the skirts and the resisting fabric of the chair until Tasfalen's arm steadied her. She stood there with her heart pounding in terror no wine could numb, suffered Ischade's direct glance, suffered a moment that Ischade put out a hand, lifted her chin with a delicate forefinger and stared her straight in the eyes.

"M-m-mis—"

"How fine you've become," Ischade said, and there was hell in that look, that sent a weakness through her bones and her sinews and made her sway against Tasfalen. Ischade let her go then, and nodded to the lord Tasfalen, as Straton came and took her arm. She walked toward the door with Straton, while everyone stayed standing and the confused kitchen started sending out another course.

A low murmur went past their backs. Slowly Tempus settled to his chair again. It was going to go on. She was left with these men after all. Moria sank back to her chair with the last strength in her legs and smiled desperately at Tasfalen.

Ischade walked for the door, paused to gather her cloak from the bannister of the stairs, and let Straton drape it about her shoulders. "Thank you," she said, and walked on toward the door. Stopped abruptly as he followed. She looked back at him and felt her whole frame shudder with the effort of calm, with the effort to keep her face composed and her movements natural. "I said," she told him carefully, "that I needed time to myself. *Don't touch me*—" As he reached his hand toward her.

"I *had* to come, dammit!"

"I said not!"

"Who is that man?"

She saw the madness in his eyes. Or it reflected hers, which pounded in her veins and grew to physical pain. He caught her arms and she flung up her head and stared him in the eyes until the hands lost the strength in their grip. But the pain grew; became madness, became the thing that killed.

She shoved him back, violently, walked with quick steps to the door and heard his steps behind her. She turned before he reached her.

"Stay away!" she hissed. "Fool!"

And jerked the door open and fled, into the wind, and on it.

CHILDREN OF ALL AGES

Lynn Abbey

It was spring in the lush forests far to the south of Sanctuary. Trees and shrubs put forth their leaves; delicate flowers swayed on gentle winds and, beneath a swag of ivory blossoms, a mongoose sneezed violently. He sneezed a second time and for a moment he was not a mongoose but something larger, something with huge, flapping ears. Then he was a mongoose again— preening his thick, musteline fur; fluffing out his tail and casting coy glances at the female a leap and a bound away. The female chattered her response and they were off along the branches, across a stream and ever further from the magical trap Randal had laid for her.

The Tysian mage had conjured and cast to exhaustion looking for her. She was the finest mongoose alive: the largest, the fastest, the boldest, and the most intelligent. She had, at least, evaded every snare he'd set from his power-web in distant Sanctuary until, in desperation, he'd transferred his essence to the forest to pursue her in person—or, rather, in mongoose. She was also, as mongooses measured such matters, the most wildly attractive creature in the forest. Giving himself over to mongoose instincts was doing Randal's vow of chastity no good at all. If he didn't lure her into the charmed sphere soon he'd forget himself completely and settle down to the business of begetting.

Forgetting Sanctuary and everything it stood for was not an entirely unattractive notion—especially when her tail flicked across his nose and he was lost enough in mongoose-ness that he didn't sneeze. Roxane was missing; Ischade was irrational and bloated with power; the Stormchildren were moribund with a venom the snake-worshiping Beysib did not understand pooling in their veins; a dead god's high priest had been revealed to be a Nisibisi warlock—and those were only Randal's magic-tainted concerns. The mage had, however, one concern that stood above all the rest; which made him secure against momentary lust and drew him, and her, back to the grove where a circle of stones glowed a faint blue. Nikodemos, the impossible Stepson whom Randal worshiped with a chaste, fervent love, was trapped at the focus of every dangerous incongruity prowling Sanctuary and anything that might help Niko was worth every risk Randal might have to take.

She had caught him when they reached the grove. They were rolling across the grass when they pierced the sphere and hurtled through nothingness back to the palace alcove where the body of Randal slumped over an embossed Nisibisi Globe of Power. The transfer back into himself was all the more uncomfortable for the mongoose teeth digging into his neck and the pottery crags of the Wizardwall mountains pressing against his breastbone. Randal slipped from the world back into nothingness and sheer panic. He had almost regained himself when a weighted net slapped over him.

"The cage, Molin. Damn you, the cage before she eats through my damned neck!"

"Coming up." The erstwhile high priest of Vashanka brandished a wicker-and-wire cage while magician and mongoose thrashed on the table.

Having the cage was not the same as having the unrequited mongoose in the cage. Both men were bloodied and torn before the bolt was thrown.

"You were supposed to have the cage ready."

"And you were supposed to be back before sundown—sundown *yesterday*, I might add."

"You're my assistant, my apprentice. Apprentices are like children: Children don't make decisions; they do as they're told. And if I tell you to have the cage ready—you have the cage ready no matter when I return," the magician complained, daubing at the wounds on his neck.

The men stared at each other until Randal looked away. Molin Torchholder was too accustomed to power to be any man's apprentice.

"I thought it best to save the globe after you and she knocked it off its pedestal," he explained, nodding toward the table where an unremarkable pottery sphere rested against a half-emptied wine glass.

Randal slumped back against the wall. "You touched an

activated Globe of Power," he mused. He possessed the globe and still hesitated before touching it, but the high priest simply picked it up. "You could have been killed—or worse," Randal added as an afterthought. His fingers wove glyphs that made the globe first shimmer, then vanish into that way-station between realities magicians called their "cabinets."

"I've made my way doing what had to be done," Molin said when the process was complete. "You've led me to believe that the destruction of that globe could unbind the planes of existence. I can see that, at its heart, the globe is nothing but a piece of poorly made pottery. Perhaps it was necessary to use magic to destroy it, as you and Ischade did with Roxane's, but, perhaps, simply falling off the pedestal would be as effective a destruction. I could not take the risk of experiment; I moved the globe."

Priesthoods, Randal considered as he met Molin's stare, did a better job of educating their acolytes than the mageguilds did with their apprentices. Aškelon, at his most magnificent, could breathe more life into the simplest phrases, making every word a threat and a promise and a truth. But Aškelon was hardly mortal anymore. Not that Molin Torchholder was exactly typical of Vashanka's priesthood. Randal had met Brachis, Molin's hierarchical superior, and been singularly unimpressed. The truth was that only Tempus, who broke mercenaries', mages', and priests' rules at his whim, could conceal more raw power in his voice and gestures.

It was a realization to make a cautious mageling look in some other convenient direction. "You might make a mistake one day, Torchholder," he said with a confidence he did not feel.

"I will make many mistakes; I already have. Someday, I expect, I will make a mistake I cannot survive—but I haven't yet."

Randal found himself staring at the unfinished portrait of Niko, Tempus, and Roxane that Molin had nailed to the wall behind his worktable. There was considerable similarity between the witch and the priest even though she had been portrayed transforming herself into her favored black eagle and Molin's facial bones showed some of the refinements of Rankan aristocratic patrimony. It wasn't surprising: the priest had been born to a Nisi witch. He had, thus far, adhered to his promise to learn only enough to defend his soul from his heritage, but if he ever wavered from that determination, now that the destruction of Roxane's globe had every latent magician in Sanctuary on the threshold of Hazard status, he would make the Wizardwall masters look like children.

Molin said, "Not if you help me," as if he'd read the younger man's thoughts. "The price is too high."

The mongoose, who in the transfer from the forest to Sanctuary had experienced being Randal as much as he had experienced being a mongoose, responded to her desired mate's distress with an eruption of motion and noise that bounced the cage onto the floor. She set her teeth into the wooden slats and splintered two of them before Randal reached her. Two were all she needed, however, to squeeze out of her confinement. She was on his shoulder in an instant, her claws finding purchase in his brocaded cloak and her tail ringing his neck.

"I'm . . . going . . . to . . . sneeze!" And he did—with an eruption that sent his defender, and a small portion of his left ear, flying across the room.

Molin dove toward the door to capture the lithe creature before it gained freedom in the endless corridors of the palace. Randal laughed through his sneezes; the sight was worth an earlobe. Nothing remained of Torchholder's intensity or his dignity as he slid along the polished stone on his belly.

Despite these losses the priest kept his reputation: he did what had to be done. Blunt fingers pinched the animal's collarbone and a well-protected arm both supported her and pinned her against his ribcage.

"Chiringee?" Molin crooned, rubbing a free finger under her chin as he got to his feet, his long robe wrinkled, twisted, and revealing the naked, muscular thighs of an experienced soldier and brawler. "So eager, are you?" He squared his shoulders, the weighted hem dropped, and he resumed his perfect lifelong disguise as priest and court functionary. "Well, let us go to the nursery then and let you meet the little ones you'll be guarding."

Randal followed, blotting his wounds with his sleeve.

The nursery was more a chaotic phenomenon of palace society than a physical location. Its denizens were moved from dungeons to rooftops, from the depths of the Beysib enclave to the warmth and abundance of the kitchens as the fears and influence of its overlords shifted. For three days a cavernceilinged hall known as the Ilsig Bedchamber had managed to contain it to everyone's satisfaction.

Protocol demanded that no one pass the guards without careful inspection. Molin, Randal, and Chiringee waited until Jihan pushed her way through the doors. She accepted the men in an eyeblink but stared hard at the mongoose, drawing on the arcane intuitions she possessed as Froth Daughter to archetypal Stormbringer only temporarily in mortal form.

"So this is the unnatural creature who is supposed to protect the children better than I? It smells of Wizardwall magic."

"Well, she is larger and more intelligent than she should be. It was an unexpected benefit from the transition—"

Randal had more to say, but Molin took command again, leading their way into the nursery.

The hour candle beside Jihan's cross-legged stool was half-burnt—nearly midnight. The chamber was silent except for the rapid, shallow breathing of the Stormchildren who should have been in their hardwood beds but had been in Jihan's arms and were now draped one over the other on the floor. She scooped them up before settling back on the stool.

"They should be in their beds," Randal complained. "How can you protect them with them sleeping in your lap?"

"They were restless with fever."

"They're two steps from death, lady. They haven't moved in a week!"

"I will protect them as I see fit—and I don't need a little mage flaunting his borrowed power and his menagerie...." Her eyes had begun to glow and the air in the bedchamber had gone frosty.

Molin dropped the mongoose and placed his hands against both of them. "Jihan, Chiringee is only another precaution, like the guards outside, to assist you. No one challenges what your father has ordained: you are the Caretaker."

Jihan's eyes cooled and the room began to warm.

In point of fact, Randal was not tremendously impressed by Jihan's caretaking. The woman, if she could be called that, was obsessed with maternal longings; she had clutched the Stormchildren to her breast when Roxane's snake made its attack rather than drawing her sword and attacking like the hellcat fighter she was. Both children had been bitten and she had taken a divine battering, but the worst injuries had fallen on Niko when he had come to her rescue.

Jihan had recovered almost at once and Sanctuary was better off with Arton and Gyskouras deep in envenomed slumber but Niko, despite Tempus's concern and Jihan's healing, looked and felt worse than the White Foal undead. He was also, because of his need for Jihan's healing touch, a permanent resident of the nursery along with the Stormchildren.

Randal didn't pretend to understand Niko's enthrallment with Roxane or his all-consuming interest in the Stormchildren—he didn't even understand his own affection for the jinxed mercenary who had rejected his friendship more than once. He had touched Chiringee when they mingled in the transfer sphere, inoculating her with his love for Niko and an awareness of Roxane's essence (an essence which, albeit neutralized, pervaded his own Globe of Power whose previous owner had loved and used the beautiful witch countless times). The mongoose might not be able to slay the snakes but she would give Niko a few moments of warning and that, not the safety of the Stormchildren, was all that mattered to Randal.

"We had a cage built for her but, with the influence of the transfer, it wasn't enough to hold her," Molin was explaining to Jihan. "We'll have Arton's father make a stronger one in the morning. In the meantime I'll tell the guards to keep the Beysib women out. She'd go after their vipers."

"Then don't build a cage," the Froth Daughter said with an icy laugh. "They need a few less snakes."

"The vipers are sacred to the Beysib and to Mother Bey. You, most especially, should respect this," Molin said sternly as the temperature continued to drop.

"Mother Bey! Mother Bey, my hind foot. Do you know where *she* found her first snake? That's all she needs, you know, a silly blood-mouth World Serpent. Not my father. No, *she* doesn't need him at all!"

When she wasn't doting on the children, Jihan fumed about her father's progressive entanglement with the fish-folk's goddess, Mother Bey. Jihan, who had never had a rival for her father's affection, was developing a dangerous resentment for all things Beysib.

Gods were the priests' problems. Randal had heard the adolescent protests before and was openly relieved to leave them to Molin. He found a fist-sized watch-lamp beside the glowing brazier, lit it, and headed toward the curtained alcove where Niko convalesced. Tempus had forbidden the direct application of magic on his partner's wounds so Jihan worked her healing through vile unguents; the taint of rotting offal drew Randal to the alcove more surely than the flickering lamplight. He swallowed his sneezes as he drew the curtain aside and stood at Niko's feet.

The mercenary thrashed on his pallet in the grip of nightmares or pain.

"Leave me be!" he gasped—and Randal pressed his back against the wall of the alcove.

Chiringee had followed the magician. She stalked across the damp, discarded linens, easily eluding Randal's cautious attempts to restrain her. Her teeth glistened and her tail quivered as it only did when she was closing on her prey. Randal set the lamp carefully on the footboard and moved closer.

"Leave me!" Niko murmured again before his words became incoherent moans and his body stiffened into an arch above the pallet.

Randal froze, horrified not merely because the creature he had enchanted to protect Niko was going to rip through the soft flesh of that Stepson's neck but because he knew, despite his chastity, that Niko was a victim of neither nightmares nor pain. The injured mercenary collapsed flaccidly on the linens; Chiringee's jaws clicked shut harmlessly and Randal watched as Niko's lips moved silently around the word he most feared:

"Roxane . . ."

The mongoose reared up and began a keening that drew Molin and Jihan to the alcove.

"He's had a relapse," Randal said, a tremor in his voice. "I'll go tell Tempus." He ran from the alcove and the nursery hoping he could reach privacy before the deceit and sick fear that had taken root in his bowels overcame him.

"I can see that," Jihan said coldly as she stared first at Molin, then at her patient. She drew the linens up to cover him. "Go now, I'll take care of him—alone."

Molin was alone in his sanctum when Illyra arrived at the palace to deliver Chiringee's new cage. She had been instructed to take it directly to the nursery, but she was the natural mother of one of Sanctuary's Stormchildren and when she insisted that she would see Vashanka's priest first no one argued with her. She dumped the iron-wire contraption on the floor and ordered Molin's scrivener, Hoxa, from the room.

"Is something wrong, Illyra? I assure you: Arton receives the same care as Gyskouras." Molin stood up from her table and gestured to take her heavy cloak.

"I have Seen things." She kept the cloak tight at her neck though braziers and windows made the sanctum one of the more comfortable private rooms in the palace. "Torchholder— it's getting worse, not better."

"Sit down, then, and tell me what you've Seen." He dragged his own chair around to the front of the worktable for her. "Hoxa! Get some mulled cyder for the lady!" Propping himself against the table, he addressed her with calculated familiarity. "Since the . . . accident?"

"That night."

"You said you Saw nothing," he chided her.

"Not about Arton or the other boy; not something I even noticed or understood at the time. But the others have felt it too." She pulled the cloak close around her; Molin understood that once again Illyra was violating some S'danzo taboo with her revelations. "There are stones—spirit stones—from the times before men needed gods. When they were lost that was when the S'danzo were born and when men began to create gods from their hopes and needs. . . .

"If men possessed these stones again there would be no need for gods."

She paused when Hoxa came into the room with two goblets.

"Thank you, Hoxa. I won't be needing you again tonight. Take the rest of the cyder and have a pleasant evening." Molin handed Illyra the goblet himself. "You think that with these stones we could free your son and Gyskouras?" he suggested when it seemed she would say no more but only stare at the twisting plumes of steam.

Illyra shook her head. Tears or the fragrant vapor of the cyder had smeared the kohl under her eyes. "It's been too long. One of the lost stones was invoked and destroyed that night— some of its magic was directed against the children, some went into a woman who came to me with death in her eyes, some of it is still falling to the ground like rain, but all of it was evil, Torchholder. It had been damaged when the demons hid it in the fires of creation. Our legends have played us false. Men can no longer live without gods.

"The other women have felt the falling but I've felt something else in the shadows. Torchholder—there's another stone in Sanctuary and it is worse than the first one."

Molin took the goblet from her trembling fingers and held her hands between his own. "What you call spirit stones are, in fact, the Nisibisi Globes of Power, the talismans of their witches and wizards. The one that was destroyed was the source of most, if not all, of the witch Roxane's power. She was evil, it is true, and the demons will have their sport with her, I'm sure. But the globes themselves are only pottery artifacts. The S'danzo needn't worry about the second one, whatever its previous owners might have been." He stopped short of telling her that Randal's globe still rested, enveloped by nothingness, on the table behind him.

Illyra shook her head until her hood fell back and her dark, curling hair fell freely around her shoulders. "It is a spirit stone and the demons have tampered with it," she insisted. "It is not safe for men to possess it."

"It could be destroyed, like the other one."

"No." She shrank back as if he had struck her. "Not destroyed—Sanctuary, the world, wouldn't survive. Send it back to the fires of creation—or to the bottom of the sea."

"It is safe, Illyra. It will hurt no one and no one will hurt it."

She stared distractedly at the table; Molin wondered what her S'danzo sight could actually reveal. "Its evil cries out in the night, Torchholder, and no one is immune." She lifted her hood and moved toward the door. "No one," she reminded him as she left.

The priest finished his cyder, then opened the parchment window. Time always passed strangely when he was with Illyra—it had seemed no later than early afternoon when she arrived, but now the sun had set and a fog bank was moving across the harbor to the town. He should have arranged an escort for her back to the Bazaar. Despite her prejudices Illyra was one of his most prized informants.

"Isn't it rather early to be sending them home, Torch?" a familiar voice inquired from behind.

Molin turned as Tempus settled himself into the chair which creaked and was dwarfed by his size.

"She is the mother of the other child. Sometimes she brings me information. I don't mix business with pleasure, Riddler."

They used mercenaries' names when they met; their personalities always created the aura of a battlefield between them.

"What was her information?"

"She is worried about the globes and their owners."

"Globes, owners: plural? Aren't we left with globe, singular, and owner, singular?"

Molin smiled and shrugged as he dragged Hoxa's stool across the room to sit beside his guest. "I suppose you'd have to ask an owner."

"Why haven't you? You're supposed to be Randal's apprentice."

"Haven't seen our long-eared Hazard since he left to find you sometime after last midnight. It seemed young Niko had some sort of relapse."

Tempus put a mild edge on his voice: "I haven't seen Randal in days and I saw Niko just before I came here. He was up and complaining about Jihan. No one mentioned any 'relapse'."

"Well, our little mage is a bit naive about these things, chaste and virgin-pure as he is. He saw something he didn't want to see, though, something he called a 'relapse', and went running from the room like he'd seen a ghost. You put it together, Riddler."

The edge, and some of the confidence, faded from Tempus's voice: "Roxane. Death doesn't stop Death's Queen. She reaches me where I cannot defend myself. Hasn't Niko suffered enough?" he asked a god who no longer listened.

"We never did find Roxane's body, you know. And by your own reports she could steal a body as easily as a soul. She pacted with demons that night; she had the power to slip inside his skull like a whisper—and we'd never know!"

"But Jihan would. She says there's not one iota of Niko that isn't pure. Pure pain. I tried to make him hate me once, and he suffered more."

"Damn you, man! He wasn't suffering when I saw him last night," Molin shouted, slamming his fist on the table to get the mercenary's attention. "If Roxane hasn't possessed Niko, then he's calling her back himself with these dreams. We could have a serious problem on our hands."

"I'd go to hell itself to set him free of her," Tempus resolved, starting to rise from his chair.

"Roxane's not in hell—she's in Niko. In his memories. In his lusts. He's bringing her back, Riddler. I don't know how but I know what I saw."

"The curse won't have him."

"Which curse? Yours, hers, or his? Or hasn't it occurred to you that Niko loves the witch-bitch far better than he loves you?"

"It is enough that he loves me at all."

"Very convenient, Riddler. This Bandaran adept, reeking of *maat*, brings the world's own chaos in his wake and it's all because he has the misfortune to admire you. I suppose you'll tell me Vashanka's gone because he loved you, too—after his fashion."

"All right," Tempus roared, but he sat down again. "My curse—all mine—on the people *I* love. Does that satisfy you?"

"Well, at least I should be safe from it," Torchholder replied with a smile.

"Don't play games with me, priest. You're not in my league."

"I'm not playing with you; I'm trying to set you free. How many years have you been dragging *that* around with you? You think the universe spins in your navel? The only curse you've got is the arrogance of believing yourself responsible for everything." It was sudden death to provoke Tempus's wrath—everyone in the Rankan Empire knew that—so the priest's audacity left the immortal mercenary flat-footed and muttering about magicians, love, and other things that passed the understanding of ordinary, uncursed, men.

"Let me tell you what I do understand, Riddler. I understand that a curse is only a threat—a potential. No wizard—no, more than that: no god—can curse a disbelieving man. No acceptance—no curse: it's as simple as that, Tempus Thales. You made some backwater mage's curse a prophecy. *You* rejected love in all its forms."

The shock was beginning to wear off; Tempus stiffened, his lips a taut line of displeasure across his face. Molin rocked back on the stool until its front legs were off the floor and his shoulders rested against the worktable: a posture so vulnerable it was insolent. "In fact," the priest said amiably, "a mutual acquaintance of ours—the highest authority in these matters, as it were—assures me that your curse is, shall we say, all in your mind. A bad habit. He says you could sleep like a babe-in-arms if you wanted to."

"Who?"

"Jihan's father: Stormbringer," Molin concluded with a smile.

"You? *Stormbringer?*"

"Don't look so surprised." The stool thumped back to its

normal alignment with the floor. "We were both, in a sense, orphans. I . . ." Molin groped for the appropriate description, "—experience him quite regularly. Now *that* is a curse. Our paternal ancestor is head-over-heels in lust with the Beysib's Mother Goddess—except they don't have a matching set of heads, heels or whatever."

"Torch, you push me too far," Tempus warned, but the power wasn't there. "The Empire's coming back. Vashanka's coming back." His voice was more hopeful than commanding.

Molin shook his head, tsk-tsk'ing as if he spoke to a child. "Open your eyes, Riddler. Unbelievable as it might seem, the future is here in Sanctuary. There's an empire coming, and a war-god as well, but it won't be Rankan and it won't be Vashanka. You came here, I imagine, to tell me to toe the line when the imperial ship arrives. Let me make a counter-proposal: Make your commitment to your son—keep Brachis, Theron, and all Ranke alive only until Sanctuary is ready to conquer it."

"You'll see your guts spinning on a windlass for that, priest," Tempus hissed as he stood up and headed for the door.

"Think it over, Riddler. Sleep on it. You look like you need some sleep."

The big man said nothing as he disappeared into the darkness beyond Molin's apartments. If he could be brought into line, or so Stormbringer said, the ultimate triumph of the Storm-children would be ensured. There were things even the primal war-god didn't know, Molin mused as he closed the window, but he might be right about Tempus.

"I tell you—she's gone mad. She's lost control. She's gathering her dead—but she can't find them all."

The young man wrung his hands together as he talked; his words slurred and broke in a constant agitation of pain and chronic drunkenness. The fog of his breath in the cold, damp air was enough to intoxicate a sober, living man. Both witches raised better looking corpses, better smelling ones for that matter, but Mor-am wasn't dead—yet.

"S-She's l-l-lost c-control. S-she's l-l-looking for s-someone to k-k-k-k—" he gasped and coughed his way into incoherence.

Walegrin sighed, poured two-fingers of cheap wine, and slid it across the barrel head. In a backwater town renowned for its depravity and despair, this one-time hawkmask had drifted beyond the pale. Mor-am needed both white-knuckled hands to get the mug to his lips; even then a dirty stream oozed out the corner of his ruined mouth. The garrison captain looked away and tried not to notice.

"You mean Ischade?" he asked when the wine was gone.

"*Seh!*" Mor-am's back straightened and his eyes cleared as he uttered the Nisi curse. "Not Her name. Not aloud. S-She's l-l-looking for s-someone to k-k-kill—someone p-powerful. I c-could find out h-his name."

Walegrin said nothing.

"I s-saw Her w-with T-T-Tempus—at m-m-my s-sister's h-h-house. S-She w-w-was angry."

Walegrin studied the stars overhead.

Mor-am gripped the cup again, throwing his head back, sucking loudly, futilely on the rim. He made a supreme effort to control his wayward tongue. "I know other things. She's looking for the witch. Got to have power—have her focus back. I can follow Her—She trusts me."

A flock of the white Beyarl made their way to the palace. A falcon's cry echoed across the rooftops. The white birds swooped back toward the harbor. Walegrin watched their slow-circling patterns and Mor-am lurched forward across the barrel head to grip his wrist with moist, sticky hands.

The young man began to speak in a rapid, malodorous whisper: "M-Moria's changed. G-G-Got f-friends w-w-who aren't Her f-friends. D-Deads at the P-Peres h-house w-w-who s-should b-b-be in h-hell. T-Taken a l-l-lover. M-Moria's a th-thief—l-l-like H-Her. H-He's a m-mage m maybe b b better th-than H-Her. S-She'll t-t-tell you w-w-what e's—"

The captain wrenched his arm away and whistled sharply. A burly soldier emerged from the inky doorway where he had been posted.

"Take him to the palace," Walegrin commanded, taking a cloth from a sack at his feet and carefully cleaning his hands.

"S-s-she'll know. When I d-d-don't come back. She'll look for me." The ex-hawkmask's voice was shrill with desperation as he was hoisted to his feet. "You said gold—you said: 'gold for information'."

"It doesn't pay to sell out your family—pud, I thought you'd've learned that by now," Walegrin replied coldly. "Take him to the palace." He nodded and another soldier stepped forward to see that the command was carried out quietly.

Walegrin threw Mor-am's mug into the garbage that lay everywhere in the burned-out, sky-roofed warehouse. It had come this low: Rankan soldiers holding forth in ruins; listening to the ramblings of the city's scum; talking to the dead and the undead. A delegation was coming from the capital. His orders were to keep Sanctuary quiet, to keep it free of surprises and, above all, to keep an ear out for rumors about the Nisi witch. He rested his hand on his sword hilt and waited for the next one.

"He might be right, you know," a voice called from the darkness.

A man separated from the shadows—mounted and armed. He came through a gap in the walls—the man's head wreathed in shifting moisture, the horse as cool and shiny as a marble statue. Walegrin stood up, his hand remaining on the sword.

"Slow up there," the stranger ordered, swinging his leg over the saddle. "Word's out you're talking to anybody—even other Rankan soldiers." His words emerged in a plume but the bay horse, though it snorted and shied from the lingering scent of the fire, made no mark on the night air.

"Strat?" Walegrin inquired and received a confirming nod. "Didn't think you came uptown much these days."

The hawk cried again. Both men glanced up past the charred, skeletal roof-beams, but the sky was empty.

"I was up here the other night at Moria's dinner party." Straton kicked the broken barrel Mor-am had used for a seat aside and selected another one from the rubble. "This place secure?" He glanced around at the gaping walls.

"It's mine."

"He might be worth listening to," Strat said, shrugging a shoulder toward Mor-am's path.

Walegrin shook his head. "He's drunk, scared, and ready to sell the only ones who've stood by him. I'm not looking to buy what he's selling."

"Especially scared—especially scared. I'd say he knows something no cheap wine can hide. I've seen the new face Moria's wearing these days; Ischade didn't put it there. I'd talk to him about that—get his confidence. Ease the burden on his mind."

Strat was known to live within the necromancer's curse—and without it, if current rumor were true. He knew Ischade's household as no other living man knew it. Likewise, he was the Stepson's interrogator—a superb judge of a man's willingness to talk and the worth of what he said.

"I'll talk to him, then," Walegrin agreed, wishing he had a larger fraction of Molin's canniness. The Stepson had gotten the upper hand in their conversation. He was sitting, silent and smiling, while Walegrin was sweating. The younger man pondered possibilities and motivations, listened to the lonely hawk, and abandoned all attempts at subtlety. "Strat, you didn't come here to help me do my job with that wrecked hawkmask and it's not safe for a Stepson to be east of the processional—so why're you here?"

"Oh, it's about a hawkmask: Jubal." Strat paused, bit an offending fingernail, and spat into the darkness for effect. "He made an agreement with me and I want you and yours to honor it."

Walegrin snorted. "Commander—this had better be good. Jubal made an agreement with the Stepsons?"

"With me," the Stepson said through taut lips. "For peace and quiet. For no confrontations while Sanctuary has imperial visitors. For business as usual as it used to be. He's pulling back; I'm pulling back. The PFLS will be exposed and we'll take care of them—permanently. Consider yourself honored that I think we need your voluntary cooperation."

"What cooperation?" Walegrin snapped. "Are we the ones rampaging through the streets? Are we running rackets? Strongarming merchants? Did we turn the town on its ear, then run off to war leaving the locals masquerading in our places? You want to take care of the PFLS—there wouldn't be any PFLS without the high-and-bloody-mighty Third Commando and there wouldn't be any Commando without you and yours. Dammit, Commander, I haven't got a headache you didn't cause one way or another."

Straton sat in stony silence. There'd never been any love lost between the regular army soldiers, enlisted to the service of the Empire, and the elite bands like the Stepsons or the Hell-Hounds, bound only to the interest of the gold that paid them. For Straton and Walegrin, whose orders—keep the peace in Sanctuary—were identical and whose positions—military commander—were untenably identical, the antagonism was especially acute.

Walegrin, having spent the better part of his life in blind admiration of the likes of Straton, Critias, or even Tempus, expected the Stepson to blast them out of their conversational impasse. He felt no relief when, after long moments of staring, enlightenment overcame him: Strat was out of his depth and sinking faster than he, himself, was.

"All right," Walegrin began, leaning across the makeshift table, forcing the anger from his voice the way Molin did. "You've got the garrison's voluntary cooperation. What else?"

"We're changing the rules—some of the players won't like it. The PFLS is going to push—"

Walegrin raised a finger for silence; the hawk's cry rose and fell in a new pattern. "Keep talking," he told the Stepson. "Don't look around—we're being watched. Thrush?" he asked the darkness.

"There was one following him—" a voice explained from the shadows behind Walegrin's back. "He's up on the roof over your right shoulder—with a bow that'll put an arrow through you both. There was another—no weapons that we could see—came up a bit later. Now the second's seen the first an' he's circling around."

"Friends of yours?"

"No, I came alone," Strat replied without confidence as a hiss that might have been an arrow crossed the open sky above them.

"Let's go," Walegrin ordered, pushing away from the barrel head.

The gods alone might know who had followed Straton, Walegrin thought as he crouched and ducked into the shadows where Thrusher was waiting for him. Every Stepson had enemies in this part of town and Strat had more than most. He might even have enemies who'd kill each other for the privilege of killing him.

Walegrin couldn't indulge in expectant curiosities, though— not with Thrusher picking a cat's path through the garbage ahead of them. His squads had patroled these warrens and knew where safe footing lay. He could only follow and hope Strat had the good sense to do the same. Thrush led them onto the nearby rooftops in time to see their bow-carying quarry land on the muddy cobblestones below.

"Recognize him?" Walegrin demanded, pointing at the receding silhouette.

"Crit."

Stepsons hunting Stepsons, was it? "After the other one," Walegrin barked at whichever of his men could hear. There were better ways to get information from Critias than risking a rooftop confrontation. He turned to follow Thrusher and realized that Strat hadn't moved since identifying his erstwhile partner.

"It's no time to be asking yourself questions, Straton."

"He came to kill me," Strat whispered, then stumbled on a loose roof tile and lurched toward the eaves.

Walegrin caught a fistful of shoulder. "He hasn't—yet. Now move it before we lose the other one, too."

Strat glowered and thrust Walegrin's arm aside.

The second interloper knew the backways of Sanctuary and was hugging darkness back toward the Maze and safety. Moonlight caught a youthful outline arching from one rooftop to the next and Thrusher's crablike scuttle as he followed.

"Not for the likes of us," Walegrin decided, judging the weight of the leather armor he and Strat wore. "We go below. It's our only chance."

He led the way, crashing through the rubble and needing Strat's help more than once to shoulder through a crumbling door or wall that threatened to block their way.

"Lost 'em," Strat muttered when they burst through a flimsy gate to find Lizard's Way deserted.

Walegrin cupped his palms around his lips and emitted a passable imitation of a hawk. "Gave it a good try, though," he added between gasps. "Worth a jug between us."

Strat was nodding when a hawk cried and a face appeared in the gutters above them.

"Round the alleys and back, Captain. We caught her."

"Her?" both men said to themselves.

Kama glared at the night from the calf-deep stench of a Maze rooftop rain cistern. Stupidity and bad luck. Another fifteen steps and she would have been so deep in the Maze they would never have found her, but not this time. This time the damn shingle had to give way and take her sliding down a rain trough. That was the bad luck. Stupidity was not knowing the trough ended in a cistern when she had taken this exact route a dozen other nights. She would have ignored the makeshift rope Thrusher dangled above her if survival weren't more important than pride or if her ankle weren't already swollen from the fall and her hands abraded by her efforts to free herself on her own.

She bore the indignity of being hauled up like a sack of dead fish, knowing that the worst was yet to come.

"O gods, no—" a familiar voice breathed softly. "Not you—"

Kama refused to look in that direction but stared instead at the young-ish officer in charge of the garrison troops who had pursued, then rescued, her.

"Well," she demanded, "are you satisfied or are you going to drag me up to the palace?"

Walegrin felt his throat tighten. Not that he wasn't accustomed to seeing a woman in men's clothing—in a thief's night-dark clothing at that. This was Sanctuary, after all. The garrison soldier guarding their flank was a woman he'd hired himself and as nasty a fighter as was ever bred in the Maze. But the young woman standing in front of him, her wet clothes plastered to her and her long hair snapping like whips when she tossed her head, was the backbone and brains behind the 3rd Commando, and probably the PFLS, for that matter. Worse—she was Tempus Thales's daughter.

"Who sent you?" he stammered, and had the god's good luck to find the one question that would leave her as uncomfortable as he was.

"Did your . . . did Tempus send you?" Strat asked, stepping into the light of a freshly kindled torch.

Kama tossed her head, barely acknowledging Strat's question, and stood silent until Thrusher stepped forward and grabbed her weapon hand.

"Lady, you want to use this again?"

"Yes—let go of me—"

"Thrush." Walegrin moved to restrain his lieutenant who had already unstoppered his wineskin. "I'm sure the lady has her own . . . resources."

Thrush turned around, exposing the wound to the torchlight. Everyone in the courtyard who carried a sword felt a twinge. The skin on Kama's palm lay in twisted spikes cross-hatched with black splinters from the cistern walls; not a wound that killed but one that stole reflexes and precision, which was just as bad. Kama shed a fraction of her composure.

"Lady," Thrush stared up into Kama's eyes, "you got a *good* doctor in there?" He shrugged a shoulder Mazeward and pointed the wineskin at her palm.

"Are you any better?"

Thrusher bared all his teeth.

"He's not bad," Walegrin confirmed, "but the demon's piss he keeps in that sack of his is guaranteed."

"Given to me by my one-eyed grandmother. . . ." Thrusher explained as a stream of colorless liquid spurted toward Kama's hand.

"It'll hurt like hell," a faceless voice warned from beyond the torchlight.

But Kama already knew that. Her face went white and rigid and stayed that way until Thrusher put the cork back in the wineskin. Strat offered a strip of his tunic as a bandage as her own clothing was as filthy as the wound had been. She seemed relieved when Strat put his hand under her arm.

"Why?" Strat asked in a voice Walegrin saw rather than heard.

"Go on back to the barracks," Walegrin ordered quickly but made no move to leave the courtyard himself. "We'll see the lady to her lodgings." He met Strat's glower and outlasted it. "You and I have a jug of wine to split," he explained when his men had vanished.

"Why, Kama?" Strat repeated. "Didn't he think Crit would carry out his orders?"

They began moving slowly toward the warehouse where Strat had left his bay horse.

"I've been following Crit," Kama admitted. "When I saw him with the bow—I don't know if he's got orders or not." She paused to tuck a hank of hair behind her ear. Whatever pain remained in her face had nothing to do with her injuries. "Nobody in the palace understands any more. They haven't set foot in the streets. They don't understand what's happening. . . ."

Like everyone else who had spent the winter *in* Sanctuary—rather than *in* the palace, or Ranke or some relatively secure war zone—Kama had lived through hell. Walegrin guessed she would have more faith and friendship for anyone who had also endured those long, dead-cold nights on the barricades, regardless of the color on their armband, than she could feel for any outsider—even her father.

"It takes someone who's been out here to understand," he agreed, sliding his arm under Kama's other arm so she didn't need to put any weight on her twisted ankle. "There's one I trust. I'd trust him at my back on the streets and I trust him in the palace. . . ."

Molin Torchholder slouched back against the outstretched wings of a gargoyle. He would have preferred to be somewhere well beyond the city walls but winter was finally yielding to Sanctuary's fifth season: the mud, and he wasn't desperate enough to brave the quagmires masquerading as streets and courtyards. The palace rooftop was deserted except for workmen and laundresses who could still be counted on to leave him alone. He closed his eyes and savored the gentle warmth of the sun.

In a methodical fashion he reviewed the conversations and rumors that had passed his way. The garrison commander, Walegrin, was finally showing promise; acting on his own initiative, he had established friendly relations with Straton and Tempus Thales's daughter, Kama. That was a good sign. Of course, the fact that Straton was on the streets, cut off from both Ischade and the Stepsons and dealing with Jubal, was a bad sign. And confirmation that Kama was the intelligence behind the PFLS was the worst information he'd had in months— even if it wasn't a surprise. Tempus, never an easy man to predict under the best of circumstances, would be chaos incarnate if any of his real or imagined family turned on one another.

The whining hawkmask the garrison had interrogated had told them everything he knew, and a good deal he did not, about Ischade. Like Straton, the priest found it interesting that Ischade had rivals within her own household—rivals who could transform an Ilsig harridan into a Rankan lady. Molin knew the necromancer had been detaching herself from her magic since her raven had appeared on his bedpost with no message and less desire to return to the White Foal. If Ischade found her focus again, the bird would let him know by its departure. If she didn't, well: Jihan could protect the children, Randal would protect his globe, and the rest of magic could destroy itself for all he cared.

On the balance, then, the thoughts percolating through his mind were satisfying. The street powers—the Stepsons, Jubal, the 3rd Commando, and the garrison—were reining in their prejudices and rivalries without overt interference from the palace. Sanctuary—flesh-and-blood Sanctuary—would be quiet when the imperial delegation made its appearance. The disorganization of magic and the broodings of Tempus Thales seemed soluble problems by comparison.

"My Lord Torchholder—there you are!"

Prince Kadakithis's relentlessly cheerful voice dragged the priest from his reverie.

"You're a devilish hard man to find sometimes, Lord Torchholder. No, don't stand—I'll sit beside you."

"I was just enjoying the sunshine—and the quiet."

"I can imagine. That's why I followed you—to get you while you were alone. My Lord Torchholder—I'm confused."

Molin cast a final glance at the glimmering harbor and gave his whole attention to the golden-haired aristocrat squatting in front of him. "I'm at your service, my prince."

"Is Roxane dead or alive?"

The young man wasn't asking easy questions today. "Neither. That is, we would know if she were dead—a soul such as hers makes quite a splash when it surfaces in hell. And we would know if she were alive—in any ordinary sense. She has, in effect, vanished which we think, on the whole, is more likely to mean that she is alive, rather than dead, but safely hidden somewhere where even Jihan can't find her—though such a place is beyond all imagining. She might, I suppose, have become Niko herself—though Jihan assures us she would know if such a thing had happened."

"Ah," the prince said with an indecisive nod. "And the Stormchildren—nothing will change with them one way or another until she's either fully dead or alive?"

"That's a rather inelegant way of summing up a week's worth of argument—but I think that you're fairly close to the heart of the matter."

"And we don't want our visitors from the capital to know about her or the Stormchildren?"

"I think it would be safe to say that whatever chaos the witch could cause on her own it would be made immeasurably worse were it witnessed by someone, as you say, 'from the capital'."

"And because we don't know where she is, or what she's going to do, or when she's going to do it; we're trying to guard against everything and starting to distrust each other. More than usual, that is—though not you and I, of course."

Molin smiled despite himself—beneath that affable denseness the prince concealed a certain degree of intelligence, leadership, and common sense. "Of course," he agreed.

"I think, then, we're making a mistake. I mean, we couldn't be making it easier for her—assuming she actually *is* planning something."

"You would suggest we do something different?"

"No," the youth chuckled, "I don't make suggestions like that—but, if I were you I'd suggest that, rather than guarding against her, we put some sort of irresistible temptation in front of her—an ambush."

"And what sort of temptation would *I* suggest?"

"The children."

"No," the priest chided, only half in jest now; the prince's suggestion had him thinking of intriguing ways to deal with both Tempus and magic. "Jihan wouldn't stand for that."

"Oh." The prince sighed and got to his feet. "I hadn't thought about her. But it was a good idea, wasn't it—as far as it went?"

Molin nodded generously. "A very good idea."

"You'll think about it then? Almost as if I had inspired you? My father said once that his job wasn't finding the solutions to all the Empire's problems but inspiring other men to find the solutions."

Molin watched the prince make his way back to the stairway, greeting each group of laborers. Kadakithis had been raised among the servants and was always more confident, and more popular, among them than his aristocratic relations suspected. He might astound them all and become the leader Sanctuary, and the Empire, needed.

The priest waited until the young man had reentered the palace before quietly making his way toward a different stairway and the Ilsig Bedchamber where he would promote the prince's notions and his own inspirations to those most able to implement them.

Jihan was bathing Gyskouras when the Beysib guard announced him. She handed the inert toddler to a nursemaid with evident reluctance and headed for the door with the long, rangy stride of a woman who had never worn anything more confining than a scale-armor tunic. Water was her element; she glowed where it had splashed against her.

For a moment Molin forgot she was a Froth Daughter, remembering only that it had been well over a month since his wife had left him and that he had always been attracted to a more predatory sort of woman than was socially acceptable. Then an involuntary shiver raced down his spine as Jihan passed judgment on him; the flash of desire vanished without a trace.

"I was expecting you," she said, stepping to the side of the doorway and allowing him into the nursery.

"I didn't know I was coming here myself until a few moments ago." He lifted her hand to his lips, as if she were any other Rankan noblewoman.

Jihan shrugged. "I can tell, that's all. The rabble," she gestured toward the doorway and the city beyond it, "aren't really alive at all. But you, and the others—you're alive enough to be interesting." She took the Stormchild, Gyskouras, from the Beysib woman's arms and went back to the obviously pleasurable task of bathing him. "I like interesting . . ."

The Froth Daughter paused. Torchholder followed her stare to its target. Seylalha, the lithe temple-dancer and mother of the motionless toddler in Jihan's arms, was doing a very attentive job of wiping the sweat from Niko's still-fevered forehead.

"Don't touch that bandage!"

Seylalha turned to meet Jihan's glower. Before becoming the mother of Vashanka's presumed heir, the young woman had only known the stifling world of a slave-dancer, trained and controlled by the bitter, mute women whom Vashanka had rejected; she seldom needed words to express her feelings. She made a properly humble obeisance, cast a longing glance at the child, her own son, Gyskouras, cradled in Jihan's arms, and went back to stroking Niko's forehead. Jihan began to tremble.

"You were saying?" Molin inquired, daring to interrupt the fuming creature who was both primal deity and spoiled adolescent.

"Saying?" Jihan looked around, her eyes shimmering.

If Jihan had not had the power to freeze his soul to the bedchamber floor, Molin would have laughed aloud. She couldn't bear to see something she wanted in the possession of anyone else and she always wanted more than even a goddess could comfortably possess.

"I wanted your advice," he began, lying and flattering her.

"I'm beginning to think that we should seize the initiative with Roxane, or her ghost or whatever she's become, before our visitors from Ranke arrive. Do you think that we could bait a trap for her and—with your assistance, of course—catch her when she came to investigate?"

"Not the children," she replied, clutching the dripping child to her breast.

"No, I think we could find something even more tempting: a Globe of Power—if it looked sufficiently, but believably, unattended."

Jihan's grip on Gyskouras relaxed, a faint smile grew on her lips; clearly she was tempted. "What do I do?" she asked, no longer thinking of children, or even men, but of the chance to do battle with Roxane again.

"At first, convince Tempus that it's a good idea to give the appearance of doing something very foolish with the Globe of Power. Suggest to him that he could solve the problems within the Stepsons by letting them prove to themselves and everyone else that Roxane is dead and powerless."

"Tempus? He spends more time with his horses than he does here with me or the Stepsons. I'd like to do more than talk to Tempus." Her smile grew broader when she mentioned the man who was, by Stormbringer's command, her lover, companion, and escort during her mortality. "The two of us alone could take the globe and the witch. . . ."

Molin felt a trickle of sweat run down his back. Jihan had taken the bait, embroidering his notions with her own, mortally incomprehensible, imagination. If he could not lure her back to plans he could shape and control, the exercise would become a disaster of monumental proportions.

"Think of the Stormchildren, dear lady," he said in what was both his most unctuous and commanding voice. "Think of your father. You can't leave them behind—not even to travel with Tempus or to destroy the Nisibisi witch."

Jihan wilted. "I couldn't leave them." She patted Gyskouras's golden curls apologetically. "I must put those thoughts behind me." With her eyes closed, the Froth Daughter focused divine determination against mortal free will until her shoulders slumped in defeat. "I have so much to learn," she admitted. "Even the children know more than I do."

"When the Stormchildren are well again, then you will travel with them to Bandara; you will learn everything that they learn.

For now, though, only you can sense Roxane through her deceits and disguises. Tempus can devise a trap for her—but only you will know if she falls into it."

She brightened and Molin almost felt sorry for Tempus. The mercenary would have no choice now but to close ranks within the Stepsons and concoct the tactics necessary to lure Roxane out of her hiding place; no one, not even a regenerating immortal, could stand for long against Jihan's enthusiasm. The priest relaxed, then caught a flicker of movement at the corner of his eye. Niko had pushed away from Seylalha's tenderness and was staring, with his one unbandaged eye, off into nothingness. Perhaps he had heard them mention Bandara? Perhaps—? Molin shook his head, preferring not to think at all about any other possibility.

The hand that reached out of the darkness to grab Molin's shoulder had the strength of an iron trap. It was only by yielding to its force, collapsing and rolling through the mud, that the priest avoided becoming a prisoner of his assailant. He scrabbled for balance, tearing a small knife free from the hem of his priest-robe's sleeve as he scanned the courtyard for some detectable sound or movement. Then he saw the silhouette and threw the knife aside; no four-finger blade would deter Tempus for long.

"I've taken all I'm going to take of your schemes, Torch." The mud squished as the big mercenary took a step forward. He leaned down and hoisted Molin to his feet by the front of his robe, then pressed him against the damp brick of the palace wall. "I warned you once—that's more than you deserve."

"Warned me of what? Warned me that you're in over your eyes with capital politics that have no meaning in *this* town? You want Sanctuary quiet when your high-and-mighty usurping friends get here—well, what are you doing about it? You started off well: you got Roxane's Nisi globe; drove her into hiding—but you haven't done anything since." Molin's voice was cracking from the pressure Tempus put against his breastbone but it could not be said that his courage had failed him as well.

"The streets will be quiet—I've seen to that."

"Straton saw to that. You can't take credit for the acts of a man who thinks you've issued orders to have him killed by his partner, Riddler."

Tempus gave the priest one last, vicious shake, then released him to slide down the wall to his proper height.

"But this scheme of Jihan's—of yours. Torch, it's beneath you, using her against me like that. We've got all our vulnerables in one place and the strength to guard them. It's no time to be traipsing through the countryside splitting our forces."

"I'm a siege engineer, Riddler. I build walls and I tear them down. It took our golden-haired light-weight, Kadakithis, to point out how predictable our tactics have become. I've got one idea for luring the bitch into the open—but I don't want to try it. I was counting on Jihan's provoking you into coming up with something better."

"And if she doesn't?"

"I'll burn the portrait that little Ilsigi painter made of you, Roxane, and Niko."

"Vashanka's balls, Torch—you aren't afraid of anything, are you? We better talk this through. Where've you got that painting now? Still here in the palace?" Tempus took Molin's arm, more gently this time, and led him toward the West Gate of the palace.

"It's where it's always seemed to be, Riddler," Molin said as he shook free of the other man's assistance. "But don't think that because you can see it you can reach it. Randal's taught me a bit about hiding things in plain sight."

They went through the gate in silence, not because of the tension between them—though it was as thick as the perennial fog—but because they were both aware that the walls were the most porous part of the palace and that nothing private should be said in their shadow. They continued in silence, Tempus leading, through the better parts of town into the Maze and toward the Vulgar Unicorn where, improbably enough, privacy was sacred.

"I'd leave that picture wherever you've hidden it if I were you, priest," Tempus warned after he'd bellowed their orders toward the bar.

"Certainly it would be cleaner if the little ginger-man had painted a simpler picture. I gather he's had more problems with things coming to life. *He* claims not to know at all what happens when his paintings cease to exist."

Molin looked at a recently replastered section of the wall, still noticeably less grimy than the rest and completely unmarked by grafitti or knife gouges. Lalo had painted the soul of the tavern there once and a score of people had died before it had been laid to rest again. Both men were thinking about the painter's unpredictable art when a warty, gray arm thrust between them.

"Good beer. Special beer for the gentlemen," the wall-eyed bouncer with the garish orange hair said with a smile that revealed corroded, and not quite human, teeth.

Tempus froze and Molin, whose aplomb was sturdier, took the mugs.

"A fiend, I should think. Not quite what Brachis and his entourage will be expecting when they order a drink. If we're lucky they'll blame it on the beer," Molin commented as the acid, lifeless brew crossed his lips.

"Hers," Tempus said and hid his face behind his hands. After a moment he raised his eyes. "And nobody notices. Roxane's fiend is ladling the Unicorn's swill and no one bloody notices!"

"A *living* fiend, my friend. You've been away too long. In this part of town being alive, in your own life, is all that really matters."

Tempus sighed. He drained the crudely made mug and motioned for another round. Now that he had adjusted to the smoky light, Molin could see that the Riddler's eyes were bloodshot and the skin around them was bruised from exhaustion.

"I should kill you for that, too," Tempus said, rubbing his eyes, making them redder. "A bad habit, you said. There's a magician—The Dream Lord, Aškelon; my brother-in-law— he overstepped himself at the Festival of Man, as you may have heard. Been exiled to Meridian by greater powers than his own. Usually I don't have to worry about him but now, thanks to you, he's always right there at the corner of my mind, waiting to get into my dreams."

"He gets into everyone else's dreams and they're none the worse for it, Riddler."

"Not into *my* dreams, damn you!" He took the second mug from the fiend without a flinch, downing it as he had the first.

"More beer? Good beer for the gentleman?" the fiend inquired. "Snapper Jo gets good beer for the gentleman. Snapper Jo remembers this gentleman, this soldier. Mistress made sure Snapper always remember . . . Tem-pus."

Tempus's hands were on Snapper Jo's throat; Molin's were

on a long, wickedly efficient knife but the fiend only smiled. He knotted the muscles in his warty neck and belched his way to freedom.

"Just where is your *Mistress?*" Tempus demanded, rubbing his knuckles.

The creature shrugged and crossed its eyes. "Don't know," he admitted. "Snapper went looking for her. Nice dark lady asked Snapper to look for the Mistress."

"Did Snapper Jo find his Mistress?" Molin asked.

"No, not find. Look everywhere—look in hell itself. Not find. No Mistress! Snapper Jo free!"

The notion overwhelmed Snapper Jo. He hugged himself, trembling with joy, and went back to the bar without another thought for the two men watching him.

"If we believe him, then she's not dead," Tempus admitted. "If I'd believe a fiend," he corrected himself. "Torch, I talked to Niko about all of this. He says he's free of her—free like he hasn't been in years. I believe Niko, Torch. There's nothing left of Roxane except memories—and bad habits."

It was Molin's turn to bury his head in his hands. "Niko and the fiend: both free of Roxane. Thank you, Riddler—I'll believe the fiend. He says he looked in hell and didn't find her; Ischade sent him to hell looking for Roxane and he didn't find her there. Now, Niko, I'll wager he not only told you that he was free of Roxane but that all our precautions were unnecessary. I'll wager he told you that he could take care of the Stormchildren all by himself."

"All right, Torch. We'll tell Niko we're moving the globe and the kids—and then we'll watch him. We'll even send a little procession out past the walls to one of the estates. But by Enlil, Vashanka, Stormbringer, and every other soldier's god—you're wrong, Torch. Niko's free of her—she's nothing but nightmares to him. Maybe there's something still after the Stormchildren—or the globe—but not Roxane and not through Niko."

Tempus set his ambush for the night of the next full moon. Walegrin muttered a number of choice, unreproducible words when half of the garrison was pulled off duty to shovel dirt, patch roofs, and in other ways make a tumble-down estate north of the city walls look like the prospective home for what Tempus called his "vulnerables." His muted protests erupted into a full-scale tirade when, by noon of the appointed day, it was clear that any advantage to having the charade on the night of the full moon would be offset by one of Sanctuary's three-day torrents.

The palace parade ground was an oozing morass which had already foundered three good horses—and it was clear sailing compared to any other street, road, or courtyard. It would be well nigh impossible to get the carriage from the stables to the gate much less up the slopes to the estate. Walegrin pointed this out to Critias as they huddled down under oiled-leather cloaks and slogged across the parade ground on foot.

"He says, use oxen," Crit replied impassively.

"Where am I supposed to get a team of oxen before sundown?"

"They're being provided."

"And who's going to drive them? Has he thought of that? Oxen aren't horses, you know."

"You are."

"The bloody hell I am, Critias."

They had reached the comparative shelter of the stable doorway, where the water gushed off the eaves in streams that could, with care, be avoided. Critias removed his dripping rain helmet and wrung it out.

"Look, pud," he said, tucking the hat into his belt, "I don't make up the orders. Orders come from the Riddler and your man, Torchholder. Now when those oxen get here, you hitch them to the carriage and drive them out to the estate. If they're," he pointed a thumb back toward the palace, "sitting tight with their gods, everything will go according to plan—somehow. And if they're not—then you could be the best bloody drover in the world and it wouldn't make a whore's heart's bit of difference."

Thus, some hours after nightfall, Walegrin found himself still in his oiled leathers standing beside the ungainly rumps of a pair of oxen. Randal was slowly making his way down the rain-slicked stairs clutching the skull-sized package containing his Nisibisi Globe of Power. The mage wore a ludicrously old-fashioned panoply which hindered his already over-cautious progress. Tempus looked uncomfortable as he waited under the stone awning with a child tucked under each arm.

"Almost there," Randal assured them, glancing back toward the torchlight and, as luck would have it, overbalancing himself just enough to slip down the last three steps.

There wasn't a person, living or dead, within Sanctuary who hadn't heard a rumor or two about the witch-globes. Walegrin dropped his torch and lunged for the package. His efforts were, however, unnecessary as the package hung politely in mid-air until Randal stumbled to his feet and reclaimed it. The effect was not lost on Walegrin or any of the dozen or so others detailed to escort the oxen—or on Tempus who came down the stairs behind Randal to deposit his silent, unmoving bundles within the ox-cart.

The mage and the mercenary commander exchanged whispers which Walegrin couldn't hear above the sound of the rain. Then Tempus shut the door and came up beside Walegrin.

"You know the route?" he inquired.

Walegrin nodded.

"Then don't move off it. Randal can take care of the magic regardless but if you want protection from anything else you stay in sight of the spotters."

With a noncommittal grunt Walegrin loosened the long whip from the bench beside him and tickled the oxen's noses. Tempus stepped quickly to one side as the cart lurched into motion. The beasts had no halters or reins, responding only to the whip and the voice of their drover. Walegrin figured he'd try to keep everything moving from the driver's bench but he imagined, accurately as it turned out, that he'd be in the mud beside the oxen before they cleared the old Headman's Gate and lumbered onto the nearly deserted Street of Red Lanterns.

"It'll be dawn before we get there," Walegrin cursed when the rightside ox paused to add its own wastes to the sludge in the street.

But the man-high solid wheels of the cart kept turning and the oxen were as strong as they were slow and stupid. Straton and a pair of Stepsons joined the procession where it cleared the last of the huge, stone-walled brothels. Strat, a lantern dangling from the pike he carried in his right hand, brought his bay horse alongside the ox-cart. Walegrin gripped at a dangling saddle-strap for some security in the treacherous footing.

It was nearly impossible to keep the torches lit. The men on horseback were having a harder time of it than Walegrin and his team. Walegrin watched the mud directly in front of them and lost track of how many checkpoints or spotters they had passed. They halted once, when the undergrowth cracked louder than the rain, but it was only a family of half-wild pigs. Everyone laughed nervously and Walegrin touched the oxen with his whip again. Another time Strat spotted shadows moving above them on the ridge, but it was only their own men breaking cover.

They had reached the stony trail leading to the estate when the oxen bellowed once in unison, then sank to their knees. Walegrin dropped the saddle-strap and went racing back to the cart where his sword was stashed. The horses panicked, rearing up and collapsing as much from the bad footing as from the metallic drone every man and beast was hearing, feeling, between his ears.

"Do something!" Walegrin yelled to his passenger as he tugged his sword free of its scabbard. The first touch of Enlibrite steel against his skin made a shower of green sparks, but it dulled the pain in his head as well. "Stop her, Randal!"

"There's no one out there," the mage replied, poking his head and shoulders through the cart's open window. His archaic armor, like Walegrin's sword, had a faintly green presence to it.

"There's damn sure someone out here!"

Walegrin stood on the drover's bench. Save for Strat all of the escort had been thrown into the mud; save for Strat's bay all the horses were either on their sides screaming or plunging into the morass of the fallow fields surrounding the estate. One horse, he couldn't tell which, shrieked louder than the rest— a broken leg most likely. Walegrin felt a rising tide of panic only marginally related to the dull roar in his skull.

Strat heeled the bay horse around as if it were a sunny day on the parade ground, then launched it at the only stand of trees in sight. Walegrin watched the bobbing lantern for a few moments before it disappeared.

"Move in. We haven't been hit yet," he yelled to the garrison men who, like himself, held the strange green-cast steel of Enlibar in their fists and were somewhat insulated from whatever assaulted them. "Well, *do* something, Randal!" he added for the benefit of the mage who had vanished back into the darkness. "Use that bloody ball of yours!"

As abruptly as it had begun, the droning ceased. Except for the one in the field, the horses quieted and got back to their feet. One of the men slogged through the mud groping for a torch, but Walegrin called him back to the circle.

"It's not over," he warned in a soft voice. "Randal?"

He crouched down by the window, expecting to see the freckled mage bathed in the glow of his magic. Instead he walloped his chin on Randal's helmet.

"Shouldn't you be doing something with that globe? Raising some sort of defense for us?"

"I don't have the globe," the mage admitted slowly. "We never intended to move it or the Stormchildren. Sorry. But there's no one out there, no one watching us in any way."

Walegrin grabbed the mage by his helmet and twisted it around until Randal was facing him. "There bloody well better be someone watching us—a whole damned estate full of some-ones watching us."

"Of course there is," Randal sighed as he freed himself. "But no one, well, magically inclined."

"What happened, then? The horses just decided to panic? The oxen just felt like sinking into the mud? I *imagined* there was a swarm of bees in my head?"

"No, no one's saying that," a familiar voice, Molin's voice, called from the nearby darkness. "We don't know what hap-pened any more than you do." He swung down from his horse, handing the reins to one of the five garrison men who'd ac-companied him down from the abandoned estate.

For once Walegrin was not about to be mollified by his patron's soothing phrases. His men had been endangered for nothing. A horse, no easy thing for the garrison to replace, was this very moment being put out of its misery. His com-plaints and opinions were still flowing freely when a lantern was seen to emerge from the trees.

"Strat?" Walegrin yelled.

There was no reply heard above the sound of the pelting rain. Each man silently put his hands back on his sword and waited until the bay was an arm's length from the ox-cart and Strat's grim, torchlit face could be seen clearly.

"Haught."

"What?"

"Haught," Strat repeated, throwing a piece of dark cloth onto the drover's bench. "And someone else—maybe Moria, maybe dead."

"Haught?" Randal poked his head out. "Not Haught. He's got Ischade's mark on him. I'd have recognized—"

"I'd recognize him before you would," Strat interrupted, and there was no one in the group who could gainsay that claim.

"Does that mean Ischade?" Molin asked nervously. They accepted the necromant as the lesser of the two witches, but even so neither was a force that any man, except Straton, was comfortable with.

"It means Haught. It means he wants the globe. It means he wants to be Roxane, Datan, or some other bloody magician. You can take the Nisi away from Wizardwall but you can't boil the treachery out of their blood."

Molin stood silent for a moment after Strat had finished. "At least, then, it wasn't Roxane. Tempus will be glad to hear that."

The other groups Tempus had assigned to guard the ox-cart's progress were beginning to appear. Crit came up with a half-dozen Stepsons, most of whom appeared to have heard Strat's accusations or at least had no desire to look their erst-while field commander full in the face. The 3rd Commando, or a good-sized part of it, rode up from behind. Whatever Tempus's opinion of the operation, he'd made certain it didn't lack for manpower.

"I think we've found out what we wanted to know," Molin said, not quite taking command away from Strat, Crit, and Walegrin, but eliminating the need for them to decide who was in command. "Randal, borrow a horse. We'll head back for the palace. They'll want to know what's happened. Straton— you should probably come along. The rest of the Stepsons can lend a shoulder to the garrison men in getting this cart turned around and back to the palace. I'll leave it to you two," he nodded toward Critias and Walegrin, "to decide if you need the Third's help. I've arranged for brandy and roast meat to be waiting at the palace barracks: Be sure that everyone— regulars, Stepsons, and the Third if they want it—gets a share."

Molin waited until Randal had directed a docile-looking horse toward Straton before turning his own gelding away from the men gathered around the ox-cart. Critias had ridden down to talk to the 3rd and Walegrin was proving himself quite capable of getting the oxen to turn the cart around. A few riders from the 3rd split off toward Strat and Randal but most of them headed back toward the General's Road and whatever billets they had Downwind or near the Bazaar.

He held the gelding to a slow walk a good number of paces behind them. They were all Rankan people, allied in one way or another to the Emperor or the remnants of the Vashankan priesthood he was no longer on good terms with. They were probably as uncomfortable around him as he was around them but here they had him outnumbered.

The riders were well beyond the ox-cart and still a good distance from the walls when Molin felt the first twinges of divine curiosity. Blood-red auroras rose from the horizon; the ground heaved and stretched, moving him further apart from the others. Despite the rain soaking through every garment he wore, the priest felt a cold, nauseous sweat break out on his forehead and spread, quickly, until it reached his weak, suddenly numb knees.

Stormbringer.

Gathering every mote and shred of determination, Molin concentrated on weaving his fingers around the saddle horn. Not there. Not on a rain-swept field with Tempus's men all around him. His heart pounded wildly. He heard, but could not feel, the loose stirrups clanking against the lace-studs of his boot.

One step. One more step. The longest journey is made of single—

The red auroras rose until they touched the zenith. Molin felt the scream trapped in his throat as the god reached out and pulled him from his body, mind and soul.

"Lord Stormbringer," he said, though he had no proper voice in the featureless, ruddy universe where he met with the primal storm god.

You tremble before me, little mortal.

The roaring came from everywhere and nowhere. Molin knew it well enough to know it could be louder, more painful, and that the present modulation revealed a certain, dangerous, humor.

"Only a foolish mortal would fail to tremble before you, Lord Stormbringer."

A foolish mortal who seeks to elude me? I do not have time to waste searching for foolish mortals.

Here, in the god's universe or perhaps within the god, there was no place for hidden thoughts or verbal gymnastics. There was only nothingness and the raw, awesome power of Stormbringer himself.

"I have been such a foolish mortal," Torchholder acknowledged.

You trouble yourself with the opinions of those not sworn to me or the children. You know that all Stormgods are but shadows of me—as Vashanka is a shadow I have abandoned, the Ilsig god a shadow I have forgotten, and the one they call "Father Enlil" a shadow which shall not fall across Sanctuary.

"I did not know, Lord Stormbringer."

Then know now! The universe throbbed with Stormbringer's pique. *I am Sanctuary's god. Until the children claim their birthright I am their, and Sanctuary's, guardian. Fear only me!*

Of course they fear you. A second presence, feminine but no less awesome, wove its way through and around the presence that was Stormbringer. *Mortals fear everything. They fear the woman's god more than they fear the man's god, and they fear a woman without a god most of all. You must tell them where to find the witch-woman who killed my snakes.*

The deities twisted around each other but did not mix or merge. Molin knew he was in the presence of what was already being called the Barren Marriage. Yet there was something like mortal affection, as well as immortal lust, between these two. He felt the part that was Stormbringer contract, and an upright figure with the head of a lion, the wings of an eagle, and the lower parts of a bull manifested itself out of the red mist.

"I cannot tell you where she is," the apparition said in a voice that was both male and female. "There are things forbidden even to me. Demonkind is brother and sister to you mortals, but no kin to gods. The S'danzo have the greater part of the truth; the Nisi witches have the rest.

"Roxane promised the souls of the children—or her own if she failed. She is not where you or I can find her—and she is not fallen among the demons. What I cannot find, what the Archdemon cannot find, must lie in Meridian or beyond."

Molin discovered that he, like Stormbringer, had become corporeal and, so far as he could tell, very much the man he had always been. Tracing his fingers along the familiar, imperfect embroidery of his sleeves, he considered what he knew of the topology of nonmortal spheres and Meridian, the realm of dreams where Aškelon held sway. He thought about Aškelon as well and reflected that if there were one entity—Aškelon hardly qualified as a man—who could both complicate and resolve their problems, the Dream Lord was that entity.

He made the mistake, however, of thinking that because he felt like himself, he was himself and slipped into rapid considerations as to which of the players would be best for the part.

"That is not for you to decide," the lion reminded Molin, baring its glistening teeth. "Aškelon has already made his choice."

"Tempus will not go."

"Give him this, then." Stormbringer laid a linen scarf across Molin's unwillingly outstretched hands.

The netherworld that was the gods' universe fractured. Molin held the scarf to his face for protection as the lion-head apparition became hard, dark pellets that beat him into a dizzying backward spiral. The scream he had left frozen in his throat tore loose and engulfed him.

"It's over now; relax."

A strong, long-fingered hand was wrapped around his wrist, pulling his hands away from his face. The hard pellets were wind-driven raindrops. His hands, Molin realized as he unclenched them, were empty. He was on his back—had fallen from his horse.

"You're back with us ordinary folk," the woman told him as she yanked on his cloak and twisted his torso until his shoulders were propped on a relatively dry pile of straw. "Are you all right? Your tongue? Your lips?"

He pushed himself up on his elbows. There wasn't a muscle, bone, or nerve that didn't ache—as it always did after Stormbringer. But it was, he told her while still trying to understand where he was and what had happened, nothing worse than that.

"They say that my . . . Tempus would bite through his lip, or break a bone. I never saw it. He wouldn't notice it, really. You're not him, though."

"Kama?" Molin guessed.

He was in some crude shelter—a lean-to the shepherds used, by the smell of it. The worst of the weather was deflected, anyway. She'd hung a lantern from the center-pole but it didn't provide much light and the priest had only seen Tempus's daughter a few times, mostly when she was considerably younger.

"I saw you stiffen up like that. I guessed what would happen. It wasn't Vashanka, was it?"

"No."

She squatted down beside him; the lantern lifted her profile from the surrounding darkness. She wore a youth's leather tunic, laced tight and revealing nothing. Her hair was twisted into a knot at the crown of her head and was clinging to her face in damp tendrils where it had come loose. She shuddered and went looking for her own cloak which, when she found it, was covered with mud and useless from the rain.

"Did the others go on?" Molin asked.

Kama nodded. "They'll have reached the palace by now. Strat knows I'm with you. He won't say anything."

Molin looked into the lantern. He should, by right, stagger to his feet and hie himself back to the palace. His life was full of gods, magic, and the intrigue that went with them. There was no room for love, or lust—especially not with Kama.

"You needn't have stayed with me," he said softly, shifting the focus of his analysis and persuasion away from politics.

"I was curious. All winter I've been hearing about the Torch. Almost everything that worked had your fingerprints on it. Nobody seems to like you very much, Molin Torchholder, but they all seem to respect you. I wanted to see for myself."

"So you saw me falling off my horse and foaming at the mouth?"

She gave him a quick half-smile. "Will the Third actually share that brandy and meat?"

"I don't have the Empire or the priesthood behind me anymore," Molin admitted. "I can't coerce a man's loyalty and I can't inspire it either—I know my limits. I bribed the cooks myself long before I left the palace." A stream of water broke through the branch-and-straw roof, hitting him full in the face. "No one, if he's done work for Sanctuary, should be out on a night like this without some reward. If the Third went to the barracks, they got their share."

"What about you?"

"Or you?"

Kama shrugged and picked at the loose threads of a bandage tied around her right palm. "I won't find what I want at the barracks."

"You won't find it with the Third—"

Kama turned to stare darkly at him.

Stormbringer, the witches, the children: everything that was important in the larger scheme of things fell from Molin's thoughts as he sat up, closing his hands over hers. "—You won't find it with any of *his* people."

It was a thought that had, apparently, already occurred to her, for she unwound into the straw beside him without a heartbeat's hesitation.

They returned to the palace after the sky had turned a soft, moist gray but before, they hoped, any of those whom Molin had to see were awake. There was nothing to set them apart from any other weary, soaked travelers coming to shelter within the palace walls. Molin did not help her from the saddle or see to the stabling of her horse. True, he found himself gripped by an emotion uncomfortably close to sudden love, but not even that was enough to make him a fool. He would have said nothing if she had wheeled her horse around and headed back toward the Maze; he said the same when she followed him up the gatehouse stairs.

He led the way to the Ilsig Bedchamber where, in consideration of all that hadn't happened during the night, he expected to find Jihan, the Stormchildren, Niko, and the bedlam residents. He found, instead, a funereally quiet chamber with only Seylalha hovering between the cradles.

"The merc's guild?" Kama inquired, reading the same omens the priest did. "The mage's?"

Molin shook his head. His mind reached out to that distant corner where his Nisi-magic heritage, the gods, or his own luck sometimes placed reliable inspirations. "With the Beysa," he said slowly, then corrected himself: "Near the snakes."

When the Beysib arrived in Sanctuary they had brought with them seventy of the mottled brown eggs of their precious beynit serpents. These eggs, packed in unspun silk, had been installed in a specially reconstructed room where a hypocaust kept the stones comfortably warm. The eggs had hatched before the start of winter and the room itself, filled with the fingerling snakes, had become the favorite haunt of the Beysa and her immediate entourage.

It had also become, because of the skill of the Beysib snake-handlers in preparing decoctions of any venom or herbal, the meeting place of all the palace healers. Jihan brewed Niko's vile unguents there and occasionally, when the other residents of the Ilsig Bedchamber objected loudly enough, administered them there as well. Molin knew he had guessed correctly when he saw Beysib snake-handlers milling forlornly in the hypocaust antechamber.

"You took your own time getting down here," Tempus grumbled as the priest entered the room. He might have added more, but he fell silent when Kama eased through the doorway as well.

Molin took advantage of the lull to look around. Crit caught his eye first because he, like Tempus, was staring at Kama as if she'd grown a second head. Jihan was here as well, though her smile was warmer than Torchholder had seen before. She set down a mortar brimming with dark, spiky leaves and embraced Kama as a long-lost friend. Her movement allowed him to see the real reason they were all in the uncomfortably warm room: Nikodemos.

The Stepson lay on his back, trussed like a roasting chicken and, though he seemed to be sleeping quietly enough now, his face was bruised and his hands covered with blood. Molin took a step closer and felt Tempus's hand close around his arm.

"Leave him be," he warned.

"What happened?" Torchholder asked, retreating until Tempus relaxed. "Randal said—"

"You guessed right," Crit interrupted with a bitterness that made the priest's blood run cold. "She made her move through Niko at about the right time."

"It was Haught," Tempus spat out the name. "Niko bolted for the window saying 'Haught'. It was a warning."

Critias ran his hand through dark, thinning hair. "But not for us. Haught was making his own moves and Roxane had to stop him."

"That's what Strat says," Jihan added.

"It doesn't matter whether Strat's right or not." Crit had begun pacing like a caged tiger. "It doesn't matter whether Haught's Ischade's catspaw or Roxane's. It doesn't matter if Jihan—"

"I didn't."

"—Told Niko about the double-shuffle with the globes. All that matters is that the witch-bitch had Niko. Again."

"What happened?" Molin repeated, though by this point he was getting a pretty good idea and was more interested in the shifting alliances of the threesome.

"When Jihan tried to keep him from jumping out the window

he went berserk. It took four guards to hold him until she could get something down his gullet to keep him quiet," Critias explained calmly.

Molin moved closer to Niko, this time without Tempus's interference. The young man had taken a beating, but the priest wasn't looking for bruises.

"What about the mongoose, Chiringee?" he asked, examining the bloody tears on Niko's hands and wrists. "Randal said it was attuned to Roxane."

Jihan looked at Tempus, Tempus looked at the wall, and Crit's voice was a monotone: "It attacked him—and he killed it. Ripped it apart and started to eat it—didn't he?"

The Froth Daughter reached back to grasp Tempus by the wrist. "He was berserk," she said softly. "He didn't know what he was doing. It doesn't mean anything." Glittering crystals of ice and water formed in her eyes.

Critias gave them a malignant stare. When he reached the door he gave Kama the same stare, for reasons Molin could not begin to understand, then he shoved her aside. Molin felt the muscles tighten along his sword arm. It would be the height of folly—Kama fought her own battles and Critias was as cold a killer as moved through the shadows—but the Stepson would answer for that gesture.

"Roxane has taken Stealth?" Kama asked the frozen room. None of the rumors circulating in the Maze had presumed so much.

Tempus pulled his arm away from Jihan. "Not yet," he muttered as he followed Crit from the room.

Molin and Kama turned to Jihan who, with a slight nod of her head, confirmed their worst suspicion. Kama sank back against the wall, shaking her head from side to side. The Froth Daughter, for her part, reclaimed her mortar and went to kneel beside the slate-haired Stepson.

"He was drunk," the dark-haired mercenary said to herself. "Too much wine. Too much krrf. Too much everything." She closed her eyes, purging herself of grief and Niko with long, ragged breaths.

"It's not over yet," Molin told her, daring to take her arm and realizing, with some surprise, that he looked straight ahead, not down, into her eyes. "Last night I was with Stormbringer."

Her eyes widened but she didn't resist as he guided her from the hypocaust and past anxious snake-handlers.

"I have to talk to Tempus—convince him to do something he doesn't want to do. But it's far from over, Kama."

She nodded and slipped from his grasp. "I'll want to see you again," she said, holding his hand lightly as she stepped away.

"I have a wife. Sabellia's priestess and a noblewoman in her own right. She's staying out at Land's End with my brother, Lowan Vigeles, and she'll make whatever trouble she can." Molin swallowed hard, knowing that Rosanda had her good qualities as well but that they no longer meant anything to him. "I am the priest of a dead god and the nephew of a dead emperor. I walk a dangerous path in full view of my enemies—and I would not walk any other."

Kama laughed, a sensuous laugh that could get a man in trouble. "If I cannot walk through your doorway wearing gowns and jewels then you'll find me as I am outside your windows or already in your bedchamber." Then, with another laugh, she was gone—heading back to Jihan and Niko.

Molin returned to his quarters, ordering Hoxa to prepare a cauldron of hot water and to find, somewhere, dry robes and boots. The young man procured the bathwater and the boots, but when he came from the wardrobe with a fresh robe he brought an unwelcome surprise as well: a scarf of linen the length of a man's outstretched arms and the color of Stormbringer's horizons.

"Have the day for yourself, Hoxa," Molin had mumbled as he drew the cloth through his fingers. "I need time alone."

He'd taken that time, sitting in a room that had been an arcane attic. Randal's Nisi globe remained *not* on his worktable; Lalo's triple portrait was *not* nailed to the wall behind him; Ischade's abandoned raven, in all its ill-tempered glory, was truly flapping from one perch to another, and now Stormbringer's gift for Tempus had made its appearance as well. Unlike the other artifacts, the strip of cloth with its ordinary, girlish embroidery seemed innocent enough—until he considered that the sight of it was supposed to convince Tempus to risk sleep and a visit to the realm of Aškelon.

The rain finally stopped. It would be days before the streets dried—if they dried at all before the next storm swept through. Molin tucked the scarf in a pouch and threw a cloak over his shoulder. There wouldn't be a better time to find Tempus. He didn't have to go far, just a sidelong glance out the window. The Riddler, followed closely by an exceptionally grim looking Critias, was coming to pay him a visit.

"That picture," the nearly immortal mercenary snarled, pointing above Molin's head as the heavy wood door slammed against the wall.

Pointedly ignoring the priest, Crit walked around to examine the picture closely. After touching it with his fingers he used his knife to scrape off a bit of the background—and got plaster-shavings for his efforts.

"It's not there, Critias," Molin warned.

"Get it," Crit ordered.

"You don't come in here giving me orders."

"Let him see it," Tempus asked wearily. "*I'll* make sure no harm comes to it."

Molin tried to concentrate. He'd been childishly pleased with himself when he'd hidden the actuality of the canvas while leaving its semblance plainly visible on the wall. It was hard enough for an apprentice of his experience to tuck something away in magic's shadows but now, with Tempus and Crit watching him impatiently, it was proving impossible to find it again. He had almost located the frayed edges when the door slammed open again and he lost them.

"You can't burn it," Randal said, the words coming between gasps for air. "No one knows what will happen when you do."

"We burn the witch-bitch when we burn it—that's what happens." Critias touched his knife to the facsimile of Roxane's face as he spoke. "Find it," he added for Molin's benefit.

"We don't know what happens to Niko . . . or Tempus," Randal continued.

Critias fell silent and Molin, getting desperate, lucky, or both, closed his mind around the canvas and gave it a little tug. The image on the wall shimmered before vanishing and, with an unpleasant sulphurous discharge, the rolled canvas dropped to the floor at Tempus's feet. He reached down and held it in his fist.

"No," the big man said simply.

"We can't destroy the globe," Critias said as Randal shuddered in agreement. "We can't kill the Stormchildren." Molin's knuckles went white. "And now you're telling me we can't burn the picture. Commander, what can we do?"

Molin saw his opportunity open before him. Opening the

pouch, he laid the scarf across the worktable and waited for reaction. Randal stared, Crit looked nervous, and Tempus jerked upright.

"Mother of us all," he sighed, laying the canvas on the table, taking the scarf in its place. "Where did you get this?" His fingers read the uneven stitches as he spoke.

"Stormbringer," Molin answered softly enough that only Tempus could see or hear.

"Why?"

"To convince you that you have to sleep; that you have to talk to Aškelon because Aškelon's decided he'll only talk to you. And, more important, because Stormbringer thinks Aškelon's got a way to reach Roxane."

"Thinks? The god thinks? He doesn't *know?*" He closed his eyes a moment. "Do you know what this is? Did he tell you?"

Molin shrugged. "He thought it would be sufficient to convince you to go where I'd already told him you had no intention of going."

"Damn her," Tempus said, throwing the scarf on the table and taking the picture again. "Here," he threw it at Critias, who let it drop to the floor, "do what you damned well want with it."

DEATH IN THE MEADOW

C. J. Cherryh

I

The floor creaked to the slightest step, and Stilcho moved quietly as he could across to the old warehouse door, not trying escape, no, only that it was so everlasting cold and he wanted the sun to warm his flesh, the sun that shone bright through a crack in the shutters. He wanted it, and he had thought a long time about getting up from that board floor and venturing outside—

—he had thought about going further too, but the front step would be enough, the front step was all he dared think of, because Haught sleeping back there had ways to know what he planned—

—so he thought, o gods large and small, gods of hell and gods of earth, only of getting out into that light where the sun would warm the stone step and the bricks and warm his dead flesh which right now had that lasting chill of rain and mud and misery. He could not abide the stink and the cold of mud, that made him think all too much of being dead, in the ground, in the river cold—

I'm not running, I'm not going anywhere, just the sun.... That, for Haught's benefit, should he wake—with his hand on the door.

The hair stirred at Stilcho's nape. His flesh crawled. He stopped still and turned and looked, and saw Haught sitting up in the shadows, a bedraggled Haught with a bloody scrape on his face and the whites showing dangerously round his eyes. Stilcho set his back against the door and gestured toward it with a shrug.

"Just going out to get the—"

Do you play games with me? With me, dead man?

No, he thought quickly, made that a torrent of *no,* letting nothing else through, and felt every hair on his body rise and his heart slow, time slow, the world grow fragile so that for a moment he *knew* the progress of Haught's mind, the suspicion that his one failure had diminished the fear of him, that a certain piece of walking meat needed a lesson, that this *thing* Ischade slept with (but not with him) could be dealt with, shredded and sent to the deepest hell if it needed to learn respect—

—Stilcho knew all that the way he suddenly knew Haught was running through his thoughts, knowing his doubt, his dread, his hate, everything that made him vulnerable.

"On your knees," Haught said, and Stilcho found himself going there, helplessly, the way every bone and sinew in him resonated to that voice. He stared at Haught with his living eye while the dead one held vision too, a vision of hell, of a gateway a thing wanted to pass and could not. But if he was sent there now, to that gate, to meet that thing—

"Say you beg my pardon," Haught said.

"I b-beg your pardon." Stilcho did not even hesitate. A fool would hesitate. There was no hope for a fool. Ischade would banish him down to hell to confront that thing if he went back to her now after what Haught had done, and Haught would tear his soul to slow shreds before he let it go to the same fate. Stilcho knelt on the bare boards and mouthed whatever words Haught wanted.

For now. *(No, no, Haught, for always.)*

Haught gathered himself to his feet and ran a hand through his disordered hair. His pale, elegant face had a gaunt look. The hair fell again to stream about it. The smile on his face was fevered.

He's crazy, Stilcho thought, having seen that look in hospital and in Sanctuary's own street lunatics. And then: *O, no, no, no, not Haught! No!*

The prickling of his skin grew painful and ceased. Haught came closer to him, came up to him and squatted down and put his hand on Stilcho's cheek, on the blind side. Chill followed that touch, and a deep pain in his missing eye, but Stilcho dared not move, dared not look anywhere but into Haught's face.

"You're still useful," Haught said. "You mustn't think of leaving."

"I don't."

"Don't lie to me." Silken-soft. And the pain stabbed deep.

"What can I give you to make you stay?"

"L-life. F-for that."

"No gold. No money. No woman. None of that."

"To b-be alive—"

"That's still our bargain. Isn't it? They know about us. They took care enough to set a trap for us. You think then that She doesn't know? You think then that we have infinite time? I've covered us thus far. They might not know who we are. But careful as I am, dead man, *Straton* came close to us. He probably knew us. He probably passed that on. And that damnable priest and that damnable mage may know who they're looking for now. They might have thought it was Her. Now they may go to Her and tell Her our business. And that won't be good for us at all, will it, dead man?"

"No." It came out hoarse and strangled. "It won't."

"So let's don't take chances in the daylight, you and I. I have my means. Let's just be patient, shall we? I'll take the Mistress. I'll deal with Her. You wait and see." Gently Haught patted him on the cheek and smiled again, not pleasantly. "The thing we need went back to the priest. It's not there and it is. I know how it works now. And I know where it went. Right now we need to move a little closer uptown—when it's dark, do you see?"

"Yes," Stilcho said. If Haught asked him if pigs flew he would have said yes. Anything, to make Haught go away satisfied short of what he could do, and what he could ask.

"But in the meanwhile there's a trip for you to take."

"Oh gods, no, *no*, Haught—there's this thing, I see it, *gods, I see it*—"

Haught slapped him. The blow was faint against his cheek. The dark gateway was more real, the thing ripping at it was clearer, and if it looked his way—

"When it's dark. To Moria's house."

Stilcho slumped aside on his knees, rested his back against the door, his heart hammering away in his chest. And Haught grinned with white teeth.

The old stairs creaked under any step (they were set that way deliberately, for more than one Stepson used the mage-quarter stables and the room above)—and Straton trod them carelessly, which was the best way to come at the man whose sorrel horse was stabled below.

He had left the bay standing in the courtyard. It would stand.
He left it just under the stairs, out of line of the dirty window
above, if Crit had come to look, if he were wary. But perhaps
he would be careless. Once.

Or perhaps Crit was waiting behind the door.

Strat reached the top landing and tried the latch. It gave.
That should tell him enough. He flung the door inward, hard;
it banged against the wall and rebounded halfway.

And Crit was standing there in the center of the room with
the crossbow aimed at the middle of his chest.

The stream Janni followed ran bubbling over the rocks,
among the trees, cold and clear; and a wind sighed in the leaves
with a plaintive sound, like old ghosts, lost friends. The trees
stood, some unnaturally straight, some twisted, like old mon-
uments. Or memories. They afforded cover, and the place had
a good feel to it, this shade, this shadow of green leaves.

The brook left that place and flowed into sunlit grass. The
meadow beyond hummed with the sound of bees, was dotted
with wildflowers, was eerily still, no wind at all moving the
grass, and Janni looked out into that place with a profound
sense of terror. That meadow stretched on and on, lit in un-
compromising day, and the grass that showed so trackless now
would betray every step. There was no cover out there.

If he were so foolish she could find him, Roxane could track
him down in whatever shape she chose, and he could not stand
against her. He knew that he could not. He had failed once
before, and that failure gnawed at his pride, but he was not
fool enough to try it twice. Not fool enough to go out where
Roxane waited in the bright sunlight, in a center defended by
such emptiness and calm that there was no surprise possible;
but he had the most terrible feeling that the sun which had
stood overhead had at last begun to move toward its setting,
and that that sunset would signal a change and a fading of life
in this place. The moment he conceptualized it, that movement
seemed true, though he could not see it clearly through the
trees—he saw shadows at this margin of the woods, cast out
on the yellow grass, and they inclined by some degree.

"Roxane!" he called out, and *Roxane-ane-ane* the forest
gave back behind him; or the sky echoed it, or the silence in
his heart. He felt small of a sudden and more vulnerable than
before. He had to keep moving in the woods, constantly seeking

some place of vantage, some place where the trees ran nearer to the heart of that meadow where the trouble lurked.

But wherever he went, however far he circled this place, the brook reappeared in its meanderings. He knew what it was, and that if there was a place where it did not exist, then it would be very bad news indeed.

It ran slower than it had, and more shallow. Now and again some dead branch floated down it, which presaged something. He was afraid to guess.

"Come in," Crit said. "Keep your hands in sight."

Strat held his hands in view and walked into the doorway of the mage-quarter office. He kept the door open at his back. That much chance he gave himself, which was precious little. In fact there was such an ache in him it was unlikely that he could run. It had been anger on the way here. It had been resolution going up the stairs. Right now it was outright pain, as if that bolt had already sped. But he cherished a little hope.

"You want to put that damn thing down, Crit? You want to talk?"

"We'll talk." But the crossbow never wavered. "Where'd she go, Strat?"

"I don't know. To hell, how should I know?"

Crit drew a deep breath and let it go. If the crossbow moved it was no more than a finger's width. "So. And what are you here for?"

"To talk."

"That's real nice."

"Dammit, Crit, put that thing down. I came here. I'm *here,* dammit! You want a better target?"

"Stay where you are!" The bow centered hard and tendons stood out on Crit's hands. "Don't move. Don't."

It was as close as he had ever come to death. He knew Crit and what he knew sent sweat running on him. "Why?" he asked. "Your idea, or the Riddler's?" If it was the one, reason was possible; if it was the other. . . . "Dammit, Crit, I've *kept* this town—"

"You've tried. That much is true."

"So you try to kill me off a friggin' *roof?*"

The bow did move. It lifted a little. About as much as centered it on his face. "What roof?"

"Over there by the warehouse. And come bloody friggin'

along with me last night, that's why I came here, dammit, this morning, to see whether you'd gone crazy or whether you think I didn't bloody see you up there yesterday. I figured I'd give you a good chance. And ask you why. *His* orders?"

Crit shook his head slowly. "Damn, Ace, I saved your life."

"When?"

"On that roof. It was Kama, you understand me? It was *Kama* that was at your back."

A little chill went through him. And a minuscule touch of relief. "I hoped. Why, Crit? Is *she* under his orders?"

"You think the Riddler'd do it like that?"

"You might. If *he* was going to. I don't know about her. You tell me."

Crit swung the bow off a little to the side, turned it back again, then aimed it away and let it angle to the floor. He looked tired. Lines furrowed his brow as he stared back. "She's into something of her own. Into—gods, something. That's all. The Third's got interests here and she has, and gods know— What the bloody *hell* is it about this town? Damn woman goes crazy, up on the roofs with a bow—. It's Walegrin she's after, I'm thinking; and then I'm not so sure—"

"You were following me."

"Damn right I was following you. So was she. She bends that bow, I put a shot right across to discourage her and put the wind up you, what the hell d'you think I'm doing? If I'd've meant to shoot you I'd have hit you, dammit!"

Strat wanted to think that. He wanted to believe every word of it. It was all tangled, Kama with Crit—that was old business; but maybe not so old to either of them. And Kama the Riddler's daughter. He saw the trouble in Crit's eyes, saw the pain which was the real Crit, behind the nothing-mask. "I guess you would," he said hoarsely. It was not so easily patched up. There was nothing mended but maybe the roughest of the edges. "I guess that was what set me to thinking. It didn't feel right."

"Dammit, wake up! What does it take? Tempus *is* going to have your guts for string if you don't solve it, hear me? He's given you more room than you've got a right to, he's left you your rank, he's left you in titular command, for godssake, how long is he going to be patient, waiting for you? You know how patient he's being? You know what he'd have done with another man?"

"He left me in command. I still am. Till he takes it." The

last came out hard, and left a dull shock behind. Tempus could ask. And get nothing from him. He knew that, the way he knew rain fell down and sun came up. He was hollow inside. Crit could have shot him. That would have been all right. That would have solved things. As it was, he failed to care. He walked over to the table and the cheap bottles of wine they had here because it kept and the water here tasted like lye and copper. He pulled a loose cork and poured a little glass, knowing it was a deadly man at his back and matters were no more resolved now than they had been. He turned and held it out to Crit. "Want one?"

"No." Crit still stood there with the bow aimed at the floor. "Where's the horse? You leave that damned horse down there in the yard in full view?"

"I don't plan to stay." Strat drank a mouthful of the sour wine and made a face. His gut was empty. Even a little wine hit it hard. "I've patched up a peace in this town. I figured it could make me some enemies. And Kama has contacts in the Front, doesn't she? I figure—I figure maybe she's got her answers, and they're not mine."

"She tried to shoot you in the back. I stopped it. You come in here madder than hell at *me;* and her, you just—No. You're *not* bloody mad, are you? You came in here—what for? *Why* did you walk in, if that was what you expected?"

"I told you. I thought if you'd meant to hit me you would have. Didn't get a chance to talk to you last night. That's all." He downed the rest of the wine in the cup and set it down before he looked around again at Crit, at the bow and the open door. "I'd better go. My horse is in the yard."

"That damn horse—that damn *spook,* Ace, the damn thing doesn't sweat, it doesn't half work, like the zombies, f'godssake, Ace, stay here."

"Are you going to stop me?"

"Where are you going?"

He had not truly considered that. He had not known whether there was truly any time beyond this room. Nothing he did presently made sense: there was no need to have come, no need to have patched things up with Crit, only it was something he had not been able to avoid thinking on since yesterday and last night, and now there was no more need to think about that. His partner was not trying to kill him. Tempus was not. Unless Tempus had sent Kama, but somehow other things rang more true. Like the PFLS. The Front. Like the agencies that wanted chaos in Sanctuary. He felt himself carrying the whole town on his back, felt his life as charmed as if the gods that watched over this town watched over him, who was trying to save it. And they both were corrupt, and they both were wreckage, he and the town. He perceived compromises that he had made, by degrees. He knew where he was now, and it was on the other side of a wall from Crit and all his old ties.

He had not seen Ischade since that day outside Moria's. Since he had blinked and lost her round a corner. Or somewhere. Somewhere. The wards drove him from the river house. He hunted Haught and failed to find him. He was altogether alone, and altogether losing everything he had thought he had his hands on.

"I don't know," he said to Crit. "I don't know where I'm going. To find a few contacts. See what I can turn up. If you haven't figured it out, it's my peace that's holding so far. The bodies that've turned up—aren't significant. Or they are. It means that certain people are keeping their word. Keeping the peace in their districts. You could walk the Maze blind drunk right now and come out unrobbed. That's progress. Isn't it?"

"That's something," Crit admitted. And stopped him with a hand on his arm when he tried to walk past him. Not a hard hand. Just a pressure. "Ace. I'm listening to you. You want my help, I'll give it to you."

"What kind of trap is it?" It was an ingenuous question. He meant it to be. The whole affair, Kama, the shot from the roof, had ceased to trouble him acutely, had become part of the ennui that surrounded him, everywhere, in every inconsequential move he made, every damned, foredoomed, futile move he made since She had turned her back on him and decided to play bitter games with him. Haught had given him the ring; Haught had made a move which might be Her move, gods knew, gods knew what she was up to. The whole world seemed dark and confused. And this man, this distant, small voice, wanted to hold onto his arm and argue with him, which was all right as far as it went: he had a little patience left, while it asked nothing more complicated than it did. "Whose orders, Crit?"

"I'm on my own. I'll go with you. Easier than following you. I'll do that, you know. I've been doing it."

"You've been pretty good."

"You want the company?"

"No," he said, and shrugged the hand off. "I've got places to go, rounds to make. Stay off my track. I'd hate for somebody to put a knife into you. And it could happen."

"But not to you."

"Not so likely."

"You hunting that Nisi bastard?"

It was more complicated than that. Ischade was involved. It was all too complicated to answer. "Among others," he said. "Just stay off my track. Hear?"

He walked on out the door.

The bow thunked at his back, the air whispered by him and the quarrel stood buried in a single crash in the stout railing just ahead of him. He stopped dead still, then turned around to Crit and the empty bow. His knees had gone weak for a moment. Now the anger came.

"I just wondered if you'd wake up," Crit said.

"I am awake. I assure you." He turned on his heel and headed down the stairs with his knees gone undependable agair., so that he used the lefthand rail, shaking and shaken, and hoping with the only acute feeling he had left, that between the wine and the shock he would not stumble on the way. That it was Crit up there watching him, Crit who knew how to read that white-knuckled grip on the rail, made his shame complete.

Damn Crit to hell.

Damn Tempus and all such righteous godsridden prigs. *Tempus* had dealt with Ischade. Tempus had said something to her at that table, in that room, and she had said something to him at great length, concluded her business like some visiting queen, before she went running off, leaving him for a fool in front of the whole damned company. He had not gone back after his cloak. Had not been able to face that room.

But suddenly it occurred to him that Crit might know what Tempus and Ischade had said together. He stopped at the bottom, by the bay horse, his hand on its neck, and looked up the stairs where Crit stood with the unarmed bow dangling by his side.

"What's the Riddler's dealing with her?" Strat asked.

"Who? Kama?"

Strat frowned, wondering whether it was deliberate obtuseness. *"Her,* dammit, at the Peres. What was she after?"

"Maybe you ought to ask him. You want to shout his business up and down the stairs? Where's your sense, for gods-sake?"

"That's all right." He turned and gathered up the bay's dangling reins. "I'll manage. Maybe I will ask him." He flung himself up to the bay's back, felt the life in it like a waking out of sleep, a huge and moving strength under him. "It's all right." He turned the bay and rode out of the courtyard, down the narrow alley.

Then the malaise came back again, so that the street began to go away from his vision, like an attack of fever. He touched his waist, where he carried the little ring, the ring that would fit only his smallest finger.

She had sent it by Haught.

Haught attacked the column and tried for—whatever Tempus was on the other side of. Tempus and the priest. And the gods.

Damn, it shaped itself into pattern, it shaped all too well: Ischade owned no gods. Haught and the dead man, who made a try that might, succeeding at whatever they were after—have shaken the town.

Ischade had sent him back to Crit that night Crit came to the riverhouse and nothing had been the same.

He slipped the ring into the light and slipped it onto his finger, the breath going short in his throat and the touch of it all but unbearable; it was like a drug. He had not dared wear it into Crit's sight, a token like that. But he wore it when he thought there was no one to see, no one but the Ilsigi passersby who might see him only as the faceless rider all Stepsons were to the town: he was a type, that was all, he was a power, he was a man with a sword and everyone in town wanted to pretend they had no special reason to look anxiously at a Rankan rider too tall and too hard to be other than what he was. So if that man's eyes were out of focus and all but senseless, no one noticed. It was only for a moment. It was always, in the last two days, only for a moment, because when he held that metal in his hand he had a sense of contact with her and his soul was in one piece again.

He shivered and looked up where a rare straightness of a Sanctuary street afforded a sliver of sunlight, the gleam of uptown walls.

• • •

There was a rattle at the window, a spatter of gravel against the second-story bedroom shutters, and Moria started, her hand to her heart. For a moment she had thought of some great bird, of claws against her shutters; she expected some such visitation, even in the daylight. But she came up off her bed where she had flung herself, dressed as she was in the stifling, tight-laced satins that were what a lady in Sanctuary had to wear, O Shalpa and Shipri, so that her head reeled and her senses wanted to leave her every time she climbed stairs or thought too much on her situation.

Now she knew that rattle of gravel for what it was: someone down in the side lane that led back toward the rear of the house and the stable. Someone who knew where her bedroom was, maybe that importunate lord who had beseiged her step; maybe— Shalpa! maybe it was Mor-am come back. Maybe he was in some dire trouble, maybe he needed her, maybe *he* would try that window, the only one off the street except the servants' and the kitchen at the back.

She went and flung the inside shutters open, looked out and saw a lately-familiar, handsome face staring up at her with adoring eyes. At one breath it drove her to rage that he was back, rage and fear and grief at once, for what he was, and what a fool he was, and how handsome and how helpless in Her spells which had somehow gone all amiss.

"Oh, *damn!*" She flung open the casement and leaned out, her corset-hard middle leant across the sill and the compression of her ribs all but choking the wind out of her as she set her palms on the rough stone. Cold wind stung her face and her exposed front and blew her hair. Loose ribbons hit her in the face. "Go away!" she cried. "Hasn't my doorkeeper told you? Go away!"

The lord Tasfalen looked up with a flourish of his elegant hands, a glance of his eyes that would melt a harder heart than an ex-thief's. "My lady, forgive me—no! Listen to me. I know a secret—"

She had started to pull back. Now she leaned there all dizzy in the wind, with the air chilling her upper breasts and her bare arms, and her heart beating so that the whole scene took on an air of unreality, as if something thrummed unnaturally in her veins, as if the feeling that had come on her when Haught touched her and turned her like this went on happening and happening and growing in her, so that she was a danger and a Power herself, poor Moria of the gutters, a candle to singe this poor lord's wings, when a conflagration waited for him, a burning that was *Power* of a scope to drink them both down. . . .

"O fool," she moaned, seeing that face, hearing that word *secret* and that urgency in his voice. It had as well be both of them in the fire. "Come round back," she hissed, and closed the casement and the shutters without thinking until then that she had just asked a lord of Sanctuary to come in by the scullery, and that at her merest word he was going to do it.

She stepped into her slippers, unable to bend in the corset, and worked one and the other on with a perilous hop and a catch-step as she headed out to the stairs, saving herself on the railings as she flew down in a flurry of too many damned Beysib petticoats that kept her from seeing her feet or the steps. She fetched up at the bottom out of breath, with a catch at the newel-post and an anguished glance at a thief-maid who gawped at her.

"There's a man out back," Moria said, and pointed. "Go let him in."

"Aye, mum," the gaptoothed girl said, and tucked up her curls under her scarf and went clattering off in unaccustomed, too-large shoes to see to that. The maid was one of those who had come for the Dinner; and stayed, Moria not knowing anything else to do with her. Like the new chef. As if She had forgotten about everything, and left her with this huge staff and all these people to take care of, and, gods, she had given Mor-am part of the house accounts, had given him too much. Ischade would find it out. She would find *this* out. . . .

Moria heard the maid clattering and clumping along the back hall, heard the door open, and went into the drawing room where there was a mirror. She stood there hunting her hair for pins to put the curls back in place.

O gods, is that me? Am I like this, this ain't me, outside, this is Haught's doing and She's got Haught by now, She has. Maybe She's outright killed him, taken him into Her bed and thrown him in the river an' all—like She'll throw me, all these damn' beggars to come on me in the night and cut my throat— O gods, look at my face, I'm prettier'n Her, She must've seen that—

A step sounded in the hall. A face appeared in the mirror beside her own. She turned, dropping her hands as a curl tumbled loose, her breast heaved—she suddenly knew what effect she projected, natural as breathing and dangerous as a spider.

She saw adoration glowing in Tasfalen's face, and the terrified pounding of her heart and the constriction of the laces brought on that faintness again.

"What secret?" she asked. And Tasfalen came and seized up her hand in his, in one move closer to her than she had planned to let him get. He smelled of spices and roses.

Like a flower seller. Or a funeral.

"That I want you," Tasfalen said, "and that you're in deadly danger."

"What—danger?"

He let go her hand and took her by both shoulders, staring closely into her eyes. "Gossip. Rumors. You've become known in town and someone has slandered you—incredible slander. I won't repeat all of it. Say that you've been accused of—trafficking with terrorists. Of being catspaw for—Is that part true? That woman, that dark woman—I know her name, dear lady. My sources are highly placed. And they mention your name—" His eyes rolled toward the uptown height, toward the palace, the while he slid his hands to hers and drew them against him. "I want to take you into my house. You understand, you'll be safe there. In all uncertainties. I have connections, and resources. I place them all at your disposal."

"I can't, I daren't, I daren't leave—"

"Moria." He gathered her against him, hugged her so tightly that the sense half-left her, tilted her face up and brought his mouth down on hers, which was perhaps all he could do, being a fool; and perhaps there was something wrong with her too, because his touching her did something to her that only Haught had done before, of many, many men, some for money and some for need and most of them come to grief and no good in the scattering of the hawkmasks. That was a world that had nothing to do with the silk and the perfume and the smell and the craziness of the uptown lord who smothered the breath that was left in her and ran his hands over her with an abandon that would have gotten him a knife in the gut back in her old wild days, but which now, through the lacings and the silk and the lace, made her think nothing in the world so desirable as shedding all that binding and breathing and doing what she had wanted to do with this man since first she had laid eyes on him there on her doorstep. He would not be like Haught, not reserved, not holding so much of himself back: this man was fever-mad, and it was all going to happen right here in the drawing-room for the servants and all to gawk at if she did not prevent him. . . .

"Upstairs," she murmured, fending off his hands from her. "Upstairs."

Somehow they got there, him carrying her part of the way, till she lost a shoe and he stopped for it; and she pulled him up the steps by the hand, damning the shoe and the laces and all, which he started undoing at the top of the stairs. She shed ribbons all the way to the bedroom, and they fell down together in a cloud of silk sheets and her petticoats, which he made shift to shove out of their way, layer after layer.

He got the last laces of her bodice and the damned corset finally, and she lay there with her ribs heaving in the sheer sensuous pleasure of clear breaths and the feel of his hands on her bare skin.

She knew, when the sense had gotten back to her along with her wind, that she was the most utter fool. But it had all gone too far for more thinking than that.

"I love you," he said, "Moria."

He had to, of course. She knew that, the way that the air thrummed and whispered and the blood ran in her veins with that kind of magic Haught had put into her.

Am I a witch myself? What's happening to me?

She stared into Tasfalen's face, that of a man bewitched.

Or what is he? O gods, save him! Shalpa, save me!

"He's quiet again," Randal said. Randal's foolish face was beaded with sweat and white under its freckles, and his hair hung down in sweat-damp points; and Tempus stared bleakly at the mage, his hand curled round a cup that sat on a polished table, there amongst his maps and his charts. Behind the mage in the doorway Kama stood, looking frayed herself.

Kama. Gods alone remembered how many others gone to bones and dust. She was smart as she was likely to be: she had that hard shining in her eyes, about her face, that he knew all too well: it was youth's conviction it was without sin or error; and if he troubled he could think his way through the maze of all the things she thought, but he did not trouble: there was enough to occupy his mind, and Kama was only a shallow part of it, shallow as a young fool was likely to be, though complex in her potentials. She had the potential for surprises to an enemy; was one part crazy and one part calculating and he had not missed the gravitation of the two points that were her and Molin. The look of a young woman in love? Not in Kama. The look of a young woman with a complex of things seething in a still-callow mind, which muddle he evaded with a mental shrug of something close to pain: another complex fool, not born to be a fool ultimately, but at that stage of growing when the wisest were prone to the most wearisome, repetitious mistakes as if they were new in the world. He knew what she had come to say. He read it before she opened her mouth, and that irritated him to the point of fury.

"I'm going back into the town," she said. "I can't sit still here."

Of course she couldn't. Who of her age and her nature could? The battle was going on here, but it was nothing she could get her hands into, so she went out to find trouble.

"I'm going to find this Haught," she said, and he could have mouthed the words a second before they left her mouth.

"Of course you are," he said. And did not ask *Where are you going to look?* because of course she had no particular idea. Haught was the witch's servant; Haught was the trouble they had had previous; and Ischade—was by far the more interesting question.

Ischade was keeping a promise. Or she was not, and a bargain was off. That was something it would take time to learn. The souls of his dead, she had promised him. And the safety of his living comrades as far as she could guarantee it. There was something deadly dangerous in the wind and the woman was onto it, doing battle with it—if she had told the truth. The possibility that she had lied was one of those lines down which he was quite willing to think, down which he had been thinking continually.

"Find Ischade while you're at it," he said. "Ask her whose Haught is."

Kama blinked. He watched her put it together. He watched the caution dawn in her immature-preternaturally mature mind, and watched the predictable thoughts go on, how she would do this, how she would need more caution than she had planned on in the other business.

Good. Things in the lower town wanted more caution than Kama was wont to use.

"Get out of here," he said then, staring past her and thinking what the world would be like without Niko, if they lost; if they lost Niko they would lose a great deal more than one man; and he, personally—Niko was one who engaged him on all levels, on too many levels. Niko was one who could cause him pain because he could give him so much else, and without Niko, that magnet for the world's troubles, that fool of fools who thought the world his responsibility—Niko almost made him feel it was, when he knew better. Niko was vulnerable the way his kind was when the uncaring little fools got past his guard; when the holding-action stopped and the god came thundering in to wrench the world apart again and Niko was the one standing rearguard to fools more vulnerable than himself. One like Kama was walking around and Niko was lying there in a bed losing a fight far too abstract for Kama to understand. She went out to do battle.

He did his fighting from this table, with a cup in hand. And could not, now that he wanted to surrender, find the god. Even that, he might have foreseen.

Randal stayed when Kama had gone. Randal was a fool of Niko's breed; and for a moment Randal, sweating and white as he was, looked at him with Niko's kind of understanding, and came and took the cup out of his hand, which gesture might have gotten another man killed. Foolish man. Foolish little mage. Who blundered his way along with more deftness and a keener sight and more guts than most ever had at their best.

So Tempus let him do it.

"You won't dream," Randal said, "if you pass out."

"I won't pass out," Tempus said, patiently, oh so patiently. "I *heal*, remember. There isn't any damn way. Now I want the damn god I can't get there."

"I've got a drug might . . . put you down a bit. If you let it."

"Try it." It took patience to say that. He already knew it would not work, but Randal was trying.

No god answered him. Not even Stormbringer, who was—gods knew where. There was not a cloud to be had out there.

Randal went away to find—whatever concoction he meant to try. Tempus filled his glass again, perversely, in a cold fury at his own vitality, a fury on the edge of panic. His body was not even in his control when the god was out of it. He could not do so simple a thing as fall asleep, when the ache of the world got too much. He *healed,* and that was what he did. He healed of the very need of sleep and the effects of alcohol and the effects of drugs and every other mortality. Aškelon could have come and claimed him by force. But the gods were not answering today.

None of them bloody cared.

Even Abarsis failed him. Or was held, somewhere.

II

A door opened somewhere far away. Ordinarily this would have alarmed Moria, though servants came and went for their own reasons. This sounded deeper and heavier than inside doors.

But just at that moment Tasfalen did something which quite took her senses inside out; and in the danger in which they both pursued this moment she cursed herself for butterflies and turned her mind to doing something which she had learned off a hawkmask lover—easy to pick a man's brain when he was feeling that good. Then Tasfalen gave as good back, and better—Shalpa and Shipri, she had never known a man with his ways, never bedded with a man who knew what he knew, not even Haught, never Haught—

"Oh," she said, "oh," and "O *gods!"*—when she brought her head up from the pillows and saw the dark figure standing in the doorway.

Ischade said not a thing. The air became charged and heavy, copper-edged. Tasfalen turned on an elbow. "Damn—" he said, and that was all, as if more than that had strangled somewhere in his chest.

Moria caught at her bodice, caught her clothing together against a chill in the air that breathed through from the hall. A scent of incense had come in, heavy and foreign, recalling the riverhouse so acutely that the present walls seemed darkened and she seemed to be in that room, strewn with its gaudy silks and hangings and the spoils of dead lovers. . . .

"Moria," Ischade said, in a voice that hardly whispered and

yet filled all the room. "You may go. Now."

It was life and not instant extinction. It was an order that sent her wriggling amongst the sheets and her rumpled petticoats as if there were hot irons behind her. Tasfalen caught at her arm, and his fingers fell away as she reached the edge of the bed and her bare feet hit the floor.

Ischade moved out of the doorway, and extended a dark-sleeved arm toward her freedom and the hall.

Moria fled in a cloud of her undone clothing, barefoot down the stairs, not for the downstairs hall but for the door, for anywhere, o gods, anywhere in all the world but this house, Her servants, Her law—

It was not where Ischade would have chosen to be—here, standing in a doorway, in a ludicrous situation in her own house: because the uptown house was hers, and Moria one of her more expensive servants who had considerably exceeded her authority.

This man who sat half-naked and staring at her—this lord of Sanctuary and Ranke, who lived his delicate life on the backs and the sweat of the downtown and the harbor and the ministerings of Ilsigi servants, this perfect, golden lord—she felt him straining at the spell of silence she wove, saw him try to shift his eyes away. But he was at once too arrogant to clutch the covers to him like a frightened stableboy and far too arrogant to be caught in the situation he was in. She let the spell go.

"It's supposed to be an outraged husband," he said, from his disadvantage.

She smiled. For a moment the black edges cleared back from her mind. *I'll walk out*, she thought. *There's more to him than I thought. I could even like this man*. But the power strained at her fingers, at her temples, the soles of her feet and ran in red tides in her gut. She felt Strat's attention, somewhere, felt the essence of him trying to get at her, to tear at her and wound like something gnawing its own flesh to get at the iron that ringed it; Strat would find her, he would kill himself finding her and that, for her, was her wound. She could walk out and find another victim, find anyone else, anywhere, stave off the hunger an hour, a day, another few days. . . .

Tasfalen patted the sheets beside him. "We might discuss the matter," he said with his own arrogant humor. And tipped the balance and sealed his fate.

She walked in, and smiled in a different, darker way. Tasfalen stared at her, the humor dying from his face, eyes quite fixed on hers in a mesmeric fascination. His lust became evident.

Hers was uncontrollable.

Pavings tore Moria's bare feet, a dozen passersby stared in shock, and Moria burst past a gaggle of old housekeepers on their way up from market. Apples and potatoes tumbled and bounced after her on the pavement, old women yelled after her, but Moria dived into an alley down a track she knew, ran dirty-puddled cobbles and squelched through mud and cut herself on glass and rubbish, mud spattering up on her satin skirts and silk petticoats, blood as well, while the breath ripped in and out of her unlaced chest.

The old warehouse was there. She prayed Haught was. She flung herself against that door, bleeding on the step, pounded with both her fists. "Haught! Haught, o be here, please be here—"

The door opened inward. She gaped at the dead man's eye-patched face and screamed a tiny strangled sound.

"Moria," Stilcho said, and grabbed her by the arms, dragged her across the threshold and into the dark where Haught waited, in this only refuge they knew, the place Haught had told her to come if ever there was a time she had to escape. He was here.

And the change in him was so grim and so profound that she found herself clinging to Stilcho's dead arm and pressing herself against him for dread of that stare Haught gave her.

"She," Moria said, and pointed up the hill, toward the house, *"She—"*

Only then in her terror did it sink in that she was half-naked from another lover's bed, and that it was rage which turned Haught's face pale and terrible.

"What happened?" Haught asked in a still, steely voice.

She had to tell him. Ischade's anger was worth her life. It was all their lives. "Tasfalen," she said. "He—forced his way in. She—"

A dizziness came over her. *No,* she heard Haught saying, though he was not saying a thing. She saw Tasfalen leaning over her in the bed, saw Ischade as a shadow in the doorway, felt all her terror again, but this time Haught was there, in her skull, looking out her eyes and running his fingers over Tasfalen's skin—Haught's anger swelled and swelled and she felt her temples like to burst. *"Gods!"* she cried, and: "Stop it!" Stilcho was shouting, his dead arms around her, holding her up while the blood loss from her wounded foot sent a chill up that leg and into her knees. She was falling, and Stilcho was shouting: "Gods, she's bleeding, she's all over blood, for the gods' sake, Haught—"

"Fool," Haught said, and took her arm, gripping her wrist so hard the feeling left her hand. The pain in her foot grew acute, became heat, became agony so great that she threw back her head and screamed.

The bay horse clattered up the street and sent fragments of apple and potato flying, sent a clutch of slavewomen screaming and cursing out of its path, and Straton did not so much as turn his head. The ring had no need to be on his finger. He *felt*. He felt all of it, lust running in tides through his blood and blinding his vision so that he had only the dimmest realization what street he was on or what house he had come to. He slid down from the saddle as the bay came right up on the walk and the jolt when his feet hit the ground was physical agony, much beyond any pleasure, as if sex would never again be pleasure to him, as if it had always been pain masquerading as enjoyment and now he was on the other side of that line. He came up the steps, grabbed the latch with all his strength, expecting a locked door.

It gave way and let him in. A fat woman stood in the hall, mouth agape. He never focused on her, only lifted his eyes toward the stairs and the next floor and went that way, knowing where he was going because there was at the moment only one focus in all creation. He grabbed the bannister and started up, blind in the shaft of sunlight that flooded in there through a high small window, and feeling the pounding of his blood as if he breathed awareness in with every breath, like the dust that danced in the light.

"Ischade!" he cried. It was a wounded sound. *"Ischade!"*

The woods were held in a terrible stillness. Janni stopped, having worked himself to the edge again, that margin where the sunlight and the meadow began. But the sun was surely sinking. It was sinking rapidly, and the breeze had stopped.

He looked down at the stream which always guided him and it was still. The water had stopped running at all, and stood invisible except for the sky-reflection and the light-reflection on its surface, which showed the maze of interlocked and breathless branches overhead.

A leaf fell and another and another, disturbing that surface, breaking up the mirror in which he and the sky were true. It began to be a shower of leaves, falling everywhere in the forest.

"Niko!" he cried. He abandoned hope of attack. He tried to wake the sleeper, back deep in the safe shadow, in the dark. *"Niko, wake up, wake up, for the gods' sake, Niko—"*

A breeze stirred from off the meadow, loosening more leaves, which turned yellow and tumbled and lay like a carpet, covering the stream.

Then the water began to move, reversed its former course and flowed out of the meadow into the forest, moving sluggishly at first, sweeping the leaves on in a golden sheet. Then the current gathered force and swept all the leaves away as he hastened into the dark.

A red thread had begun to run through the water, a curling wisp of blood that ran the clear depths and grew to an arm-thick skein.

Janni ran and ran, breaking branches and stumbling over falling branches and the slickness of the dying leaves.

"Ischade!"

Strat ran the stairs and nearly took the fragile bannister post down as he spun round it on his way to the bedroom. He hit the doorframe with his arm as he fetched up in it and stopped still at the sight of the figures in the tumbled bed, the dark and the light entangled.

He stood with his mouth open, with the words choking him. And then waded forward in a blind rage and grabbed the man by the shoulders with both his hands, hurled him over and confronted a face he had seen before in this house.

"Strat!" Ischade shouted at him. It had the grotesquerie of comedy, himself, the shocked uptown lord, the woman's shout in his ears. He had never looked to be made a fool of, dealt with the way she and Haught had dealt with him, made a partner to her rutting with another man—who for one moment hung shocked in his grasp and in the next flung up both arms to break his grip. "Damn you," Tasfalen yelled at him, "damn you and damn this lunatic house to hell!"

And the man tumbled against him, collapsing in a way that nothing alive ever felt. Straton caught him in first reflex, recoiled on the second with the dead man tumbling down off the bed and onto his feet. Movement drew his eye and his reflexes: he seized Ischade's wrist in an access of disgust and horror as she got to her knees; he jerked her off the bed and to her feet in her disarray and the entanglement of the sheets and the lord lying on his face on the floor against his feet.

"Damn!" he cried, and shook her by both arms till her black hair flew and her slitted eyes rolled white in her head. "Damn you, bitch, what do you think you're doing, what have you *done?*"

Her eyes opened wider, still showing whites, blinked again with the dark where it belonged, a widening dark, a dark that filled all their centers and turned those eyes into the pit of hell. "Get out of here." It was not the voice he knew. It was a feral snarl. *"Out!* Get out, get out, get out—"

The blood pounded in his veins. He shoved at her, flinging her onto the bed in a flood of grief and rage and outright hate. She scrambled to get to the other side, and he dived after her to stop her, hurling his weight on her, felt her under him and himself in control for a moment, himself in a position to teach her once for all that he was not hers to tell to come and go and do her errands and do it all her way, when she wanted it, if she wanted it. . . .

"Get off me!" she yelled at him, and hit him like any woman, with her fist. His own hand cracked open across her face and blood spattered from her mouth, red flecks on the pale satin pillow, her black hair flung in webs across her face with the recoil. He jerked with one hand at his own clothing, pinned her with his weight and his forearm, and elbowed her hard when she twisted like a cat and tried to bite his arm. In that distraction she came within a little of getting her knee into him, but he got his where it counted instead, and got both her hands pinned.

"Fool!" she screamed into his face. *"No!"*

He looked into her eyes. And knew suddenly that it was a terrible mistake.

"Let me go," Niko whispered to Randal, while Jihan was off doing something, while Jihan flitted somewhere about the countless things that somehow diverted the Froth Daughter in wild gyrations of attention. It might be Tempus, who still courted unwilling sleep, and who was, in his present state, a magnet for Stormbringer's daughter. It might be some other difficulty. She was likely where trouble was. And Niko, so wan and wasted, so miserable his voice sounded childlike soft, wrung at Randal's heart.

"I can't, you know," Randal said. "I'm sorry, Niko."

"Please." Niko strained at the ropes. His unbandaged eye was open, bleary and glistening with Jihan's godsawful unguents. His skin was white and glistened with sweat. "I'm all right, Randal. I hurt. In the gods' mercy give me some relief. I've got to—"

"I'll get a pot, it's all right."

"Let me up. Randal. My back hurts, you know what it's like to lie like this? Just let me shift my arms a little. Just a moment or two. I'm fine now. I'll lie back down, I'll let you put the ropes back again, oh, for the gods' own sake, Randal, it's not your joints that feel like they've got knives in them. Have a little pity, man. Just let me sit up a moment. Do for myself. All right?"

"I'll have to put you back again."

"That's all right. I know that. I know you have to." Niko made a face and shifted his shoulders. "O gods. My back."

Randal bit his lip and put out a little magical effort on the strain-tightened knots. They loosened, one after the other. He got the two closest, which tied Niko's feet to the bedframe. And got up off the end of the bed and carefully undid the one on the left wrist, carefully, around the thick padding they had put there to protect the skin. Niko sighed and flexed his legs and dragged his arm down to his chest while Randal went around the bed to get the other one. "Thanks," Niko said, a ghost of a voice. "Ah. That's better. That's a relief."

"Ought to give you a rubdown, that's what." Randal unwound the last rope, and held onto Niko's hand to work a little life into the arm.

Then something hit him in the side of the head and he went down blind and numb and dazed from the impact of his skull on a marble floor.

"Niko," he cried, trying to focus his eyes or his talent or to organize his defenses, but the dark and the daze swirled around him in clouds and gray and shooting flashes of red.

He heard bare feet, going away at speed.

"Ischade!" He shouted the name aloud, silently, threw all he had of talent into that scream. *"Ischade! Help!"*

Two men lay motionless in the bedchamber. Tasfalen was one, already chilling, his eyes half-open, his body curled up like a child where he had fallen, wrapped half in the bedspread and the sheets. The other lay sprawled in a twist where she had pushed him when he lost consciousness. He was still breathing. His face ticced in what might be dream, in such dreams as she gave him, filled his nights with, confused the truth with.

And Ischade was trembling all over, shuddering and shaking from sheer fright and aborted rage and the rush of power that, given time, would have done more than wrenched the life away from the uptown libertine, would have wrenched his soul out and shredded it beyond any power of demons or fiends to locate it.

As it was something got to it, something that wanted that kind of rage as it had known when it died. That something wanted *through,* wanted the essence of a god, wanted to *be* a god, or something like. It wanted a witch's soul at second best, and got Tasfalen's, which was far from enough to pay what Roxane had raised. It scented Straton's soul unguarded, loosened from its ordinary resistance, and Ischade flung power about him, a shrug as she caught her cloak up from under his legs and jerked it free in a series of violent, angry pulls.

Ischade!

The appeal hit her like a scream at her back. She physically turned and looked in the direction from which it had come. It was Randal's voice. It was blue light. It was...

She ran to the window, flung open the shutters, flung wide the window and launched herself from the floor of the bedroom to the incoming wind that swept the curtains, never questioning whether she had the control or knew where she was going: Randal's outpouring was a shriek of utter panic, shuddering and wavering in and out of focus in a wild undulation across the whole of the town.

Ischade! Help!
It's Roxane!

"She's gone," Haught whispered, gathering himself to his feet. "Her attention's elsewhere. It all is—"

"What are you doing?" Moria gathered herself up off the dust of the warehouse floor and the mouldering sacking which was the seating Stilcho had provided her. Her foot still hurt, though the bleeding had stopped. She staggered, blinked at the ex-slave turned magician, *her* Haught, who had stood straight up and looked off toward a blank wall of the rotting building as if his eyes saw through walls. Stilcho caught her arm when she wobbled on her feet, his hand cool but not cold, certainly not the deathly cold she always expected to feel. He held her there; she held onto him a moment; then Haught just stopped being there.

There was a thunderclap that rocked the building, a wind jerked roughly and once at her clothing and her hair toward the spot where Haught had been, and her skull all but split with Haught's voice thundering in it and into her soul and her bones and her gut.

Go home. She's not there now. I'll find you at the house.

There was threat implicit in that order. There was rage and jealousy and all promise what that power that racketed about her skull could do.

That and disgust for her soiling. Haught was always fastidious.

Dead man and damned drab. Wait for me.

She sobbed. It was different than a voice. It got into her soul and she had never felt so dirty and so small and so worthless to the world.

Stilcho hugged her head against his chest, hard. She heard his heart beating, which, through all her pain and her confusion, confounded her further; she had not thought it beat at all.

The door to Molin's office slammed wide, hit the wall and started a cascade of books and papers about the feet of the apparition which staggered into the room half-naked and wild and going straight for him, his desk, his life.

And the pottery globe which was/was not there.

Molin flung himself in a dive which intercepted Niko in mid-lunge as they both skidded over the desktop and off it. The sick man rolled and twisted and it was Molin who hit the ground on the bottom, Molin who had the wind half knocked from him and his skull cracked on the rebound of his neck as he tried to curl and save himself. Sparks exploded across his vision; Niko was trying to rip free, sweating, naked skin offering precious little purchase as he surged to his feet.

Molin grabbed Niko's leg with both arms, rolled and brought the Stepson down in another scrape and clatter of furniture. The chair this time. As shouting closed in on the room and he had hope of help if he could only hang on to the madman who was trying to scrabble and twist round to get at him. He bent the leg and grabbed the ankle and got his own foot around to slam into Niko's face.

"Get him," someone yelled from the doorway.

"Niko!" That shout was Tempus.

And something exploded through the window in a shower of glass, something that existed a moment in midair and then toppled in a tumble of black cloak, black hair and dusky skin that landed with a thump in front of Molin's dazed eyes.

Ischade lay on the floor like a dead thing, eyes open, lips apart, a strand of her black hair lying across her open eyes without a reaction at all, her bare arm outflung, fingers curled in the light of the broken window. Blood welled up in cuts on that arm—did not spurt, but only leaked, slowly, to pool under the arm, amid the fragments of glass. All this he had time to see: Niko had suddenly gone limp as Molin sprawled atop him. Ischade lay not breathing at all and he was desperately afraid that Niko was not breathing either.

He pushed himself up on his arms, had help as a strong hand grabbed him and pulled, and Tempus waded in, shoved the oak desk aside to get room and grabbed Niko up in his arms.

"He collapsed," Molin said, "he—just—"

Reason tottered. He felt himself pulled up and set aside like a child, and the Froth Daughter let him go and sank down to grab Tempus's arm as he held onto Niko.

"I can't get through," Tempus shouted in desperation. "Dammit, *Stormbringer—let me get to him!*"

"You can't go in there," Jihan yelled. Her fingers closed on his arm and dented the muscle. "She's *there,* Riddler, she's in there, and you want it too much—*Stay here!*"

It was wreckage, everywhere wreckage. Ischade cast about her in the woods, with the wind blowing everything to wrack and the trees creaking and groaning in the gusts. A stream ran there, and it was clear water around its edges, but its center was blood; and in the center of the blood was a thread of black, like corruption.

She knew where the attack came from. She clutched her cloak about her to shield herself from it as best she could and ran with her back to the wind, trying to find the lost soul whose refuge this was. A little bit of hell had crept in and settled in the meadow. A great deal of it was not that far away, and there was in a place this numinous a great deal of what it could use, if her enemy was an utter fool and let it in.

A tree gave way at the roots and crashed down, taking others with it, showering her with its ruin. She had no magic in this place. She had nothing but her mind, and that was unfocused, chaotic as this place was chaotic: she was the worst of helps for it, a raw Power without a center of her own, an existence without a reason. It was the worst of places for her to come.

The ground quaked. Thunder rolled and a voice pursued her without words, a shrieking shout that impelled the winds and stung with mortal cold.

She stumbled upon a tumble of rocks, a little rise, a place where a guardian waited, faceless, selfless, a pale shape that shone with inner light and its hands glowing more terribly than its face as it lifted them to bar her way, light against her black, certainty against her doubt. It had had a name once, and she suddenly knew it: once she knew that name, it took on shape and became Janni, a torn and failing ghost that blew in tatters in the wind.

"I need his help," she said. "Janni, I need yours."

She had raised only his Seeming out of hell; the part of Janni that stood there flaring with light came on loan from elsewhere, an elsewhere with which she had as little to do as possible, wanting its expensive bargains no more than hell's.

But he had come for this. To stand here. For hell's reason: revenge; and a reason out of that other place: raw devotion. It shone out of him like a candle through paper, and made his face unbearable: she flinched and avoided the sight of it. He blinded. He burned the eyes and left his imprint when she looked aside, so that a shadow-Janni drifted in front of her eyes when a shining hand at the edge of her vision indicated the sleeper by the streamside.

"Niko," she said, and exerted all the power she had stored, one vast push against the wind and the accumulated ruin of this place. "Niko. Nikodemos. *Stealth, it's not your time. Do you hear me?*"

Mine, a voice said on the wind. *Damn you. Damn you, Ischade.*

It was, delivered out of a witch's power, a curse that wrenched at the locks on hell.

"*Fool!*" Ischade whirled in the echoing gust and shoved back with all that was in her, keeping that Gate shut. It strained. It manifested, over across the stream, a barred door in the stone cliff beside the stream, a door bent and creaking under the blows of what might be a shoulder, an arm, a fragment of night itself reaching for Niko's soul—

"*Niko!*" she shouted. And: "*Roxane, you utter fool!*"

Niko's back arched. It was Jihan and Tempus who held him. Molin attempted to get his jaws open and to stop him choking while an occasional flutter of white betokened a priest dithering this way and that in the doorway, between help and hindrance. "Get *her!*" Molin snarled at the priest, applying all his strength to Niko's spasmed jaws, and nodding with a toss of his head toward the crumpled black-cloaked form on the floor. "Keep her warm, I don't care if she isn't breathing, tie up those wounds, *shut her eyes, she'll go blind, for godssakes—*" Niko spasmed again and Tempus swore and yelled his name as another staggering form appeared in the doorway.

Randal came reeling in, with blood all down his chin and down the front of him.

"*Nooo!*" Randal cried, his eyes lighting suddenly as if they had spied something, and he made a wild lunge toward the desk, but the priest got in his way, staggered him and knocked him reeling into a chair against the wall as something which was not-there burst with light.

Fire came back, blue and scorching as Randal recoiled out of the chair and threw power at it. White light blazed out, for a moment illumining a figure that clutched a Globe in its hands. The Globe spun without moving. It lit the whole room.

And when it and the holder vanished the contents of bookshelves came pouring out in a thunderclap.

"He put himself into it," Randal yelled, his hands clenched, his hair standing up in blood-matted spikes. "Into the cabinet! He put himself in and he *moved* it!"

"I'll get it," Jihan cried, and: "Dammit, no!" Tempus shouted at her, for Niko flung out the arm she let go: she grabbed it again, grabbed all of him and held onto him with bonecrushing strength, her unnatural skin aglow and her eyes full of violence for whoever had done this thing.

It was still going on, in whatever Place that racked body contained or was linked to: Molin could not describe it. He had only the conviction it existed, and it was coming apart under their hands: Roxane was tearing it apart from inside, he understood that much, while Niko's joints and muscles cracked and strained. Niko would shatter his own bones, rip tendons from their moorings, break his own spine in the extremity of the convulsions: it was a preternatural strength. It destroyed the body it lodged in; and the mind—

A wind was blowing through the room, the air was cold where it met bare skin, and Straton came up from his abyss with a gasp after air and a wild motion of his arm that sought after Ischade.

It met chill, empty sheets.

"Damn!" he cried and rolled off the bed, staggering on the rumpled rug and the sheets and the forgotten obstacle of Tasfalen's body lying there stark and cooling with the chill.

It was true. It was all true, what they said about Ischade, she had left him with her dead and gone off somewhere to sleep it off. He felt of his throat and felt of his chest with a chilled hand and staggered about with a throbbing headache and no concept of direction while he got his clothes to rights.

Damn her. Damn, damn, and damn her to bloody *hell*.

Am I alive? Am I like that poor sod Stilcho, alive-dead, killed and brought back out of hell, o gods—

A door opened downstairs; wind sucked in a chill gust from the window.

"Ischade," he yelled, and flung himself past Tasfalen's corpse, out the door, toward the stairs. He caught himself at the top, looking down on Moria in a torn and muddy gown, on Stilcho standing there ghastly as the truth in that bedroom.

He came down the stairs, broke through between them and headed out the door where the bay horse stood curiously nosing the remnants of an apple core on the walk. He ran for it, took the reins in his hand with no idea in heaven or hell where he was going.

To Crit, maybe, to that place where Crit was waiting for him.

He got his foot in the stirrup and heard a sound he had heard on a score of battlefields and a hundred ambushes. An arrow hit the wall and shattered. He dropped from the stirrup, whacked the bay to get it out of fire, already knowing it was stupid; he should have the horse for cover, the damned, foolish horse which was the only thing in all the world which had never betrayed him.

It snorted and shied up and stayed. That was what made him hesitate in his dive for cover, one half-heartbeat of disbelief...

... that persisted when the arrow smashed high into his chest and he staggered back and fell on the pavings. There was a smell of apples. The pavings were cold. The sky showed a clear, strange glow, going lavenders and white, and the upper stories of the buildings went all dim. It did not particularly hurt. They said those were the really bad ones.

III

Moria saw him fall. She never thought. She ran out onto the walk with Stilcho shouting after her and the bay horse rearing and plunging in hysterics over Straton's body. She ran; and a man's arm grabbed her around the waist and swept her back to the safety of the doorway. In that moment she had time to realize that she had just risked her life for a man she knew for another of Hers, for a man she had seen only twice in her life, who had burst past her down her own stairs, shoved her painfully against a wall and run out like the devils of hell were after him.

She could comprehend pain that strong. Ischade's service was full of it. It was that fellowship which sent her pelting out after him, no other reason; and now Stilcho in a terrible slowing of time and motion drew his hands from her waist, turned in a flying of his cloak, a falling of the hood that normally hid his eye-patched face—for a moment it was the good side toward her, the sighted side, mouth open in a gasp for air, legs already driving in a lunge back to the street. He skidded in low almost under the bay's legs, grabbed the Stepson by the collar and one hand and dragged him toward the door—he looked up as he came, his half-sighted face wild and pale, the dark hair flying, and his mouth opened.

"Get out of there!" he yelled at her, "get out of the way!"

An arrow whisked past with a bloodchilling sound she had heard described and instantly recognized. She spun back around the corner to the door and the inside wall, and saw the arrow lying spent on the rug as Stilcho dragged the Stepson in past her to drop him in the hall.

Moria hurled herself at the door and slammed it with all her might, shot the bolt and went and shuttered the drawing-room window in haste, ducking down beneath to slam the shutters tight and shoot the deadbolts. "Shiey!" she screamed. "Shutter the downstairs! Quick!"

Something banged back in the kitchens. Outside on the street she heard the clatter of hooves, the horse still outside the window: it whinnied loud and stamped this way and that. Hooves struck stone pavings up close to the window; and another shutter banged shut at the rear of the house.

"Upstairs," Stilcho said. He squatted over the unconscious Stepson. He had a knife out and he was cutting away the cloth from around a wound that might have been high enough to miss the lung but which might have cut the great artery under the collarbone—there was blood everywhere, on him, on the carpet. Stilcho lifted a pale face contorted in haste and effort. "The upstairs shutters, woman! And be careful!"

Moria gasped a breath. "Help him," she yelled as Cook came waddling out in panic, one-handed Shiey, who was worse as a cook than she had been as a thief. But they knew wounds in this house. There were servants who knew a dozen uses for a knife and a rope. She never looked back to see what Shiey did, only flew round the newel-post, never minding at all the pain of her sore foot. She had only the new and overwhelming fear that a shutter might be open, someone might find a way in even on the upper floor—

She reached the bedroom and froze in the doorway, dead-stopped against the doorframe.

Not a sound came out of her throat. She was Moria of the streets and she had seen corpses and made a few herself.

But the sight of a man who had lately made love to her lying dead on the floor in her bedspread—her heart clenched and loosed and sent a flood of nausea up into her throat. Then she swallowed it down and ducked down low, got across the room to get the shutters closed and bolted—for the window itself she did not try.

Then she ran, past the dreadful death on the floor, out of that place and down the stairs again for the comfort of Stilcho's presence, for the dead-alive man who was the only ally she had left, and to the Stepson who had come running out of that upstairs room the same as she.

He was still lying on the hall floor, there beside the stairs, with Stilcho's cloak wadded under his head and Stilcho crouching over him. Stilcho looked up as she came down the last steps, and his face and the face of the Stepson on the floor were the same pale color.

"Name's Straton," Stilcho said. "Her lover."

"T-Tasfalen's d-dead," Moria said. She had almost said *my* lover, but that was not true, Tasfalen was only a decent man who had treated her better than any man ever had, and who had died a fool. Of *her* doing, never this Straton's fault: Moria knew who she had left him with; and suddenly Moria the thief felt a pang of tears and the sting and ache of all her wounds. "What'll we do?" She leaned with her arms about the bottom newel-post and stared helplessly at Stilcho and stared at the man who was dying on her hall rug. Stilcho had gotten the shaft broken. The remnant of the arrow stood in the wound, with bloodstained flesh swelling it in tight. High in the ribs with bone to help lock it up and gods knew what it had hit. "O gods, gods, he's done, isn't he?"

Stilcho held up the fletching-end of the arrow from beside him. It had been dipped in blue dye. "Jubal," he said.

She felt a twinge of chill. Jubal was another who had owned a piece of her soul, once. Before Ischade took her and set her in this house that no longer seemed safe from anything. "You know how to pull it?" she asked.

"I know how. I don't know what I'm cutting into. Your staff—that cook of yours—ran back in the kitchen after another knife. I need two to get on either side of this thing. I need waddings and I need hot oil. Can you get them moving back there?"

"They've locked themselves in the cellar, that's where they are!" The silence out of the servants' end of the house suddenly interpreted itself and filled her with blind rage. She knew her staff. She flung herself from the newel-post and started down the hall.

And screamed as a light and a thunderclap burst into the drawing-room beyond the arch beside them. Wind hit her.

She turned and saw Haught there, Haught disheveled and without his cloak, and holding a pottery sphere in his hands, a sphere that by odd seconds seemed not to be there at all and at others seemed to spin and glow.

Haught grinned at them, a wolf's grin. And he let go the globe which hung where he had left it, in midair, spinning and glowing white and a thousand colors. The light fell on him and on her drawing room and paled everything. Then he tucked it up again under his arm and ran one hand through his hair, sweeping it from his face in that child-gesture that was like the Haught she had known, the Haught who had shared her bed and been kind to her. Both of them stood there on the same two feet, the mage she feared and the man who had given her gifts and loved her and gotten her and him into this damned mess.

Whatever it was he had gotten, it was not a natural thing and it was not something the Mistress meant him to have, Moria knew that by the look of it and of him. And she was cold inside and full of a despair so old it made her only tired and angry.

"Dammit, Haught, what the *hell* are you into?"

He grinned at her. Delight radiated from him. And he looked from her to Stilcho to the man on the floor, the grin fading to curiosity.

"Well," he said, and came closer, his precious strange globe tucked up in his arms. "Well," he said again when he looked down at Straton. "Look what we've got."

"You can help him." Moria remembered her foot and a touch of hope came to her. "You can help him. Do something."

"Oh, I will." Haught bent down and laid one hand on the Stepson's booted ankle. And the Stepson's whole body seemed to come back from that diminished, shrunken look of something dead, to draw a larger breath and to run into pain when it did. "How did this happen?"

She opened her mouth to say.

"That's all right," Haught said. "You've told me." He still had his hand on the Stepson's ankle, and closed it down till his fingers went white. "Hello, Straton."

Straton's eyes opened. He made a small move to lift his head from the wadded cloak, and perhaps he saw Haught, before the pain got him and twisted his face. "Oh, damn," he said, letting his head back, "damn."

"Damned for sure," Haught said. "How does it feel, Rankan?"

"Haught!" Moria cried, as the Stepson made a sound nothing human ought to make. She jerked with both hands at Haught's shoulders. "Don't! *Haught!*"

Haught stopped. He stood up, slowly, the globe still beneath his arm. And Moria flinched in the first backward step, then stood her ground, jaw clenched, muscles shaking in the threat of this utter stranger who stared at her with eyes that held nothing of the Haught she had known. There was something terrible inside. Something that burned and touched her inside her skull in ways that ran constantly through her nerves.

"Oh, I know what you've done, I know everything you'll say, and what you really think. It's more than a little trying, Moria." He reached and brought a finger under her chin. "It can be a damned bore, Moria, it really can."

"Haught—"

"Ischade doesn't own you anymore. I do. I own you, I own Stilcho, I own this house and everything in it."

"There's a dead man in my bedroom! Dammit, Haught—"

"A dead man in your bedroom." Haught's mouth tightened in the ghost of an old smile. "You want me to move him?"

"O my gods, no, no—" She backed away from Haught's hand. He could. He would. She saw that in his eyes, saw something like Ischade mixed with Haught's prankish humor and a slave's dire hate. "O gods, Haught—"

"Stilcho," Haught said, turning his face to him, "you've just acquired company."

Stilcho said nothing at all. His mouth was clamped to a hard line.

While upstairs something thumped, and that board that always creaked near the bed—creaked; and sent ice down Moria's back.

"Gods, stop it!"

"You don't want your lover back?"

"He's not my lover, he wasn't my lover, he was a poor, damned man She got her hands on, I just—I just—I was *sorry* for him, that's what, I was sorry for him and he was good, and I don't give a damn, Haught, I'm not your damn property, I'm not Hers, you can blast me to hell if you like, I've had all I'll take from all of you!"

Her shouting died. Her fists were still clenched. She waited for the blow or the blast or whatever it was wizards did and knew she was a fool. But Haught's face stressed and it smoothed, and something flowed over her mind like tepid water. "Congratulations," he said. "But you don't get those kind of choices. The world doesn't give them to you. *I* can. I have the power to do whatever I like. And you know that. Stilcho knows it. You want power, Moria? If you've got a shred of talent I can give you that. You want lovers, I can give you those, whatever amuses you. And I'll amuse you myself when the mood takes us. Maybe you'd like Stilcho. Ischade's probably taught him a lot of interesting things. I'm not jealous."

The hell you're not.

Haught's eyebrow twitched. Dangerously. And the cold eyes took on a little amusement. "Only of your loyalty," he said. "That, I'll have. What you have in your bed is your business. As long as I have the other. I don't hold anybody my *property,* Moria."

Slave, she remembered, remembered the whip-scars on him, and saw his face grow hard.

"I was apprenticed on Wizardwall," he said. "And Ischade was fool enough to take me on. Now I have what I need. I have this house, I have hands to do what I want, and I have one of my enemies. That's a beginning, isn't it?"

He looked up toward the head of the stairs. Moria did, unwillingly, and saw Tasfalen standing there naked to the waist and with his hair all rumpled as if he had just risen from sleep.

But there was something wrong in the way he stood there, in the lack of reaction, in the way the hand reached out listlessly for the bannister, all the reactions of life but no reaction to what ought to stir a man. As if he did not know that there was anything amiss with him or in what his eyes must register in the hall below him.

"The body's working," Haught said. "The mind's rather spotty, I'm afraid. Memory's not what it was. The soul might retain the missing bits—decay sets in very soon, you know; some tiny bits of him have just rotted, already. So a lot it had is gone. But it doesn't need a soul, does it? It doesn't need one for what I want."

"You said you'd help me," Stilcho said from where he knelt by the wounded Stepson.

"Oh. That. Yes. Eventually." As the body that had been Tasfalen came down the stairs in total disinterest. And stopped and stood at the bottom. "It doesn't have much volition. But it doesn't need that either. Does it?"

Niko's body went into still another spasm. Jihan had gotten his jaws open and Tempus had forced a small wooden rod there—gods knew where Randal had come up with it, out of what debris of the office. It kept Niko from biting his tongue through. And Randal had pulled another thing out of that other-where of a mage's storage—had gotten bits and pieces of that armor he had worn and tried to fit the breastplate to a body that kept trying to break its own spine.

Niko screamed when that touched him. He screamed and flung himself into a spasm that Molin would not have thought was left in that wracked body; his own muscles ached with pity and his hands sweated. "It's killing him," Tempus yelled, and shoved Randal and the collection of metal aside. "Dammit, let him be; Jihan, hold onto him, *hold onto him*—"

Tempus hugged him hard against him and shut his eyes and tried. Molin saw what he was trying, sensed the effort to break through the barrier that existed in Niko now. He threw his own strength into it, and felt Randal add his.

Trees groaned in the wind, crashed and fell, and the ground quaked. Ischade put out all her effort to stay others, her arms about the sleeper, Janni's white shape holding him from the other side. The wind grew colder, and the thing battering at the gate grew more powerful.

Even Roxane was afraid now. Ischade knew it.

"Get out of him!" Ischade yelled into the wind. "Witch, you've lost, get out of him, leave this place!"

I'll know when to go, the voice came back. *Give me Niko.*

"Fool," Ischade murmured, holding tight. "Fool, fool—*You won't get him, Roxane, I'll send his soul to hell before you get your hands on it, hear me?*"

And then a gate would exist indeed, snake swallowing its tail, a gaping hole in the world's substance which would pull them all in. She said it and knew it was not bluff, that she was not going to let go; she did not know how to let go, in the way that Roxane did not know how; and at the end that was what would-happen, the thing would find its way up out of the pit that had opened in this place and take the sleeper, and when it did, when it did, that snake-swallowing-tail effect would envelop them all. Her doing, and Roxane's.

Storm broke overhead.

Something else had manifested. Lightnings crashed. The ground shook; and of a sudden a bolt crashed down nearby, where the gate was. All of existence shuddered.

And there was sudden nothingness in her arms and in Janni's. The sleeper melted from them. The sky dissolved in rack and lightnings.

And a dark shape flew from the direction of the meadow to mingle with it, one fused whirling mass of lightnings, of gray cloud, and of night that shot destruction everywhere. . . .

Niko's unbandaged eye opened. He flung himself in a spasm against Jihan's strength and Tempus's inert weight and Molin flinched at the scream that came past the gag. *Let him die,* he prayed, was praying, when Randal scrambled out of his disarray with the armor and reached after something else. The painting manifested in his grip.

"Get a light," Randal yelled at him. In one dullwitted moment Molin knew what Randal was after, recoiled from the thought of the deed and wondered in the same numb-minded flicker why a candle, why not call fire: but a candle was apt for fire, the canvas was magical and unapt, it *resisted* destruction. "Light!" Molin bellowed at the priest who hovered terrified in custody of Ischade's body. The priest cast about this way and that, and in that selfsame moment Randal snatched up a handful of papers and blasted them into flame. The fire whumphed up and took the corner of the canvas on which Tempus and Niko and Roxane existed in triad, and Molin clenched his hands on the back of the chair in front of him and flinched as the smoke poured up from it, as Randal held onto burning paper and burning canvas, his face twisted in the pain of the burning that went up and up, the fire licking out at sleeves, at robe, at hair, at anything it could get while Randal turned and twisted in what looked like some grotesque dancer's contortions, keeping it away from himself and what else it reached for. Silver smoke poured up, mingled unnaturally with black. There was a stench of sulphur, and a shadow poured out of that smoke, a presence of intolerable menace. The priest screamed and covered his head. Then that darkness went— somewhere.

At the same moment Niko's body went limp as the dead and a slow trickle of blood flowed down from his nose and around the corner of his mouth where the stick was set between his jaws. Jihan looked puzzled and Randal stood there breathing in great gasps with the sweat standing on his white face and his hands all black and red, his lips drawn back in a grimace of pain and doubt.

Cloth whispered. Molin glanced aside in his distress and saw Ischade move and rise on one elbow and the opposing hand. Her dark hair hid her face. She looked up then, toward Niko, and that face was drawn and grim.

Tempus stirred and shoved himself up off the floor. His jaw clenched and knotted as he looked into Niko's face; while Jihan carefully pulled the stick from between Niko's jaws and closed his mouth, down which a ribbon of blood still poured.

"He's alive," Ischade said. Her voice was ragged and hoarse. "He's free of her."

"But not of *it,*" Tempus snarled, "dammit, not of *it*—"

"Let it alone!" Ischade shouted. Her voice broke. She reached out a forbidding hand and straightened the other arm, supporting herself. "It's not loose. Yet. Don't meddle with it. It's not something you can handle. Or that I can. I don't make that kind of bargain."

"Do it!"

"No!" She got herself up on her knees and staggered to her feet. "He's got Janni still. And Janni on that ground is power enough to keep him till he wakes. She's still loose, do you hear me? Roxane's still free, and she's pacted with that thing. She's somewhere, and your meddling in that Place can only make it worse: she's still got ties there. She doesn't want that gate open any more than we do: not unless she can get it what she promised. *Then* she'll open it. She's lost her power, she's lost her hiding-place, we're that much better off, but not if you go head-on against her ally—"

"That's not the worst of it," Randal said. "Your apprentice just stole the globe in all the confusion. I heard him coming and I couldn't get here in time. I do trust it wasn't your idea."

Ischade opened her mouth to say something. The air shuddered and Niko choked and moaned. Then she shut it and her jaw went hard, her fists clenched. "It wasn't," she said. And did not speak any curse, which restraint sent a chill down Molin's back and reminded him what she was. "Well," she said, "now we know where Roxane's gone, don't we?"

"Don't hurt him," Moria said, "Haught, don't."

"Another of your lovers?" Haught asked, and prodded Straton's side with his booted toe.

"No. For Shalpa's sake—"

"Your old patron." Haught shifted the globe he held to the crook of his arm and touched her under the chin. "Really, Moria, I make you a lady and look at you, you smell like a whore and you swear like a gutter-rat. Carry a knife in your garter, do you? No? Your brother stole it. What a life you lead."

"Stay out of my mind, dammit!"

"You're going to have to learn to control yourself, you know. Stilcho does. He thinks about things when I ask him questions. He thinks about things other than what I'm asking, he's gotten very good at it. Sometimes he remembers being dead. That's his greatest weapon. Sometimes I see other things in his head, like what it feels like to have people flinch away from you— bothers you terribly, doesn't it, Stilcho? You ran right out there to collect this bit of dogmeat just because Moria was going to do it, just because death doesn't mean a damn to you and you wanted to do something she wanted, you wanted her to look at you and not flinch, you *want* her, don't you, you sorry excuse for a living man?"

"Stop it," Moria cried.

"I just want the ones I love to know themselves the way I know them. Isn't that fair? I think we ought all to know where we stand. You want to go to bed with him? He's dying to."

"That's very funny," Stilcho said. "Excuse him, Moria, he's not himself."

She clenched her hands together to stop their shaking and clenched her jaw and stared up the bit she had to go to stare Haught in the eyes. "Well, dead, he's still got a heart in him. Where's yours? They beat it out of you?"

It scored. It scored all too well. For a moment she thought she would die for that, and she ought to be scared; but she was what he had said, she was a gutter-rat, and a rat was a coward until it got cornered, its back to two walls. Then it would fight anything. And these were her walls. This was her house. "My house, damn you, and mind your manners, I don't care what you've brought in with that damn jug. Get this man off my floor, put him to bed where he belongs, get this other poor thing set down somewhere where he won't scare my servants, and let me go up and take a bath, I've had enough of this goings-on."

"There's a love." Haught chucked her under the chin. She hit at his hand. "Go clean up. I'll take care of the rest."

She tightened her lips as if she would spit at him. It occurred to her. Childhood reflex. Then her eyes fixed on a move behind his shoulder. On Tasfalen, who had stood listless till then; now Tasfalen's head lifted and the eyes focused sharp; the chest gave with a wider breath and the whole body straightened. *Damned trick of his*, she thought, *to scare me with it*.

"Not a trick," Haught said, turning even while that cold touch ran over her mind. "We have a visitor. Hello, Roxane."

IV
Crit slid down from the saddle breathless and sweating, was on the marble steps at the second stride, and took them two at a time. "Watch my horse," he yelled at men whose proper job at the doors was not hostelry, but one of them ran to do that, and Crit kept going, inside the building in long strides—he wanted to run. Being what he was, where he was, he refused to show that much of his anguish to the locals.

He grabbed a middle-aged man by the arm, a Beysib who turned and stared at him in that way a Beysib had to, with eyes that had no white and no way to turn in their sockets. "Tempus," Crit spat. "Where?" His haste was such that he had no time to waste hunting; no time even to hunt an honest Rankan: he took the first thing he could get.

"Torchholder's office," the Beysib lisped, and Crit let him go and strode on.

Broke finally into a jog, his steel-studded boots ringing down the marble hall and echoing off the central vault. He saw the room, saw white-robed priests hanging about outside its open door, and came up on them in his haste.

"Wait," one said, but he shoved through and into the stench

of burning and the tumble of chaos in the room.

Tempus was there. Ischade. Molin. And a couple of priests. Molin and the priests he ignored; he ignored the stink of fire, the ashes, the strewn papers and tumbled books.

"They shot Strat," he said. "Riddler, your damned daughter's friends've shot Strat, they got him in Peres, someone in Peres pulled him in and we're trying to pick the snipers off the street so we can get in there. They've got it ringed, only thing they can't hit is that damned horse, they got Dolon in the arm and Ephis got two in the leg—"

"Damn, *who?*" Tempus grabbed him by the arm. "What in hell's happened?"

"The Front, the damned piffles! They made one try on him, this time they shot him. News is all over town, we got barricades going back up, we got every precinct flaring up, we haven't got the men to cover the whole damn city *and* fight a sniper action: they got that whole damn street and I had to come way wide and around to get in here."

"My house," Ischade said. "Strat's there?"

"The Peres house. They got him in. We don't know whether he's alive or not—"

"Gods blast it!" Tempus shouted. "What's your intelligence doing?"

Crit sucked in his breath. *Walking rings around your daughter,* was the thing that leaped up behind his teeth, but he stopped it before it got out. "We fouled up," he said. That was all there was to say.

"Tempus." Molin thrust out a hand to stop him on his way out. "Niko. Niko's at risk, you understand me."

"Haught's there," Ischade said. "So's Roxane by now. Right in the middle of it. And Roxane's got her ally poised here. In Niko. You need me for either and we could lose it in either place. You choose. You're the strategists."

The witch stirred a step, looked down at her/his own body, and up again. Tasfalen's eyes burned with a preternatural clarity. "Give me that," Tasfalen/Roxane said, taking a second step toward Haught; and Haught clutched the pottery globe the tighter and backed that step away while Moria shrank back against the outside of the bannister.

"Oh, no," said Haught. "Not so readily as that—compatriot. You may even be outranked. Do you want to try me? Or do you want to take the gift I've already given you and be reasonable?"

The witch laid a hand on her own naked chest, ran it down to the belly. "Is this your sense of humor, man? I assure you I'm not amused."

"I worked with what I had at hand. If you've seen the staff in this house you know I did quite well. This one—" Haught grasped Moria by the arm and dragged her behind him. "—is mine. The body is Tasfalen Lancothis. He's quite rich. And with your tastes I'm sure you'll find amusement one way or the other."

Tasfalen's eyes looked up from under the brows and all hell looked out.

"We'll do better," Haught said, "if we both live that long." He nodded toward the street. "There's considerable disturbance out there. They're back at it again. I found you, I offer you a body. I have the globe. For two wizards, this is an opportune place and an opportune time: Ranke is dying in the streets out there by what I gather. And here—" he moved his foot aside, against Straton's leg. "Here's Tempus's own lieutenant. His chief interrogator. His gatherer of secrets. I think we have something to discuss with him, you and I. Don't we?"

Tasfalen's nostrils flared. The face seemed hollowed. "I want a drink," Roxane said. "I'm parched."

"Moria," Haught said.

"I'm not your damned servant!"

"I'll get it," Stilcho said, and got up from beside the unconscious Stepson and went for the drawing room.

"Moria," Haught said. "Don't be a total fool." His hand caressed her shoulder but he never looked her way. "Lover's quarrel," he said to Roxane.

"Who are you?" Roxane asked, and Haught stiffened; his hand stopped its motion and Tasfalen's face went hard and careful.

"Answer enough?" Haught asked. "You knew my father. We're *almost* cousins."

Roxane/Tasfalen said nothing to that. But the expression became thoughtful, and then something else again, that sent a shiver up Moria's Ilsigi spine. The face of the man she had lately made love with began to take on different lines, flush with lifelike color, and settle into expressions alien to its personality.

Stilcho brought the drink in a glass, from the carafe and service on the drawing room sideboard. Tasfalen reached for it; Roxane took it and lifted it with a lingering suspicion in the look she turned toward Haught. Then she sipped at it carefully, and let go a small sigh.

"Better," she said. "Better." And finished the glass and gave it to Stilcho. She put out her male hand in the next instant and stayed him in his departure, then turned the hand as if it had suddenly interested her as much as Stilcho. The fingers ran up the fabric of Stilcho's sleeve. And he stared back with a hard, revolted stare. Of a sudden Tasfalen's face broke into Tasfalen's grin, and a small short laugh came out. "Well." Then the hand dropped and the face turned to them again with the eyes aglitter. "You hold onto that globe so tightly—cousin. You're young, you're handling something you're only half able to use, and you're vulnerable, my young friend. This house is Ischade's property. Anything she's ever handled is a focus she can use; and this is a place she *owns,* you understand me. I felt your wards when I came through them, a nice little bit of work for what they are, but that streetwalking whore isn't what she was, either. Now do we put something around this house she'll have trouble breaking, or do we just stand here playing power games? Because she's on her way here, you can believe me that she is."

Haught tucked the pottery globe the more tightly in his arms, then slowly reached out and set it in the air between them. It spun and glowed and Moria flinched away, her arm flung up between herself and that *thing.* It hummed and throbbed and hung there defying reason; it beat like a heart as it spun, and her own hurt in her chest; her tangled hair lifted on its own with a prickling eerie life, her silken, muddy-hemmed petticoats crackled and stood away from her body with a life of their own. All their hair stood up like that, Tasfalen's, Stilcho's, Haught's, as blue sparks leapt from Tasfalen's outstretched hand, from Haught's fingertips, flying against the globe and spattering outward against the walls, lining the crack of the door, whirling up the stairs and into the drawing room and everywhere. From somewhere in the cellars and the rear of the house there was a general outcry of panic; it had gotten to the servants.

The sound became pain. It throbbed in time to the pulse. It

screamed with a high thin shriek like wind and became her own scream. "No," she cried, "make it stop—"

Strat moved. It was the hardest thing he had ever done, torn muscles and swollen flesh tensing round the shaft in his chest; something else tore, and the swirl of light spotted with black and went all to gray, but he knew where his enemy stood and he had coordination enough to brace his good hand against the floor, draw up the opposite leg while the pain turned every move weak and fluttery, muscles shaking and weak: one good push, his foot behind the damned Nisi's leg—

He shoved, with all that was in him. Haught screamed; he thought that was the scream he heard, or it was his own.

Tasfalen's hands clutched the globe. Tasfalen's face grinned a wolf's grin. "There, wizardling."

Moria made herself as small as she could against the side of the stairs: she shut both eyes, expecting a burst of fire, and opened one, between her fingers. Haught and the witch stood facing each other, Stilcho was down on his knees by the writhing Stepson, but no fire flew.

"You've a bit to learn," Tasfalen said. "Most of all, a sense of perspective. But I'm willing to take an apprentice."

From Haught, a long silence: then, quietly: "Is it mistress or master?"

Tasfalen's right eyebrow jerked in wrath. Then a grin spread over his face. "Oh, I like you well, upstart. I do like you." The pottery globe vanished from his/her hands. "First lesson: don't leave a thing like that in reach."

"Where *is* it?" There was the ghost of panic in Haught's voice, and Tasfalen's grin widened. Male hand touched male chest.

"Here," Tasfalen said. "Or as close as hardly matters. I learned that trick of a Bandaran." He—Moria shuddered: it was impossible to look at that virile body and think *she*—walked closer and stood looking down at the Stepson, who lay white and still by Stilcho's knee. "Ischade's lover. Oh, you are a find, aren't you? And you're not going to die on us, oh, no, not a chance of that—"

* * *

"... A chance of that," a strange voice said; and another, hated: "I've no intentions of it. Not with what he knows."

"He has uses other than that. Her lover, after all. It has to play havoc with her concentration. Even if personal pride is all that bothers her."

"Oh, it's more than that." A grip closed on Strat's wrist, lifted that, let go and lifted the other, the wounded hand, with a pain that drove Strat far under for a moment; he came back with the feeling of someone's hands on him, roughly probing among his clothing. "Ah. *Here* it is."

"Hers?"

"I gave it to him. It should have come to you. In your other life."

He thought what it was then. He would have kept the ring. He was sorry to lose it. He had been a fool. He was sorry for that too. *Play havoc with her concentration.*

With what he knows.

He understood that well too. He had asked the questions for years. His turn now. He thought of a dozen of his own cases and had no illusions about himself. He tried to die. He thought of it as hard as he could. Probably his own cases had thought the identical thought at some stage.

"He wants to leave us," the one voice said. A feathery touch came at Strat's throat, over the great artery. "That won't do." A warmth spread out from it, his heart sped, a hateful, momentary surge of strength, like a tide carrying him up out of the dark. "Wake up, come on. We're not even started yet. Open the eyes. Or just think about what I'd like to know about your friends. Where they are, what they'll do—it's awfully hard, isn't it, *not* to think about a thing?"

Crit. O gods. Crit. Was it you after all?

"We can take him into the kitchen," one suggested. "Plenty of room to work in there."

"No," a woman cried.

"Let's not be difficult, shall we? There's a love. Go wash. You'd rather be taking a bath than stay for this, wouldn't you? You do look a mess, Moria."

THE SMALL POWERS
THAT ENDURE

Lynn Abbey

Battlefield chaos reigned in what had once been Molin Torchholder's private retreat from disorder. Niko lay on the worktable while Jihan brought her healing energies to bear on one tortured joint after another. Now and again the mercenary's eyes would bulge open and the sounds of hell would explode from his mouth. The others would cease their arguings until the Froth Daughter had him quiet; then the frantic bickering would begin again.

Crit's simple statement, "We fouled up," applied to everyone in the room—none of whom were accustomed to failure on such a grand scale. Niko's physical pain was the least of their worries. The demon erupting in his *maat*-molded rest-place had the power to reshape all creation—if Roxane didn't do something preemptive with the Globe of Power or the mortal anarchy of the PFLS-inspired riots didn't overwhelm them all first.

None of then noticed a new shadow at the threshold.

"Divine Mother! This is intolerable!"

Shupansea, exiled Beysib Empress and, by virtue of foreign gold and the strong arms of clan Burek, de facto ruler of Sanctuary, stopped short in the open doorway. She *stared*—knowing that it discomfitted these drylanders, but there was no other way. Her mind, moving behind glazed, amber eyes, scanned from one shadowed corner of the room to the other, from the floor to the ceiling, absorbing every detail without the distraction of movement.

They had been arguing, singly and severally, but the sight of her united them in silence. She knew them all, except for the dark-clad, disheveled woman sitting on a low stool with a half-full goblet leaning out of her hands. Their combined presence in such a small, private room could only mean disaster.

Shupansea was caught in an undertow of emotion as the

173

images of violence patterned themselves against her memories of the Beysa's court those last few days before her supporters in clan Burek had effected her rescue, and exile. Not even the silken touch of her familiar serpent moving between her breasts could break her horror-struck fascination with Niko's broken, blood-streaked body. The tears and shrieks of terror she had resolutely concealed from her own people could not be withheld from this insignificant drylander.

Divine Mother, she repeated, this time a prayer as the silent undertow swept her back toward incapacitating fear. *Help me!*

The downward surge was broken by the soft strength of Mother Bey cradling her mortal daughter. Shupansea felt her pulse quicken as the goddess' vitality flowed within her own envenomed blood. She ascended through the Aspects: Girl, Maiden, Mother and Crone, to Sisterhood, then broke through to Self-ness. She blinked and stared across the room again.

"He yet lives," the Presence said to her, and through her to the still-silent assembly. "The mortal soul survives."

Shupansea took long, gliding steps toward Niko. Tempus moved away from his self-assigned post at Niko's side in a slow, graceful fury, determined to stop her. She paused and stared—seeing him clearly for the first time: this nearly supernatural man now spiritually naked and silently invoking the names of puny, man-shaped gods. She lifted a finger of Power but was spared its use when Another reached out to restrain him.

"That's the snake-bitch goddess within her," Jihan hissed, getting a handful of Tempus's biceps and squeezing it hard.

The Beysa reached out to catch a drop of Niko's blood in the curve of her long fingernail, then brought it to her lips. Blood was sacred to Mother Bey. She savored the taste of it and absorbed all it told about Niko, his rest-place, and the uneasy truce which held there. Visions of the handiwork of *maat*, the Bandaran imitation of divine paradise, came as an unwelcome—indeed, unimaginable—surprise.

You should be ashamed of yourselves, she, who tolerated no other deities in that portion of paradise she called her own, roared at the pantheons and protogods who shared a suddenly imperfect omniscience with her. *THAT.* An ephemeral finger pointed toward the blazing column that was Janni and the ominous bulge beneath it. *That is what comes of giving mortals their own dreams. That is what they have built with free will:*

a gateway for demons—for the destruction of us all!

Mother Bey reserved special ire for her erstwhile lover, Stormbringer, but her mortal avatar was spared that confrontation. The goddess withdrew, leaving Shupansea somewhat flushed and tingling with righteous indignation.

"How could you allow this to happen?" she demanded of Molin.

Molin straightened his robe and his dignity. "You knew all that we knew. Roxane took control of Niko's body; another magician has stolen the Globe of Power. The rest, the consequences, we are only just beginning to understand."

"I have seen with my mother's eye, and the force within that young man," she gestured toward Niko with a blood stained finger, "has nothing to do with witches! Can't you fools tell the difference between a demon and a witch?"

Tempus freed himself from Jihan's restraint. He towered over Shupansea. "We know exactly what we're dealing with, bitch," he said in a softly menacing voice.

"Well, what are we dealing with?" Shupansea replied, her head tilted back and glowering with a stare he could not hope to break. Her serpent made its way up the stiff wires of her headdress. Its tongue flickered; Tempus blinked and Molin spoke instead.

"Roxane promised the Stormchildren to the demon. She poisoned the children but she couldn't deliver their souls and got herself wounded in the bargain. We knew she was hiding; some of us thought she had a hold on Niko but we didn't guess she'd gotten *behind* him until it was too late and the demon'd come to collect its payment from *her*. That was Aškelon's message for Tempus: that she'd gotten behind him somehow."

Ischade shook her head. "It was never so simple. Roxane promised the demon a gateway in exchange for Niko. The only gateway she knew about was the Stormchildren. She thought she was safe from everything where she was—and that Niko was safe as well. Now that it's trying to take Niko, as it would have taken the Stormchildren, she's frantic herself. She understands less than we do—but, with a globe again, she has vastly more power."

"We understand the demon must be destroyed and the rest-place with it," Shupansea agreed.

Randal staggered forward, his face swollen and glistening from the fire, bits of charred canvas and flesh trailing from his clawed fingers. "Not destroyed." He had breathed the flames; his voice rasped and gurgled in his throat. "It will go someplace less defended. We need the globe. We can make it right with the globe." Passion exhausted him; he slumped forward into Jihan's outstretched arms.

"Is this true?" the Beysa demanded.

"It is likely," Jihan admitted, trying to divide her ministrations between the stricken mage and Niko, who moaned when her hands weren't resting against his flesh. "We can defend the rest-place, or the Stormchildren, but if Roxane has the globe she'll always be one step ahead."

"Roxane, Niko, or your son, Riddler," Ischade interrupted, focusing her own, and everyone else's, attention on Tempus. "You must make your choice. No matter what I do, I will need time. I cannot wait any longer!"

But Tempus only shook his head. He took Niko's hand and the unconscious Stepson seemed to breathe easier. "Go where you want," he said slowly.

Ischade set the goblet down and made ready to leave the room.

"Guards!" Shupansea shouted, and a pair of the shaven-pated Burek warriors appeared in the doorway. "Provide her with shoes and clothing. Escort her wherever she wishes to go."

The necromant stared across the room, hell-dark eyes flashing rejection of Beysib hospitality.

"You ought not squander yourself by leaving the same way you arrived," the Beysa said gently, a faint smile on her lips; her eyes still defended against the power of *that* stare.

Ischade lowered her eyes and picked her way carefully across the shattered glass. The great black raven, which had arrived moments after the first Globe of Power had been shattered and had held itself aloof from all the commotion since, spread its wings and flapped out the window its mistress had broken by her entrance.

"How did Roxane get in there?" Tempus asked once Ischade was gone. "How? Not even the gods can violate *maat*'s sanctuary."

"Randal?" Molin asked.

The mage pushed himself away from Jihan's healing hands. He started to speak but the words were too great an effort. Quivering, he sank back to his knees; tears ate their way down his cheeks. "They had him for a year, Riddler," he pleaded for understanding. "He hates her. He remembers and he hates her but when she comes for him. . . . A year, Riddler. O gods, after a year he remembers; he hates but he can't—won't—refuse."

Critias pounded the windowframe. "*Seh!*" he said, watching the smoke rising from the city's rooftops. The Nisi obscenity was somehow appropriate. If the gods, what remained of them, had intended to cripple what remained of order and competence in Sanctuary they could not have done a better job. He had even allowed the fatal thought—that the situation could not possibly get worse—to percolate through his consciousness.

"Commander," he said with a heavy sigh. "You'd better take a look at this."

Tempus followed the lines of his lieutenant's outstretched arm. He said nothing, so the others—Molin, Jihan, Shupansea, and finally Randal—crowded around the broken window.

"It's all up now." Torchholder turned away and slouched against the wall.

Jihan closed her eyes, reaching deep into her primal knowledge of all water and salt water in particular. "We've got a bit of time. With the tides they won't be able to enter the harbor until after sundown."

"I don't expect you'd be able to send them back the way they came?" Molin asked.

Shupansea tried looking, *staring,* and leaning perilously far out the window and saw nothing but the myopic fuzziness of the wharves and the ocean beyond it. "Send what back?" she inquired with evident irritation.

"The Rankan Empire, my lady," Tempus explained. "Come to find out what's going on in this forsaken backwater."

"How many ships?"

"Lots," the big man said with a feral grin.

The Beysa stepped back from the window, suddenly remembering that she had dismissed her guard and that none of those between herself and the door could be considered willing allies to her cause. "We must make preparations," she said, edging backward toward escape.

"You put the fear of Ranke's strong right arm into her," Crit snorted, once the nervous woman had disappeared down the narrow steps. The lone ship fighting its way through the tidal currents carried no more than two hundred men, including oarsmen, and was equipped for tribute, not combat.

"I should have killed her," Jihan muttered.

"You would never have left this room alive," Tempus informed her.

"I? *I* would never have left this room? I could have frozen that little bitch before she knew what happened to her."

"And what would your father have said to that?" Tempus retorted.

The Froth Daughter went red-eyed and icy for a moment. She raised a fist toward the Stepson's commander and shook it at him. Her scale armor creaked as she stomped back to the table where Niko was moaning softly. Molin peered intently out the window lest she see his smile; Crit was fighting laughter himself and nearly lost the battle when he glimpsed the priest biting his lower lip.

"I'm taking Stealth back downstairs," Stormbringer's daughter announced, effortlessly holding the grown man in her arms. "Is anyone coming with me?"

She had strength and power it was dangerous to mock, however immature its manifestation. Not even Randal, who of the men was the most clearly respectful of gods and magic, dared to answer her.

"What now?" Randal asked, easing himself onto the stool Ischade had used. Jihan's touch had cleansed and sealed the surfaces of his wounds; he had his own healing resources to call on but his continuing tremors indicated that the little mage had not yet paid the full price for the day's exertions.

With the last of the women departed, Tempus felt his confidence returning: "For you—rest. If we need you again we'll need you healthy. Go stay with Jihan and Niko if you can't finish the job yourself over at the Mageguild. Crit, you get someone in that damn house of hers. And get Kama—however you have to do it. The rest of us will see about restoring the appearance of order in this damn place before that ship docks."

He looked out the window again as trumpets blared from the gateways; Shupansea had evidently reached her advisors. Squads of Burek fighters, deadly swordsmen and archers despite their baggy silk pantaloons and polished scalps, were double-timing across the courtyards. Either all Beysib were nearsighted like their empress and believed the entire Rankan fleet loomed beyond the horizon, or they were taking no chances.

When the triple portrait had burned, the fire had touched Tempus—not as it had touched Randal, but purging him of the dark associations between Death's Queen, Niko, and himself. The shock, and the pain, were still strong—he'd kill the witch when he could for the crippling scars she'd left in Niko—but the compulsion he'd felt since the black storms in the capital was fading.

"Damn plague town," he said to himself. "Infecting everything it touches with its disease. Let the fish people have it."

Torchholder looked over at him. "You just might have something there, Riddler." He liked the idea coalescing in his thoughts; unconsciously he tugged at his sleeves as a sense of competence returned to him. "Now, then—whatever we might feel about the long-term implications of Theron's delegation I think we all agree that this is not the time to have any outsider wandering around. Right?"

The other men nodded reluctant agreement.

"We also know them well enough to know that once they suspect we're hiding anything they'll make imperial nuisances out of themselves. And they're suspicious right now just from the smoke." He didn't wait for them to nod this time. "They'll want to be out there unless we give them a bloody good reason for staying exactly where we put them: plague—quarantined for their own protection."

Critias arched an eyebrow. "Priest, I could find myself liking you."

Ischade made her way to the White Foal alone. She'd separated from her Beysib escort near the Peres house when the anarchists and so-called revolutionaries had challenged them. With their twirling swords they'd seemed more than a match for the poorly-armed quartet that had come charging out of the alley and she had been grateful for the opportunity to slide into the shadows unnoticed.

The house had called out to her: her possessions, her lover, her magic, the tiny ring now on Haught's slender finger. Not long before—before her explosive journey to the palace—the call would have been irresistible. She would have had the power to sunder any wards Roxane had concocted. And she would have done just that: gone blundering into another abortive confrontation with the Nisi witch.

If the battle within Niko's rest-place had done nothing else it had vented the excess of power which had blighted her vision since Tempus had returned to Sanctuary and ordered the de-

struction of the Globes of Power. Purged and refreshed, she
perceived the wards not simply as Haught's betrayal or Roxane's arrogance but as the finely strung trap that they were.

They think I am still blind to the finer workings, she'd said
to the raven perched on the stone finial beside her. *Their first
mistake. Let's see if there are others.*

No one bothered her as she picked her way across the open
expanse of mud surrounding the new White Foal bridge. It was
probable that none of the bravos running between Downwind
and the more profitable riots uptown could see her though even
she was uncertain how far her magic, or her curse, extended
in such directions, now that her power had resumed its normal
proportions.

Her house showed signs of her indisposition. The black roses
brawled with each other, sending up bloomless canes armed
with wicked thorns that flaked the rusted iron fence where they
rubbed against it. And the wards? Ischade shuddered at the
sight of the heavy blotches of power smeared stridently across
her personal domain. With small movements of her hands,
hands now less powerful but once again skilled and certain,
she constrained the roses and reshaped the wards into a more
acceptable pattern.

The gate swung open to greet her; the raven preceded her
to the porch.

Once across the threshold, Ischade kicked the heavy-soled
boots the Beysib soldier had given her into a corner where, in
time, her magic would twist them into something delicate and
brightly colored. She retrieved her candles, lit them, and settled
into the small mountain of shimmering silk that was, in the
final sense, her home.

Inhaling the familiarity—the rightness—of it, she gathered
the tangled skein of imaginary silk which bound the Peres house
to her and studied her options. She touched each strand gently,
so gently that no one in the uptown house would suspect her
interest as she reacquainted herself with what rightly belonged
to her. Then she drew the thread that bound her to Straton as
surely as it bound him to her.

Straton!

Ischade lived at the fringes of time, as she lived at the fringes
of the greater magics practiced by the likes of Roxane or even
Randal. She was older than she looked; probably older than
she remembered. Straton was not the first who cut through her

defenses—even her curse—to hurt her, but anguish had no sense of proportion: it was *now*. The Peres house, Moria, Stilcho, even Haught; she wanted those back through pride but the sandy-haired man who hated magic had a different claim. Not love.

Partnership, perhaps—someone who, because he had shattered the walls which surrounded her, lessened the loneliness of existence at the fringes. Someone whose demands and responses were *simple* and who, like all the others, eventually broke the rules which were not. She'd sent Straton away for his own good and he'd come back, like all the others, with his simple, impossible demands. But, unlike the others, he hadn't died and that, the necromant realized with a shiver, might be—for want of a better word—love.

He would not die, or be stripped of his dignity, in the Peres house, if she had to destroy the world to stop it.

Walegrin paced the length of the dark, malodorous cellar. Life, specifically combat, had been much easier when he had been responsible for no more than the handful of men he personally led. Now he was a commander, forced to stay behind the lines of imminent danger coordinating the activities of the entire garrison. They said he did the job well but all he felt was a vicious burning in his gut as bad as any arrow.

"Any sign?" he shouted through the slit window to the street.

"More smoke," the lookout shouted back so Walegrin missed Thrusher's hawk-call.

The wiry little man swung himself feet first through another window, landing lightly but not before Walegrin had his knife drawn. Thrush took the arrows out of his mouth and laughed.

"Too slow, chief. Way too slow."

"Damn, Thrush—what's going on out there?"

"Nothing good. See this?" He handed the blond man one of his arrows. "That's what the piffle-shit are using. Blue fletchings—like the one that took Strat down up near the wall."

"So it wasn't Jubal starting all this?"

"Hell no—but they're in it now: them, piffles, fish, Stepsons—anyone with an edge or a stick. They're giving no quarter. It's startin' to burn out there, chief."

"Are we holding?"

"Holding what—" Thrusher began, only to be interrupted by the lookout and the arrival of a messenger with a scroll from the palace. "There's no territory bigger than the ground under your feet."

Walegrin read Molin's message, crumpled the paper, and stomped it into the offal. "Shit-on-a-stick," he grumbled. "It's gonna get worse—a lot worse. The palace wants plague sign posted on Wideway and the Processional; seems our visitors have arrived."

"Plague sign?" Thrusher whistled and broke his remaining arrow. "Why not just burn the whole place to the ground? Shit—where're we supposed to get paint?"

"Use charcoal, or blood. Hell, don't worry about it; I'll take care of it. I got to get out of here anyway. You find me Kama."

The little man's face blanched beneath his black beard. "Kama—she started the whole thing . . . taking Strat down with Jubal's arrow! There isn't a blade or arrow out there not marked for her back!"

"Yeah—well, I don't believe she did it, so you get her back to the barracks for safe-keeping. You and Cythen."

"Your orders, chief? She's probably meat by now anyway."

"She'll be alive—hiding somewhere near where we caught her that night."

"An' if she's not?"

"Then I'm wrong and she did start it. My orders, Thrush: Find her before someone else does."

Walegrin endured Thrush's disappointed sigh and watched as the little man left the same way he'd come; then he went up to the street.

Plague sign: the palace wanted plague sign to keep the visitors on the straight and narrow. It might work. It might keep the Imperials tight on their ship, away from the madness that was Sanctuary. But it would sure as hell bring panic to what was left of the law-abiding community and, the way things were going, it would probably bring plague as well.

He wrenched a burning brand out of a neighboring building and, after sending the lookout down to the cellar, headed off to the wharves. It wasn't two hours since the afternoon sky had been split by a dark apparition streaking between the Peres house and the palace. Damn witches. Damn magic. Damn every last one of them who made honest men die while they played games with gods.

* * *

Understanding came slowly to Stilcho, which was not at all surprising. There was no peace in Ischade's one-time house for understanding and a man, once he understood himself to be dead, did not reconsider the issue. Indeed, his first reaction on seeing Straton there with an arrow by his heart was considerably less than charitable. This bleeding hulk who had supplanted him in Her affections; this murder-dealing Stepson who had massacred his comrades was getting naught but what he deserved.

His opinion hardened further when the globe was spinning madness into all of them and the injured Stepson had summoned the strength to reach into that dazzling blue array of magic to disrupt it. At first, all Stilcho had seen was the globe passing from Haught to Roxane: from bad to worse; he had cursed Straton with all the latent power his hell-seeing eye possessed. He had not been gentle getting his hands under Strat's shoulders and dragging him along the hallway while Roxane gloated and Haught wore a superficial obsequiousness.

Then he saw the little things they did not: the subtle wrongness in the globe-wrought wards, the holes through which She might be yet able to reach. He felt the pulse of fear and anticipation pounding at his temples, making his hands sweat—and *that* he had never expected to feel again; he even remembered, distantly, what it meant.

Haught had said She had cut him loose—had proved it— but now Haught had nothing except what Roxane had allowed and Death's Queen would surely have claimed him . . . if he'd been dead.

"I'm alive?"

He paused for a heartbeat's time and went immediately back to moving the Stepson, as they had ordered. What man could bear to lose such a precious gift? But he tugged more gently now; Strat, whatever he had meant with his gesture, had given him life. He pushed the kitchen door shut with his foot and wiped the spittle from the fallen man's chin.

"Kill me," Strat begged when Stilcho bent over him.

Their eyes locked. Stilcho felt himself assaulted and dragged to a level of consciousness he had never, living or dead, imagined.

Strat was going to be tortured; was going to be systematically stripped of every image his memory held. Death would spare him nothing but the pain and, for Strat, the pain would not be the true torture. Stilcho remembered his own torture at Moruth's hands. He shrank with the knowledge that no little heroics, like a slash to the carotid, would spare this man. He had never, at his best, risen above little heroics but he would now, for Straton. The determination came instantaneously and suffused the resurrected man with a glow that would have chilled the Nisi witches beyond the door—had they seen it.

"It won't work, Ace," he informed the Stepson as he contrived to make him a bit more comfortable on the floor. "Think of something else. Think of lies until you believe them. Haught can't see the truth; he can only see what *you* believe is the truth." He ripped a corner from Strat's blood-soaked tunic and tucked it up his sleeve. "Don't fight them; just lie."

Strat blinked and groaned. Stilcho hoped he'd understood. There wasn't time for more. The door was opening. He prayed he wouldn't have to watch.

"I said the table," Haught said in his soft, malice-laden voice.

Stilcho shrugged and thought, carefully, about being dead. But Haught had no energy for the likes of him, not with Roxane—Stilcho's empty eye *saw* Roxane, not Tasfalen—hovering behind him and Strat helpless at his feet.

"Find me Tempus's secrets," a man's voice with strange, menacing inflections commanded. "If they hide the son from me, I'll have the father."

The witch produced the globe from wherever she had hidden it. Stilcho clutched his sleeve where the bloody cloth was hidden and backed toward the door. They didn't notice him leaving—or perhaps they did. They were laughing, a laughter that rose in pitch until it blended with the maniacal whine of the globe itself. But they didn't call him back as he edged around the newel-post and slunk upstairs.

It was not difficult to find Moria. She had only gotten to her bedroom doorway before succumbing to the horror around her. Stilcho found her with her arms wrapped around her ankles and her Rankan-gold hair spilling past her knees onto the floor.

"Moria!"

She lifted her head to look at him—blankly at first, then wide-eyed. Her breath sucked in and held, ready to scream if he came any closer.

"Moria, snap out of it," he demanded in an urgent whisper. Her scream was nothing more than a series of mewling squeaks as she scuttled away from him. She froze, except for her eyes, when her spine butted into the wainscoting. Stilcho, no stranger to utter terror himself, felt pity for her but had no time to give in to it. Grabbing her wrist he hauled her, one-handed, to her feet and slapped her hard when the mewling threatened to become something louder.

"For godssakes get control of yourself—if you want to live through this at all." He shook her hard and she went silent, but alert, in his arms. "Where's a window that overlooks the street?" He had never willingly come to the uptown house, never wanted to remember the times that he had.

Moria pulled back from him. Her bodice, much torn and retied, fell down from her shoulders. She did not seem to notice but Stilcho, with death still in his nostrils and hell itself downstairs in the kitchen, knew beyond all doubt that he was as alive as he had ever been.

"Moria, help me." He took her arm again. Haught hadn't slighted her with his magic: tear-streaked and disheveled she retained her beauty. O gods, he wanted to go on living.

"You're . . . you're—" She put a hand out to touch the good side of his face.

"A window," he repeated even after she fell against him, burying her face in a shirt that had seen better days. "Moria, a window—if we're going to help him and save ourselves."

She pointed at the window beyond her bed and sank back to the floor when he left her to fight, oh so silently, with its casement.

Stilcho panicked for a second when the salt-rusted window swung wide open. Not from the noise, because Strat screamed then, but from the wards he could see shimmering like whorehouse silks flush against the outer walls. He forgot to breathe until his heart pounded and his vision blurred, but it seemed the wards were for larger forces and were not affected by the iron-and-glass casement.

The horse was still out there: Strat's bay horse that Ischade had painstakingly restored to life. It danced away from the fires burning beyond the wards and the occasional bravo racing down the street but it had no intention of abandoning its vigil—not even when Stilcho reached out to it as he had learned to reach for all of Ischade's creations. Eyes that were red, vengeful, and not at all equine regarded him for a moment, then turned away.

Stilcho stepped back from the window, smiling. He retained the ability to see the workings of magic but magic no longer took notice of him. It was a very small price to pay for the ordinary sensations returning to him. Moreover, it was one he had anticipated. He grabbed a handful of rumpled linen from the bed and had begun tearing it into strips before he noticed Moria huddled on the floor.

"Get dressed."

She stood up, examining the tangled ribbons of her bodice. Heaving an exasperated sigh, Stilcho dropped the sheets and gripped her wrists. The soft flesh of her breasts rested against his hands.

"Gods, Moria—your clothes, *Moria's* clothes! You can't get out of here dressed like that."

Moria's face lost its complete vacantness as the idea penetrated through her terror that Stilcho—living, breathing Stilcho—would somehow get her out of here. She yanked the ribbons free, tearing the dress and its memories from her, diving into the ornate chests where, beneath the courtesan's trappings which Ischade had endowed her with, her stained and tattered street clothes remained.

She made a fair amount of noise in her industry, hurling unwanted lace and satin to the floor behind her, but between the globe's whine and Strat's screams it was doubtful that anyone in the kitchen heard or cared about the commotion upstairs. Stilcho finished ripping the linen.

Blood would draw the bay horse. Stilcho pulled the bloody rag from his sleeve and tied it to the linen. He'd used blood to bring the dead across water into the upper town. Strat's blood would bring the horse into conflict with the wards, chipping away at the flaws in them.

"What are you doing?" Moria demanded, forcing the last of the rounded, Rankan contours into a now snug Ilsigi tunic.

"Making a blood lure," he replied, lowering the makeshift rope and swinging the dull red knot at its end toward the horse.

She bounded across the room. "No. No!" she protested, struggling to take the cloth from him. "They'll see; they'll know. We can get out across the roof."

Stilcho held her off with one arm and went back to swinging the lure. "Wards," he muttered. He had the bay's attention now. Its eyes, in his other vision, were brighter; its coat rippled with crimson anger.

But wards and warding had no meaning to Moria, though she was one of Ischade's. She rammed stiff fingers into his gut and made a lunge for freedom. It was all he could go to grab her around the waist, keeping her barely inside the house. The linen slipped from his hands and fluttered to the street below. Moria whimpered; he pressed her face against his chest to muffle the sound. Ward-fire, invisible to her but excruciating nonetheless, dazzled her hands and forearms.

"We're trapped!" she gasped. "Trapped!"

Hysteria rose in her face again. He grabbed her wrists, knowing the pain would shock her into silence.

"That's Strat down there. *Straton!* They'll come for him. The horse will bring them, Moria. Ischade, Tempus: they'll all come for him—and us."

"No, no," she repeated, her eyes white all around. "Not Her. Not *Her*—"

Stilcho hesitated. He remembered that fear; that all-consuming fear he felt of Ischade, of Haught, of everything that had had power over him—but he'd forgotten it as well. Death had burned the fear out of him. He felt danger, desperation, and the latent death that pervaded this house and this afternoon—but bowel-numbing fear no longer had a claim on him.

"I'm going to save Strat—hide him until they come for him. I'm going to save me, too. I'm lucky today, Moria: I'm alive and I'm lucky. Even without the horse. . . ."

But he wasn't without the bay horse. The bloody rag had landed on the carved stone steps that had been, many years ago, the Peres family's pride. The bay pounded on the steps, surrounded but unaffected by ward-fire. It scented Strat's blood soaking into the wood planks of the lower hallway and heard his anguish. Trumpeting a loyalty that transcended life and death, it reared, flailing at the ephemeral flames which engulfed it. Stilcho watched as the mortal image of the horse vanished and the *other* one became a black void.

"Moria, the back stairs, the servant's stairs to the kitchen, where are they? It's only a matter of time."

Candlelight flickered over Ischade's dark-clad body. She had collapsed backwards into her silken lair. Her hair made tangled webs around her face and shoulders. One arm arced around her head, the other fell limply across her waist; both were marked with dark gashes where the priest's glass had cut her. Ischade had death-magic, not healing.

She was, if not oblivious to her exhausted body, unmindful of it. If her efforts were successful there would be time enough for rest and recovery. She continued manipulating the bonds which made all she had ever owned a focus for her power. She set resonances at each flawed boundary, reinforced them as motes of warding eroded away and tried not to feel the tremors that were Straton.

It was not her way to move with such delicate precision— but it was the only way she had left. Balancing her power through every focal object within the Peres house which could contain it, she hoped to build her presence until she could pull from all directions and burst the warding sphere Roxane had created. She had discarded the thread tying her to the bay horse. She had never regarded the creature as *hers* but only as a gift, a rare gift, to her lover. Thus the moment when it had scented Strat's blood passed unnoticed but the instant when it penetrated the wards was seared into her awareness.

Her first response was a heartfelt curse for whatever was causing havoc in her neat, tedious work. The curse soared and circled the wards until Ischade understood she had an ally within the house. She examined the small skein of living and dead within whom she had a focus and found that one, Stilcho, was no longer anchored. Stilcho, whom Haught had stolen and fate had set to living freedom.

Smiling, she pushed her imperceptible awareness past the ward-consuming emptiness.

"Haught," she whispered, weaving into his mind. *"Remember your father. Remember Wizardwall. Remember slavery. Remember the feel of the globe in your hands before she stole it from you. She does not love you, Haught. Does not love your fine Nisi face while she wears a Rankan one. Does not love your aptness while she is trapped in a body that has none. Oh, remember, Haught; remember every time you look on that face."*

The ambitious mind of the ex-slave, ex-dancer, ex-apprentice shivered when Ischade touched it. Foolish child—he had believed she would not look for him again and had taken none of the simple steps to ensure that she could not. She sealed her hypnotic surgery with a gentle caress on the ring he wore: the ring he had thought to use against her.

Ischade retreated, then, behind the little statues, the gewgaws and the sharp knives she had scattered throughout the house. Her thoughts would eat at a mind already disposed to treason just as the essence of the bay horse ate the ward-fire. It was only a matter of time.

"You have to eat. Magic can't do everything."

Randal opened his mouth to agree and received a great wooden spoonful of Jihan's latest aromatic posset. His eyes bulged, his ears reddened, and he wanted nothing more than to spit the godsawful curdled lump to the floor. But the Froth Daughter was watching him and he dared do nothing but swallow it in one horrendous gulp. His hands were immobilized in gauze slings, suspended in oval buckets filled with a salted solution of the Froth Daughter's devising. His own magical resources were insufficient to guide the spoon to his mouth— if he had been so inclined in the first place.

He had been to the Mageguild and found his treatment there even less pleasant. Get rid of the globe; get rid of the demon; get rid of the witches, his colleagues had told him—and don't come home again until you do. So he'd come back to the palace to be tended by Jihan and to fret over the way fate was unfolding for him.

"You tried," Jihan assured him, setting the bowl aside. "You did your best."

"I failed. I knew what happened and I let her trick me. Niko would have understood; I knew that Niko would have understood why we had him down here. But I listened to her instead." He shook his head in misery; a lock of hair fell down to cover his eyes. Jihan leaned forward to brush it back, moving carefully to avoid the shiny, less severe burns on his face or the singed, almost bald, portion of his scalp that still smelled of the fire.

"We've all made more than our share of mistakes in this," Tempus commiserated from the doorway. He unfastened his cloak, letting it drop to the floor as he strode across the room. The hypocaust fires had been banked for two days but the room was still the warmest, by far, in the palace. "How is he?" he asked when he stood beside Niko.

The young man's body showed few traces of his ordeal. The swellings and bruises had all but disappeared; his face, in sleep, was serene and almost smiling.

"Better than he should be," Jihan said sadly. She laid her hand lightly on Niko's forehead. The half-smile vanished and the hell-haunted mercenary strained against the leather straps binding him to the pallet. "The demon has his body completely now and heals as it wishes," she acknowledged, lifting her hand. Niko, or his body, quieted.

"You're sure?"

She shrugged, reached for Niko again, then restrained that impulse by gripping Tempus's arm instead. "As sure as I am of anything where he's concerned."

"Riddler?" The hazel eyes flickered open but they did not focus and the voice, though it had the right timbre, was not Niko's. "Riddler, is that you?"

"Gods—no," Tempus took a step forward then hesitated. "Janni?" he whispered.

The body that contained the demon and Janni and whatever remained of Nikodemos writhed and pulled its lips back into a skull-like grin.

"The globe, Riddler. Abarsis. The globe. Break the globe!"

Its fingers splayed backwards, seeming to have no bone within them; its neck snapped from side to side with force enough to make the wooden slats jump. Tempus rushed to weave his hands through Niko's slate-gray hair, cushioning the other-world tortures with his own flesh.

"Do something for him!" he bellowed as the spasms rocked Niko's body and blood began to seep from his nose and lips.

"Do something for him!"

The demon's mocking echo erupted from somewhere in Niko's gut. Sparks sizzled along Tempus's forearm, paralyzing him. Niko's arms, no longer trembling, strained purposefully against the leather straps.

"It's going to transfer!" Randal screamed, leaping up from his chair. He gestured with burn-twisted fingers. His will called forth fire but his ruined flesh could not support it. Groaning, he sank to his knees.

"Poor little mageling," the familiar voice issuing from a shimmering blue globe chuckled with strychnine sweetness. "Let me fix that for you." A tongue of indigo flame licked out from the globe; Randal, like Tempus, was motionless.

Jihan took a deep breath that formed ice in the salt-water buckets an arm's length away. She had been patient with these mortals, abiding by their constraints, accepting their wisdom even when it contradicted everything her instincts demanded, and now that they were finally helpless she was going to do things *her* way.

Niko turned endless, empty eyes toward the blue sphere, asking a silent question.

"Stormbringer's Froth," Roxane replied, with the malice and disdain reserved by women for lesser women.

A frigid wind swirled through the once-warm room. No one, especially a Nisi witch or a nameless demon, spoke that way about Jihan and survived. No matter that Stormbringer had created his parthenogenic offspring from an arctic sea storm, Jihan knew an insult when she felt one. She pelted the sphere with a thick glaze of ice, then she leaned her palms on Niko's chest.

"I'm here!" she announced, bringing a howl of cold air into Niko's rest-place. "I'm here, damn you."

She rode her anger across the once-beautiful landscape of a *maat*-endowed mind. The dark crystal stream roiled and froze in agonized shapes. Charred trees snapped and crashed to the ground under the burden of the ice that came in her wake. She reached the meadow where the pure light of Janni guarded the gate.

"I'm going in," she told him, though she had no communion with such spirits and could not hear nor understand his reply.

The heavy door with its man-thick iron bars loomed before her. Leaving a pattern of rime on the metal, she passed beyond it to confront an eternity as vast and empty as the demon-Niko's eyes had been.

"Coward!" the Froth Daughter shrieked as nothingness, which was the essence of all demonkind, leeched her substance away. She lashed out blindly, stupidly expending herself against an enemy whose chief attribute was its absence. *"Cowar—"*

She retreated, a ragged wisp streaming back to the frost-bound doorway, and collapsed in the meadow, her fury and her confidence equally diminished. Demonic laughter using her own stolen voice compounded her shame. In her impotence Jihan gathered shards of ice and hurled them at the gate.

"I'll be back," she told it as the ice melted into the thawing crystal stream. "You'll see."

She sniffled and wiped her eyes on a damp forearm. The ground was slick with melting ice; she slipped more than once. Pain and cold became part of her mortal vocabulary as she made her way home, never once looking back to see that the meadow was brighter or the crystal stream rushing fast and clear.

"I thought we'd lost her," Tempus admitted as he watched the Froth Daughter pick her way slowly across the hillside.

We? Do we care? Stormbringer inquired in a dangerously friendly tone.

Tempus didn't bother to turn around. He wouldn't be wherever he suddenly was without some god or another's interference; and he was no longer awed by interference. "I care— isn't that obvious? She damn near annihilated herself for me."

Your care is not enough. She is mortal now and requires something less abstract. If love is beyond you, surely you remember rape? The Father-of-Weather manifested himself before Tempus: all blood-red eyes and parts that did not become a single whole.

The man who had been Vashanka's minion shrugged his nonexistent shoulders and gave the god a critical glance. "It is an option *I* retain," he said defiantly.

You are a nasty little man—but I have need of you—

"No."

She is a goddess.

"No."

I'll attend to this abomination.

"You'll do that regardless—for what it did to her. The answer's still no."

I'll turn my daughter's eyes toward another.

"It's a deal."

The Stormchildren lay in state on a velvet-covered dais in the vault-ceilinged room known as the Ilsig Bedchamber. Musicians gathered in an alcove, playing the reedy, discordant melodies beloved by the Beysib and guaranteed to set Molin Torchholder's neck hairs on end. He pressed his forefingers against the bridge of his nose and sought a pleasant thought, any pleasant thought, that might make the waiting easier.

Shupansea, in a curtained alcove opposite the musicians, was equally anxious but had not the luxury of isolation. Her waiting-women swarmed around her fussing with her hair, her jewels, and the splendor of her *cosa*. She was the Beysa this evening—as she had not been since her cousin's execution in the summer. Her breasts had been dusted with luminous powders and gilt with gold and silver; her normally slender hips were augmented by the swaying brocade-jeweled panniers in which her personal vipers were accustomed to ride. Her thigh-length fair hair had been supported and wired until it hung about her like a cloak and condemned her to look neither up nor down, nor side to side, but only straight ahead. It was a costume she had worn since childhood but now, after a season in the modest attire of the Rankan nobility, she felt awkward and feared for the outcome of the rites they were about to perform.

"You must not sweat," her aunt chided her, reminding her of the physical discipline demanded of Mother Bey's avatar.

She steeled herself and the offending perspiration ceased.

Footsteps came through the tiny doorway behind her. "You're nervous," a welcome voice consoled her as the prince reached out to take her hand.

"Our priests would have us wait until the fifth decoction has been made but we dare not. Not after this afternoon. We have countermanded the priests; it is the first time we have done so. They are anxious but we think the waiting is more dangerous than success or failure."

"Mother Bey guides you," Kadakithis assured her, squeezing the be-ringed fingers ever so gently.

Shupansca lifted her shoulders a fraction. "She says only that I must not be alone afterwards."

The prince, who had finally edged his way through her women to stand where she could see him, made a wry face. "You are never alone, Shu-sea."

She smiled and gave him a stare which proved Beysib eyes could be erotic and unsettling at the same time. "I will be alone tonight—with you."

The music changed abruptly. Before the golden-haired prince could express his surprise or pleasure he was politely, but firmly, shoved to one side.

"It is time."

The Beysa came forward onto a cloth-of-gold carpet laid between the alcove and the altar. Her first steps were tentative; she tottered between the outstretched arms of her waiting-women. Her glazed eyes held no power, only simple terror of the ancient bald priest who waited for her with a delicate glass vial and a knife of razor-sharp obsidian.

Her beynit vipers, tasting the incense and the music, rose from the panniers to begin their own journey. Shupansea trembled involuntarily as the scales slid coldly between her thighs—for the *cosa* was meant for the display and convenience of the snakes, not the avatar. Three sets of fangs sank deep into sensitive skin: the beynit did not approve of her anxiety. Venom enough for the deaths of a dozen men shot into her. She gasped then relaxed as the languid strength of Mother Bey enveloped her.

She raised her arms, lifting the *cosa* away from her body. The serpents emerged, baring their moist fangs and their vermilion mouths. It was her priest's turn to tremble anxiously. The Beysib priest summoned Molin to the altar where, without ceremony or explanation, the ancient, bald man transferred the ritual artifacts from the old order to the new and ran from the room.

Molin held both with evident discomfort and outright fear. "What do I do?" he whispered hoarsely.

"Complete the ceremony," the voice he had last heard in Stormbringer's swirling universe informed him from Shupansea's mouth. "Carefully."

Torchholder nodded. The vial contained blood from the Stormchildren, venom from the snake Niko had slain with Aškelon's weapons, and ichor from Roxane's giant serpent which had been combined and distilled four times over with powders the Beysib priests knew but had no names for. The scent of its vapors could kill a man; a drop of the fluid might poison an army. Molin intended to be very careful.

"The vial first," the avatar informed him. "Poured on the knife edge and offered to each of our children."

Molin remained slack-jawed and motionless.

"The snakes," Shupansea's normal voice whispered, but the Rankan priest did not begin to move. "Hold your breath," she added after a long pause.

He had once said to Randal that he did whatever had to be done, be it moving the Globe of Power or unstoppering the lethal glass teardrop. He held his breath and tried not to notice the green-tinged fumes or the sizzling sound the liquid made as it ate through the carpet and on into the granite beneath. The obsidian shook when he extended it toward the smallest of the serpents—the one with its leaf-nosed head resting on the Beysa's right nipple. He was prepared to die in any number of unpleasant ways.

The beynit's tongue flicked a half-dozen or more times before it consented to add a glistening drop of venom to the sulphurous ooze already congealing on the knife edge—and it was the most decisive of the lot. His lungs strained to bursting and his vision drifting amid black motes of unconsciousness, Molin faced the avatar again.

Shupansea held her hands out palms upward. He looked down and saw the lattice-work of uncountable knife-scars there. During his youthful days with the armies he had killed more times than he cared to remember, and killed women more than once as well, but he hesitated—for once unable to do what had to be done.

"Quickly!" Shupansea commanded.

But he did not move and it fell to her to grab the knife, letting its noisome edges sink deep. *O Mother!* she prayed as her blood carried its searing burden toward her heart. It was too soon. The priests had said wait for the fifth decoction; they had abandoned their offices rather than preside at her death. The serpents plunged their fangs into her breasts many times over but it would not be enough. Not even the presence of Mother Bey within her would be enough to change the malignancy Roxane had created. Clenching her fingers together, the Beysa heard the rough edge of the knife grind into bone but she felt nothing.

She fainted, although the lifelong discipline of Mother Bey's avatar was such that she did not topple to the ground. Still, she was oblivious to the agony when the imperfect decoction reached her heart and stopped it.

She did not hear the collective gasp that rose from Beysib and Rankan alike when her eyes rolled white and the three serpents stiffened to rise two-thirds of their length above her shuddering breasts.

She did not feel Molin let go of the knife or see him ignore the hissing beynit to hold her upright when even discipline faded.

She did not hear Kadakithis's enraged shout or the slapping of his sandals across the stone as he raced to take her from the priest's arms.

She experienced nothing at all until the prince's tears fell into her open eyes then she blinked and *stared* up at him.

"We've done it," she explained with a faint smile, letting
the now-harmless knife fall from her scarred, but uncut, hands.

But barely. Shupansea lacked the strength to gather the drops
of blood now welling up on her breast in a second, pristine
vial; nor could she take that vial and place its contents on the
lips of first Gyskouras, then Arton. Her eyes were closed while
everyone else prayed that the changed blood would awaken the
Stormchildren and they remained that way when the two boys
began to move and a chorus of thanks rose from the assembly.

"She needs rest," the prince told the *staring* women around
them. "Call her guards and have her carried back to her rooms."

"She is alone with All-Mother," the eldest of the women
explained. "We do not interfere."

Kadakithis blinked with disbelief. "The goddess isn't going
to carry her to bed, is she?" he demanded of their glass-eyed
silence. "Well, dammit, then—*I'll* carry her."

He was a slight young man compared to any of the profes-
sional soldiers in his service, but he'd been trained in all the
manly arts and lifted her weight with ease. The trailing *cosa*
tangled in his legs, very nearly defeating him until he planted
both feet on the gilt brocade and ripped the cloth from its
frames. The beynit, their venom temporarily expended, slithered quickly out of his way.

"She is alone with me," he informed them all, striding out
of the bedchamber with the Beysa cradled in his arms.

Molin watched as they went through the doorway—turning
left for the prince's suite rather than right toward hers. He sup-
pressed a smile as the snakes found safe harbor with the other
Beysib women, not all of whom were so comfortable with a serpent spiraling under their garments as Shupansea had been.

Unimpressed by the ceremony surrounding them, the Stormchildren behaved as if just awakened from their daily nap. They
had already pulled the velvet hangings from the altar. Arton
twisted the cloth around his head in unconscious imitation of
his S'danzo mother's headgear while Gyskouras put all his
efforts into wrenching the golden tassels free from its corners.

The archpriest turned to his single acolyte, Isambard, who
could scarcely be expected to control the Stormchildren when
they became either adventurous or cantankerous—which they
were certain to do. "Isambard, go downstairs to the hypocaust
room and remind Jihan that the children need her more than

anyone else." The young man bowed, backed away, then scampered from the room.

Molin then turned his attention to the Beysibs in the room. The musicians he dismissed immediately, sending them on their way with only the most perfunctory of compliments. The women *stared* at him, defying him to give them orders as they gathered up the discarded *cosa* and bore it reverently from the chamber. This left him with a double-handful of priests, their foreheads still bent to the ground, who had been left to him by Mother Bey's high priest.

Ignoring the holes and the sacrilege, he paced the length of the gold carpet and back again. "I think a feast is in order: a private feast. Something delicate and easily shared: shellfish, perhaps, and such fruit as remains in the pantries. And wine— watered, I should think. It would not do to dull their appetites." He paused, waiting to see which shiny head would move first.

"You'll see to this." He pointed his finger at the most curious of the lot; with their bald skulls, bulging eyes, billowing tunics, and pantaloons, the Beysib men all looked alike to him. He seldom thought of them as individuals.

The Beysib he had addressed cleared his throat nervously and the one at the front of their triangular formation pushed himself slowly to his knees. "The priests of All-Mother Bey serve only Her transcending aspects. We . . . that is, You, the Regum Bey, do not serve the Avatar," he explained.

Torchholder leaned forward to grip the other man's pectoral ornament. Reversing it with a quick snap, he used the golden chain as a simple garrotte. "The Beysa will be hungry. My prince will be hungry," he said in the soft, intense voice his own people had come to fear.

"It has never been so," the Beysib protested, his face darkening as the Rankan priest hauled him to his feet.

"There is a first time for everything. This could be the first time you visit the kitchens or it could be the first time you die. . . ." Molin gave the pectoral another quarter turn.

It was true that the Beysib could show white all around their eyes even when they were *staring*. The priest gasped and clung to Torchholder's wrist with both hands. "Yes, Lord Torch- holder."

The mosaic floor of the hypocaust room was hidden under icy, ankle-deep water. Isambard removed his one-and-only pair of sandals and tied them together over his shoulder before stepping into it. With his lantern held high he moved cautiously, knowing there had been snakes down here once and not knowing if the cold water would stop them.

"Most Reverend Lady Jihan?" he inquired into the darkness, addressing her as he would have addressed Molin's long-absent wife.

Silence.

"Most Reverend Lady?" he repeated, sloshing a few steps further.

They were all heaped together on the pallet where they had tied the demon-possessed mercenary, Nikodemos: Jihan, Tempus, Randal, and possibly Nikodemos himself—Isambard couldn't be sure in this light. They weren't dead, or not all of them anyway, because someone was snoring.

"Great Vashanka—Giver of Victories; Gatherer of Souls—abide with me on Your battlefield."

Lantern rattling in his hand, the acolyte moved forward. He cleared one of the great columns that continued upward all the way to the Hall of Justice. A faint light reflected off the water—a faint *blue* light such as his lantern could never cast. His heart seized with panic and his gut tumbling with fear, Isambard turned around.

A column of ice loomed midway between the bodies and the far wall. Within it a blue sphere the size and height of his head throbbed; water cascaded to the floor with each rising pulse. The light grew brighter, calling to him. He walked toward it: one step, two steps, three—and put his foot down squarely on the sharpened clasp of Tempus's discarded cloak. The pain jolted him backward and backward and broke the spell.

He had left the room before he had time to scream.

Roxane had been within the Globe of Power longer than was prudent especially since her bond with life was through Tasfalen—who was dead and already beginning to ripen. With her reacquisition of a globe, the Nisi witch was powerful beyond comparison but even she could not do all the things which Sanctuary's situation required at once. She had a demon hounding her now, as well as all the other enemies she had accumulated since the first battles were fought along Wizardwall. The strain of uprooting her soul so many times was starting to show. She was getting careless—being gone so long, leaving a freshly claimed sack of bones like Tasfalen without ensuring that it was life-worthy.

Haught, who was frequently foolish but never careless, knelt beside Straton's unconscious body on the floor of the Peres house kitchen. The interrogation Haught had promised his new mistress/master was going worse than slowly. In his delirium, the Stepson made no distinctions between truth and imagination; wandering, his mind had given Haught no more than tantalizing hints about Ischade or Tempus—plus a throbbing headache.

He comprehended smaller healings like the slash on Moria's foot; he could tamper with the magic of his betters as he had when he'd exerted his control over Stilcho but he lacked the complex magical vocabulary necessary to contend directly with the inertia of a dead or mortally wounded body. He had failed with Tasfalen; the Rankan noble's body had turned a pasty shade of blue and its stiffness, when Roxane returned, would be far more serious than muscle cramps. But Tasfalen had been Haught's first attempt; he had already learned from those mistakes—and Straton was not dead.

The would-be witch studied Tasfalen's silver-white eyes. A touch from the globe and he'd have the power to mend Strat's body enough that the Stepson would no longer have his retreat into delirium and imagination. He'd unwind the man's secrets like so much silk from a cocoon and present his mistress/master with a portion of it.

Just a touch.

A piece of Haught swiped out toward the Globe of Power like a child dragging a finger through the icing on a cake. He had enough to heal and a bit to hide for the future but he hesitated. The wards were wrong: weakened, eroded, vanishing. He reached a little farther and had a vision of an equine face surrounded by ward-fire; consuming the ward-fire—

"Impudent slime! Ice water! Damn *her!* And you—"

The voice was Tasfalen's but the inflection was all Nisi and malice. The witch swung a clublike open hand at him, striking with the force of a Wizardwall avalanche. Haught heard his spine crack against the far wall and felt the blood streaming from his nose and mouth.

She does not love you, a nameless voice rose out of Haught's memory. *Remember your father:* a wind-filled husk of flayed skin when the Wizardwall masters had finished with him. Haught shook the blood from his hand and healed as the witch ranted, cursed, and swallowed the globe.

Haught was against the cupboard where Shiey kept the knives. Silently he called one to his sleeve and held it against his forearm when he meekly rose and followed his mistress/master from the room. He said nothing about the wards or his vision.

Stilcho crept back up the stairway to the dark landing where Moria waited.

"It's now or never," he told the quiet woman, grateful he could not see her face when he found her wrist and led her back down the stairs.

There were two stairways leading to the kitchen of the Peres house: one came up from the larder and pantries in the basement, the other ascended to the servant's quarters under the eaves. Both had been occupied. Stilcho opened the door to face the malevolent leer of the household's cook, Shiey. He knew that face—the last face his missing eye had seen—and it turned his bowels to ice. His resolve and his courage vanished; Moria's hand fell from his trembling fingers.

"We're taking Straton to the stables," Moria said in a soft but firm whisper as she stepped out of Stilcho's shadow. She had her own fears of these servants whom the beggar-king Moruth had provided for the house and she had learned how to hide those fears long ago. "You and you," she pointed to the burliest pair, "take his feet." She looked up to Stilcho.

Giving the one-handed cook a lingering glower, the one-eyed man took position at the Stepson's shoulders.

"We'll get him into the lofts, if we can. And we'll wait for the help that's going to be coming—from everywhere."

"An' if'n it don't?" Shiey demanded.

"We burn the stables around us."

They grumbled but they had been listening as well; none disagreed. Moria held the outer door for the men while Shiey gave her cupboards a final inspection.

"Took my best cleaver, didn't he?" She prowled quickly through the cutlery, slipping her favorite implements through the leather loops of her belt. "Here, lady." She spun around and flipped a serrated poultry knife the length of the room. Moria felt the hardwood hilt smack into her palm before she'd consciously decided to catch the knife rather than dodge it. "Ain't nothin' can't be hurt wi' a good knife," Shiey informed her with a grin.

• • •

Walegrin shoved the trencher to one side. Whatever the barracks' cooks had thrown into the dinner pot smelled as bad as the smoke he had breathed all afternoon, and tasted worse. He had men still out in the streets—more than a dozen good men, not including Thrusher, who had yet to return from his special private assignment. Maybe the palace had good reason for wanting plague sign splashed over every other color of graffiti out there; he hoped they did. The populace was reacting with predictable panic.

He'd kept his men busy fighting but now the sun was down. A Rankan oar-barge flying Vashanka's long-absent standard had tied up at the wharf, its passengers and cargo under imaginary quarantine. No one had yet seen a disease-slain corpse; rumors were getting wilder and darker with each retelling. So far Walegrin didn't believe any of them, but some of the men were showing doubt at the edges and the night had just begun.

Before he could decide on a course of action, the door to his quarters slammed open admitting one of the veterans who'd been with him for years.

"Thrush's at the West Gate with Cythen. They've got a body between 'em an' they say they won't give it over."

"Bloody hells," the commander exclaimed, crumpling his cloak in one fist. "Watch the pot, Zump. I'll be back."

He went down the stairs at a run. He'd believed in Kama; believed in the mugs of ale she'd downed with Strat and him a scant week ago. He'd believed she hadn't put an arrow in Straton and believed she was smart and wary enough to keep herself alive after it'd happened.

The temporary palace morgue was just beyond the public gallows. It glowed faintly in the late twilight. With plague sign up the gravesmen were taking no chances and had laid a fair carpet of quicklime beneath their feet. Thrush was arguing loudly with his escort as Walegrin approached.

"As you were," he commanded, positioning himself carefully between the gravesmen and the shrouded corpse. "What's the problem?"

"It's gotta stay here," the chief digger said, pointing to the dark object behind Walegrin's feet.

Thrusher sucked on his teeth. "But, Commander, he's one of ours: Malm. He deserves the rites inside—beside the men he served with for the last time."

Malm had died two years back and had never stood high in Thrush's estimation. Walegrin peered into the darkness. His friend's face was unreadable. Still, he'd known Thrusher for thirteen years: if the little man wouldn't leave Kama's body with the gravedigger's there had to be a good reason.

"We tend our own," he told the gravesmen.

"The plague, sir. Orders: *your* orders."

It was easy for the straw-blond commander to lose his temper. "My man hasn't got the plague, damn you. He's got a big, bloody hole where his stomach used to be! Take him to the barracks, Thrush—*now!*"

Thrush and Cythen needed no urging to heave the sagging burden to their shoulders and double-time it across the parade-ground while Walegrin dueled silently with the gravediggers.

"Got to tell 'em," the gravesman said, looking away as he cocked a thumb toward the Hall of Justice dome. "Orders're orders. Even them's that make 'em can't break 'em."

Walegrin ran a hand through the ragged hair that had escaped the bronze circlet on his brow. "Take the message to Molin Torchholder, personally then. Tell him Vashanka's rites want performing in the barracks—plague or no plague."

The least of the diggers headed for the hall. Walegrin waited a moment, then turned back toward the barracks, quite pleased with himself. Until the gravesman threatened him, he hadn't been certain how he was going to get a message to his mentor without drawing the wrong kind of attention.

"Upstairs—Cythen's room," Zump said as soon as he'd crossed the barracks' threshold. Every one of the half-dozen men in the room was watching him. But at least they weren't thinking about plague or imperial barges. Walegrin forced himself to walk slowly as he climbed the half-flight of stairs to where Cythen, the only woman billeted with the regular garrison, slept.

Thrush and Cythen stood guard outside the open door.

"How is she?" Walegrin asked as they slid the bolt open.

"I'm fine," Kama assured him herself, swinging long, leather-clad legs off of Cythen's bed.

A dark smear covered most of the right side of her face but it seemed mostly soot. She wasn't moving like she'd taken too much punishment.

"I guess I owe you my life," she said uncomfortably.

"I didn't think you'd kill Strat. You'd had too many opportunities before—better opportunities. And you wouldn't care if he was shacked up with the witch."

She scowled. "You're right on the first, anyway."

"Piffles, Chief," Thrusher interjected from the open doorway. "Two of them guarding the cellar we found her in."

Kama stood in front of Walegrin, looking through and beyond him. She had that way about her—even dressed in scratched and rag-tied leather she had elegance and, however unconsciously, the powerful demeanor of her father. The garrison commander never had the upper hand with her.

"Personal?" he stammered.

"Personal? *Personal?* Gods, no. They saw me with Strat and you. They thought I'd sold out—nothing personal about that," she snapped.

Then why lock her up and put an arrow in Strat? And why Strat and not him?—he was every bit as easy to find. It was personal, all right, as personal as the sharp-faced PFLS leader could make it.

"You've got worse problems," Walegrin told her.

Finally she turned away, watching the lamp-flame as if it were the center of the universe. "Yeah, so they tell me. He used one of Jubal's arrows, didn't he? All hell broke loose, didn't it?"

Walegrin couldn't suppress a bitter laugh. "Not quite. Came close. Seems someone came out of the witch's house an' dragged Strat back in. Stepsons thought they'd go in to rescue him. Found the place'd been warded: Nisi warded—like you'd remember, I guess. Old Critias lit back for the palace and found out that Roxane'd broken out of wherever she'd been hiding and went there 'cause some slave-apprentice of Ischade's'd stolen a Globe of Power and stashed it there. So, no, hell didn't quite break out—it's sort of holed up there in the old Peres place."

Kama ran her hands through her hair. Her shoulders sagged and when she turned around again she looked straight at Walegrin. "There's more, isn't there." She didn't make it a question.

"Yeah. There's a boat down at the wharf with Vashanka's arrows flying from its mast. They say it's Brachis at the least and maybe our new Emperor as well. Can't be sure because we've told them the town's under plague sign: no one from Sanctuary's been on board; no one's gotten off either. Whatever it is, it's got the whole damn palace fired up. They mean to have the town quiet if they have to kill every known trouble-maker before sunrise—and your name's at the top of everyone's list. Word was that you didn't even have to be brought in alive."

"Crit?" she asked. "Tempus?"

Walegrin nodded after both names. "Kama, the only Stepson who might not want you dead is inside the witch's house with bigger problems than you've got. The nabobs were in trouble anyway; Strat's arrow didn't make *their* problems but the way it's comin' down you'd think *you* stole the globe and let Roxane out."

"So what am I supposed to do? Hide the rest of my life? Climb to the highest rooftop and leap to my ignominious death? Maybe I'll just go back to Zip and the rest. I can take care of *that* myself, at least." She began pacing, though there was barely enough space between the bed and the wall for her to take two steps before turning. "I could get on that boat. Reach Theron, if he's there—"

The garrison regulars exchanged glances. Under no circumstances was anyone who knew what had been going on in Sanctuary going anywhere near that wharf without an arm-long scroll of permissions. Walegrin took a step forward, blocking Kama's path.

"I've sent word to Molin Torchholder. I told you about him. If there's anyone in the palace who'll understand the truth of this, it's him."

Kama stared in disbelief. "Molin's coming here?"

"To perform your funerary rites. The diggers went to get him. He'll come. He might not be too popular with you Wizardwall veterans but he takes care of Sanctuary. You can trust him—I told you that," Walegrin assured her, misreading the shadows that fell across Kama's face.

"How long?"

"I've sent word. He'll come as soon as he can. The Interiors," by whom he meant the few Rankan soldiers still on detail within the palace, "say there was some sort of big Beysib gathering around sunset—some sort of ritual. I don't know if he was involved or not. If he's got to eat with them he may not get here till midnight."

Kama strode to the little window overlooking the stables and a corner of the parade ground. She popped the shutters and leaned out into the night air.

"I'd just as soon you kept the windows closed and stayed out of sight," Walegrin requested, unable to give her a direct order.

An inaudible sigh ran the length of her back. She pulled the boards closed and stared expectantly at him. "I'm your prisoner, then?"

"Damn, woman—it's for your own good. No one's going to think of looking for you here—but I can't keep them out if they get a notion to look. If you've got any close friends you think you'd be safer with you just tell me about them and I'll see that you spend the night there."

Kama had pushed as hard and far as she dared—more from habit than grand design. "Is there any food left below?" she asked in a more civil voice, "or water?"

"Fish stew with fat-back, some wine. I'll send some up."

"And water, please—I'd like to wash before my funeral rites." She flashed the smile that made men forget she was deadly.

Torchholder, still garbed in the regalia he had worn when the Beysa had healed the Stormchildren, came to the garrison barracks flanked by the gravediggers. The diggers demanded to view the body but Molin, once he saw Walegrin's anxiety, dismissed them with a wave of his hand.

"Not before the rites," he snarled contemptuously. "Until the spirit is sanctified and released, the impure may not view the remains."

"Ain't no 'Shankan funeral *I've* ever heard of," the second of the gravediggers complained to his superior.

"The man was an initiate into Vashanka's Brotherhood. Would you risk the Stormgod's wrath?"

The gravediggers, like everyone else in Sanctuary, suspected that the Stormgod was impotent or vanquished but none of the trio was about to say so to a palace nobleman whose power in the simple matters of life and death was not in question. They agreed to return to their posts and await the delivery of the body. Molin watched the door close behind them, then pulled Walegrin back into the shadows.

"What in seven hells is going on here?"

"There's a bit of a problem," the younger man explained, drawing the priest up the stairs. "Someone you should talk to."

"Who've you got—?" Molin demanded as Walegrin knocked once, then shoved the door open.

Kama had put her time and the water to good use. The soot and grime were gone from her leathers and her face; her hair framed her face in a smooth, ebony curtain. Walegrin saw something he did not immediately understand pass silently between them.

"Kama," Torchholder said softly, refusing for the moment to cross the threshold. Throughout the afternoon and into the evening he had forced any thought of her from his mind; had, in effect, abandoned her to fate. He believed she would not have expected, or appreciated, anything else and saw by her face that he had believed correctly—but correctness did nothing to alleviate the backlash of self-imposed guilt which swept up around him.

"Shall I leave?" Walegrin asked, piecing the situation together finally.

Molin started; weighed a dozen responses and their probable consequences in his mind, and said: "No, stay here," before anyone could guess he had considered some other course of action. "Kama, why are you here, of all places?" he asked, closing the door behind him.

With Walegrin's help, she explained her situation. How the PFLS leader, Zip, had misinterpreted her encounter with Straton and Walegrin and how that mistake had started the downward spiral of events which culminated with not merely the attempt on the Stepson's life but the sabotage of all he had tried to accomplish.

Molin, though he listened attentively, took a few moments to congratulate himself. Had he dismissed Walegrin, he would have helped Kama because he loved her—and, in time, she would have rejected him for it. Now, he could help her because he had heard and believed her story before witnesses. She might still reject him—she would always prefer action to intrigue, he suspected—but it wouldn't be through the weakness called love.

"You have two choices, Kama," he explained when both she and Walegrin were silent. "No one would be surprised if you had died today. I could easily see to it that *everyone* believed that you had. You could take a horse from the stables and no one would ever think to come looking for you." He paused. "Or you can clear your name."

"I want my name," she replied without hesitation. "I'll appeal to the Emperor's justice. . . ." It was her turn to pause and calculate options. "Brachis—" She looked around the room and remembered the Stormchildren, the witches, and the irremedial absence of Vashanka. "I'll get the truth out of Zip," she concluded.

Molin shook his head and turned to Walegrin. "Would you believe anything that young man told you?"

Walegrin shook his head.

"No, Kama, maybe if Strat's still alive in there and *he* says it wasn't you, you'd be believed, but no one else's word will count for enough. You'll do best coming in to face your accusers."

"Under your protection?"

"Under Tempus's protection."

Walegrin broke into the conversation: "He's one of the ones who've ordered her dead!"

"He ordered her captured—the rest is the enthusiasm of his subordinates. He's got caught in another skirmish with the demon—and Roxane—for Niko's soul. Jihan barely pulled him out and she is, until the next sea storm at any rate, as mortal as you or I. Tempus is in no mood for death right now."

"You're wrong if you think he'd go lightly with me," Kama warned in a low voice. "He acknowledges my existence—nothing more than that. It would be easier for him if I did die."

It cost her to admit that to anyone, stranger or lover. Molin knew better than to deny it. "I'm not interested in making things easier for that man," he said in his own low, measured voice. "He will not dare to judge you himself, so he will be scrupulously honest in seeing that justice is done by someone else."

Kama tossed her hair behind her shoulders. "Let's go to him now."

"Tomorrow," Molin averred. "He has other obligations tonight."

Prince Kadakithis took the tray from the Beysib priest. He was gracious, but firm: no one besides himself was attending Shupansea. It was her wish; it was his wish; and it was time everyone got used to the idea that he gave orders too. The bald priest had seen too much upheaval in one day to argue successfully. He bowed, gave his blessing, and backed out of the antechamber. The prince set the careful arrangement of chilled morsels beside the bed and returned his attention to the Beysa.

Streaks of opalescent powder shot across the bleached white

imperial bedlinen. Brushing aside a blue-green swirl, Kadakithis resumed his vigil, waiting for her eyes to open and more
than half-expecting that he'd made a terrible mistake. He
smoothed her hair across the pillows; smiled; dared to kiss her
breasts lightly as he'd never dared to do at any of the few other
times they'd stolen moments alone together and jerked upright
when he felt something move against the back of his neck.

The Beysa ran orchid-colored fingertips down his forearm.
"We are alone, aren't we?" she inquired.

"Quite," he agreed. "They've sent food up for us. Are you
hungry?"

He reached for the dinner-tray and found himself restrained.
Shupansea raised herself up and began dealing with the clasps
on his tunic.

"Kith-us, I have two half-grown children and you have had
a wife and concubines since you were fourteen. I surrendered
my virginity in a ritual that was witnessed by at least forty
priests and relations—tell me the first time wasn't just as bad
for you."

The prince blushed crimson.

"Very well, then. We're pawns. The cheapest whore has
more freedom than I've had. But everything's in flux now.
Even Mother Bey is affected. She says not to be alone tonight;
I don't think she can absorb your stormgod into herself as She
has done with all our heroes and man-gods. I could choose to
be with a priest or one of the Burek—but I've chosen to be
with you."

She stripped the loose tunic back from the prince's shoulders
and pulled him toward her. He resisted, fumbling with the
accursed buckles on his sandals, then committed himself to the
changes she promised.

It was night at last, with the darker emotions of the mortal
spirit obscuring the heavens as surely as the smoke and the
eternal fog. Ischade extinguished her candles and gathered her
dark robes around her. She had planned and deliberated as she
had seldom done, choosing decision over reaction despite its
risks and unfamiliarity.

She sealed the White Foal house with a delicate touch; if
she failed, the dawn would find nothing more than rotting
boards rising from the overgrown marshes. The black roses
opened as she passed them, giving her their arcane beauty for

what might be the last time. With a caress she savored their death-sweet perfume and sent them back where she had found them.

Across the bridge, deep within the better part of town, the bay horse consumed the last of the ward-fire, leaving the Peres house naked to whatever moved in the darkness. Ischade clung to the shadows with more than her usual caution; she was not immune to mortal forms of death and there were others migrating instinctively to the house now that its defenses had vanished. Crouched in a doorway, she lit a single candle and studied the wisps of magic rising through the ruins of Roxane's wards.

At her unspoken command the front door faded from its hinges. Ischade crept through, bristling with alertness and prepared to utilize every trick in her carefully prepared arsenal. There was nothing to challenge or greet her as she glided along the hallway, vanishing amid her numerous possessions.

She found the trail Straton's blood had made and followed it through to the kitchen. Stilcho's heroism had borne fruit; but Straton's safety was not her only goal. Haught was here; the Nisi witch was here and she would not leave until she had consigned both to hell and beyond.

Continuing her search, Ischade swept from room to room to the waist-thick beams of the cluttered attic where her search had to end. Haught crouched outside the sphere, enraptured by the nether-world dazzle of the globe, his eyes as wide and glazed as any Beysib's. Shiey's cleaver lay in a twisted lump at his feet. Tasfalen sang with a dead man's voice, dragging one leg stiffly as he shambled around the perimeter of the globe's light.

Tasfalen?

Ischade did not immediately comprehend the changes which had overtaken Tasfalen Lancothis. Had Haught somehow kept the globe? Had she simply imagined Roxane's taint on the corroded wards? Surely Tasfalen's flawed resurrection had been her one-time apprentice's work; Roxane's efforts were brutal but never so crude. Concealed by shadow and the skein of magic she had spun, the necromant dared briefly to listen to the globe's song until she could piece the truth together.

She noted, even as Haught had noted, the carelessness which marked the Nisi witch's failure to protect her mortal shell and recognized the same mystic illness from which she herself had only just recovered. For a fleeting moment Ischade felt a sense of pity that one so powerful should be conquered by an accumulation of minute errors. Then she set about weaving a gossamer web to ground the globe's radiant energy in her focal possessions as fast as Roxane/Tasfalen could create it.

The faster the globe whirled, the stronger Ischade's binding threads became, until the whole house rattled and dust fell in flakes from the ancient roofbeams—and still the Nisi witch sang her curses into the artifact. The necromancer played out the last strand and stood up in the wash of blue light.

Tasfalen's dead eye gave no indication of recognition; Roxane was too deeply enmeshed in her spell-casting to spare the energy for simple words. A shriek of rage emanated from the globe itself as the Nisi witch launched her attack—a shriek that shattered abruptly as the power surged into Ischade's handiwork and made the web brilliantly visible. Curls of smoke twisted up from the weaker foci, but the web held. Ischade began to laugh, savoring her counterpart's growing terror.

Roxane flailed helplessly with Tasfalen's rigor-stricken arms, struggling to free herself from the power gnawing at her soul.

"The wards!" Roxane's disembodied voice howled above the globe's whine. "No wards! He comes for me!"

The Globe of Power spun faster, first swallowing the witch's voice, then swallowing her body within its cobalt sphere. Gouts of fire sprang up in the joists and floorboards where Ischade's web had touched them. Ischade covered her hair with her cloak as she inched away from the conflagration swirling around the globe. The Nisi witch was trapped, along with her accursed artifact; it was time to see that Straton was safely away from the house and its outbuildings. Straton—she put his face in the forefront of her mind and looked toward the corner where the stairs had been.

An orange nimbus surrounded the image Ischade formed of her lover. A demonic nimbus, she realized too late—after she had turned to face the throbbing cobalt sphere again. No wards, Roxane had screamed: no wards to keep Niko's demon at bay. It had one soul but it could claim many. Her foot scuffed against the rough planks, but Ischade moved forward as it beckoned.

"Straton."

Haught kept himself small and low against the roofbeams. Insignificant—as he had always been as a dancer or a slave; beneath the notice of witches and, certainly, of demons. He saw the thing which had been Roxane flickering between an awful emptiness and the dozen or more bodies the witch had taken during her life. He saw Ischade think to escape—and fail, and lurch inescapably forward. But mostly he saw the globe hanging midway between Ischade and the demon: motionless and, for the moment, ignored.

Still keeping himself invisible in the demon's perception, he drew himself into a compact crouch. There was no need for the globe to be destroyed by this, he thought while massaging the finger which bore Ischade's ring. One leap would take him across the sphere and down the stairs. He was a dancer still, in his body; the leap was no great feat for him.

He caught the skull-sized artifact on the tips of his fingers. The momentum of his leap brought the searing object hard against his breast as he forced the center of a very small universe to shift from one existence through an infinity of others. It clung to him; passed through him; absorbed him; shattered and expelled him utterly.

Ischade was hurled against the rafters by the force of the globe's destruction. Wrapped in the fullness of her fire-magic she barely reached the stairway when the roof itself was swallowed in the flames. Her robes were in flames before she reached the streets.

A tower of fire soared from the open roof of the Peres house to the heavens themselves. The demon, trapped in fire, warred with Stormbringer, whose thundercloud form was illuminated by each lightning-bolt He threw. A crowd was gathering, a crowd which saw her try to squeeze the flames from her hair and robes and called after her when she raced down the streets with fire still licking after her.

Molin Torchholder had been one of the first to climb to the palace rooftops for a clearer view of the flame pillar. Bracing himself against the gritty wind he looked past the light to the dark cloud beyond.

"Stormbringer?"

He nearly fell from the roof as a hand closed tightly over his shoulder. "Not tonight," Tempus said with a laugh.

There were others appearing at the myriad stairways, making their way to the railing circling the Hall of Justice: Jihan and Randal, leaning on each other for strength, with Niko close behind; Isambard, dragged forward by the exuberant Storm-

children; the functionaries, retainers, and day-servants all barefoot and in their nightclothes. The palace was no different than
the rest of Sanctuary this night—every rooftop, courtyard, and
clearing had its collection of awestruck mortals.

Brilliant light streamed into the prince's bedroom. He awoke,
sighing with the knowledge that the best must also seem the
shortest, and meant to leave Shupansea undisturbed. His heart
sank when he realized he was alone in the bed; it did not rise
when he saw her transfixed by the column of light in the open
window.

Dragging a silken blanket behind him, he came slowly to
join her.

"She has kept her promises," Shupansea explained, taking
a corner of the blanket around her shoulder and pressing close
against him. "Stormbringer fights the demon."

It did not seem like gods and demons at first glance. It
seemed like a single, great cloud spewing lightning at a flame
of impossible size and brightness—but such a vision was, in
itself, so improbable that the Beysa's explanation was as acceptable as any other. Certainly the lightning struck only the
flame and the flame directed spirals of its substance at the
cloud. The stormcloud, with its percussive thunder, deflected
the fire away from itself to the ocean and, occasionally, the
city.

"He has it trapped," the Beysa said, indicating the precision
with which the Stormgod's bolts prevented the demon-fire from
shifting its location. "They will fight until the demon accepts
annihilation."

The prince was unable to look away from the awesome
spectacle. Armed with Shupansea's explanations he could see
the flame shrinking each time it launched a missile against the
lightning. He stayed Shupansea's hand when she tried to close
the shutters.

"The end is inevitable," she assured him, holding him tightly.

A fine powder blew through the window. The Beysa protected herself but tears flowed freely from Kadakithis's eyes.

"I want to see if there's a beginning as well."

"The beginning is here," she reminded him, closing the
shutters and leading him back to the bed.

PILLAR OF FIRE

___

Janet Morris

Death was riding the feral wind that blew in off Sanctuary's
harbor—even Tempus's Trôs horse could smell it on the sooty
breeze as horse and rider picked their way down Wideway to
the wharf and the emperor's barge made fast there.

The Trôs danced and snorted, its hooves sending up sparks
from ancient cobbles that seemed, in the dusky air, to have
lives of their own. The sparks whirled round the Trôs's legs
like insects swarming; they darted hither and thither on smoky
gusts drawn seaward from the pillar of fire blazing between
the heavens and the Peres house uptown; they skittered along
Tempus's clothing like dust-motes from hell, stinging when
they touched his bare arms and legs; they lighted upon the
Trôs's distended nostrils and that horse, wiser than many human
inhabitants of this accursed thieves' world, blew bellowing
breaths to keep from inhaling whatever dust it was that glowed
like fire and burned like hot needles when it landed on the
stallion's dappled hide.

The hellish dust was the least of Tempus's troubles on this
morning that had lost its light, as if the sun had slunk away to
hide from the battle under way beneath the sky. Oh, the sun
had risen, brazen and bold, illuminating the flaming pillar raging up to heaven and the storm clouds with their lightning
ranged round it. But it had been eaten by the stormclouds and
the soot of the fire and the lightning spewing up from the
grounds around the uptown Peres house and down from the
furious heavens of the gods, who smote at witches' work and
cheeky demons with equal force.

And it was this absence of the morning, this vanquishing
of natural light, that bothered Tempus (accustomed to analyzing
omens and all too familiar with godsign) as he rode down to
greet Theron, the man he'd helped bring to Ranke's teetering

213

throne, and Brachis, High Priest of Vashanka, while around
the town civil war and infamy reigned, unabated.

If the chaos around him (which he'd once been sent here
to banish) weren't enough of an indictment of his performance,
then the skittishness of the Trôs horse made it certain: he was
failing ignominiously to bring order—even for a day—to Sanctuary.

And though some men would not have taken the responsibility and clasped the fault for all Sanctuary's catalogue of
evils to his bosom, Tempus would and almost gladly did—the
state of town and loved ones fulfilled his own dire prophecy.

Only the Trôs horse's distress truly touched him now: ani-
mals were pure and honest, not dour and divisive like the race
of men. It might not be his fault that Straton lay, somewhere,
in the clutches of the revolution (Crit was sure), dead or held
for ransom; it might not be because of Tempus, called the
Riddler, that Niko was the perennial pawn of demons and foul
witches; it might not be directly attributable to him that his
daughter, Kama, was now sought as an assassin and revolutionary by his own Stepsons and the palace guard, thus creating
a rift between her unit, the Rankan 3rd Commando, and the
other militias in the town that no amount of diplomacy would
ever bridge if she were executed; it might not be on his account
that Randal, once a Stepson and the single "white" magician
Tempus had ever trusted, was a burned-out husk, or that Niko
stared sightlessly at the pillar of flame uptown in which Janni,
his one-time partner and a Stepson who'd sworn Tempus a
solemn oath of fealty, burned eternally, or that Jihan had been
stripped of her Froth Daughter's attributes, humbled to the
lowly estate of womankind, or that Tempus's own son, Gyskouras, looked at him with fear and loathing (even trying to
shield his half-brother, Arton, from Tempus whenever the children saw him come).

But it probably was—he was the root and cause of all this
slaughter: it was his curse, habitual (as Molin Torchholder, a
Nisi-blooded slime in Rankan clothing, maintained) or invoked
by jealous gods or hostile magic. He didn't know or care which
force now drove him: he'd lost interest in which was right and
which was wrong.

Like the day around him, black and white and good and
evil had lost their character, merging like the sullen dusky noon
in an unsavory amalgam to match his mood.

But it bothered him that the Trôs was nervous, sweating, and distressed. He reined it down a side street, hoping to avoid the greater gusts of dust. For he knew that dust as he knew the voices of the gods who plagued him: each particle was a remnant of pulverized globes of Nisi power, magical talismans reduced to pinprick size and myriad in number.

If Sanctuary needed anything less than a dusty cloak of Nisi magic wafting where it willed, he couldn't think what it might be.

And then he realized what lay ahead, down a shadowed alleyway, and drew his sword: a little honest swordplay might cheer him up, and ahead, where PFLS rebels in rags and sweatbands fought Rankan regulars in the street, he knew he'd find it.

Though he was overqualified for street brawls—a man who couldn't die and had to heal, whose horse shared his more-than-human speed and more-than-mortal constitution—numbers made the odds more honest: four Rankan soldiers, against a mob of thirty, were trying to shield some woman with a child from whatever the mob had in mind.

He heard shouts over the Trôs's hoofbeats as it lifted into a lope and trumpeted its war cry as it sped gladly toward the fray.

"Give her up, the slut—it's all her doing!" cried one hoarse voice from the mob.

"That's right!" a shrill woman's voice seconded the rebel demand: "S'danzo slut! She bore the accursed Stormchild's playmate! S'danzo wickedness has taken away the sun and turned the gods' ire upon us!"

And a third voice, streetwise and dark, a man's voice Tempus thought he ought to recognize, put in: "Come on, Walegrin, give her up and you go free—you and yours. We're only killing witches and their children today!"

"Screw yourself, Zip," one of the Rankans called back. "You'll have to take her from us. And we'll have a couple lives in exchange—yours for certain. That's a promise."

Tempus had only an instant to realize that Walegrin, the garrison commander, was one of the Rankans under siege, and to add up all he'd heard and realize that the blond soldier's sister-of-record, Illyra, must be the woman whose life was the subject of a traditional Sanctuary streetcorner debate.

Then the Trôs was sighted by the rebels at the rear of the

crowd, which began to part but not disperse.

Missiles pelted him, some barbed, some jagged, some meant for rolling bread or holding wine—and some designed for war.

He ducked an arrow hurtling toward him from a crossbow, his senses so much faster that he could see the helically-fletched blue feathers on its tail as it sped toward his heart.

The Trôs was hit between the eyes with a tomato: it had seen the missile coming, but never flinched or ducked, its ears pricked like a sighting mechanism aligned upon the crowd: it was a warhorse, after all.

But Tempus found this affront unacceptable, and took exception to the brashness of the crowd. Reaching up with his left hand while still holding his reins, he plucked the arrow from the air when it was inches from his heart and, as he seldom did, flaunted his supernatural attributes before the crowd, holding the arrow high and breaking it between his fingers like a piece of straw as he bellowed in his most commanding voice: "Zip and all you rebels, disperse or face my personal wrath— a retribution that will haunt you till you die, and then some: you'll leave my fury to your descendants as a bequest."

And Zip's voice called back from a gloom in which all white faces looked alike and darker Wriggly skins faded to invisibility: "Come get me, Riddler. Your daughter did!"

He set about just that, but not before the crowd surged inward as one body, pinning the four Rankans and the girl they thought to shield against the wall.

He kneed the Trôs in among confusion, took blows, and swung back and down with his sharkskin-hilted sword, inured to the death he dealt, his conscience salved before the fact by giving warning, so that his blood-lust now reigned unimpeded and rebels fell, like wheat before a scythe, under his blade, a sword the god of war had sanctified in countless bodies just like these, across more battlefields than Tempus cared to count.

But when, finally, the crowd broke to run and none clawed at his saddle or bit at his ankle or tried to blind the Trôs horse with their sharpened sticks or hamstring it with their bread knives, he realized he'd been too late to save the day.

Oh, Walegrin, bloody and with a face pummeled beyond recognition so that Tempus could only recognize him by his braided blond locks and the tears streaming from his blackened sockets unheeded, would live to fight another day: he'd been innermost, protecting Illyra—the S'danzo seeress who should have forseen all this—with his own big body. But of the other three soldiers, one's gullet was split the way a fisherman cleans his catch, one's neck was hanging by a thread, and the third was hacked apart, limb from limb, his trunk still twitching weakly.

It was not the soldiers, however, who drew Tempus's attention, but the woman they'd tried to shield, who in turn had been protecting her child. Illyra, S'danzo skirts heavy with blood, cradled a young girl's body in her arms, and wept so silently that it was Walegrin's grief, not her own, that let Tempus know that the child was surely dead.

"Lillis," Walegrin sobbed, manliness forgotten because an innocent, his kin, was slain; "Lillis, dear gods, no . . . she's alive, 'Lyra, alive, I tell you."

But all the desperate wishes in the world would not make it so, and the S'danzo woman, whose eyes were wise and whose face was tired beyond her years and whose own belly bled profusely where the axe that had hewn her daughter had gone through child and into mother, met Tempus's eyes before she turned to the field commander who could no longer command so much as his grief.

"Tempus, isn't it? And your marvelous horse?" Illyra's voice had the sough of the seawind in it and her eyes were bleak and full of the witch-dust settling all about. "Shall I foretell your future, lord of blood, or would you rather not read the writing on the wall?"

"No, my lady," he said before he looked above her head and beyond, to where graffiti scribed in blood defaced the mudbrick. "Tell me no tales of power: If doom could be avoided, you'd have a live child in your arms."

And he reined the Trôs around, setting off again toward Wideway and the dockside, forcing his thoughts to collect and focus on the audience with Theron soon to come, and away from the writing on the wall behind the woman: "The plague is in our souls, not in our destiny. Ilsig rules. Kill the witches and the priests or perish!"

It sounded like a good idea to him, but he couldn't throw in his lot with the rebels; he'd made a truce with magic for the sake of his soldiers; he'd made a truce with gods for the sake of his soul.

And perishing wasn't an option for Tempus. Sometimes he wondered if he might manage it by getting himself eaten by fishes or chopped into tiny pieces, but the chances were good that his parts would reassemble or—worse—that each morsel of him would reconstitute an entire being.

It was bad enough existing in one discrete form; he couldn't bear to be replicated countless times. So he smothered the rebellious impulse to throw in his lot with the rebels and see if it was true that any army he joined could not lose its battles.

He was bound by oath to Theron, to the necromant Ischade in solemn pact, to Stormbringer in another, and to Enlil, patron god of the armies now that Vashanka was metamorphosing into something else within the body of Gyskouras, their common son. And he'd spent an interval with the Mother Goddess of the fishfaces in which he'd learned that Mother Bey had lusts as great as any northern deity.

So he alone, acquainted with so many of the players intimately and capable of standing up to more-than-human actors, was competent to negotiate a settlement among the heavens through supernal avatars and earthly rulers, the representatives of their respective gods.

This task was complicated, not helped, by Kadakithis's impending marriage to the Beysib ruler, as it was obstructed, not advanced, by Theron's arrival here and now, when all was far from well and men had brought their hells to life by meddling with powers they did not understand.

So he didn't care, he decided, what happened here, beyond his personal goals: to protect the souls of his Stepsons and those who loved him, to reward constancy where it had been demonstrated (even by mages and necromants), to clear his conscience so far as possible before he trekked back north, where the horses still grazed in Hidden Valley and the Successors on Wizardwall would welcome him back to what had become the closest thing to home he could remember.

But to do that, he must see Niko on the mend and on his way back to Bandara; he must do what Abarsis had counseled, and more.

He must get rid of that thrice-cursed pillar of fire burning with renewed fervor uptown, and spewing fireballs and attracting lightning and spitting bolts into the sea, before a storm blew up from the disturbance.

For if a storm came riding the wake of all this chaos, then Jihan's powers would be restored, and Tempus would be saddled with the Froth Daughter for eternity.

Now he had a chance to slip away without her and let her father, the mighty Stormbringer, keep His word: find Jihan some other lover.

So he was hurrying, as he reined the Trôs toward dockside where the Rankan lion blazon flapped in a sea-wind too strong not to be promising wild weather.

And the Trôs, scenting the sea and his mood, snorted happily, as if in agreement: the Trôs would as soon be quit of Jihan, who curried him to within an inch of his life daily, as would he.

And if a storm would bring the dust to ground, and all the magic of Nisi antiquity with it, then that was not his problem—not if he played his cards right.

For once, Crit was grateful for the witchy weather that plagued Sanctuary worse than all the factions fighting here.

"Getting Strat" was not going to be the easiest thing he'd ever done, but he wasn't arguing that the job was his to do: Ace was his partner; their souls were too bound up to chance letting Strat die with any strings on him, no matter which witch was holding the end of them.

And Strat wasn't going to die in flames, not in some burning house that wouldn't burn *down* but only burned on and on like no natural fire.

Not that common sense was saying otherwise: crouched at the heat's end, where waves of burning air licked his face despite the water he was palming over it intermittently. As he stared at the flaming funnel waiting for a plan to come clear, Crit reflected that his Sacred Band oath made no distinction between natural and unnatural peril. He hadn't sworn to stand by Strat, shoulder to shoulder, until death separated them if it must, only in cases where it was convenient, or magic wasn't involved, or Strat was behaving as a rightman ought, or the problem didn't involve an urban war zone and the possibility of being roasted alive.

The oath was binding, under any circumstances.

Watching the fiery tornado, like nothing he'd ever seen but the waterspouts of wizard weather or the cyclone that had fought in the last battle on Wizardwall, he was trying to determine whether it had a pattern to its burning and its wriggling, whether the lightning spewing from the cloud above was dependable as to target or random, and in general just how the hell he was going to get in there.

Because Strat *was* in there. Everything pointed to it; Randal was sure of it; no ransom demands had come forth from the PFLS. His orders were to fetch Strat and Kama.

Kama could wait until all the hells froze over and Sanctuary sank into the sea, for all he cared. He'd had an affair with Tempus's daughter, true: he was willing to pay for his indiscretion, not complaining. But Strat was his partner—Strat came first.

If they'd had arguments, then that was normal—they'd have them again . . . over women especially. It went with pairbond, and he'd beat Strat silly if he had to, to win his point. As soon as he had the porking bastard back where he could pull rank, they'd settle things.

But you couldn't settle anything with a dead man, unless he became *un*dead like the freakish bay horse who was partially present, trotting around the Peres house on ghostly hooves, its coat looking as if it reflected the flaming whirlwind around which it circled—or was a part of it. The horse was insubstantial, sort of. But if he could catch it, maybe he could ride it up the back stairs.

Strat had ridden it. And the horse and Crit were both here for the same reason: Strat.

He decided to follow the horse on its rounds and forsook the cover of jumbled stone, remnants of the Peres's garden wall, behind which he'd been crouching.

The heat waves emanating from that spinning horror of flame struck him with awesome force; he could feel his eyelashes singe and his lips start to blister. Head down, following echoing hoofbeats as much as the flickering glimpses he could get of this "horse," he edged along in its wake.

If the house would just burn *down*, like any normal fire did once a fire had consumed its fuel, things would be so simple: he could begin mourning.

He'd thought of just considering the whole unsightly and unnatural mess as a funeral pyre, calling for reinforcements, and making the Peres estate Strat's bier. They'd say the rites, play some funeral games, he'd put everything he owned up as prize or sacrifice.

But he couldn't do that, not until he knew for certain that

Strat really was dead, and wholly dead: not likely to be resurrected by Ischade.

For that was what he feared the most: that the necromant wouldn't be content to let Ace stay dead, that she'd pine for her lover and eventually call him up from ashes, make him an undead like poor Janni, who was somewhere in the cone of the fire—Crit couldn't imagine how or why, but he could see, if he squinted, the dead Stepson, fully formed and unconsumed, doing something that looked like bathing under a waterfall, but doing it in a heat that would melt bone in seconds.

Crit had learned, fighting magic and sometimes fighting it with magic, not to ask questions if he didn't want to hear the answers. So he left the matter of Janni to those who ought to tend it: to Ischade, who'd raised his shade after a proper Sacred Band funeral; to Abarsis, who'd come down from heaven and escorted Janni's spirit on high, and done it where the whole Band could see it. If there was an argument about propriety here, it was between the necromant and the ghost of the Slaughter Priest: it wasn't a matter for a decidedly unmagical fighter like himself. If Janni hadn't once been Niko's partner and a Sacred Bander, it wouldn't have been the business of any Stepson what Ischade had done. As things stood, all you could do, if you were so inclined, was pray for Janni's soul.

But it bothered Crit intensely because the same thing could happen to Strat—Ischade could make it happen.

He wondered idly, trailing the ghost-horse on its rounds about the Peres estate, how you went about killing a necromant. If Strat didn't come through this intact, he was going to find out. Maybe Randal would know—if Randal ever again was capable of doing more than swallowing when you put a spoon of gruel in his mouth.

There had been a few minutes, he'd been told, when it seemed that Randal and Niko had come through their battle with Roxane and the demon in good shape.

But physical flesh—even mageflesh and Bandaran adept's flesh—could take only so much. The two were alive; they'd live; whether they'd ever be as hale or as smart as they once were, only time would tell.

Rounding a burned-out wall, the heat lessened perceptibly and Crit could stop squinting and raise his head.

The ghost-horse was still right in front of him. In fact, when Crit stopped, it stopped.

When he took a linen rag and wetted it from the waterskin dangling from his belt, the specter craned its neck to look back at him, ears pricked, as if to ask what he was doing.

What he was doing was anybody's guess, but he didn't try to tell the ghost-horse that. The bay was still bay: it had a black mane and tail (although when the hot wind ruffled them they streamed out like charred cinders, not horsehair); it had a red-gold haircoat (now flame red and flickery as the patterns from the fire chased each other along its flanks); it had black stockings (which resembled burnt timbers). But it was more substantial than it had been around front, where the fire was brighter.

Then it pawed the ground and whickered, still fixing him with a fire-light centered gaze from liquid horse eyes.

The come-hither look and the forefoot pawing the ground were unmistakable to any horseman: the bay wanted Crit to hurry up, climb aboard: it wanted to go for a ride.

"Oh no, horse," he said out loud to it. "I came by myself—no reinforcements, no backup. I did that because nobody else ought to risk his life—or sacrifice it, if that's what's going to happen here . . . because this is a matter between pairbonded partners."

The horse snorted disapprovingly, as if to remind Crit that it knew he was trying to cover his own fear. Then it slowly turned around, so that its rump was no longer facing him, and ambled toward him.

The big, liquid, obling-centered eyes said: *Strat is mine, too; horses and men are partners; mount up and let's stop playing games. He's waiting.*

"Strat, damn you to hell," Crit whispered, shaking his head to clear it of horse-thoughts and horse-needs and horse-loyalties. This wasn't even a living horse, just a ghost, something Ischade had conjured from a dead animal.

But the thing kept coming, head high, feet carefully placed to avoid stepping on its dangling bridle reins.

Bridle reins? Had they been there before? He didn't think so.

The horse, now an arm's-length away, stopped still. It whickered softly and the whicker said, *I love him too.* The forefoot, pawing the ground impatiently, added, *We don't have much time.* And then the horse, in the manner of high-school horses like Tempus's Trôs, bent one foreleg at the knee, curling it and lowering his forequarters, the other front leg outstretched, while it arched its neck in a bow meant to enable a wounded man or a high-born lady to mount up without difficulty.

"Crap, all right," Crit said through clenched teeth and strode resolutely toward the bowing ghost-horse, trying hard not to think too much about what he was doing, or whether he might be imagining the whole thing—maybe a piece of timber had fallen on him, a piece of masonry collapsed so fast he hadn't had time to realize it, and he was dead too, dead but denied a peaceful rest, trapped in some netherworld with the ghost-horse, on which he'd wander forever, seeking his lost rightside partner.

But no: The sky was full of lightning, there were shouts and mutters on the breeze from somewhere near by where factions fought. There was a plague in Sanctuary, all right, but not some spurious one that turned your lips blue and made your armpits sore: it was a plague of human failing, of confusion, of greed and desire and endless power plays.

It wasn't, he admitted as he mounted the bay (which felt surprisingly substantial, for a ghost-horse), the magic or the gods which made Sanctuary such a foul pit, but human excess: magic was no more to blame than sword or spear or rock. There were enough rocks on the earth to eradicate the race; magic couldn't do a better job, only a more colorful one. But rock or spear or wand or Nisi globe didn't murder on their own, nor enslave—the weapon must be wielded; the true culprit was human greed and human will. And the killing never stopped—in the name of magic or the name of god or the name of honor or nationalism or progress or liberation, it was just killing.

And because it had always been so, and would always be so, Critias had come to the profession of arms himself: the only protection he could see was to be a perpetrator, not a victim.

That was why Strat had made him so angry when he'd become entangled with Ischade: Strat had become a victim, and Crit had a horror of helplessness. Even if Strat were just a lovesick fool, Crit still thought he'd been right when he had shot past his friend that night on the balcony—if it had served to bring Straton to his senses, then Crit wouldn't be here, pulling himself up into the sometimes-saddle of Strat's sort-of-corporeal bay, riding into he-didn't-know-what for abstracts of honor and duty that weren't going to keep him alive if the steaming stable toward which the bay was ineluctably heading crashed down upon his head.

The stables weren't exactly ablaze, but they had corn magazines and straw and hay in them and sparks smoldered on the roof.

Crit reached forward to catch up the bay's reins, but the beast had had a mouth like iron in life and it was no better in afterlife.

He sawed on the reins to no avail, then quit trying in time to duck as the horse trotted determinedly through the open stable doors and headed for wide stairs which must lead to the stable's loft.

Crit shifted his weight, thinking to throw one leg over the saddle and check out the stable loft on foot, when the horse started climbing.

"Vashanka's balls," the task force leader swore, flattening himself to the horse's neck as it climbed a flight never meant for anything of its size and boards creaked and groaned. "Horse, you'd better be right."

It was: at the stair's head was a landing, and as the bay's bulk appeared there, a woman stifled a scream.

It was hard to accustom his eyes to the dark; the climb up the stairs had been too fast—everything was still milky green to Crit's fire-dazzled vision.

But Crit heard voices and slipped from the bay's back, his sword in hand.

Together, man and ghost-horse ventured into the dimness; horse's head snaked low, man's sword paralleling its questing muzzle.

"Dear gods, what's that smell?" Crit muttered to himself.

And someone answered: "Strat. Or me, Critias. Which smell do you mean?"

And the voice of Stilcho was familiar to Critias, who had once thought him the best of his kind of Stepson. Blinking, Crit strained to see the ruined visage of the undead soldier. Stilcho was one of Ischade's minions. He should have known the witch would still have her talons in Strat, one way or the other.

He was going to swing his sword up, cut the one-eyed, ghoulish head from Stilcho's torso and hope decapitation would provide the poor soul what rest Ischade had denied—not be-

cause he expected his poor quotidian blade to do the job against
magic, but because he was a soldier and he could only do what
he was trained to do, when his vision cleared enough to see
that Stilcho's face was neither so ruined nor so hostile as it
ought to be.

And a hand touched his right shoulder, squeezed, and rested
there—Stilcho's hand, warm and with the pulse of mortal blood
in it so strong Crit fancied he could feel it coursing.

"That's right," said Stilcho softly through a mouth hardly
scarred, "I'm alive—again. Don't ask—"

Crit's question, *"How?"* hung in the air until Stilcho vol-
unteered, "It's just too complicated, Stepson. Ask about Strat,
that's what you're here for . . . or at least that's what *he's* here
for." Stilcho jerked a thumb toward the bay horse, head low,
snuffling, taking slow, careful steps toward a shadow that might
be a prostrate man with a woman crouched by his side.

"That's right, Stilcho—Strat. That's all I want. Not you or
your witch woman." It was Ischade there, hulking over Strat—
it must be. Ischade's ghost-man and ghost-horse, and the necromant herself, ringing Strat round with magic.

Crit considered seriously for the first time the possibility
that he was going to die here. He didn't believe for a moment
that Stilcho was "alive" in the way that Crit—or Strat, please
gods—was alive.

He said to Stilcho, "That's him, then? He's alive, if he can't
control his bowels. I'll just take him and be—"

A voice from the shadowed loft said, "Shit, Stilcho, he'll
kill me," as a hand which was also Strat's reached up feebly
to stroke the ghost-horse's questing muzzle and the horse started
to bow down again, not realizing that Strat was too badly
wounded to mount, no matter how easy the ghost-horse tried
to make it.

Crit found that he was blinking back tears. Unreasonably,
he wanted to sit down crosslegged where he was, let things
take their course—even if it meant burning to death in this
damned loft with a partner too sick to be moved but well enough
to remember that Crit had shot at him.

Crit said, "I wouldn't—couldn't. I busted my butt getting
here, Strat," but it came out hoarse and low and he said it to
the straw scattered on the loft's floor at his feet.

The woman was trying to help Straton, who didn't realize
he couldn't get on that horse by himself.

Crit sheathed his sword and put his hands in the air, then walked over to the place where the ghost-horse nuzzled its master encouragingly.

Strat, half-prone, was staring at him. The big fighter's hand was clutched to his chest or belly—Crit couldn't tell from all the blood in the way.

"Strat . . . Ace, for pity's sake, let me help you," Crit said, bending down on one knee, empty hands outstretched.

The ghost-horse neighed impatiently and butted Straton's shoulder. Behind the pair, the woman stood—the woman named Moria from the Peres estate, but dressed in street rags so that he hardly recognized her.

Stilcho said, "Strat, maybe you'd better . . . it's not going to be safe here much longer. They can take care of you better than we—"

"Stilcho," Moria hissed, "come away. It's for them to talk out."

"Talk?" Strat laughed and the laugh choked him, so that he gurgled and wiped his mouth with a hand that came away bloody. "We just did."

The wounded fighter reached with his bloody hand to take one of Crit's. "Well, Crit, you going to watch, or you going to give me some help?"

"Strat . . ." Crit embraced his partner, oblivious of might-be enemies about him, searching for harm, testing strength, mouthing harsh words that covered too much emotion: "You stupid bastard, when I get you fixed up I'm going to beat some sense into you."

And Strat said, "You do that," just about the time the bay horse trumpeted joyously as he felt Strat's weight on his back and Crit began the arduous process of leading the mounted, wounded man out of the stable's attic to safety—at least of the sort a Sacred Band partner could provide.

Fire raged inside Ischade, now that she had quenched it in her clothing and her hair. It might have been her wrath that caused the houses across the alleys on either side of her to flame up as she passed—uptown alleys she'd traveled before and now again on her way to Tasfalen's velvet stronghold.

An ache and a fury was in Ischade and perhaps it spread around her. But perhaps it was just the pillar of flame and the young fires it set, so that better uptown streets (where Sanctuary's troubles never spread and rebels never sped) were a smoking labyrinth like some upscale version of the Maze.

Rebels skulked here now, and peasants, looting: Wrigglies, arms laden with pilfered, sooty treasure, jostled her, saw whom they bumped, and slunk away.

She saw rape and nearly stopped to feed—these mortal murderers wasted the best part of their victims, let the manna go, let the essence, precious soul and energy, escape. Ischade was weakened by the struggle in Peres's, somewhat. Somewhat. But not too much.

She moved on, through a day mercifully veiled in clouds and soot and a storm now rising off the sea. She wondered, as the sky blackened with thunderheads boiling up, if the storm was natural or summoned—then thought it didn't matter: it was convenient, either way.

She saw an enclosed Beysib wagon, overturned by brigands. Bald heads of Beysib males littered the environs like playballs from some devil's game, their accustomed torsos near but not attached. She saw what fate was dealt a pair of Beysib women, and wondered what the rebels thought to gain. If they kept their war to downtown, they might win it. Up here, they asked for retribution that would last for generations.

Amid pathetic cries, she stopped awhile, and closed her eyes—trusting to a cloaking spell to hide her. When she moved on, she was emboldened, strengthened, but sick at heart: for her to be reduced to scavenging was demeaning. But war did what it willed.

Thunder wracked the streets and she looked upward, grateful for the lowering, stormy dark but wary: she'd finish what she started, unless the stormgods intervened. She owed Tempus something. And she owed Haught a different thing.

She had her word to make good. She had her interests to secure. She had work to do before retiring to the White Foal's edge.

It was not painless for Ischade, this sneaking to Tasfalen's in the daylight. Janni, one of hers, was still trapped in the cone of flame, where Stormbringer and demons argued, where Roxane had been and now was not.

What would Tempus, who wanted the souls of his soldiers freed of strings and tortures, make of Janni's plight? Hardly an honorable rest, in his terms. But a piece of bravery, in hers, the like of which she'd never seen.

All for Niko, or for something more abstract? she wondered as she found Tasfalen's gate and then his steps and her thoughts turned to Haught and Roxane and what lay ahead, as she dealt with locks of natural and other kinds, and doors likewise doubled, and, as the last portal opened to her will, a raindrop struck her cheek, and then another, and thunder rolled.

The storm would ground the dust and douse the fires and she knew it was too great a luck for Sanctuary, the most luckless town she'd ever seen. She knew also that, inside the flaming pillar back at the Peres's, evil was held at bay by one whose name could not be spoken but could be approximated: Stormbringer, the Weather-Gods' father—Stormbringer, whose daughter Jihan was close at hand.

And then there was no time to put it all together: there was a ring on the finger of Haught which she could see with her inner eye.

This she stroked and called home to her. Its spell, still strong, would bring the scheming apprentice—if he was not already here.

In the ground hall full of shadows she paused. The door behind her closed at a gust's whim. The slam it made was daunting.

Her hackles rose—she hadn't thought of the ring Haught had until she'd entered. Was it her will, or only her perception, that saw him here?

Why had she come here? Suddenly, she wasn't sure. She shook her head, on the ground floor landing, and touched her brow with her palm. She owed Tempus none of this—not so much. Tasfalen was dead, a minion to be summoned to the river house. Why, then, had she risked the streets and come up here?

Why? She couldn't fathom it.

And then she did, when Haught's silken voice oozed down the stairs from a shadow at their head.

"Ah, Mistress, how kind of you to visit sickbeds with so much at stake."

She reached out for the ring he wore, but the apprentice was reaching on his own: grown desperate, he was full of pain, and wanted to make her a gift of it.

Suddenly (more because she underestimated what lay behind him and what hid within him than because of Haught himself) she was dizzy, spinning in another place, a place of blood and

murky water—of ice and great gates whose bars were rent as
if a giant shape had bent them out of its way.

Niko's rest-place! How had she come here?...not by
Haught's strength.

And a laugh tinkled—a laugh with razor edges that cut her
soul: Roxane.

Yes, Roxane—but something less and something more hob-
bled through that gate, misshapen and huge, and shrunk until
Tasfalen's beauty masked it.

And then the thing...for it was part highborn, mortal lord,
part witch, and part Haught...held out its hand to take her
arm as if to escort her to some formal fête.

She met its eyes and gripped her own ribs with both her
hands: to touch it might imprison her here. This was where
Janni had lost the last shreds of self-concern that made him act
predictably in the interest of what life he still led.

The eyes that bored into hers were gold and slitted; deep
behind them glowed a purple fire she knew wasn't right.

She forced her leaden limbs to work and backed a step,
watching first her feet and then scanning the horizons, winding
wards that worked in Sanctuary which were much weaker here.

Niko's star-shaped meadow, once ever-green and pastoral,
the very essence of spirit peace, was frostbitten, brown, and
gray and riddled with ice like arrows. Where trees had spread
rustling leaves, their boughs now held shards of flesh and
writhing things resembling tiny men who cried like kittens
being drowned.

And the stream which was his life's ebb and flow ran with
swirls of red and blue and pink and gold: blood shed and to
be shed; magic winding it round and chasing it; Niko's faith
and the love of gods bringing up behind.

Tasfalen was cajoling: "Come, my love. My beauteous one.
We'll feast." He flicked a glance to the trees hung with anguished, living things. "The boughs are ripe for picking, the
fruit is sweet."

And she knew the only salvation here, for her, was in the
stream.

She didn't know the consequence if she should do what her
wisdom told her: take a drink.

Before she could lose her nerve or be mesmerized, she
whirled about and flung herself knee deep in running water.

And bent. And drank.

And saw Niko, when she raised her dripping lips, sitting on the stream's far side, his face calm, unravaged. His quick, canny smile came and went and she noticed he wore his panoply: the enameled cuirass, sword and dirk forged by the entelechy of dreams.

"It's a dream, then?" she said, feeling the icy water with its four distinct and different tastes run down her chin and hearing a lumbering behind her much louder, and a rasping breath much deeper, than Tasfalen's form could make.

"Don't turn around," Niko advised as if he were training a student in the martial arts; "don't look at it; don't listen. This is my rest-place, after all—not theirs."

"And me? It's not mine, fighter. Nor are you."

"And they are. I know." There was no abhorrence in the Bandaran fighter's glance, just infinite patience. And as Ischade looked, his visage changed, contorting through a metamorphosis that seemed to include all the tortures of his recent past— eyes rolled up, cheeks split over bone, lips purpled and torn, teeth cracked and crumbled, bruises filled with blood.

Then the entire process reversed itself, and a handsome man still in the last bloom of youth regarded Ischade once more.

"You're very beautiful, you know—in your soul," Niko said. "It shows here. In spite of everything."

Behind her, the Tasfalen-thing was shambling closer; she could hear it splash into the stream. She almost whirled to fight it; her fingers spread into a shape suitable for throwing counterspells.

Niko shook his head chidingly: "Trust me. This is my place. As for your welcome here—when I needed help, you came here, where risk is greater than mortals know, and tried to aid me. I haven't forgotten."

"Are you dead?" she asked flatly, though it was impolite.

His smooth brow furrowed. "No, I'm sure not. I'm reclaiming what's mine . . . with a little help." Behind the fighter, the semblance of the pillar of fire came to be.

He knew it was there without looking. He said, "See, you must trust. We're giving Janni his proper funeral, you and I. At last. And you, who kept him from worse and soothed his conscience, ought to be here."

"And . . . *that?*" Ischade meant what was behind her. All her hackles risen, she found her mouth dry and eyes aching—

if she had a mouth here, or eyes. It seemed she did.

"We'll put them back where they belong—not here. They're yours to deal with, in the World."

He must have seen her frown, for he leaned forward on one straight and scarless arm that might never have been shattered when a demon raged inside him: "Roxane is . . . special. Different. Less. I'm free of all but my own feelings. For that I don't apologize. Like you, I deal in more than one reality. But I ask you for mercy on her behalf . . ."

"*Mercy!*" Incredulous, Ischade nearly burst out laughing. The thing that was part Haught, part Tasfalen (who was dead and had housed Roxane once and now again, if Ischade understood the rules by which Niko's magic games were played), was shuffling close behind now, intent on biting off her head or munching on her soul. It had been one with a demon; it had merged with devils; it had taken fire out of the hands of archmages such as Randal and used it even against her. All of this, Ischade was sure, was Roxane's twisted evil come to ground. And Niko wanted mercy for the witch that had made his life a living hell and wouldn't offer him so much mercy as clean death would bring.

"That's right—mercy. I'm not like you, but we've helped each other. Tolerance, balance—good and evil: each resides within the other, part and parcel."

Ischade, who'd seen too much evil, shook her head. "You *must* be dead, or still possessed."

"Look." Niko's diction slipped into mercenary argot. "It's all the same—no good without evil, no balance . . . no *maat*. If we lose one, we lose the other. It's just life, that's all. And as for death—we get what we expect."

"And you *expect* what?" Now she realized that Niko himself was not naive, or helpless, or entirely benign. "From me, I mean?"

"Mercy, I already told you." The firewell behind him began to shimmer and to dance, swinging its hips like a temple girl. "To your kind; for the record. For the balance of the thing. Janni we will take now."

"We?" It was one of the hardest things Ischade had ever done to engage in philosophical discussion with Nikodemos while, behind, the shambling thing had come so close she could feel its fetid breath upon her neck, and fancied that breath moist and felt, she thought, a strand of drool land in her hair. *Don't look at it; don't turn around—it's Niko's rest-place and his rules, not mine, apply.*

"We," Niko said as if it were a simple lesson any child should understand. And then she did: behind him, a ghost appeared.

She knew ghosts when she saw them: this one was a spirit of supernal power, a fabled strength, a glossy being of such beauty that tears came to Ischade's eyes when it sat down beside Niko, ruffling his hair with a fawn-colored hand.

"I am Abarsis," it smiled in introduction, and she saw the wizard blood there, ancient lineage, and love so strong it made her heart hurt: she'd given up such options as this ghost had thrived on, long ago.

"We need Janni's soul in heaven; it's earned its peace. Give it that, and we will restore you totally—all you were, all you had . . . including this northern pair of witches . . . this amalgam behind you of all their hate—*if*, as Niko asks, you show them mercy, then the gods will be well pleased."

"And if not?" This was no place for Ischade—she had no truck with gods or ghosts of dead priests. *Damn Tempus, who muddled all the sides and made ridiculous demands.*

"That's done long since," said the ghost, unabashedly reading her mind. "We're here for Janni only, and to give a gift for your safekeeping him until we could take him home. Now name it, Ischade of Downwind. Choose well."

She wanted only to get out of there, to be whole and well and fighting on her own terms, dealing with her own kind. And before she could say that, or think of something better, Abarsis, one arm around Niko, raised his other hand to her, saying: "It is done. Go with strength and purpose. Life to you, Sister, and everlasting glory."

And the rest-place went out like a light. The icy stream of colored water, the pillar of fire which aped reality, the snuffling horror at her back which she'd never truly glimpsed but only felt—and the two fighters, one spirit, one man of balance: all were gone as if they'd never been.

She was standing on the dry floor of Tasfalen's house and Haught was taunting her to come up the stairs.

Mercy, Niko had asked of her. She wondered if she knew, still, what it was and how to show it to creatures like these.

"Ischade . . . Mistress, aren't you curious?" Haught was rubbing the ring and she could feel the feedback of magic twisted, a deadly loop fashioned by a brash and foolish child.

Temptation made her shift from foot to foot. She was stronger, she could feel it: Niko and his guardian spirit had given her that. She could end them, here and now—Haught and whatever animated Tasfalen. For, though she hadn't seen *him* yet, she knew he must be here: the rest-place revelation was like a map, a schematic, a design which fit over human ones. So he was here, reborn, animated by some power. And Niko had wanted mercy for Roxane. . . .

Two and two fit together with a snap.

Ischade whirled on her heel and fled out the door. For a moment it resisted, but her strength prevailed.

Haught, behind her, came running down the stairs with a shout.

But she was faster: she wrenched the door open, slipped through, and bolted it with magic from the farther side.

Then, stepping back, Ischade considered mercy in all its meanings: if Tasfalen and Roxane were with Haught, in any stage of being whatsoever, mercy could only take one form.

And with strength loaned her from the rest-place of a mystery she didn't understand and under the benediction of the high priest of a god in whom she had no faith, Ischade began to weave a spell so strong and fast she had no doubt about it holding.

All about Tasfalen's house she wove the ward—a special one, one that would keep the house sealed and keep those within locked up until they learned what mercy meant.

When it was over, she realized she had worked her spells in the midst of a downpour which had soaked her to the skin.

Picking up her heavy robes, she headed homeward. Perhaps she should have found the Riddler and told him what she'd done. But there were Crit and Strat to think of, and she didn't want to think of Strat—who was with Tempus by now, alive or dead.

She wanted to think only of herself for now. She wanted things to be just as they always had been before. And she wanted to think about mercy, a quality quite strained and strange, but strengthening, in its way.

In Tasfalen's house, what had been Roxane lay abed in Tasfalen's body, half-conscious, rent in memory and power, a mere fragment knowing only that it wanted to survive.

"Duuu," it mumbled, and tried again to move the lips of a corpse twice resurrected. "Dusss." And: "Dusssst. Haughttt . . . dussst."

The ex-slave was rattling windows barred by magic, cursing horrid spells that couldn't get outside, but bounced around the corners of the house and back upon him like ricochets, so that each one was more trouble than it was worth.

Eventually his panic ebbed and he stalked over to the bedside, looking down at the fish-white pallor of the man who'd brought him here.

Snatched him from somewhere—from *else*where . . . perchance from oblivion. Someone else might have been grateful, but Haught was too wise, too angry: he knew that all witches took their price.

He'd thought to win; he'd lost. He was captive now, captive in a mansion with fine stuffs around him, true. But he was caged like an animal by his former mistress. And he was here only because of Tasfalen.

Nothing else could have done it. So he crouched down, thinking of ways to kill the already-dead, ways to get the Roxane out of Tasfalen, where it was bodiless and weak.

But then he began to listen, to try to understand what the thing on the bed was saying:

"Duuussss, duuussss, duuussss . . ."

"Dust?" he guessed. "Do you mean dust?"

The eyes of the revivified corpse blinked open, startling him so that he fell back and caught himself on his hands.

"Duuussss," the blue lips said, "on tonnnn."

"Dust. On your . . . tongue?" Of course. That was it. The dust. It wanted the dust.

Not ordinary dust, Haught realized: the hot dust, the bright dust, the fragments of the Nisi Globes of Power. And the corpse was right: the dust was their only hope—his as well as . . . hers.

For the first time, Haught thought about what it meant, being caged with Roxane, the Nisibisi witch-in-man's-body—or what was left of her. If she perished, those who held her soul would come for her. And Haught might be embroiled. Entangled. Taken. Swallowed. Absorbed like interest payments.

His skin horripilated: there was enough intelligence in that body to have seen the answer before he did.

What else was there, he was in no hurry to find out.

And he had a long, trying task ahead of him: the dust in question must be collected, mote by mote.

It was going to be arduous: the place was full of dust, most of it nonmagical. It might take days, or weeks, or years, to gather enough—especially when he had no idea how much *was* enough.

And when he had it, what would he do with it? Give it to the invalid ex-corpse? Or find a way to make use of it himself?

He didn't know, but he knew he had plenty of time to decide.

And, since he had nothing better to do, he thought, he might as well start collecting what dust he could, mote by mote by mote. . . .

The storm pelted Sanctuary with all the fury of affronted gods. Rain sheeted so hard that it punctured skin windows in the Maze; it ran so thick and wild in the gutters that the tunnels filled up and sewers overflowed in the better streets while, in the palace, servitors ran with buckets and barrels to place under leaks that were veritable waterfalls.

On the dockside, everything was awash in tide and downpour, which gave Tempus the perfect opportunity to suggest that Theron, Emperor of Ranke, Brachis, High Priest, and all the functionaries forget protocol and begin their procession now, to higher ground and drier quarters.

By the time the Rankan entourage reached the palace gates, Molin Torchholder had already arrived; Kama in tow.

In the palace temple's quiet, he was giving grateful thanks for the storm which had come to quench the fires (that, unattended by gods, threatened to burn the whole town down) while, at the casement, Kama stared out over smoking rooftops toward uptown, where the pillar of fire spat and wriggled.

She had sidled into the alcove, away from priestly ritual, and she couldn't have said whether it was the cold storm winds with their blinding sheets of rain so fierce that she could see it bounce knee-high when it struck the palace roof, or the demonic twistings of the fiery cone which resisted quenching that made her hair stand on end.

She was more conscious of Molin than she should have been. Perhaps that was the reason for the superstitious chill she felt: she was about to be indicted for attempted assassination and what-have-you, and she was worried about what the priest really felt in his heart—about how she looked and whether he believed her and what he thought of her . . . about whether anyone of her lineage ought to be thinking infatuated thoughts about anyone of his.

It wouldn't work; he was a worse choice for her than Critias. But, like Critias, it was impossible to convince Molin of that.

It was nothing he'd said—it was everything he did, the way their bodies reacted when their flesh touched. And it frightened Kama beyond measure: she'd need all her wits now just to stay alive. Her father would take Crit's word over hers without hesitation; oath-bond and honor outweighted any claim she had on the Riddler.

If she'd been born a manchild, it might have been otherwise. But things were as they were, and Torchholder was her only hope.

He'd said so. He knew it for a fact. She didn't like feeling weak, being perceived as vulnerable. And yet, she admitted, she'd spread her legs on the god's altar for the man now coming up behind her, who slid his arm round her shivering shoulders and kissed her ear.

"It's wonderful, the timely workings of the gods," he said in an intimate undertone. "And it's a good omen—our good omen. You must . . . Kama, you're shaking."

"I'm cold, wet, and bedraggled," she protested as he turned her gently to face him. Then she added: "While you were communing with the Stormgod, my father and Theron's party came through the palace gates. My time is at hand, Molin. Don't hold out false hope to me, or gods' gifts. The gods of the armies won't overlook the fact that I'm a woman—they never have."

"Thanks to all the Weather Gods that you *are,*" said the priest feelingly and, after peering into her eyes for an uncomfortably long instant, pulled her against him. "I'll take care of you, as I have taken care of this town and its gods and even Kadakithis. Put your faith in me."

Had anyone else said that to her, she would have laughed. But from Molin it sounded believable. Or she wanted so to believe it that she didn't care how it sounded.

They were standing thus, arms locked about one another, when a commotion of feet and then a discreet "Hrrmph" sounded.

Both turned, but it was Kama who whooped a short bark of disbelieving laughter before she thought to choke it off:

Before them were Jihan and Randal, the Tysian Hazard, arms around each other.

Or, more exactly, Jihan's arms were around Randal's slight and battered frame. She was holding the mage easily, so that his feet hardly touched the floor. His glazed eyes roamed a little but he was conscious—his quizzical, all-suffering looking confirmed it.

Jihan's eyes were full of red flames and Kama heard Molin exclaim under his breath, "The storm—of course, it's brought her powers back."

"Powers?" Kama whispered through unmoving lips. "Were they gone? Back from where?" and Molin answered, just as low, "Never mind. I'll tell you later, beloved."

Then he said, in his most ringing priestly voice, "Jihan, my lady, what brings you to the Stormgod's sanctuary? Are the children well? Is something amiss with Niko?"

"Priest," Jihan stamped her foot, "isn't it obvious? Randal and I are in love and we wish to be married by the tenets of your . . . faith . . . god, whatever. Now!"

Randal hiccoughed in surprise and his eyes widened. Kama would have been more concerned with the exhausted little wizard if she wasn't still reeling from shock: *Beloved,* Molin had called her.

Randal raised a feeble hand to his brow and Kama wondered whether the casualty was capable of standing under his own power, let alone making any decision about marriage.

So she said, "Randal? Seh, Witchy-Ears, are you awake? My father isn't going to like you marrying his girl ranger, not considering the use he tends to make of her. I'd—"

Jihan's free hand outstretched, pointing, and Kama's flesh began to chill.

Molin stepped in front of Kama. "Jihan, Kama meant no slight. She's in dire straits herself. With our help, Froth Daughter, you shall be able to wed your chosen mage before . . ." He craned his neck to peer out the window, where no sun could be seen, just the demonic pillar of fire and the lightning of Stormbringer. ". . . before sundown, if that's your desire, and I will wed mine. If you aid me, my gratitude and that of my tutelary god will be inscribed in the heavens forever and—"

"You're marrying a mage?" Jihan's winglike brows knitted, but her pointing finger, with its deadly cold, wavered, and her hand came to rest on her own hip.

"Not a mage. Kama, here. I can divest myself of Rosanda easily enough: she's abandoned me. But I'll need your help in securing Tempus's permission . . . he's your guardian as well as Kama's."

"Guardian?" Both women snapped in unison as two feminine spines stiffened and two wily women considered alternatives.

"Someone," Torchholder intoned through the objections of the two women, "must set the seal on the betrothal pacts," thinking that he'd found a way to free Tempus from Jihan and, for that boon alone, Tempus owed him any favor he cared to ask.

And for Kama's hand, Kama's freedom, and Kama's honor, he'd be glad to call their debt even. But for Kama's willing love he needed more. Standing behind her, his arms circling her in the proper pose of the protective husband, he whispered: "Trust me in this; accept a formal betrothal. I am sacerdote of Mother Bey, Vashanka, and Stormbringer. It will take a month to untangle the necessary rituals. It will take longer—if you desire."

The tension along her spine eased. She let her breath out with a careful sigh.

Once more, Molin Torchholder gave fervid thanks to the Stormgod, who had seen fit to visit rain upon this paltry thieves' world in all His bounty, to quench the fires of chaos, and even to restore Jihan's powers.

Over Kama's head, as he looked out the window, it seemed to him that even the demonic pillar of fire was shrinking under the onslaught of the god's blessed rain.

Tempus was still trying to explain to Theron, who'd come down here to the empire's nether-parts because of that black, ominous rain falling in the capital of Ranke, Abarsis's visit, and because it was the tendency of omens to make or break a regent's rule, that the plague had been specious (a handy way to keep Brachis under wraps) and the storm merely natural; that the fires and the looting were simply consequences of the demonic pillar of flame, which had much to do with Nikodemos and nothing at all to do with Theron's arrival; and that "No one will construe it otherwise, my friend, unless we show weakness," when they came upon Molin Torchholder in Kadakithis's palace hall.

"My lord and emperor," Molin purred, and bowed, and
Tempus stifled an urge to let Theron know that Sanctuary's
architect/priest was a Nisi wizardling in disguise, a pretender
and defiler, and a loudmouthed meddler to boot.

Theron, who didn't quite remember Molin but recognized
the ornate robes of office, said sharply, "Priest, what's wrong
with your acolytes that this place is accursed by weather, witch,
and demon? If you can't restore order to your little backwater
of the heavens, I'll replace you with someone who can. You've
till New Year's day to set things right here—and no argument."
Theron's leonine visage reddened: he'd found someone to blame
for at least part of what was wrong here.

Only Tempus noticed the humor dancing in the shadows
round the emperor's mouth as the Lion of Ranke bawled: "See
Brachis, this is his mess as well, and tell him my decree: either
Sanctuary is made pleasing in the sight of gods and their chosen
representative—me—or you'll both be out looking for new
jobs come year's end."

Molin Torchholder was too smart to wince or bridle. He
stood stolidly, eyes fixed on Theron's hairy left ear until he
was certain that the emperor was finished.

Then he responded, "Very good, my lord emperor. I'll see
to it. But while I have your ear—and Tempus's—some news:
Last night Prince/Governor Kadakithis pledged his troth to the
Beysib queen, Shupansea . . . an alliance is ours now for the
asking."

"Really?" Theron's manner mellowed; he rubbed his hands.
"That's the sort of omen worth retelling."

Tempus found his dagger in his fingers; he cleaned dirt from
its chased hilt absently, waiting for Molin's other shoe to drop.

And drop it did: "Moreover, if I have leave to continue,
sire? Many thanks. Then: The esteemed Froth Daughter, spawn
of Stormbringer who is father of all the Weather Gods, will
marry our own archmage, the Hazard Randal. This alliance,
too, is fortuitous for—"

"What?" Tempus could scarcely believe his ears—or his
good fortune. Stormbringer, at least, kept His word.

Molin continued, not deigning to notice the Riddler's out
burst: "—for us all. And to make a threesome of favorable
omens, I myself propose to marry—with all suitable ceremony
and with Tempus's permission, of course—the lady Kama
of the Third Commando, daughter of the Riddler. Thus the

armies and the priesthood will be wed as well, and internal strife ended . . ."

"You're going to *what?* You're mad. Crit says she tried to mur—" Tempus bit off words of accusation, thinking matters through as quickly as he fought in battle. Torchholder was canny; the move was one sure to bring him power, consolidate his position, put him beyond Tempus's retribution and above reproach. But it would also save Tempus's daughter from a lengthy inquisition: even Crit would admit that, since Strat was alive and would recover, Kama was more useful to them alive than dead, if she shared Torchholder's bed.

And Crit had sent word to him that there was some evidence that PFLS members had used the blue-fletched arrows: the task force leader had warned against hasty action, using all his operator's wiles to posit misdirection, to give Tempus an honorable way out of accusing his own daughter of an attempt at murder.

"So you'll make an honest woman of my . . . daughter. Just don't expect a dowry, congratulations, or any leniency on my part if you later wish you hadn't: a divorce will get you killed. So will unfaithfulness, or perfidy of any sort." It was the least he could do for his daughter. And, said before the emperor, Tempus's conditions bound like law. It was a good thing that a priest of Vashanka could have more than one wife, though Tempus wouldn't have wanted to be Molin when that one's first wife heard this news.

Torchholder blanched, but smiled and said, "I'm off to tell her, then. And you'll take care of the other matter . . . the little misunderstanding she had with certain troops of yours?"

"That goes without saying," Tempus growled while Theron looked back and forth between the two, uncomprehending.

When Molin had hurried away in a swish of robes, Theron elbowed Tempus and said, light eyes sparkling, "Don't suppose you'd tell an old warhorse what all that was about?"

"Petty squabbles, unimportant. Now tell me about this expedition you want to mount—the one to the uncharted east, beyond the sea. It interests me; I'm restless. My men need some mortal enemies to fight—this going up against magics and the gods tends to dull an army's spirit. They want a battle they can win upon their own."

And Theron was glad to do that. They worked it out, on the way down to see Nikodemos and the fabled Stormchildren in their nursery: Tempus would take his forces—Stepsons and 3rd Commando and whomever else he chose from the empire's legions, and strike east. He'd ship the horses such cavalry must have, and weapons and provisions; he'd bring back intelligence and rare goods, if there were any; he'd set up embassies for trade and size up weak principalities for conquest. And he'd do it without any help from witch or god—taking just Jihan (and Randal) and his fighters.

The two old friends shook hands as they came down a flight of stairs and headed for the nursery, with Theron sighing wistfully, "I only wish that I could join you, Riddler. This kinging is even less than it's cracked up to be. But it makes me feel less trapped, setting you free, even for a few months. . . ."

Tempus pushed the door inward and Theron fell silent.

The Rankan emperor remembered Nikodemos from the battle for the throne at the Festival of Man. He'd been with Tempus once when the Riddler had had to bail his Stepson out of a Rankan jail.

The ashen-haired youth sitting with a babe on either knee looked tired, wan, and somehow much too gentle to be the same much-lauded fighter. But when Niko raised his head and wished them life and glory, it was clearly the youngster whose fate was dogged by a Nisibisi witch.

Tempus left Theron's side and strode to where Niko sat.

As he did, Gyskouras buried his young head in Niko's chiton and began to weep at the sight of his natural father, and Arton, understanding more than children should, shook his dark-haired head and told his blond companion: "'Kouras, be brave. Don't cry."

"Let him. They're clear tears, and that's a blessing," Niko said softly to the children, then looked up at Tempus and beyond, to Theron: "You'll excuse me for not rising, lords. They're tired. They're undisciplined. They've had too many adventures for boys so young."

"So have you, we've heard, Stealth," Theron said kindly, remembering all that went on upcountry to win him the throne from Abakithis, and how much Niko had sacrificed to that end.

"You're still taking them to Bandara, Niko?" Tempus asked offhandedly.

"If you still agree, Commander. If you'll give me leave."

Tempus almost said that Abarsis had usurped command from him in the matter, but he was too pleased with the outcome of his talk with Theron. "Leave you have, and leave to meet us in three months back in the capital—we're mounting an expedition and I'll want you along."

Something changed in Niko's face, as if a tension had been drained. "You do? You will?" Niko let the children slide off his lap and got slowly, carefully, to his feet. The signs of all he'd been through then showed clearly: bruised bones, favored muscles, a stiffness time would have to heal. "I'm glad . . . I mean . . . you might have thought me too much trouble—all I bring with me, wherever . . . my witch-curse and my ghosts and all."

"You're the best I've got, Niko," said Tempus levelly. "And the only man I've called partner in a century. Some things can't be changed."

And although Theron might not have understood the last bit, Niko did, and moved painfully to embrace him, stepped back, bowed as best he could to Theron, and then, with a blush of humility, mumbled that he'd best begin preparations to take the boys and make away.

Tempus took Theron out of there, then, and on the way back upstairs they chanced to glimpse the skyline out the palace window, where a hair-thin column of fire, a weakened pillar of flame, blew far right, then left, and then winked out.